Ghada Samman w Syria. She was edu American Universi, She began to write in the early 1960s and worked as a journalist and columnist in Beirut. She has written over thirty volumes of short stories, novels, poetry and non-fiction. She founded her own publishing house and lives at present in Paris.

Nancy N. Roberts studied Arabic language and literature in the United States. She currently lives in Mafraq, Jordan, and teaches English at Al al-Bayt University.

GHADA SAMMAN

Translated from the Arabic by Nancy N. Roberts

Beirut Nightmares

Quartet Books

First published in English by Quartet Books Limited in 1997
A member of the Namara Group
27 Goodge Street
London W1P 2LD

Reprinted 2010

Originally published in Arabic as *Kawabis Beirut*
Dar al-Adab, Beirut 1976

Copyright © Ghada Samman 1976
Translation copyright © Nancy N. Roberts 1997

All rights reserved. No part of this book may be reproduced in any form or by any means without prior written permission of the publisher.

A catalogue record for this book is available from the British Library

ISBN 978 0 7043 8065 3

Printed and bound in Great Britain by
TJ International Ltd, Padstow, Cornwall

Dedication

I dedicate this novel
to the workers in the typesetting room
who at the moment are putting its words in order,
and who do so despite the storm of rockets and bombs swirling about them,
knowing that this book
will not bear their names.

Ghada

9 February, 1976

Translator's Introduction

Ghada Samman has rightly been referred to by one critic as 'the most prominent Syrian woman writer of fiction,'[1] and by another as modern Arabic literature's 'prose poet of female despair'[2] (though I would also add, hope). She was born in 1942 in Damascus. Her mother died when she was a young child, after which she was raised by her father, Ahmad Samman, and her paternal grandmother. For ten years her father was Dean of the Faculty of Law at Damascus University, after which he became Syria's Minister of Education. She describes him as having been a hard-working, self-made man who raised her on a lifestyle of Sufi-like asceticism, which exerted a powerful influence over her life and thinking. To her father she attributes her 'hatred for all bourgeois theatrics' and her dedication to hard work and self-discipline. From her days as a university student, Samman has worked as a librarian, a lecturer in English at Damascus University, and as a journalist and columnist, in which profession she has continued ever since.

Although she learned French as her first language, her father immersed her in the study of Arabic classics as well, and made her memorize the Qur'an to ensure her mastery of Arabic. Initially obliged by her father to study sciences with a view to becoming a doctor, eventually she rebelled and turned to English literature. She completed her MA at the American University of Beirut in the mid-1960s.

In the summer of 1966 her father died. At this time, while she was in London, she was sentenced *in absentia* to three months' imprisonment in Syria for having broken a law forbidding those holding advanced degrees to leave the country without official permission. She also learned that she had lost her job as a journalist with a Lebanese magazine and was ostracized by her family because of her insistence on leading a free and independent life. As she states: 'That summer I had to face the question of whether I really meant every word I had written about freedom, facing the world as it is, and translating one's principles into action no matter what the cost...'[3] From 1966 to 1969 she was working and travelling back and forth between Lebanon and a number of European countries. These were formative years for her, during which, she says, she discovered once and for all the pettiness of the guiding principles of bourgeois Damascene society, which now considered her a 'fallen woman' when in fact she was a woman just beginning to live, an artist with a growing awareness of reality. 'Perhaps I was perishing – "fallen" – before, and wouldn't have survived had I not gone through this.'[4]

One student of Samman's writings[5] divides her works into two periods: pre-1967 (the year of the Arabs' defeat at the hands of the Israelis resulting in the occupation of the entire West Bank, Gaza Strip, Golan Heights and Sinai peninsula) and post-1967. Her pre-1967 works focus more exclusively on male–female relations within Arab society, highlighting women's oppressed, inferior status and what she sees as the (positive) contrast offered by Western society. In her post-1967 works she expands her focus, developing a vision of Arab society encompassing political, economic and social issues which include relations between the sexes. In this broader vision, both men and women are seen as victims of forces such as economic injustice, class inequality and outmoded traditions, forces which are depicted against the backdrop of two primary events: the Arab defeat of 1967 and the Lebanese civil war. One may also see a development in Samman's female characters, from their being 'tearful, weak-kneed' and more or less shallow and escapist to their being stronger, more politically aware and self-determining. There is also a marked development in her style, from a romantic idealism in her earlier fiction to greater realism in her later works.[6]

In her fourth collection of short stories *Departure of the Ancient Ports* (Beirut: Dar al–Adab, 1973), which is representative of this later period, Samman deals with the causes and effects of the 1967 defeat as she sees them, drawing connections between this event and other, ongoing socio-political problems within the Arab world, of which women's oppression is only one. Other works published during this period include *Love* (Beirut, 1973),[7] a collection of free poetic texts written between 1960 and 1973, and *Beirut '75* (Beirut, 1975;

published in English by the University of Arkansas Press, 1995, trans. Nancy N. Roberts), a novel prophetically depicting the social and political causes of the Lebanese civil war which broke out in 1975. The personal aspirations and struggles of the novel's five protagonists are seen to be inseparable from the wider context of the Lebanese civil war, with its concomitant socio-political unrest, strife and class inequalities. Samman's *Incomplete Works* (Beirut, 1978-80), a thirteen-volume collection of travel accounts, book reviews and social and political analyses, focuses on such issues as crime, law, supernatural phenomena and social conditions in war-torn Lebanon, as well as the condition of women in Arab society.

Samman's second novel, *Beirut Nightmares*, is a personal account of and reflection on the events of Lebanon's civil war. Presented as a series of 'nightmares', each of which forms a sort of mini-chapter, it is in part a diary-like account of events in the life of the narrator over a two-week period during which she is trapped in her house after street battles and sniper fire have turned her neighbourhood into a virtual prison. However, unlike a traditional diary detailing one individual's daily experiences, the book is peopled by a variety of characters, some real, some fantastic. Moreover, some of the 'nightmares' are self-contained, while others form episodes in an ongoing series of events that lends cohesion to the work as a whole.

A recurring theme of the novel is the narrator's preoccupation with the animals in the pet shop next to her house. The animals' sufferings parallel those of the unarmed, defenceless civilians of Beirut. The narrator's repeated visits to the pet shop, where the abandoned animals are becoming increasingly hungry and are gradually returning to a state of wildness, become a nightly ritual, and she comes to see the animals' ordeal as a kind of microcosm of what is happening to the human society outside the pet-shop walls. Initially drawn to the pet shop by the sounds being made by the animals in their misery, she experiences a growing sense of their common destiny and compassion for their undeserved suffering.

Intermingled with surrealist elements and internal dialogue, *Beirut Nightmares* is an account not only of events but also of the author's understanding of the social, political, psychological and spiritual effects of civil war on a people and their country: a sense of disorientation and disintegration; loss of trust; alienation; the questioning of previously held values and priorities; and the unmasking of the 'dark' side of the human soul and the superficiality of human ties such that violence becomes a way of life and self-preservation the sole criterion by which one's actions are judged. The author exposes the absurdity of allowing religious affiliation to become a basis for mutual enmity, especially at a time when those fighting each other should rather see that they are united by a common plight: their humanity and shared experience of poverty and oppression.

Thus Samman makes it clear that the root causes of Lebanon's civil war go far beyond religious differences, which she sees as a mere smokescreen, a mask for other, more fundamental causes, such as class divisions, economic injustice and the search for a more stable sense of cultural identity by members of Arab society affected by the encroachment of Western values and influence. She seeks to disabuse the reader of the notion that:

> 'Beirut was living through a kind of "golden age" prior to the war, which brought it abruptly to an end. The "good life" associated with Beirut in the minds of so many was enjoyed only by a tiny minority of the city's

population, most of whom were suffering hunger, ignorance, illness, injustice and poverty. If the civil war was a "dirty war" ... then the peace which Beirut enjoyed before the war was a "dirty peace". It was a peace born of the enjoyment of the "sweet life" by some at the expense of the deprivation of the majority.'[8]

The translation of *Beirut Nightmares* into no fewer than five other languages – Polish (1984), German (1988; reprinted in 1990 and 1993), Russian (1988), Italian (1993) and French (1994) – attests eloquently to both its literary merit and the power and importance of its content and message. As the second volume of a trilogy dealing with Lebanon's civil war (preceded by *Beirut '75* and followed by *Night of the Trillion, Beirut, 1976*), *Beirut Nightmares* is a worthy addition to the growing number of modern Arabic literary works being made available to the English-reading public.

---

1 Mineke Schipper, *Unheard Words* (London, New York: Allison & Busby, 1984), p. 83.
2 Hanan A. Awwad, *Arab Causes in the Fiction of Ghadah Al-Samman (1961–1975)* (Quebec: Sherbrooke, 1983), p. 72.
3 Ghali Shukri, *Ghadah Al-Samman bila Ajnihah* (Beirut: Dar al-Tali'ah li'l-Tiba'ah wa'l-Nashr, 1977), p. 42.
4 Ibid., pp. 42–3.
5 Awwad, *Arab Causes*.
6 Ibid., p. 117.
7 This and all subsequent books where no other publisher is given have been published by Manshurat Ghada Samman.
8 *Beirut Nightmares* (Beirut: Dar Al-Adab, 1976), p. 400.

Nightmare 1

When dawn broke, we were all staring at each other in amazement, wondering: How did we stay alive? How did we survive that night?

We'd spent a night during which bombs, explosives and rockets had been galloping around our house as if the elements had gone mad. The explosions were coming so thick and fast you might have thought we were in some tacky, overdone war film.

We hadn't yet fully awakened from our 'non-sleep' when we made a quick decision: to get the children and the old people out of the house. So after ten minutes of hysterical running back and forth between the various rooms of the house – to gather up belongings which we would no doubt discover later were unnecessary – the caravan descended the stairs leading from the house to the garden, and from there to my ancient car. The windscreen had a bullet hole in it right at the place where the driver's head – my head, that is – would have been, while the back window was shattered although still in place. I ran my hands over my head and was overjoyed to find it still there and with no additional holes in it. The sight of the bullet hole in the glass made us all the more determined to smuggle out the very young and very old. It was as if the sounds of the explosives had a mysterious, drug-like effect ... releasing a hidden strength stored somewhere deep inside us, while at the same time silencing the voice of everyday logic and common sense...

We must have closed the car doors really hard once we'd got in, because the shattered glass that had been in place in spite of the cracks now began falling in, showering down on us in little white pieces like some sort of wicked snow.

My only fear was that my old car would decide to play one of its tricks, like clinging to the street where it was parked and going on strike for the day. As I turned the key in the ignition, my heart was pounding as wildly as an African drum. But the car started and, like someone in a hypnotic trance, I began driving with one single thought in my head: to deposit our human cargo – those of us least capable of enduring the terror – and get back home.

I dropped them off at the house of some relatives, then returned by the same way I'd come, like a doll that's been wound up and follows her pre-set course without stopping – even if she bumps into the edge of a rug or a chair leg, she keeps up her mechanical movements as if nothing has happened. That's exactly how I was as I passed through the innumerable new checkpoints guarded by armed men. I didn't stop and I didn't speed up. I didn't even feel that I'd seen them. As for them, the only expression on their faces was one of bewilderment and dismay. It was obvious that the car had been bombarded by a hail of bullets, especially in the spot where my head was, and amazingly I was still alive and driving the thing around without any expression on my face. Maybe they thought I'd died when the car was shot at, yet here I was driving it, on my way to the afterlife. The road to eternity was the only one that was passable, safe and free of checkpoints. Consequently, no one even stopped me.

Nightmare 2

When I left my car that morning and went into the house safe and sound – until further notice, at least – I didn't know that this was the last time I'd leave my house for a number of very long days, and that the moment I closed the door behind me I was also shutting myself off from life and hope on the other side. I'd become the prisoner of a nightmare that was to drag on and on...

My brother and I didn't know that we'd come home only to play the role of captives. If we'd known, we would have stocked up on food on the way back. And if we'd known, maybe we wouldn't have come back at all...And if...and if...So we planted 'if' in the fields of regret and up sprouted 'if only'!

Nightmare 3

We hadn't heard the radio reports yet. Only when I got back

to the house did I remember that, for the first time in a month, I'd left home without listening to the instructions given by Sharif, the radio announcer, and without even washing my face for that matter.

When I did tune in, it was too late. Armed men had occupied the Holiday Inn, across the road from our tiny old house. The hotel overlooked the top floor of our three-storey building like a mountain of cement and iron towering above some peaceful peasants' shanty at the bottom of a ravine.

Only then did I wake up to what was happening, realizing that I was like a defenceless noncombatant who'd been sentenced to house arrest in the middle of a battlefield! So I called the grocer to order some supplies. No answer. I telephoned all the shops in the neighbourhood. No one answered anywhere. I called the neighbours' house and the phone was answered by their son, Amin. Aghast, he asked me, 'Where have you been living? Don't you realize what's going on around you?'

Nightmare 4

Where have I been living?

His question cast me back into a frightful reality. I was living on a battlefield without a single weapon to my name. Nor had I mastered the use of anything other than this skinny little object that went scurrying over the paper between my fingers, leaving quivering lines behind it like the trail of blood left by a wounded man crawling over a field of white cotton.

Where have I been living?

It seemed that I was living in a verse of poetry. My pillow was stuffed with myths and fairy tales, and my blanket was made of tomes full of philosophical treatises. All my revolutions took place and all my slain met their end in fields strewn with letters of the alphabet and bombshells made of words ...

'Where have you been living?' he asked.

Then an explosion went off and I felt a twinge of remorse. Why hadn't I learned how to take up arms – not just the pen – for the sake of what I believed in? Whenever some explosion went off, the scratching sound made by my pen on the paper seemed so faint. But I decided that now was not the time for self-reproach after the manner of writers who fall into crises of conscience whenever fighting breaks out and they become aware of the futility of the pen. The important thing was for me to survive. After all, life alone could guarantee the opportunity to correct any of my errors if I became convinced that I'd been in the wrong. This wasn't the time for introspection or philosophical debates. By now the explosions were coming in steady succession, so I decided to face the concrete reality before me and determine my position on the battlefield in proper 'military' and statistical fashion.

Nightmare 5

I sat writing on a piece of paper:

1) There are no weapons at all in the house. Even the kitchen knives are blunt. So then, there's no need to investigate any approach other than fighting Gandhi-style! (Note: this isn't an invitation to murder me!)
2) There's only one small fire extinguisher in the house. I looked for it and found it in the library. I've noticed that it's smaller than I'd imagined, and about all it's good for is to put out a cigarette.

3) Our food supply will last for five days – that is, if we eat like birds!
4) The drinking water has been cut off, which means that I'll have to drink contaminated water that's been boiled – that is, provided the gas needed to light the burner doesn't run out!
5) There are two candles in the house, one of which happens to be burned down, which means that in the event of a power cut I'll have to depend on the light of rockets and bombs!
6) I'm afraid.
7) I'm really afraid.

I shredded the paper into tiny, tiny pieces. Then, in an attempt to distract myself from the sound of the shooting, I tried to put it back together the way it had been before by placing one word next to another. But it was hard, like trying to revive a relationship after we've thoroughly torn it asunder, or like trying to restore joy to a heart 'sheathed with arrows'.

I laughed at myself. Here I was living on a battlefield and seeking to protect my body by reciting verses from Al-Mutanabbi as if they were some kind of incantation that would shield me from harm!

Nightmare 6

The shooting died down a little, and I went up to the window. So did the mother living on the third floor of the building facing mine. The elderly grocer was putting some loaves of bread in a basket for her with a rope tied to it. She was standing behind the wooden shutter and had lowered the rope to him without even putting her hand out. As for him, he was keeping himself safely hidden inside the entrance to the building.

Everything was utterly still. I figured the fighters must be washing their faces and letting their guns cool off, so I decided to call out to the adventurous grocer and do the same thing that he and my neighbour were doing...

Very slowly, the woman began raising the basket tied to the rope. I thought to myself, her hands must be trembling now! Nevertheless, the basket kept going up and up, even though the rope from which it hung was so thin that the basket seemed to be ascending unaided towards the terror-stricken people above, bearing the loaf of peace. I noticed that the eyes of the rest of our neighbours hidden behind their windows were also following the journey of the basket of bread through midair. We were like a single heart praying for it; it was as if the basket had become a tiny infant, the child of love, security and communication with the world of the guileless and pure of heart.

A tense silence prevailed as the basket rose higher and higher until it reached the lower edge of the second floor.

Then suddenly a shot was fired.

I don't know whether we heard the shot first or whether we first saw the basket plunging through space like a man who'd fallen from the balcony. But in a flash we all understood the significance of what had happened. Some sniper had fired a shot at the rope and in so doing had demonstrated his prowess for everyone in the neighbourhood to see. He'd said to us all: I'm capable of hitting any target, however tiny or delicate it may be. Every one of your hearts is within my range. I could put bullet holes through your arteries one by one. I could aim inside the very pupils of your eyes without missing the mark. I can aim my bullets at any part of your bodies I choose.

When the basket fell, I felt as though the entire neighbourhood had been transformed into a single heart that breathed an agonized sigh. We realized that we were all prisoners of that mysterious ghoul, hidden somewhere, who now held sway over not only the circulation of the blood in our veins but also the course of our very minds and souls. And he possessed this power for no other reason than that he happened to have a rifle with a sight on it that he'd spent a bit of time being trained to use. And to hell with all the hours we'd spent being trained and educated in universities and laboratories!

When the basket fell, our hopes fell with it, collapsing in a heap on the pavement like someone breathing his last. When it fell, we grieved as if a tiny child had fallen off the Ferris wheel at an amusement park, causing all lights to be extinguished and all laughter to cease at a stroke.

It was obvious that we'd all understood the message, since from that moment on the wooden shutters on all the windows in the neighbourhood stayed shut tight, not to be cracked again. Goodbye, sun!

Nightmare 7

The bullet that had come flying from somewhere or other to sever the rope bearing the basket of bread meant, simply stated, that we were captives. It had become impossible to flee the battlefield, and even obtaining a loaf of bread was now too much to hope for.

One step into the street and we'd suffer the same fate as those loaves of bread.

I found myself thinking of my body as material that could be pierced by a bullet, or broken, or burned, or torn to ribbons. I don't know why, but it made me think of advertisements for watches that are 'unbreakable' and 'waterproof', and I felt envious of them. It grieved me to think that the human body is so fragile, that life is unrepeatable. Death is the only loss that can never be recovered. I remembered a saying to the effect that 'Old age is the only funeral procession in which the deceased marches on his own two feet', and I felt a longing to be elderly. I pictured myself and my friends once we'd passed the age of seventy, our hair grown white, reminiscing about these bitter days. How distressing for old age to become one of our highest aspirations!

My brother and I didn't exchange any conversation. It was as if the sound of bullets flying through the air had rendered language ineffectual, or had created some sort of insulating wall, increasing each person's awareness of his individuality and isolation, an isolation in which each of us had fallen into his own personal well ...

Nightmare 8

I fell into my well, into that inner place where nightmares are ...

The door opened, and in came my boyfriend with his taut physique, looking like an arrow straight out of Africa. I wanted to tell him that I'd missed him, but I didn't open my mouth or make a sound. Still, he understood what I wanted to say and, without uttering a word, replied: And I miss you, and love you ...

His body was covered with blood and on his bare chest there were pieces of broken glass. My body had also begun to bleed from all its pores. I don't know whether it hurt or not. His coming was a joy beyond belief... I'd called out to him: Come, wherever your are, however you are ...

And here he was. He'd come. I took him in my arms. The pieces of shattered glass sank into my own chest as well and I felt that we'd been joined, fused.

Then there was an explosion and the nightmare was shredded to pieces. The explosion threw me to the floor, and I was afraid and alone, but bleeding only on the inside!

Nightmare 9

I decided to wage war on the nightmares by working.

However, dusk had already begun casting its grey cloak over the neighbourhood's wounds.

I looked stealthily out the window. The basket was still where it had fallen on the ground, like a motionless corpse... The little piece of the sea that was still visible to me after they built the Holiday Inn wasn't its usual lovely red horizon. Instead, smoke was ascending and blocking it from view.

Nightmare 10

The gunfire died down a bit ...

Nothing remained now but the night and the silence – a mysterious, tense silence. Then I began to hear faint voices, cries for help. At first I thought I was imagining things, but then I remembered the pet shop next to our house. Perhaps its owner, working as a sniper, had been distracted from taking care of the animals and feeding them by his new job of manufacturing destruction. Or was he just not able to get to them?

I pictured the animals inside their cages, smelling the odour of gunpowder and fire and picking up the danger-charged electrons that filled the air. Yet they were incapable of fleeing or defending themselves. Where was their owner, who'd earned his living by buying and selling them?

Hadn't he imprisoned them under the pretext of ensuring a 'life of dignity' for them? So why should he hide from them simply because his customers and deals had vanished and danger had come to take their place? Where was the pet-shop owner? Might he have gathered up the fortune he'd amassed from selling them and then fled with it to Europe, along with all the others who'd made their getaway?

I remembered him. In his face there was a cruel hardness that wasn't fully concealed even by his ceremonially proper politeness with customers. Once I went to his shop with a colleague of mine who wanted to buy a Siamese cat. She knew what she wanted down to the last detail: it had to have blue eyes and brown ears, a white body and a brown tail. In vain I tried to convince her that what she needed was to have a baby rather than running away from something by adopting a cat. She was still passionately attached to her married boyfriend who wouldn't divorce the mother of his children and would never marry her. He showered her with money as a way of compensating her for 'damages and loss', including her wasted youth. Apparently, however, she was content to accept things on his terms, and had decided to add the crowning touch to their love story by adopting a cat – that is, as long as she couldn't give birth to it!

We went into the shop. The section designated for strangers – those coming in from outside to conduct their business – was as clean, neat and attractive as if one were in some shop in Switzerland. It contained all the consumer-age diversions that you might find, say, on Beirut's Hamra Street, Airport Road or the seaside Rawsheh district, or in some fancy transit lounge or casino. My friend stood inside this tidy, modern section complete with stainless-steel cages and shag rugs. As for me, I passed through the shop's tourist façade and went further inside.

I could hear my friend's voice wafting back to me as she put in her order: 'I want a Siamese cat – with a good pedigree – that has blue eyes, black whiskers, a brown tail and a white body.'

'We've got just what you're looking for,' the shop owner replied, 'and our prices are quite reasonable. I'll bring out three cats for you to choose from.'

'I'll leave it to you to choose one that suits your taste,' she said.

Then the phone rang, and while he was busily engaged in a conversation about the sale of some hunting dogs, I slipped behind the decorative wall that concealed the true condition of his merchandise.

There were cages of various sizes and shapes arranged in such tight rows that there was virtually no space between them, like the graves in some paupers' cemetery. Neither sun nor wind nor dew nor blue sky could reach them. Inside the cages was a motley group of living creatures that resembled human beings in their diversity: poodles and hunting dogs, grey cats, 'home-grown' cats and cats imported from Syria, white rabbits with red eyes, grey and black rabbits, white mice and coloured mice, goldfish swimming in a lit-up aquarium like so many aquatic butterflies, sparrows with broken spirits and broken wings, a nightingale, a goldfinch, a parrot and others... Animals of various colours, shapes and temperaments had been brought together by a cage – a prison – and misery. It was clear that they were weary, since the cats didn't meow with any gusto, the dogs didn't whine or howl very well and the sparrows didn't sing. And I wondered: Do you suppose he puts some kind of sedative in their water dishes? Or does he just not feed them enough for them to keep up their strength? That way, they can't rise up in rebellion, bang their heads against the bars of their cages or bite the hands of the prison-keeper and the customer, the seller and the buyer.

By now my eyes had begun adjusting to the relative darkness inside, and in spite of the loud dance music that the shop owner insisted on playing in the tourist wing of his shop, I could still hear the mournful, collective voice of the 'pet people' in their cages. It sounded something like a demonstration being staged by the ill, the wounded and the weary. But at the same time it was a ferocious sound full of ominous threat. It was obvious that the shop owner fed them just barely enough to keep them alive so as to be able to continue selling them. He gave them half-contaminated water to drink and would bring them out into the light only when they were about to expire, his one concern being to keep them from dying and robbing him of his business. But what kind of life was this? That was another issue which was none of his concern. These creatures' relationship with sun and moon, forest and jungle, with the seas, the night, the joys of changing seasons and freedom — all these were matters which didn't concern him in the least.

Then suddenly I found him behind me. He'd come to get the animal that my friend had requested. He opened one of the cages and took out a cat. It had been stuffed like a sardine into a narrow living space with seven other cats of the same variety. I noticed that some of them were wounded. Perhaps when they were at the height of frustration and distress over their imprisonment, misery and wretched living conditions, they would start fighting among themselves. No doubt the shop owner was happy to have the wretched and miserable bite each other rather than all gang up together on him — their true enemy.

He took the cat out of the cage, then carefully closed it again. Our eyes met. It was obvious that he understood that I understood what was going on and that he didn't like it one bit.

He said pompously, 'No customers are allowed in the storeroom!'

'I'm not a customer,' I said. 'I'm on the "other team".'

Then he handed his choice to my friend – an emotional outcast seeking distraction from the truth of what was happening around her by drowning herself in her own personal anxieties and concerns. After having been supplied by the shop owner with the name of a veterinarian, she paid for the cat and came out. She was supposed to go to the vet straight away to have the cat vaccinated and get its claws trimmed. First the salesman, then the veterinarian, then perhaps after that the pharmacist, and after him who knows who else in this Mafia ring of beneficiaries. When she finally left with the cat, I noticed that the pet shop's guardian heaved a sigh of relief. He was no doubt pleased to be rid of an extra mouth to feed. I didn't sense any emotional bond between him and his tribe of domesticated animals. He would take them out of their cages and put them back in without his heart skipping a beat. Even in prisons, some sort of affinity develops between the prison guard and the inmate, since both of them are generally from the same downtrodden class. But as for this shop owner, I didn't notice a single hint of affection between him and his charges. Nothing bridged the chasm between them but the desire for personal gain ...

And he was capable of taming them all, docile and ferocious alike, through starvation, imprisonment, degradation and bad living conditions, until they had no strength left to resist his tyranny and indifference.

From the pet shop we went to a luxurious, immaculate

veterinarian's clinic reserved for that class of cat that is accustomed to a life of comfort and ease. It made me think of a woman I'd seen in labour under a tent in Akkar. She was screaming and clinging to the branch of a tree, without a doctor or anyone else to come to her aid. She didn't even have a single piece of cotton... The day I saw her, I'd gone out to prepare a newspaper report on the outlying areas of Akkar. When I was there I saw how, immediately after their children are born, they're baptized in the dust. After this woman had given birth to her baby, it was received by the field floor, his blood mingled with thorns. Then she grabbed a rock and cut the umbilical cord. Meanwhile, I stood there in a daze, looking into her tough, courageous face, which looked exactly like the boulder I was standing next to: petrified!

We took the cat into the clinic and, assisted by my friend and the nurse, the vet managed to hold on to the cat and trim its claws. It was screaming with all the strength it had left, struggling to hold on to its only natural weapon in the face of the unknown that now surrounded it on every side.

Once the claw-trimming operation was over, the vet produced a needle, which he stuck into the cat's thigh. As I looked on, I remembered in horror that the baby of the Akkarite peasant woman might have died by now because there was no one to vaccinate him. After this, the doctor decided it would be necessary to give the cat Valium so that she wouldn't go looking for a tom-cat and 'do what cats do'. After all, he said, she was still young and pregnancy would be dangerous to her precious health!

When my friend heard this, she flew into a rage. What? A female cat! She'd wanted a male. The pet-shop owner had sold her this 'brother cat' claiming that it was a male rather than a female. My friend received the news with such profound grief, you might have thought she was a woman who'd just given birth to her seventh daughter after her husband had sworn to divorce her if she didn't bear him a son!

But finally she accepted her fate, and as the veterinarian gave the cat its doses of Valium, she began cursing that humbug of a pet-shop owner. When the nurse demanded that she pay the bill, my friend laid into the vet too.

Nightmare 11

No, I wasn't imagining things. The sound I'd been hearing, which resembled a collective cry for help, was coming from the pet shop next door.

The animals weren't hungry yet, but they were afraid, just like everyone else now being held prisoner in this neighbourhood. Every family was in its own cage and none could pinpoint the whereabouts of the person who held its well-being in his hands. What was he doing? Did he see the fires burning? Did he hear their voices? And so on, in an unending series of unanswered questions... The houses in the neighbourhood had become cages, and all of us – except for the men bearing arms – were his simple-souled subjects. Was it a mistake for us to have believed that there's a difference between the jungle and the pet shop?

I felt the walls of my own cage closing in on me more and more until I started banging my head against the bars...

Then a huge boom rang out, shattering the solemn, tense silence with a horrendous series of explosions.

I made up my mind there and then that next time I wasn't going to let anybody trim my claws. I wouldn't believe the claims made by the shop owner. I wouldn't be left defenceless!

Nightmare 12

The cascade of fire kept pouring forth unabated...

I noticed that I was sitting on the floor, curled up under the window. I decided that since I had no way of knowing where the bullet that was going to land in my chest would come from, I might as well stretch out on my bed and learn how to sleep while bullets were flying...

After all, I'd endured indescribably harsh conditions before. I'd been obliged to sleep in places haunted by cold, homesickness and grey phantoms, and I'd taught myself how to adjust to whatever suffering happened to surround me... Once I'd even trained myself to sleep with a bright electric lamp shining in my face.

And now I'd have to learn to sleep on a battlefield. So I mustered all the will-power I could and tried to recall everything I knew about yoga. Then I began dismantling my body, detaching one limb after another as if I were a mannequin in a display window. First I commanded my right leg to go to sleep, then my left. Then, one at a time, I began ordering the remaining parts of my body to migrate out of time and space into the untamed expanses of the world of slumber. I was certain that the experiment could succeed. Yet I also knew that it required a great deal of practice... Just then there was a violent explosion, and the braid of nerves that I'd been plaiting one strand at a time, using it to gradually bring my whole body under control, suddenly went slipping out of my mind's tenuous grasp.

After this failure I suffered a setback and began to hear the explosions as louder than they really were, or so it seemed to me.

Then something strange happened. Into the room came a foreign body – a being possessed of a hot vitality and terrifying strength. I heard the sound of it striking the wooden door, then the chair, the bed and finally the other door. At first I didn't understand exactly what had taken place. The room was filled with the peculiar odour of something burning. Either a bullet or a piece of shrapnel had pierced one edge of the door leading into the room. After entering the room, it had blown the chair leg apart, then collided with the bed and ricocheted off it on to the other door, punching a hole through it. I stood there in a daze, staring at the aftermath. Splinters of wood covered the floor, the bed and my hair, as well as the magazines scattered all over the floor, and I stared in horror at the places where the object had been. It had dug into the wood to a depth of at least ten centimetres. And as for the low chair it had struck, some pieces of melted, broken nails were now scattered throughout its splintered remains, just exactly as if it had been pounded by some infernal hammer.

There was something else that terrified me also... I'd always thought that bullets (with which this was my first real-life encounter) took off in a straight line, then kept on going until they hit their target. However, this bullet (or splinter) had moved through the room like a billiard ball or a frightened cat. It shot in all directions, destroying my military theories about the safety of staying at ground level or of lying down flat. And the most shocking thing was that this bullet (or splinter of something) had exploded at an extremely low elevation, not more than thirty centimetres above the ground. So I was bewildered. Where had it come in? And how? It perplexed me so much that I forgot how afraid I was. I went into the room where the object had begun its excursion, and it occurred to me that perhaps it had been shot from inside the house. On the wall facing the first door it had struck, I was surprised to find a scar where some plaster and dirt had fallen on to the floor. So the bullet had passed by here. But where could it have come in when the shutters on all the windows were closed and none of the glass was broken? I'd just begun taking a good look at the windows when another explosion went off. At this point I decided to discontinue my military investigations, close the case temporarily and flee to the other end of the house ...

Now I was truly afraid. For the first time, I'd become aware that bullets don't follow the straight and narrow, as it were, but at times take a winding, tortuous path, like a rat scurrying from one side of a room to the other. I also realized that bullets don't necessarily fly above window level. Instead, I could see that matters were far more complicated than I'd been led to believe by the superficial information I'd gleaned from police films and novels. I now realized I was up against an enemy I knew absolutely nothing about. And with this miserable thought, I stretched out in resignation on a sofa in the living room.

Nightmare 13

I lay down on the couch in the living room. It was pitch dark and all the lights were out. My gaze was fixed on the cracks in the windows, whose shutters were shut tight but whose glass portion had been left open. I'd read in some police novel that in the event of an explosion, it's best to leave the glass windows in a room open so that the pressure created by the explosion won't transform the windowpanes into knives that go flying everywhere and plant themselves in your body. I shuddered at the thought. Meanwhile, I kept on looking thoughtfully at the cracks in the shutters, and at the 'moon windows' – the small, round, shutterless windows located just beneath the ceiling in most old houses in Beirut and Damascus. Their primary purpose is to allow more daylight into rooms with very high walls, as well as to let in the moonlight by night.

Now, however, the tiny stained-glass skylights seemed more like deadly weapons to me than anything else, like scores of daggers that at any moment might be let loose by an explosion from the cords that held them in place...

With thoughts like this running through my mind, I lay down alone in the heart of the darkness. Meanwhile, there was an astounding spectacle coming in through the moon windows. The rockets and bombs going off in the sky were illuminating the night like lightning, flashing through the tiny windows like a hellish thunder storm that refused to abate. I felt extremely afraid. But in spite of everything, I couldn't help but be impressed with the beauty of the sight. The multicoloured skylights would suddenly release a brilliant glow, then grow dim, then quickly light up again in a bewitching, psychedelic display of colour.

I decided that I must be like someone plunging to the bottom of Niagara Falls who's still captivated by the beauty of the scenery, or like someone falling from the fiftieth floor of a skyscraper who finds himself admiring the flowers on the balconies as he passes by them on his way to death...

It was an extraordinary nightmare with a kind of sadistic, aesthetic appeal. And with the madness of the lightning, my slain beloved came to me, still covered with bloody wounds. I took him in my arms and kissed him, indifferent to the fact that his body was cold and caked with blood. Together we writhed and twisted to the sounds of flying bullets, which had turned into frigid, metallic knife blades. And I cried out to him: 'I still love you!'

Nightmare 14

It was autumn and I was a prisoner just like the creatures held captive in the pet shop. Those green mountains... I wouldn't be shooting through them like a joy-laden arrow any more. All those mountain roads leading to outlying villages, and the ravines, pasturelands and plains – I might die before seeing them again...

I was now in my third day of captivity. Maybe I'd always been a captive without noticing it, just like the creatures in the pet shop. Or maybe I'd always been aware of my captivity and had been constantly trying to break the bars of my cell. If so, then my constant longing to reach out for the horizon and the sky beyond it is really nothing but a part of my longing for inner freedom: real freedom, not merely the freedom to roam about inside a huge prison with borders for walls – commonly known as 'the homeland'!

I remembered my boyfriend, as if the thunder had caused an image of him to spring up from deep inside me like a wild mushroom. He and I were among autumn's loyal subjects. After other people had withdrawn from the sea and the mountains, we'd go and take possession of them. We'd run around with the sheep and join in their bleating – 'Baa, baa!' – then giggle with delight over this pure, unsullied language.

It was raining now and the shelling had died down a bit. It was as if those waging war on the land were pausing for a few minutes to mourn the passing of the season they were about to put to death the moment it arrived from heaven.

Nightmare 15

The lull didn't last long... Soon intermittent shots could be heard again in a sprightly rhythm, serving notice that an even fiercer and more violent performance was about to begin. With the first huge explosion, I picked myself up off the sofa where I'd spent the previous night.

I tried to get hold of my nerves so as to be able to spend as normal a day as possible, knowing that otherwise I'd go insane! But this proved to be impossible. In the past I'd always begun my day by reading the newspapers and of course I didn't find them outside the door. They couldn't, for example, distribute them by armoured car! And even if the newspaper sellers had put on bullet-proof vests, they still wouldn't have been able to get to my door, located as it was in the middle of the war zone.

And though I knew full well that even the alley cats wouldn't dare go out roaming on our street, I still made phone calls to all the neighbouring grocery shops. And of course no one answered... Then I went up to the window and cracked it open a bit.

When I looked out, I was confronted by a dreadful sight. All the houses had their windows shut, as if everyone in the entire neighbourhood had fled, stealing away under cover of darkness until not a soul was left.

When the shooting had quietened down and the rain had ceased its coughing, a tense, frightening silence prevailed. It was an unbelievably nightmarish silence, like the stillness that must reign inside coffins that have been shut up for hundreds of years. It was a silence that would make you long to hear any sound, even if it happened to be the report of a gun. I wanted to hear the sound of something that was alive – any sound.

My brother was still asleep, or maybe he just had his eyes closed. As for me, I decided to listen to the radio, a gadget that I ordinarily had no dealings with. I'd recently begun listening to it more often, but only so as to be able to hear what Sharif, the radio announcer, had to say. He was the only one who would give us straight, honest talk instead of a load of revolting pseudo-intellectual rhetoric. Consequently, I'd always turn the volume down until I couldn't tell the difference between singing, instrumental music and chatter. But I knew the timbre of Sharif's voice, and as soon as I heard it I'd turn the volume back up. Then when he was finished speaking, I'd stuff cotton in the radio's mouth again. And so on it went...

Today, though, I was so lonely I turned it on. When it came on the announcer was saying: 'The capital enjoyed a peaceful night except for intermittent gunfire in the area of Qantari and around the Holiday Inn hotel.'

'Aren't you ashamed to tell a lie like that?' I shouted at him.

He didn't answer me, but instead continued reading the news report, then went on immediately to speak at length about the civil war in...Portugal.

I yelled at him again, saying: 'But I don't blame you! You're nothing but a voicebox that they stuff full of false information. You're just an instrument of the crime.'

He made no reply, but just kept reading the news, this time about Angola...

Finally I screamed: 'You're the revolver and they're the hand that fires the shot! And when a crime is committed, they ought to imprison the murderer, not the gun he used...'

He still didn't reply, but started going on in long-winded detail about the weather conditions in the Canary Islands...

Finally the explosions began coming in quick succession, each louder than the one before. Terrified, my brother got up and came looking for me...

After this I concluded that the only genuine news report is what comes to us borne on the wind, not what we hear on the radio.

Nightmare 16

Two long hours of calm went by, during which I heard

nothing but the moans and wails of the creatures in the pet shop. Their voices seemed laden with fear, anxiety, anger and confusion. Or was I just hearing my own inner voice? Logically speaking, it wouldn't have been possible for me to hear them. The pet shop was located on the other side of the garden next to our house. It was a large, unkempt garden that stood between our back door and the back door to the room where the animals were kept. I'd never heard their voices before... but perhaps that was because of the amount of noise created by the activity in the street: the screeching of cars day and night, the chatter of pedestrians and vendors, and the general symphony of everyday life. In this absolute stillness, the kind that must have prevailed in this area half a century ago, when it was still nothing but open fields – that is, before this neighbourhood was built – then it might have been at least theoretically possible to hear them. Or do you suppose it was some sort of mysterious sixth sense on my part that was picking up their vibrations? What was it that had created this bond between us? And why were their voices gradually getting louder and louder until I could hear them enveloping the entire neighbourhood, coming out of every cage, out of every one of these peaceable, mild-tempered creatures wounded by terror, wariness and anticipation? Their voices kept growing louder and louder until I stuck my fingers in my ears and went running towards the window in search of a meadow in the sky... But the sky was nothing but the lid of a steel box!

Nightmare 17

Once the deadly storm had drifted away, the rain abated and the sky turned cloudless and blue. It was weather ill-suited for dying. There hadn't been any shooting for more than two hours. Maybe the fighters were so exhausted they'd fallen asleep behind their machine guns. Or maybe they were out of ammunition. In either case, why didn't we get out of this cage before we were burned to death or died of fright or hunger?

As I stared out at the street from the window, I made up my mind that if a single car or human being passed by and wasn't shot at, then I'd leave this place immediately, either with my brother or without him.

It was exactly one o'clock at the time and until one-thirty neither a car nor any living creature passed by. Nor did a single head emerge from any of the windows in the building facing us. A feeling of anguish, terror and dread came over me and I decided to get out of the house.

Then all of a sudden a dog appeared on the street corner. It approached a pile of garbage in hopes of finding something to sustain it for the day. Then it began walking down the pavement at a snail's pace. I wondered: Do you suppose he notices that the street has changed — that it's devoid of pedestrians and cars? If so, is he happy about the change, upset or indifferent?

Then, without forewarning, a bullet shot from who knows where hit the dog. He fell on to the pavement, shrieking in brutish, heart-rending agony. The echoes of his cries reverberated through the empty streets and came bouncing back off the walls as if they were covered with scores of microphones...

It was the same sniper. The day before he'd killed a loaf of bread and today he'd reaffirmed his existence by murdering the one living thing that had dared to stir in our lifeless street!

Nightmare 18

I could see the hat shop. I could also see bullets going through all the hats until every one of them was riddled with holes. Elsewhere I saw the heads that had been destined to buy and wear these hats as they continued living their lives in various faraway places. I could see the bullets piercing the heads also, until each head bore a bullet hole in the very same spot as the hat which it had been destined to buy!

Nightmare 19

I saw them lead a young man over to the pavement. His only 'crime' was to have gone down a street where, just a few minutes earlier, a car carrying some armed men had parked. One of the armed men had a brother who'd been killed and he was on the look-out for any scapegoat he could find. The person's name was of no importance; the only thing that mattered was that he be of a different religion...

The brother of the slain man took hold of the youth-now-turned-scapegoat and began cursing his religion. As for the youth, he was perplexed. He was a philosophy student and believed in God, but he saw every religion as a means by which people could come closer to God. At those moments when he felt a need to draw near to his Maker, he'd pray in the first place of worship he happened to come to, be it a church or a mosque. However, he preferred to kneel on the seashore and speak privately with his Creator far from man-made edifices. Then he'd let the wind scatter the vibrations of his prayer throughout the vast universe, thereby creating a few drops of light that might dissipate a little of the darkness of hatred and brutality that hang over our world like a cloud of evil.

They dragged him on to the pavement.

'What have I done wrong?' he asked them.

Enraged, the brother of the slain man replied with curses and insults. The armed men nearly came to blows over whether they should kill him there and then or take him with them, over who should kill him and how.

One of them asked him: 'How do you prefer to die?'

'I'd prefer not to,' he replied.

One of them suggested that they put a quick bullet through his head, then get moving right away before some other gang came along.

'I don't want to die,' he said to them.

The bereaved brother insisted that he was the one who should have the privilege of killing him.

'I don't want to die,' the young man repeated.

One of them asked him: 'Which party do you belong to?'

'I belong to the party of life,' he replied.

'What's your name?' they asked.

'Lebanon.'

'Family name?'

'Arab.'

Finally they shouted at him: 'Come on, this is no time for joking! Who are you?'

He repeated: 'My name is "Arab Lebanon", and I don't want to die.'

One of them said: 'It would be better to kidnap him, interrogate him, then get rid of him.'

They continued to disagree over whether to kill him right away or to wait, and before long they were all pointing their guns at each other. Making the most of the situation, the youth resorted to the only style of combat he knew: flight.

He took off, running down the road like a madman. He kept going for quite a distance, but always he heard the sound of footsteps running behind him. Finally he tripped and fell to the ground. It wasn't pitch dark, since a streetlamp was shining nearby. When he became aware of the light, he was amazed, since he'd been feeling as if he were in a jungle back in the days before electricity was discovered, or even fire... The footsteps that he'd heard pursuing him stopped and he saw the face of the armed man who was hellbent on killing him, this time with shocking clarity. And the armed man was crying just as he was.

'My brother was a fireman,' he said. 'The last time he went to put out a fire, they killed him and sent him back to us a corpse.'

Thinking that the man was confiding his woes to him, the youth almost felt sorry for him, and was going to encourage him to say more. But then the brother's face was suddenly transformed into that of a ruthless murderer as he said: 'And you're going to die for it. The ones who killed my brother belonged to your religion.'

The youth wanted to say something in reply, to tell him many things, to explain to him what the matter of 'religion' was really all about. But he also realized that now wasn't the time for philosophical debate, but rather for taking up arms. However, arms were something he didn't have.

He was still lying on the pavement on the spot where he'd fallen. He exerted a tremendous effort to free himself from the butcher's grip and stand up, and found himself grabbing on to a marble moulding on a nearby wall. His senses were in a state of high alert and by the dim light of the streetlamp he read an inscription engraved in the marble: 'This fountain was presented as a gift for the glory of God by Salim Fakhoury, 1955.'

The fountain was bone dry, without a single drop of water in it. But the armed man twisted the youth's neck until it was up against the fountain's marble rim, then in a flash his knife came down on the major artery in his neck. The youth gasped, and that was that. But the armed man continued to cut into the youth's neck even after his body had fallen limp, while blood came pouring out of the fountain, which may have been dry for years. The blood gushed forth, bursting out in copious torrents... It flooded the streets, then rose higher and higher until it was lapping at people's windows and finally came pouring into the rooms of the houses. It was like some sort of mythical spring that never runs dry. As it rose, it immersed my knees, then my waist, then my chest, then my neck... As I choked on the blood, I began to gasp and scream... Then finally I woke up...

Nightmare 20

I wondered: Don't these men ever get tired? Don't their fingers ever take a rest from pressing against the trigger?

The periods of calm were so brief as to be hardly worth mentioning, and I concluded that the fleeting moments of tense silence must be when replacements were being brought in for the fighters.

That terrifying, charged silence had come back again. I listened hard and could hear some men shouting, but I couldn't make out what they were saying. All I could catch were shrill, high-pitched calls coming in rapid succession, like the warning cries uttered by birds in the wild.

Unfortunately for me, my house was located exactly midway between the two groups of fighters. Right smack in the middle... I thought of the person who'd spoken in praise of the 'golden mean' and pitied him for his short-sightedness. If he'd lived in our house, he might have said something different. I knew that the fighters located in the streets behind us must surely be in contact with people. They might even have got hold of a few *mana'iche*[1] to pass around between them. As for our house being located right in the centre of the battlefield, on top of a hill exposed on all sides and surrounded by gardens overgrown with wild grasses, all of these factors made it impossible for either of the two sides to get to us. It would even have been impossible for the 'third side' – namely, the scavengers who made it their profession to loot war-stricken houses.

We were like the inhabitants of a leper colony. No one would have dared come near us, not even a thief! Shells and bombs were the only things willing to hazard paying us a visit, to come knocking on our doors and walls...

Nightmare 21

It was dusk...
My beloved would always come to me at dusk... at dawn... with the thunder... with the rain... with everything that was awe-inspiring and timeless...

My beloved would always come to me with the autumn, as if that season were his footprints on the ground... He would come down to me out of the mad symphony of death and explosives then come in lacerated with bullets, just as he had been the last time I saw him. Then I'd run to him and cling to his chest, which had been sown with shattered, jagged pieces of glass as a field is sown with seed. The closer he drew me to him, the more deeply the splinters of glass would sink into my own chest. We were fused in death and pain, and the knives of glass were transformed into bridges, into arteries shared in common by our two bodies... Then little by little the darkness would descend upon us, and right there in my arms he'd vanish into thin air as I cried out: 'But I still love you!'

Nightmare 22

'But I love you!' I said.

We were speeding along in the car through the streets of Beirut late last spring (the spring of 1975). It was the day the violence broke out – round one...

'But I love you!'

We were talking about an absurd joke that we'd discovered after we got to know each other – namely, that the word written in the box for 'Religion' on his identity card wasn't the same as the one written on mine.

'But I love you!' I insisted.

He was telling me about his father's absolute refusal to think of us getting married – because of the religious difference!

'But I love you!'

I couldn't believe that religions had come into existence to destroy love rather than to stoke its fires...

'But I love you!'

'We'll get married anyway, then,' he said. 'We'll marry once in the desert under the stars. For witnesses we'll have the cosmos, ourselves, and the God that lives inside us and everywhere. Then we'll get married in a church and then in a mosque. That way, maybe we'll please everybody.'

'It's impossible to please everybody,' I protested, 'And besides, it's immoral even to try. It's our duty to put a stop to this crazy obsession that people have with divisions, not to go along with them.'

Then all of a sudden we were stopped by the strangest, most peculiar barrier... A thin piece of string had been stretched from one side of the street to the other and in front of this extraordinary checkpoint there stood a group of children whose leader and oldest member was ten years old.

We were laughing. It pained us to think of tearing up their war string, so we stopped. They were all holding sticks as if they were rifles, which made us laugh all the more. Then they asked to see our 'tickets' (that is, our identity cards), so we got them out, amused by the act they were putting on.

My boyfriend said: 'They remind me of the naughty pupils I had when I used to teach in the lower grades.'

Then the ten-year-old said to us: 'The woman should be kidnapped and murdered. She's of a different religion from ours.'

Then, addressing my boyfriend, he added: 'As for you, though, you can pass through.' His voice was fearsome and sharp, like the fangs of a little wildcat.

We sat there studying their faces. They looked like adult faces that had been mounted on children's bodies. Then they began to sprout beards, their fingernails grew out, their faces developed wrinkles and sweat came streaming down their foreheads. Suddenly they'd turned into a gang of pygmy highway robbers...

As my beloved pulled away, I screamed in terror.

'What's got into you?' he asked.

Nightmare 23

Several weeks later, with the battles still blazing as fiercely as ever, we were halted in the same spot by another checkpoint. This time, though, the people who stopped us weren't little midgets and the rifles were real. And this time they really were my beloved's students. Yousif breathed a sigh of relief when he saw their faces, and as he opened the car door to get out and speak to them he said to me: 'They're my students – don't worry.'

As for them, though, they spoke to us in the same way that the children at the first checkpoint had: with the same tone of voice and with the same trance-like look in their eyes, as if they were under the influence of some sort of mysterious, wicked magic. They asked for our identity cards, and Yousif said to them: 'What! Don't you remember me? I'm your professor... I'm Yousif.'

But his student just repeated the question, this time enunciating more clearly than before. I gave them my card and so did their professor, my beloved. Then one of them started insulting me because I was going out with someone of a different religion. Angered, Yousif shouted at him: 'Even you?'

I was taken aback by the student's response. With astonishing, metallic coldness, he replied: 'All we know now is that you're of a different religion from ours – the religion of the ones who kidnapped my cousin, then tortured and killed him.'

Yousif shouted at them: 'You idiots! Don't you see that you're poor like me? Poverty – that's our primary "religion"! Poverty should make us allies against people who have a vested interest in continuing to rip us off, then numbing us to what's really going on by playing up religious differences! Listen, sons ...'

The youngest of them, who hadn't even sprouted a beard yet, replied: 'We've had enough of your lectures, Prof. Come with me, please...'

Scarcely had my beloved turned his back and stepped on to the pavement than the shot rang out. The night air seemed to make it all the louder, like the sound of hungry birds of prey screeching over a floating corpse. Right before my very eyes, my beloved was torn to shreds. His shoulders, his arms, his back, his chest – every part of his body that I'd kissed was torn asunder. As the bullet penetrated him it thrust him forward. He collapsed on to an airline display window, which shattered and turned into knives of glass that pierced him.

I was too stunned to scream. It was a nightmare beyond belief. I ran over to where he was and, as I bent down over him, I suddenly burst out laughing. I laughed and I laughed and I laughed... His death was an absurd joke. In the airline display window there was a miniature aeroplane that kept blinking on and off, on and off. For so long we'd dreamed of going away together... But love's aeroplanes are made only of paper, while reality's bullets are made of fire.

Then one of the young men slapped me in the face several times, saying that that ought to knock some sense into me. Then he took his knife and engraved the symbol of my religion on my arm. The pain was excruciating.

He said to me: 'That's so that from now on, you won't forget where you belong and go out with some guy of another religion.'

Then I took off running through the darkened streets screaming: 'But I belong to love and to life! And it's engraved on the inside, deep in my bones, not on my skin!'

Nightmare 24

Someone was knocking on the door. It was our elderly neighbour, Amm Fu'ad.

'Has your brother come back yet?' he inquired.

'My brother!' I replied. 'But he went down to see you!'

In a dejected-sounding voice, he said: 'Yes, he came down to see us, and we hadn't laid in a good food supply, so he decided to go and get some things for us. He said we'd die of hunger if these battles kept up for another two days!'

'What do you mean, he left?' I shouted. 'How could he have done that? And in which direction could he have gone? Don't you realize that they even shot a dog that had the nerve to cross the street?'

'He slipped out through the back garden, where the pet shop is. It's a narrow back street, so it's relatively safe from watchful eyes.'

'But how could you have let him go?' I shouted. 'He isn't armed!'

Amm Fu'ad said sorrowfully: 'He insisted on going and he took my pistol with him.'

'But your pistol is an antique! It dates back to the First World War – and that was ages ago! The world has changed... Against modern weapons, your pistol would offer about as much protection as a mosquito would against an attacking lion.'

He replied serenely: 'But the mosquito can bloody the lion's eye!'

I cursed the poetry he'd appealed to, but I respected his old age. I knew that trying to discuss the matter with him would be an exercise in futility. After all, we belonged to worlds that were light-years apart. The gulf that lay between us was vast indeed.

And I found myself wondering: Do you suppose my brother really went on some sort of heroic mission to bring back food? Or is it just that, like me, he's scared to death, so much so that he lost his nerve and decided to grab the chance to make his getaway without taking any responsibility for me?

I figured that the latter possibility was the more likely one. But I didn't blame him. In fact, I envied him for his courage! In this kind of hell, perhaps the only sort of heroism possible for unarmed people like us was to do exactly what my brother had done: flee! To stay alive... alive... alive...

Nightmare 25

It was nearly sunset and my brother hadn't come back...
Meanwhile, I sat reading a pile of old newspapers that I'd found heaped in the corner of the kitchen. They were two and three months old, and all of them spoke about death, murder, cadavers, kidnappings and our bitter, intractable civil war. All of them were nightmares, nightmares, nightmares...

A world of horror opened up before me, as if I'd stepped inside the dank cellars of the past and suddenly found myself reliving the horrors of the previous months...

As I kept on reading, nightmares of horror sprouted inside my head, then began growing and spreading, putting out new shoots with the untamed savagery of some abominable, carnivorous plant...

These newspapers had an odd feel to them, as if they were recounting the story of every bullet that I'd heard whiz by since the beginning of hostilities... as if all the nightmares that had beset the city were now sliding over my chest once more with the weight of a tombstone. They were like an aged storyteller in some deserted coffee shop in which I was the only listener... Or like the stories of warrior-poet Antara bin Shaddad and the clay water jug, and Joseph being thrown into the well by his brothers, now transmuted into a tale of unspeakable horror...

And Yousif... here was the picture of his dead body, with a caption saying that he'd been killed by armed men at a checkpoint. Just like that, for no reason... As far as my heart was concerned, he'd really suffered two deaths in one: the first because he'd died, and the second, because he'd died meaninglessly.

Nightmare 26

Night had now fallen and my brother still wasn't home yet.

The bed I was sleeping in wasn't mine, nor was the room. The creaking of the cupboard door was unfamiliar to me and I didn't know how to work the iron latch on the window. The dreary brown furniture wasn't mine and the walls weren't my walls. However, I was going to spend the night in this room and begin a new page in the record of my homeless wanderings...

Amm Fu'ad had insisted that I sleep in his flat on the ground floor. He said that our third-floor flat was more vulnerable to being hit by rockets, and that he and his son, Amin, wouldn't leave me alone in the 'house of terror' that my flat had become...

So I went down to their flat, which was oh so gloomy. Like all houses occupied solely by males, it lacked that tender woman's touch that might have lent a bit of warmth to the place. Three years earlier, Amm Fu'ad's young daughter had died while giving birth to her first child. Then three days later she was followed by her mother, and from that day on the ageing gardener lost all interest in growing violets and pansies. The elderly patriarch began to wither and waste away, and his laughter ceased to be laughter... Now he was content to live in semi-isolation with his Sudanese servant and his only son, Amin, the perennial bachelor...

So here I was again, hanging up my clothes on a clothes rack that didn't belong to me and washing my face in a bathroom whose tap I didn't know exactly how to use, not being sure just how much to turn it so as to keep water from either gushing out in torrents or coming down in a feeble trickle. I was using unfamiliar soap, drying my face on a towel that I was seeing for the first time and the smell of which I detested, and stretching out on a bed that I didn't know who'd slept on last... As I lay there, I stared at the cracks in the ceiling, which were different from the ones I'd grown used to in my own house. All these little details were like faint messages over a telegraph wire, coming through from the kingdom of exile into which I was setting foot once more... Here I was, a vagabond again...

A feeling of unspeakable gloom came over me... Perhaps it was on account of the ageing furniture, whose brown hue was suffused with grief and sorrow. Or maybe it was because I'd seen Amm Fu'ad's wife dying in this room. I'd watched her breathe her last on this very bed... Her head had been exactly where mine was now – possibly even on the same pillow – and her body had been stretched out in exactly the same spot. She'd been a bit taller than me, but since death had made her body contract, perhaps her feet also had been in the same place as mine. The bed remained, while one corpse replaced another, to be replaced by still another... And all the while, the bed grew more and more melancholy and dejected.

I thought to myself: It's as if a bed turns into a coffin as soon as it comes out of the factory, or at least as soon as someone uses it for the first time. As long as every one of us is a corpse in the making, and as long as every human being alive carries his own death around with him, then why do we even have beds? Why not sleep in our coffins from the start instead of going through so many detours and evasions in an attempt to get around the undeniable facts of life?

I felt that death was my only true mother, that the sounds of the bullets whizzing through the air were the lullaby she sang as she rocked me to sleep... Then something inside me began slipping away. It receded further and further into the distance, leaving my body behind, piled in a heap on the bed. And I realized that I was like someone condemned to death who's been granted a temporary stay of execution...

Nightmare 27

Oh... where am I?

What happened...?

I'd been awakened by a horrendous explosion... I screamed... In fact, I heard myself screaming even before I was completely awake, and the sound of my own voice frightened me more than the explosion itself... Then all at once I understood what was going on...

It was an explosion that sounded exactly like thunder... Maybe what I was hearing were 160mm field artillery pieces, or might it have been a rocket-propelled grenade, or 'sagger' missiles? Were they 120mm or 82mm mortar pieces?

Alas! My ear had always loved music with a passion. I could distinguish the special features peculiar to all the geniuses of classical composition and could identify the style of any one of them after listening for just a minute or so. But in this Beirut nightmare music was the sound of gunfire and explosives, and here I was memorizing the range of notes that could be produced by deadly weapons... In fact, I could tell just from the way the shots sounded which of the two sides was shooting at which, since I knew what types of weapon each side did and did not have... Now that I'd graduated from the Civil War School, I knew that the man-made thunder called a 160mm artillery piece was just like the thunder of the gods, and that the shot that sounded like the cawing of crows came from the Belgian 'H and K' rifle or the American M-16. As for the shots that came pouring forth like a cloudburst, they were produced by modern automatic rifles. Still, though, whenever I heard them I'd think back to the cowboy films I'd seen as a child, and I'd picture some fighter spinning a steel cylinder, shooting out scores of bullets with every spin of the wheel...

By now the shots were being fired nonstop and without mercy. I was counting them to keep from going out of my mind, the way pampered rich people count sheep when they're suffering from insomnia. I was dying of drowsiness, while sleep was just a bullet's throw away, as it were. This was my third sleepless night.

Then, after the twenty-first shot had been fired, a deep silence prevailed. What a coincidence... it was as if the shells were being fired in mourning for some great man who'd died. But who had died on this night? And what was his name? What sorts of unseen catastrophes were taking place on this night of unfathomable sorrow and mystery?

I didn't get out of bed and neither did anyone else in the house. No light went on and not a soul knocked on my door. Perhaps everyone else in the house was like me: too frightened even to stand up or move.

I remained alone in the inky darkness, trembling. I didn't hold it against my brother that he'd left me alone. Ever since I was a teenager I'd been supporting myself financially, living my life like any other 'guy' in the family. And now I was afraid just the way any unarmed young man might have been on this night of madness. After all, fear is a human phenomenon, not just a female one. Still, though, I couldn't get the image of my beloved Yousif out of my mind – and that broad chest of his which had invaded my lonely existence. I sincerely wished he could hold me close and that I could do the same for him. It wasn't that I wanted to hide by burying myself in his bosom. Rather, I wanted each of us to find protection in the other, like the two leaves of a double window that close together in the face of the storm. I didn't dream, for example, of fainting in his arms. But the night would have been less dark and the roaring of the bombs less fearsome for both of us if we'd been able to hold hands. After all, in an earthquake even wild animals huddle close together. To die communally, as it were, is less terrifying than to die as a solitary individual. He who dies alone dies twice: first because he's alone and then again because... he's died!

Nightmare 28

The bombs had stopped going off and the shooting had ceased, allowing an all-embracing silence to settle over everything once more. Yet I still couldn't go back to sleep.

Silence had begun to frighten me even more than the sound of explosions. In the silence I could hear my heart beating... In the silence I could hear the constant bleeding of some unseen part of my body... I could hear the blood dripping on to the cold tile floor in the darkness... drop by drop... Or might it have been the partially open tap in the bathroom next to my room? In the silence I could hear the sounds being made by the creatures in the pet shop. They'd begun to get hungry and thirsty and were pining away for the sun. Meanwhile, their hopes were fading and their patience was wearing thin. I heard some of them beating their heads against the sides of their cages in protest, while others sat quietly, awaiting the unfolding of events to come. Some were praying, while others were dreaming or blaspheming or trying to escape or delivering speeches and sermons... just like people... exactly like us, the residents of this tame, domesticated neighbourhood...

It was a long, mournful silence... Then little by little, the sound of gunfire resumed. It was very close to where we were and I suspected that a battle of some sort was taking place in the street in front of our house. Then suddenly a car began honking its horn... Coming as it did in the midst of the shooting, it sounded strange and comical – almost human, like the howling of a man who'd been shot. Yet surrounded as I was on all sides by darkness, gunfire and explosions, I took comfort in the sound, although I was saddened by it as well. For five minutes straight, the horn wailed at the top of its lungs, then ever so gradually it began growing fainter and fainter, like someone in the throes of death. Apparently the sound annoyed one of the fighters, since it was followed by several heavy sprays of bullets, after which the car fell completely silent. And now it was dead...

I missed the sound of the horn. I missed life... I missed the traffic, the crowded pavements and the screeching of horns when I used to drive along the mountain road with Yousif at my side. We'd laugh with malicious glee wherever we saw some 'official' car that had been in an accident and now lay upside-down on the side of the road. And I found myself singing softly,

> 'May the rain bless you abundantly, if the rain should so choose,
> Ye days of lovers' reunions in Andalusia!'

My eyes were filled with Yousif's image and with tears. Then suddenly I thought in dismay: Do you suppose I've started to lose my mind? And is this a song I'm singing or a dying person's last gasp?

Nightmare 29

When I woke up, I was inundated with a burning anxiety...

The room was both strange and familiar to me at the same time. Then I remembered everything. For a long time I remained stretched out just as I was, watching the luminous spot that was shining in through a hole in the window where it had been pierced by a bullet. Could this be reality, plain and simple? Was it true that the light would come in only if we bored through the walls of our prisons with bullets and explosives? I slipped out of bed. The cold was intense and came pouring out of all the unfamiliar pieces of furniture surrounding me. Then suddenly a profound misery flooded over me. How many times had I dressed in cold, strange rooms in faraway lands, a new room every day and a meal of gloom and loneliness every morning? I went out into the hallway. It was obvious that Amm Fu'ad had been awake for some time. However, it didn't appear that he'd been up all night. I envied him for his poor hearing. Only the deaf, having been freed from one of their senses, would be able to live with Beirut's nightmares. After all, once life becomes a nightmare, the senses are instruments of torture.

Standing in front of the window, he greeted me with a sort of lifeless amiability, while outside a luxuriant jasmine plant shimmered in the light of the not yet risen sun. There wasn't a single person among us who would have dared go out to the garden to inquire after the sun's health. I wished I could bury my face in the jasmine flowers, close my eyes and fly away to a night of tender affection, to Yousif's night ('Good evening, my bygone yet unforgettable love. Oh, good evening!'). I began to chant the tune in a funereal tone of voice. I didn't know why, but ever since Yousif's death, all the songs of the past had begun to taste like ashes and tears in my mouth.

Amm Fu'ad told me he was going out to pick me a jasmine flower. I begged him not to, fearful for both his life and the flower's. So he changed his mind, seeming to be happy that I hadn't let him pay with his life for this sweet whim of his... or be obliged to retreat like a frightened child.

And so it was that to touch the jasmine plant became a wish and a hope, to stand under the open sky a cherished ambition. Then Amin got up too and stood beside his father. Together they made a picture of terror and misery. Besides that, it always seems like the end of the world when men don't shave off their whiskers, so I implored them both to do so!

Nightmare 30

I went up the stairs to my flat on the third floor, and for the first time I noticed how many large windows lined the stairwell. This meant, of course, that anyone who passed in front of them would be an easy target for a sniper in one of the modern cement buildings surrounding our house which, like most of Beirut's old residences, was made of sandstone. Whenever I passed a window, I would unconsciously lower my head, despite my recent discovery that the bullets used in modern weaponry don't believe that a straight line is the shortest path to the target, preferring instead the rat's method of running from one wall to another, or that of a billiard ball...

I heard the telephone ring inside our flat. Thinking it might be my brother, I rushed to open the door. I could see that my hand was trembling, and I wasn't having any luck getting the key into the lock. When I finally succeeded in opening the door, the telephone had stopped ringing. It grieved me deeply – I'd been in such need to hear an outside voice, any voice. Then it began ringing again. I ran over to it eagerly. It was

Salwa, the sister of a colleague of mine named Maryam. Salwa was a young, pretty, pleasant girl.

'Yes, Salwa. What can I do for you? Is Maryam all right?'

'Oh, yes,' she replied, 'and she gave me your phone number.'

I assumed she was in need of a loaf of bread, just as I was, or military assistance to get her out of a bind similar to mine. In fact she was in need of some help. And what do you suppose it was?

She said, 'I wanted to see if you would speak to your friend Professor Sabri for me and ask him if he'd let me join his folk-dancing troupe! I love dancing with a passion...'

Nightmare 31

Salwa kept pleading with me to put in a good word for her so she'd be able to dance the *dabka*. I remained silent, too perplexed to say a word, while through the glass skylight set high in the wall I could see frightful clouds of smoke. I don't know how I managed to be civil, to not scream at her, 'The city is going up in flames and you're just aflame to dance the *dabka*!' Instead, I asked her politely, 'Where's your sister? And why didn't she call me herself?'

She replied sarcastically, 'Because she went to fight with the militia.'

I didn't say anything to this. I only wished Salwa well, then said goodbye with the understanding that she'd call me the next day (!). Then I rushed over to look stealthily out of the window. Fire was ascending from the Holiday Inn across from our house. I began counting the floors in the gargantuan building. There was a huge tongue of flame coming out of the eighth-floor balcony, and before long it had entered the mouth of the ninth floor, then the tenth... The blaze was spreading with incredible speed, while black smoke covered the face of the sea and the sound of exploding shells rang out. Meanwhile, I was being torn to pieces by dismay and alarm.

Then something shattered. It was the window in the adjoining room. I went running through the house in search of a room without windows and was astounded to discover that there wasn't a single windowless room in the whole place. For the first time I noticed that the entire front of the house was made of glass, half of it being stained glass of the old-fashioned type. In times of peace, stained glass might create an enchanting, spiritual, 'Byzantine' sort of atmosphere. But in times of war, it's likely to turn into small daggers flying in all directions if an explosion should occur. I also noted that all the windows in the house were huge. The man who'd built it hadn't been thinking of war. He'd been thinking about love, peace and the beautiful horizon, so he made sure that the sea could peek in through every single window, even the ones in the bathroom. The hallway alone had no windows at all. But what good would it do to use that as a shelter when there were three doors opening on to it? The explosions continued rocking the house, while the sounds of shattering glass in the neighbourhood could be heard clearly between one boom and the next.

I found myself sitting on the hallway floor. Then I got up, fetched a chair and sat down on it. In front of me I placed a packet of cigarettes and a box of matches, then gave myself over to the madness of the explosions. I was well aware that, perhaps for the third time, I was standing on that fine line that divides life from death, and a marvellous tranquillity washed over me. In that narrow hallway, explosions following one on the other were illumining the depths of my soul.

Nightmare 32

Doors that had been closed inside me began opening one after the other. I found myself looking at things and seeing beyond them...

In front of me there was a library extending the entire length of the corridor wall and reaching from the floor to the ceiling. The hallway wasn't as safe as I'd supposed, though, since in the event of an explosion inside the house all the books might come crashing down on top of me and kill me. As for the remainder of the wall, it was covered with a huge poster containing a picture of dense, leafy trees. I could have stepped inside it, fleeing from the hell of my own world to a lush European forest. I could have climbed the trees, fused with the fog and gone to sleep for a while.

But I didn't. Life had taught me that it was no use running away from where I truly belonged. I was a daughter of this land, a daughter of this Arab region so ridden with unrest and turmoil that it threatened to boil over at any moment. I was also a daughter of this war. This was my destiny.

My gaze was fixed on the shelf that held the books I'd written, as well as scores of others that I'd translated over a period of ten years of work in a revolutionary publishing house. I found myself whispering: And I also had a part in bringing about this war. True, I'd never carried a weapon in my entire life. It was also true that I was as terrified as a mouse in a pet shop. Yet the lines I'd penned had always conveyed a call for change, a call to cleanse the face of this homeland of ours of all ugliness, washing it with justice, joy, freedom and equality. All the fighters were doing was carrying this out in their own way. These were my words. They had emerged from inside my books to take on flesh as human beings who were now bearing arms and fighting.

Had I really wanted a revolution without blood? Of course ... like all artists, I'm full of contradictions. I want revolution but I don't want blood. I want the deluge to come, but I don't want to accept the fact that people will drown as a result of it... I thought to myself:

– But what's happening here is nothing but a nightmare, not a revolution.

– All revolutions are born this way, baptized in blood. Even the birth of a child takes place only through a baptism of blood.

– But a huge number of innocent and defenceless people are dying.

– No one is innocent in a guilty society.

The sound of bombs exploding continued to reverberate everywhere and I remained seated in the hallway, seeking protection behind its walls. They seemed like the walls of a womb of stone, but I was no longer terrified like a mouse in hiding. The books were looking down at me from the shelves and I was looking back at them, but neither of us possessed any part of the other. They were nothing but empty covers now, their words having fled from their pages to be transformed into fighting men. I picked up one of the books that I'd translated, opened it and found what I'd suspected – blank pages. The words had taken to the streets to lead their own lives. They'd become fighters, transforming ideas into practice. So what was frightening me?

Brilliant, luminous explosions coming in steady succession continued to go off deep inside me, while doors that had been closed within my spirit were opening up one after the other. Voices continued to ring out inside me, carrying on their discussion within that tiny, well-locked box called my brain... Shouts rang out one after another and I imagined that the corridor walls and the book-laden shelves were returning their echo...

– But a huge number of innocent, defenceless people are dying...

– No one is innocent in a guilty society.

– What about those who remain neutral?

– There can be no neutrality in a society devoid of justice. There can be no neutrality in the city of nudity and the veil, the city of hunger and surfeit. Those who remain neutral are the principal offenders. The silent majority is the criminal majority. It sees the injustice and even suffers from it, yet it opts for cheap safety rather than exposing itself to 'noble' danger...

– Some people aren't psychologically equipped to endure the sight of blood.

– When they take a good look at their inner wounds and their own bleeding, they'll have no choice but to learn to watch their enemy bleed under the force of their blows...

– 'If anyone strikes you on your right cheek, turn to him the other also...'

– Rather, 'An eye for an eye, and a tooth for a tooth,' and he who offends first is the greater wrongdoer.

– But what sin is the peaceable, safe, silent majority guilty of?

– Its 'sin' is that it has remained silent and conciliatory, living in the illusion of safety... Every attempt to maintain neutrality is actually participation in an act of murder committed by some oppressor against someone who is oppressed. The silent majority is the criminal majority... It presents the oppressor with an irresistible temptation to persist in his practice of injustice. And it's this silent majority that arouses evil impulses in the souls of 'human wolves'. A spirit of conciliation is an incitement to murder, which is a crime. Passivity is the first step towards suicide. And that also is a crime.

– But I haven't been neutral. On the contrary, I've been partial to one side against another. I'm on the side of the sun, of justice, of freedom, of joy, of equality. And I've spent my whole life serving these causes with the only weapon I know how to use well...

– You should have learned how to use other weapons for a time such as this.

– But a well-used pen is better than a stray bullet.

– What good does the pen do in the whirlpool of fire that we find ourselves in now?

– I'm waiting until the gunfire falls silent and the pen regains its voice...

– You mean you're going to sit in this dark corridor like the rats do, then, when the war ends, you'll go on playing the same absurd part that you did before: applauding or whistling from the safety of your office, then, when an explosion goes off, ducking and hiding under your desk!

– But what good would it do for writers to be killed in the war when most of them aren't cut out to be good fighters anyway? Byron was a great poet, but a failure as a fighter. He died in the civil war in Greece after his own side – rather than that of the enemy – had suffered heavy losses. But if he'd lived and written on behalf of the ideas he believed in, he would have benefited others and benefited from them. Instead, he died and began to rot an hour later, and his hand – which was his 'lamp', as it were – was extinguished. It's the artist's duty to remain alive in order to continue fulfilling his mission: writing!

– But why do you cling to this one example? What about other artists who've chosen to fight?

– Hemingway was a bad fighter too. True, his literature benefited from his experience on the battlefield. But as for the side he fought for, no doubt it paid dearly for his ineptness when it came to using a weapon or practising the arts of war. Perhaps the only time Hemingway used his weapon well was the moment he committed suicide!

– You'll find scores of examples to justify this instinctive aversion of yours to blood and physical violence.

– I don't want to fall prey to a sense of guilt because I don't fight. I can think of scores of educated French people who were overcome with this feeling during the days of the civil war in Spain. But then when they volunteered to fight, they ended up being a burden to the revolutionaries. One of them, a famous poetess, wasn't good for anything on the battlefield, not even cooking for the soldiers. So to drag the artist to war would be like dragging Marie Curie out of her laboratory and into the kitchen on the pretext that the country was suffering from a shortage of cooks!

– So then, you believe that the mission of the artist is to pour out the fuel and light the fire, then flee?

– Just about! That's true in a way. The artist's function is to create the revolution, not to carry it out. President Gamal Abdul Nasser declared that Tawfik Hakim's book *Return of the Spirit* was a major contributory factor in the outbreak of the Free Officers' revolution which he led in 1952. The book served to light the spark. The artist is the spark that ignites the revolution and its herald as well.

– And its fuel!

– The artist's dying like a rat wouldn't do anyone any good. But what usually happens is that the artist is a unique sort of revolutionary. He manufactures revolutions, then in one way or another inevitably finds himself to be fodder for those same revolutions. He ignites them with the knowledge that he'll be the first to be consumed in the fire. And even if the artist isn't killed during the revolution, he'll lose the tools of his trade: his library, reference books, archives... Even the relative degree of inner peace he's known will be torn away from him as he is driven out of house and home – and add to all this the constant spiritual homelessness he endures...

– But when war does break out, why doesn't the artist fight like any other member of society would? There are good fighters and there are bad ones. So why can't he just be one of the bad ones? That would at least protect him from dying alone and from the torment of listening to the contradictory voices in his head.

– Because the kind of psychological purification that makes him a good artist is also the very thing that prevents him from being a good fighter! I for one couldn't kill or torture anyone. I'd think about how once upon a time the person had been an innocent child. I'd think about how it wasn't his fault he'd turned into the monster I saw before me, but how instead there were all sorts of factors outside his control that went into making him such a scoundrel. I'd also think about his mother and about his sweetheart, and I wouldn't be able to inflict pain on him. I'd bring to mind how his face might look while he was laughing, praying, making love... I'd imagine that he was some sort of self-contained star and that to kill him would be tantamount to a cosmic catastrophe...

Voices, voices, voices, exploding inside my head and arguing out loud! With every voice I heard, I'd feel that a new woman had emerged from inside me. I was no longer just one woman in the hallway. Instead, I'd reproduced and multiplied until the entire corridor was swarming with 'us'. Then there was a horrendous explosion I was certain had come from somewhere inside the house went off, so I went back to being a single women, alone in the corridor on the dividing line between life and death. Looking at my library shelves, I spied the word 'revolution' in most of the titles there. But a voice inside me shouted: This is just a bad dream, not a revolution! These are sadistic nightmares, not a war of liberation!

To which another voice replied: Every revolution in history

has seemed this way from the inside. What matters where a revolution is concerned is the generation that will reap its fruits. There can be no revolution without one generation to serve as its victims...

Then I heard the unmistakable sound of a wall falling down... The explosion drowned out the voices in my head, and I got up and started running. At first, it seemed as if thick smoke was rising from my grandmother's room. I didn't know I had it in me to be brave... but without being aware of what I was doing, I picked up the small fire extinguisher and rushed to her room. Both the ceiling and the wall opposite the window had been gouged out. Initially, I assumed that a shell had fallen on the roof. I ran towards the kitchen, then climbed the wooden stairs leading to the roof. I was surprised to find that it was unscathed. There wasn't even a hole in it. I went back down to my grandmother's room, where clouds of dust had settled on the floor and the furniture. Then, upon closer inspection, I discovered that something had passed through the window pane, boring a hole in it without breaking it, then collided with the ceiling and bounced off on to the wall. And as for what I'd imagined to be smoke, it turned out to be nothing more than dust that had been falling steadily from the cracks in the wall and ceiling. After searching about on the floor, I found three metallic pieces that were still hot. One of them was pointed and so small that I was astounded to think it could have wreaked all this destruction...

Only then did I notice that my knees were shaking as if they'd been detached from both my body and my will. Kneeling on the floor, I buried my face in my hands and began to weep.

Nightmare 33

I hate the way I sound when I cry...

My brain went to work immediately against my weakness and started to chase down the unruly, rebellious elements in my body. I decided that my nerves must be frayed because I hadn't eaten anything.

I went into the kitchen and turned on the gas ring. My hand was shaking so badly that I burned the tip of one of my fingers. It caught fire with incredible speed and gave off a peculiar odour. I didn't feel any pain, yet still went into a frightful panic. How easily the human body can go up in flames! And when I broke an egg into the frying pan, I was startled to find that its white was pink and that its yolk was made of blood. My senses weren't deceiving me. The egg really was full of blood. There might have been scientific explanations for it, but I was convinced that even the chickens in our city had been so terrorized that they'd stopped laying eggs and had begun bleeding instead!

The eggs had turned into a mess of clotted blood...

However, I still ate, swallowing my bloody breakfast without grumbling or complaining. My will had taken over again. And I knew what that meant...

I was fourteen years old when I grabbed a needle and, with a steady hand, pierced holes in my earlobes. First the right, then the left. The pain was phenomenal, but my hand didn't shake. Nor did I quail at the thought of piercing my left ear within just seconds of having pierced the right, even before the pounding of my heart had subsided and the blood had stopped rushing to my head because of the intensity of the pain. I'd placed the needle in a flame and sterilized it, and I didn't put strings in the holes in my ears until the wound healed. Instead, I sterilized two little gold earrings and put them in right away. I was in pain for days, but then the wound healed. From that time on, I was aware of the tremendous power that resides deep inside every one of us, that power called the will. Perhaps the tragic thing in my case was that I'd pitted my will against the desires of my heart for so long that there had come to be a deep-seated, intractable enmity between them!

Nightmare 34

After I'd consumed my meal of coagulated blood, my 'will' decided that I should carry on with my normal life lest I break down and go mad. Work first... So I wrote my diary. Then I remembered that today was Monday, which meant that I had to write my weekly column for the magazine I was working for. The gunfire was going on nonstop. But when I grabbed the pen and sat down on the floor near my table (that is, under the table!) to begin writing, the shooting became all the more savage. It was as if the battle were taking place between my pen and the bullets, as if each of them were challenging the other, like two wrestlers in some arena of ancient Rome. Perhaps we were simultaneously working towards one and the same end: I was writing and they were shooting for the sake of a single goal. Perhaps each of us was waging war in his own way, yet for the same reasons. But at the same time, I sensed that the pen and the bullet were, at best, like brothers who are enemies. After all, it was difficult for my pen to go racing along with ease while bullets were pounding their nails into my skull.

Still, I began to write and write. And as I did so, it felt as if the act of writing were enclosing me on all sides like a coat of mail, garbing me with plate armour, and making me strong, like an ancient boulder in the face of a storm. Soon after this

I stopped hearing the gunfire and instead heard nothing but the sound of my pen, my conscience, and the cry coming from deep inside me and out on to the innocent paper. I was writing with fiery passion about our leaders, who seek to treat a cancer with an aspirin, and about that corrupt class that thinks of the homeland as some sort of suitcase in which it can pack up its wealth, then flee... I no longer felt anything, yet I kept on writing and writing and writing... When I finished, a sharp pain had begun to pierce my head. Concentrating was an awesome task in the midst of the street war that was no doubt going on around my house.

Then I found myself bursting out laughing... I'd written my article now, but how was I supposed to get it to the printer when I couldn't even open a window?

Remembering fairy tales I'd read, I thought: I'll tie the article to my long hair and let it down from the window. Then along will come a horseman on a bullet-proof horse and climb up to the window on my braided tresses. He'll ask me if I'm in need of anything, then climb back down my braids to read the article and whisk it away to the printer. I chuckled. The only modern-day bullet-proof horse was the armoured car. But the armoured cars in this sorrowing homeland of ours couldn't start playing mailman and taxi!

Then I thought of 'the disappearing hat'...

Perhaps the person who came up with the notion hadn't been thinking of the dilemma of a writer caught in the middle of a civil war. No doubt he'd had other ideas in mind. Even so, if I owned 'the disappearing hat', I'd put it on and go out, and no sniper would be able to touch me no matter what kind of sight he happened to be using. But who knows? By now they may have invented X-ray sights that can spot even the people wearing disappearing hats. I went to my bedroom and, standing in front of the mirror, started trying on all my hats, one after the other. Each hat I tried, I expected to be the one, and waited for my image to disappear from the mirror. But that didn't happen. So, I don't own the disappearing hat after all!

I also thought back to tales about witches who turn into sheep or black cats. If I had the capacity to turn myself into some other kind of being, or to take non-human form, I'd be safe, I thought. But then I remembered that the sniper is the enemy of life in all its forms. Hadn't he shot the poor dog just the day before? Do you suppose that dog was a human being held captive like me, who'd turned himself into something else, changing his appearance and taking on another body? If so, then his magic hadn't succeeded in delivering him from the dreaded sniper...

I pictured the sniper's head. He had a single eye in the middle of his forehead, like the ogres in fairy tales, and the body of a robot, like the ogres of modern times!

So how was I going to get my article to press?

Just then the telephone rang, bringing me the answer through the voice of my friend Bilqis.

Nightmare 35

It was as if I were the Prisoner of Zenda, or the Count of Monte Cristo as he rapped on the wall of his dungeon in a plea for help from his fellow prisoner. It was as if I myself were all those whose communication with the outside world had come to require a superhuman, creative effort. Or as if I were a butterfly imprisoned within a cocoon of fire...

As I dictated my weekly article to my friend Bilqis, the telephone wires that connected us were the walls of the Count of Monte Cristo's dungeon. Only he'd been pounding on the wall in a world of silence. As for me, I had to shout at the top of my voice in order for Bilqis to hear what I was saying and transfer it on to a piece of paper in front of her in her famous hieroglyphic handwriting. The shooting was extremely loud. No doubt a battle was being fought in the street right outside the window, as if the bullets wanted to sever the telephone wires and, along with them, the wires of compassion and human fellowship...

When I wrote that article, I hadn't given up all hope of getting it to press. Now, though, as I dictated it to Bilqis so that she could pass it on for me, I realized that henceforth we would have to be more succinct. We'd have to start writing telegrams as it were, rather than lengthy odes. Bilqis wrote nonstop for no less than forty-five minutes. Now and then we'd laugh bitterly when the shooting got so loud that even beating on walls and wires became an exercise in futility. Then finally the phone call came to an end.

In my mind's eye I pictured Bilqis as a white carrier pigeon, flying through the skies of Beirut that were now polluted with the madness of destruction. As she flew to the magazine's printer bearing my message, I said a prayer for her white wings and her golden beak. It was true that she lived in a (relatively) safer neighbourhood than I did. Yet the mere act of venturing out into the street in Beirut had become a life-threatening exercise. In fact, the various neighbourhoods of the city had come to be called simply 'war fronts'. So I decided that if things went on this way, I ought to think seriously about adopting the homing pigeon as a means of sending articles, messages and letters. I imagined the whole population of Beirut giving up their cats, their dogs, their telephones and their cars and breeding homing pigeons instead...

Oh, armed men... if you happen to see a pigeon with white wings, a golden beak and green eyes flying in the direction of a printer's in the Zaydaniya district, please don't shoot at it. That's my friend Bilqis!

Nightmare 36

Once again a vague sense of danger came over me, a sense that some hot presence had penetrated the room. I felt something hot touch my right ear, then collide with the wall behind me just as some glass was shattering. Such things happen quickly – with breathtaking speed... Soon afterwards I realized that a bullet had grazed me, wounding the tip of my ear, and had then rammed into the wall behind me. The strange thing was that I didn't feel any pain. All I felt was a very hot sensation all over my body, a wakeful vigilance in every cell and every limb, and a sort of sinfully delicious exhilaration. I didn't understand the true meaning of what had happened until I saw a few drops of blood on my hand. The bullet had gone straight into my university diploma, which was in a silver frame. It shattered the glass cover, then ripped the paper to shreds at the spot where it read: 'We hereby attest that... has earned such and such a degree in literature...'

I stood there staring at it in a daze. It was as if the bullet had wanted to tell me something, and had chosen deliberately to wipe out the academic qualifications I was so proud to hang on my wall. Or perhaps this was an invitation to me to earn a degree of some other type before it was too late... The degree now required for survival was one's ability to kill and exterminate. Something else that perplexed me about the bullet was the way in which it moved and the fantastic speed with which everything had taken place. I could feel the fire ablaze in my ear even before I was aware that a bullet had stolen into the house. So I figured that all those who were being shot to death weren't even aware that it had happened to them. After all, they were dying so quickly that their brains would have no time to prepare its report on the event!

Nightmare 37

Within a few minutes, the sensation of warmth and scandalous exhilaration had left me. The wound had begun to cool, and with the cooling came pain and a descent from the invigoration I'd experienced initially. It was a minor, superficial wound. Yet it was one more solemn reminder of the fragility of the poor human body, on account of which all these instruments of destruction had been invented. I felt grieved, not because I was wounded but rather because I was woundable, as it were, and killable as well. And it could happen just like that, without the least justification. If, for example, a fly had happened to pass by at the moment when the bullet entered the room and I'd jerked my head a few centimetres to one side in order to avoid it, the bullet would have gone into the middle of my forehead. In so doing, it would have wiped out my memory and, along with it, worlds of love, fears and hopes that had inhabited the little chest – no larger than a can of sardines – which they call my brain!

I took the bullet in my hand and placed it beside my pen. Put a bullet beside a pen and you'll find that the pen is larger. But this bullet in particular looked to me at first as if it were the same length as my pen. Then it grew larger and larger until it became a pillar of fire. Meanwhile, my pen quaked before it, growing thinner and thinner until it had no more substance than the feather of a wounded bird, helpless in the face of a storm of fire.

Nightmare 38

The shooting abated somewhat and, as happened during every lull in the fighting (each of which generally lasted about a quarter of an hour), I heard men calling out to each other but without understanding exactly what they were saying. I figured they must be bringing replacements for fighters who'd grown weary. They would probably go off somewhere to get some sleep, talking on the phone to their worried sweethearts or dropping by to see them. As for me, my sweetheart had gone away for ever, and sleep hadn't fully overtaken me for three nights. This was my only major concern, since someone who doesn't sleep well doesn't think or behave well either, and if he chooses to die or to flee, then it's his instincts that are doing the choosing... And I hated the thought of allowing my instincts to decide my fate...

I found solace in the sound of the fighters calling out to each other. Whenever that sound was absent, an awful, tense silence would reign, a silence which I knew for certain would be followed by more explosions. Meanwhile, the sounds of the creatures in the pet shop grew louder and I could hear them clearly as they cried out in their cages. They were getting hungrier and more frightened, wondering in bewilderment what had become of their owner, who for so long had made his living by selling them and then had run off somewhere now that they found themselves in danger. I heard their voices joining in unison with the murmurs and growls of the domesticated families imprisoned in the neighbourhood until at last it became a single chorus, like the chorus in a Greek play telling the story of a city stricken by the plague of madness.

I felt a strange desire to sneak over to the pet shop and take a look at the creatures inside. At first I convinced myself that I was going to go feed them and save their lives. But then I had no choice but to admit that I wasn't going to save anyone's life! Nor did I know what sort of gravitational force was drawing me to them. Perhaps it was mere curiosity, or a sense of common destiny that bound me to them. Or it might have been the need I felt to seek out their company – I the lone stranger in the world of human wolves. Besides that, the pet shop was the only neighbour's house (apart from Amm Fu'ad's) that I could sneak over to visit in safety. So I decided to take the animals some water, at least. But first I'd wait until darkness fell.

What I didn't know was that the modern sniper, with the eyes of an owl, can see in the dark!

Nightmare 39

The telephone rang. I ran over to it in hope that it would be my brother. I pressed the receiver hard against my ear, only to suffer excruciating pain from my wound, which I'd temporarily forgotten about. I was also pained because it wasn't my brother! It was my friend Maryam, who'd called to ask how I was and to apologize on behalf of Salwa for her insistence on discussing dancing the *'dabka'* at a time like this. I told her that her sister could be excused since she was still just a teenager, a child. The big-time criminals, I said, were those who had been insisting on dancing the *dabka* on our dead bodies for half a century without so much as a change of leadership. And if such a change did occur, then their descendants simply inherited the kingdom of their fathers, cloaking themselves in the same Ottoman-like mentality and manners which with age had grown musty and putrid. And so it was that no one was dying but the people themselves. There is no such thing as the innocent people or nation. Rather, our

people had wronged themselves by being content for decades and decades to bear their executioners on their shoulders...
In a tone full of conviction Maryam replied: 'As for me, I've decided to take up arms and fight. So I won't be going back to journalism right now. The pen is powerless to confront a situation like this. Why don't you join us?'

Nightmare 40

I discovered that there wasn't any sterilized gauze in the house, nor was there any kerosene to use as a disinfectant. All I had was some Mecuriochrome and some cotton. Instead of spending all my money on books, as I normally did, I would have to fit out the house with the trappings of a fully equipped hospital! And in place of my car, from which all the doors had been removed, I would have to save up to buy an armoured vehicle that would close me in on all sides and protect me like a coat of mail. Rather than staying in the house, I would have to live in a fall-out shelter. And instead of my university degree in literature, I would have to become the bearer of a degree from a military academy...

I stood there rubbing my wound. It was quite minor and superficial, so I concluded that it wasn't my ear that was causing me pain. Rather, it was other ears. And I closed my eyes so as to be able to see better ...

I saw them after they had drunk from the spring poisoned with the powder of madness... I saw them cutting off the ears of the newspaper vendor who used to stand in front of our house every morning in order to be able to pay his school fees every evening. I saw ears being severed and cut to pieces in every darkened corner of the city. I saw fire and knives inscribing figures on people's bodies, figures which were supposedly religious symbols. What God is this who is pleased to have his name pounded with nails into people's skulls and burned on to the bodies of his worshippers with the flame of a soldering iron? Go to the churches, to the mosques and to the seashore, travel to the depths of the cosmos and ask Him whether He is pleased. I saw ears piling up in the streets, in front of the doors until they blocked them off like snowdrifts in the winter. I saw gouged-out eyes floating on top of the cup of coffee I was preparing. I saw the remains of dismembered bodies pouring into the streets and accumulating in mounds that towered higher than rubbish heaps. I saw severed legs running away without their bodies and disconnected forearms waving along the roads, bearing white flags or stretching out their hands in search of someone to come to their rescue. I saw fingers floating through the empty streets and pointing accusingly at their executioners. I saw men whose blood had been drawn from their veins so that it could be given to others, running along as bluish corpses. I saw others who had been decapitated, scurrying down the pavements of this grieving homeland of ours in search of their heads, which had been cut off on some dark night. I saw heads whose features had been erased, so severely had they been tortured, heads which had been cut off and were now floating on a sea of blood and darkness in search of their tongues, which had been extracted with pincers. I saw them emerging from the ovens of torture and fire, running along with their bodies in flames and reeking of burnt flesh.

I saw the city being transformed into a witch's cauldron. The cauldron and all it contained boiled and boiled and spun around and around in a whirlpool of bloody shrieks. Meanwhile, bullets pierced through every mouth that wished to utter anything contrary to the logic of the bullets themselves. I saw the poor dying, the innocent poor alone. As for their butchers, they had fled from the city of nightmares and madness to the cabarets of Paris, London and Geneva.

I saw my beloved looking out at me from the cauldron. They brought me his bullet-riddled body and I drew him close to me as I cried out: 'I still love you!'

Nightmare 41

Ah, nightmares, nightmares...

They were sprouting inside my head and climbing the walls of my brain like some sort of wicked, mythical plant...

Ah, nightmares, nightmares...

They were erupting from inside my head (or might they have been outside as well?). At first I would see them only when I closed my eyes, especially after reading the stacks of old newspapers from the preceding months since the war had begun. Nightmares would assail me from time to time like seasonal plagues of locusts.

But now I was seeing them constantly, even when I had my eyes wide open. I'd stand in front of the mirror and see ants coming out of my mouth, my nose and my eyes, consuming me as if I'd died long ago. On this particular day I wanted to put on some eyeliner but was astonished to find that my head had turned into a bony skull. I no longer saw myself in the mirror, but rather a cloud of fire and smoke. Then I grew smaller and smaller until I was the size of a fly, while the mirror grew larger and larger until it became like a translucent curtain in a theatre of madness. I stepped forward into the mirror. Then, roaming about inside, I came to an immense field of trees whose branches were rifles. I saw masked men picking the rifles off the trees and gathering bullets off the ground as if they were heaps of ripe fruit. They were melting down the iron from the ploughs, hoes and scythes and turning them into more bullets – many, many bullets.

The bullet-strewn threshing floors stretched out to infinity. I remembered the wheat, the summertime and the threshing floors from my childhood, and how I used to sit on top of the wooden plank that the mule would drag along over the wheat on the threshing floor. The mule would go around and around, and the golden ears of grain would gleam under the rays of the sun. I'd been determined to enjoy this fantasy ride through the field of blessing as the peasants' songs mingled with my childlike gasps of delight. This time, however, the threshing floors were covered with gunpowder and filled with the stench of wrath, while the sky had become a field of rusty iron. And singing? There was none. There was nothing now but either cries of woe and destruction or matters too trivial to mention!

Then the men emerged from the field of madness carrying with them the fruits of the bitter summer season of Beirut 1975 – the harvest of blood.

Nightmare 42

I remembered...

I once went on a journalistic assignment to a city in Lebanon which I'd been told was to be the main site of a new university. A springtime tranquillity had settled over the suburb where I found myself and, as I went in search of the place where the dream university was to be located, I got lost – as usual – among unfamiliar streets and byways. However, I found being lost quite enjoyable, as long as the road was pretty and teeming with life in all its lush, rejuvenated spring hues...

Then I heard a gunshot...

The sound of gunfire seemed dissonant and out of place in those fields bursting with life and newness. But then I heard a second shot, then a third... Finally, showers of bullets could be heard, while the gun reports continued to echo long after the shots had been fired. It was as if they were bouncing peevishly off every green branch, off the eyes of the sheep in the field, the birds, the lizards, the cats and all the creatures that inhabited this amazing natural abode.

I was still searching for the site of the dream university when, to my surprise, I came upon five armed men playing with their revolvers. Some were throwing them into the air then catching them again, like jugglers in a circus.

'What are you looking for?' they asked me.

I implored them to redirect the black pipes being pointed at me, laden as they were with the emissaries of death. They laughed hilariously at my fear of their weapons... I told them I was looking for the headquarters of the university which, as rumour had it, was going to be established here. One of them mocked me. However, the one who had asked me for my name and the name of the magazine I worked for didn't make fun. Instead, he pointed with the barrel of his revolver towards the road that I needed to take. I noticed that in his other hand he was holding a small wounded sparrow. I asked him in turn for his name and where he worked. They all said that they were bodyguards for a certain VIP.

'But why are you shooting?' I asked.

'Because the boss is off on a visit, so we're having some fun! But there aren't many sparrows, as you can see.'

It astounded me to think that there was anyone who could take pleasure in killing, even if the victim was only a sparrow...

I felt upset for the rest of the day. I didn't know that during the next hunting season, the targets wouldn't be sparrows, but rather... us!

Nightmare 43

The woman hadn't said a thing to her husband. However, when he got up at dawn, his heart was weighed down with a feeling of deep distress. His powerful muscles, his towering height, a moustache that could stop a falcon in midair, his copious chest hair – none of these outward signs of manliness did him a bit of good in his battle with... her body.

He still hadn't been able to occupy the tender-skinned fortresses of this soft, mild young woman whom he'd taken as his third wife. It had been fifteen days now and this hand of his which could slaughter a sheep with a single stroke still fell limp when it came up against her body. In fact, his entire body would droop and sag when it encountered hers. He didn't know what had come over him. It was true that he was forty-seven years old now, but his father had married his fifth wife when he was sixty.

And as if to make his suffering all the more unbearable, this poor young thing (even poorer than he was – in fact, he'd bought her) remained utterly silent. She didn't say a word – she didn't object, she didn't explain, she didn't complain. Yet in her eyes he glimpsed a womanly look of frightful hardness and scorn. In fact, during the past few days he'd begun imagining that the sheep's heads were actually hers, and when he finished them off with a single blow, he'd do it with a boundless, lusty passion.

Early one morning, his bitterness was turning into such a volcano of physical violence that he thought of cutting off her head instead of the sheep's, accusing her of immorality and unfaithfulness. But he couldn't do that yet, since she was still a virgin. With all of Beirut in chaos on account of the civil war, there wouldn't be any qualified medical experts around to examine her corpse. So... why not just shoot her on her way home from the market some day? Then, of course, suspicion would fall on a sniper. Yes, that was it. It would be better to kill her in the street, because then she'd just die like so many thousands of others in the city, without anyone taking the least notice. In fact, her body would stay right where it fell for days and begin to rot. She wouldn't be among the lucky ones whose corpses were taken to the government's cold-storage vaults.

He was roused from his day-dream by the ringing of the telephone. The bey who'd hired him wanted a 'service'. Without being told, he knew where to go.

'At your service, Bey. I'll be there in quarter of an hour.'

Fifteen minutes later, they handed over to him five youths, none of them more than fifteen years old. They asked him to 'teach them a lesson', then to 'take care of them'. Delighted with his new assignment, he took off his shirt, exposing his powerful muscles. Next off came his belt.

Three hours later, five corpses were found in a Beirut side-street. Their heads had been severed and what remained of their bodies bore the marks of brutal torture.

The butcher went home and slept as soundly as if he'd conquered five virgins, one after the other. He slept from noon that day till the following morning. As for his little wife, she didn't worry him any more, since his new work filled up his life nicely, and his pockets as well.

Nightmare 44

It was no surprise – to me, at least – to hear my brother announcing his determination to emigrate on that night in particular – the night of his birthday. For all his friends who were there had taken up arms, and weapons were the main topic of conversation throughout the entire get-together. My brother was the butt of everyone's jokes because he didn't own a single weapon and weapons (as everybody knows!) are what make a man a man.

He said to them: 'OK, then, weapons are for men, not for toddlers, eunuchs, fools and boys...'

A fight might have broken out if one of them hadn't hastened to poke fun even at the blunt knives in our house, which were nearer to being spoons than weapons of destruction! My brother had recently graduated from college after having obtained a scholarship. He was extremely bright in his field, electrical engineering, and extremely dull in anything that required physical exertion. Besides that, he hated weapons and couldn't watch a violent film without getting nauseous.

That night he told me: 'There's no place for us in this city.'

'But this is *our* city,' I protested. 'We'll hold out! We'll fight — each one of us with his own type of weapon.'

'Don't you still believe that "the pen is mightier than the bullet"?' he asked me.

'A Palestinian acquaintance of mine once said to me, "The important thing is to endure. Beware of leaving Beirut." And when I asked him if he would be leaving Beirut, he answered sarcastically, "From now on you won't find a single Palestinian vacating his house until the day we return — to Palestine."'

From then on my brother stopped talking about emigrating, although his face took on a distant expression, as if he'd already left.

But where do you suppose he was now? Had he really gone out to get food? Had he gone away for ever? Or was he lying in a nearby gutter with a sniper's bullet in his head?

Nightmare 45

The chief of police stood at the window in misery. In spite of the shooting and the explosions that were tearing everything around him apart, he'd been given orders not to interfere! From the window he could see them coming — armed and masked. He saw them stealing the police cars. Then he saw them return, come to where he was and strip him of his weapons and his companions. So he didn't interfere. Those were the orders he'd received. Besides, why should he interfere? In whose interest would it be for him to do so? On whose side would he be and against whom? The important thing was for this madness to come to an end and fast. Otherwise he'd die of blood poisoning...

One of his kidneys no longer functioned and the other one didn't work very well either. He had to go at specified times to the dialysis centre. The treatment was costing him a fortune. So when he carried out some of the 'extra' orders that had come down to him, he didn't feel that he was breaking his military oath. After all, he hadn't sworn to commit suicide. But not to accept the money he was getting on the side would have meant just that — suicide. His salary was miserable and so was he. He'd been secretly pleased when they'd stripped him of his weapons, since in so doing they'd also relieved him of the obligation to think.

But what was taking place now right before his very eyes was causing him great anguish. From the time the armed men had set up their barricades right under the police-station window, and ever since they'd stopped that gentle young man and started slapping him around, a voice inside had begun crying out and had refused to stop...

He was young and had innocent-looking eyes. Lifting his gaze towards the police-station window, he'd cried out with utter confidence that he would be rescued: 'Police! Come and save me, please!'

It was obvious that he still believed everything he'd learned in school about how policemen preserve order, defend the oppressed and deal with oppressors. The chief of police remained standing there on the balcony in a state of confusion, the young man's cry having reawakened someone sleeping deep inside him. As for the armed men below, they just burst out laughing. Here was a man seeking protection from the police... What a joke! Once again the young man began calling out to the policeman in a voice filled with childlike trust – he was a little boy appealing to his father for help. Then they began slapping him. One of them hit him across the shoulder with his rifle. He fell to the ground and began to weep. Yet even then his gaze remained fixed on the policeman peeking out of the window and on the half-burned Lebanese flag flying over the station. The policeman didn't want to believe the nightmare he was seeing. They beat the young man until his screams turned to death rattles. Yet he still continued to cry out: 'Police!'

Then suddenly the policeman found himself hurtling out of the police station like a madman in defence of... of... he wasn't sure what exactly.

And after that he didn't feel a thing. Nor did he feel anything when he was taken in an armoured car to the cold-storage room where corpses were kept. And since he didn't read the newspapers the next day, nor did he see his picture in the obituary column.

Nightmare 46

The telephone rang...

I bolted over to it like a mad woman, thinking it might be my brother. It wasn't. It was an unfamiliar voice saying: 'Your brother asked me to call this number and to tell you that he's in prison.'

'In prison? Why? What did he do?'

'He was arrested for carrying an unlicensed weapon.'

I laughed, and laughed, and laughed until I choked on my tears. Oh, Beirut! Oh, theatre of the absurd!

Nightmare 47

'But that pistol is an antique – just some rare piece that people might collect as a hobby the way they do stamps. It's useless, and I don't even think it would shoot. No doubt the ancient gunpowder in it is damp and mildewed after a quarter of a century of disuse...'

That was what our neighbour, Amm Fu'ad, said when I asked him about the revolver that he'd supplied my brother with before he went out!

Then he added fervently: 'It's a miserable, laughable gun, especially if you compare it to modern weapons like M-16 rifles, machine-guns, or Colt or Magnum revolvers. I only gave it to him to lift his spirits!'

At this point I had no choice but to break the news to him. 'My brother is in jail now,' I said. 'He managed to get out of the neighbourhood alive and to get past the armed men and the snipers, and then he was arrested for possession of an unlicensed weapon!'

Amm Fu'ad didn't seem to believe me. At first he just burst out laughing and said I had 'a good sense of humour'! Then his face began to betray signs of fatigue and exhaustion. He closed his eyes half-way, trying to recall a verse of poetry, and managed to pick up the beginning of the thread in the 'hanging ode' that he had in mind.[2] Then he started reciting aloud: 'He whose time has come... He whose time has come...' He began repeating the phrase over and over, his tongue gradually growing heavier and heavier until at last he fell into a deep slumber.

I looked over at him thoughtfully. I was envious. It isn't true what they say about the fragility of the old. On the contrary, they're as solid as oak trees and have an astounding inner strength. From the beginning Amm Fu'ad had declared that no one would leave his house. All the old people in the neighbourhood had made the same decision. As for the young people, they'd fallen prey to confusion. However, confusion is also a sign of health. It's a sign of life, of openness to all currents of thought and a willingness to release one's inner voices, which in turn leads to greater knowledge of oneself and where one stands with respect to all these realities. Besides, what was the use of turning one's house into an idol to be clung to at all costs? Or into a grave where we'd die the death of lazy cowards, all the while deluding ourselves into thinking that we'd paid our dues to the Almighty?

Amm Fu'ad would always sleep through the explosions that went off at night – although perhaps that wasn't because he was brave but because he was hard of hearing!

Nightmare 48

I stole Amin's radio.

Or rather, I didn't exactly steal it but replaced it with the transistor radio that belonged to me. Let's say I made a 'compulsory exchange.' This was because his radio could pick up the local short-wave bands, which meant that one could listen in on the official wireless communications taking place between the rulers and their men or between the internal security forces and their commanders, and even private telephone conversations. In obedience to his father's orders, Amin didn't listen to such things. As for me, though, I wanted to know more about what was really happening. That was how I justified to myself what I'd done. Or you might say I felt no real need to justify it, as if war imposes its own set of moral standards.

Despite the fact that they were separated by an age difference of half a century, Amin was a virtual carbon copy of his father. And that's exactly what was so bad about it – in his day, Amm Fu'ad had been a fighter as well as an important government figure. As evidence of his importance, he possessed a huge fortune that had been amassed through means which, by his generation's standards, weren't considered terribly immoral. Eventually, at the ripe old age of eighty-five, he was forced to retire. As for Amin, he was an exact replica of his father, only as he was now! He was his inseparable companion even to the point of refraining from marriage. He was a dutiful, devoted son even to the point of isolating himself from his own generation. The thread that separates family loyalty from loyalty to oneself and one's generation is a fine one indeed. Some children fail to see the distinction, with the result that they lose themselves in their quest for an illusive family unity.

Amin, for example, never listened to the taboo radio bands because his father wouldn't permit it. Still considering the state to be a true state and the ruler a true ruler, Amm Fu'ad had continued to live in the golden world of the ideals he'd been raised on since he was a child. In his blind imitation of his father, Amin didn't notice that times had changed. I, on the other hand, seemed to belong to another species. And like most members of my own family, Amin secretly hated me. He seemed to have the vague feeling that I was 'the man of the family', and was shocked to discover that physiological differences between men and women were no longer of such great importance. He'd also been faced with the fact that inner strength and endurance don't necessarily reside in a neatly groomed moustache. In fact, they might even be found crouching beneath the soft exterior of a fragile-looking woman. My manliness seemed to awaken the womanliness in him, while my freedom was a challenge to his mental lassitude.

I picked up my booty (his radio) and went up to my cave on the third floor.

The tall, window-lined stairwell didn't disturb me as it had during the first few days, and the bullet that grazed the wall behind me, then ricocheted on to the floor, didn't strike terror into my heart as it had on previous occasions. Instead, I continued up the stairs at the same speed as before. Meanwhile, the pain in my ear had come back. I'd start to feel it again whenever a bullet passed near me. Still, I kept on heading up, as cool as a cucumber. Do you suppose I'd begun to get used to the sound of the shooting? Is it possible for anyone to grow accustomed to the sound of gunfire?

Nightmare 49

The wall had been demolished and the wind had become my own secret kingdom, where I could listen to any conversation I chose anywhere in my woebegone homeland, thanks to this remarkable apparatus: the short-wave band on Amin's transistor radio.

Listening was more exhausting than I'd anticipated, so I got up to look for something to eat. When I came upon the remains of a bottle of vitamins, I was overjoyed. After all, who could tell how long my incarceration might last? Here I was nearing the end of my third day without a single soul having knocked on my door or even passed by on the pavement across the street.

When the roar of the gunfire had died down, the voices of the poor creatures in the nearby pet shop broke through to me once more. This was the third day of their isolation and imprisonment too, the third day since they'd seen the sun.

Perhaps they'd begun to get hungry. Perhaps the food in their cages had run out and the water as well. Even if the shop owner had wanted to feed them, he couldn't have in these circumstances. I didn't think anyone from outside would be able to get to them, but I thought that I might be able to via the garden behind our house. However, knowing that I'd become an enticing target for scores of snipers all around us, I decided to wait until sunset.

What was it that drew me to them? Why did their voices haunt me so? What was the common something between us? I'd always loved all sorts of creatures, from owls and squirrels to lizards and frogs. But what I was experiencing now was entirely different. I felt a bond between myself and the creatures incarcerated in the storeroom across the way, who sat in their cages quaking in terror, defenceless and bewildered. Might it have been the tie that develops between beings that share a common fate? Might I have been one of them without realizing it?

Nightmare 50

The explosions had died down a little...
I left the hallway, my 'war headquarters', and headed for my bed. When I got there, I found that bullets had ripped the pillow to shreds. A kind of hopeless indifference came over me.

I stretched out on top of the bed, which was covered with splinters of wood, iron and lead, and tried to relax a bit. I detached my head and laid it beside me on the pillow, then strove in vain to go to sleep. As I lay there, my gaze was drawn to the hourglass that dear Yousif had given me. It consisted of two spheres of clear glass separated by a narrow neck which allowed the sand to pass from one sphere to the other. It took half an hour – by modern clocks' time – for the sand to pass all the way through. It was an ethereal, silvery blue, as if that were the colour of time. On the day he gave it to me, Yousif said: 'My love for you will keep on pouring forth, just like this sand. If you ever doubt my love, just turn the clock over again, and when the sand starts flowing, that means that I love you...'

Never for a moment had I doubted Yousif's love, not even now that nothing was left of him but a mangled corpse. He would always come to me with the wind wafting through the bullet holes in his body and I'd hold him close to my heart, mustering every ounce of my soul's capacity for tenderness and unity with another spirit... Even so, I turned the clock over and the sand began flowing from the top sphere to the bottom one, slowly but steadily... steadily. I gazed at it pensively as it slid down... bleeding nonstop. After all, nothing can halt time's incessant forward march – neither calamity nor great joy, neither earthquake nor civil war, neither Yousif's death nor mine. And if at that very moment I'd been struck by a bullet that blasted my head apart, even then the sand would have continued its inevitable flow. Perhaps I was just exhausted, having been worn down by the successive explosions. By now the sand had emptied out of the upper sphere and had accumulated in the bottom. Even so, I knew that time's invisible sands were still pursuing their course through the infinite expanses of the cosmic sphere...

I sat staring at the silvery-blue granules heaped in the

bottom of the lower sphere. Then all of a sudden the most peculiar thing happened. The sand began rising to the upper sphere, without the slightest alteration in its rate of flow – as if time were moving backwards. Then the sand's upward flow began to accelerate, going faster and faster and faster.

Suddenly I found myself with Yousif on the seashore. No longer was his body riddled with bullets. Instead, here we were, reliving our sweet days together. Everything was repeating itself, exactly as it had been.

Nightmare 51

As I waited for it to be time to visit my neighbours, the creatures in the pet shop, I read the old newspapers piled up in our house. It seemed to be the only available source of entertainment, and at the same time it was a kind of torture. I read and I read... in fact, I'd been re-reading them ever since the first day I was confined to the house. And as I did so, I saw them with new eyes. Every piece of news took on new meaning, a significance it had never had before.

For example, one announcement read: 'From Muslimani and Samir to their family in the Nabatiyah region: We're fine. Please don't worry!'

When I read it, I was filled with a terror that knew no bounds. There wasn't a trace of civilization anywhere in sight. Perhaps the only reason I'd been reading old newspapers and running my hands over my books was the need to reassure myself that I was truly living in what was supposedly the space age. Perhaps at this very moment some spaceship was taking off from Earth to discover another planet or star. Yet at the very same moment there were still people on our own planet living through the torments of the Stone Age. The newspapers alone enabled me to believe, if only for just a moment, that I was still living in my own era and that the wheel of time hadn't suddenly gone awry and sent Beirut hurtling a thousand years into the past. What a tragedy to live in a country where one's mere survival is considered a newsworthy event. If the newspapers all went out of print – which was exactly what might happen if their offices continued to be the targets of sabateurs – how would people like Hasan, Samir, Muhammad or anyone else contact their loved ones? How would they manage to inform their families living on the other edge of the jungle that they'd escaped unharmed from the clutches of the wild beasts? With smoke signals American Indian-style? By beating the message out on drums? Via carrier pigeon?

Then I read the following: 'Ali Fadi Yousif would like it to be known that he is from Urmati and is not to be confused with the Ali Yousif whose body was discovered after his throat had been slit at the hands of...' I was taken by the wording of the announcement and decided that if I survived I'd publish one of my own. It would read: 'I hereby declare that I am the same woman who was found with her throat slit at various stages of her life and who expired several times only to emerge once more from her ashes. I likewise declare that I am still alive and well, and capable of having my throat slit several times more in the future.'

By this time the sun had begun gathering up her golden robes; before long nature would be casting the black cloak of nightfall over the city. It was time for me to pay my daily visit to the pet shop.

It was night-time... the time of explosions and of terror. The time of wandering, vexed spirits whose screams had been etched into the face of the heavens in the language of iron and fire.

As I slipped out of the house and descended the stairway, I

noted to my dismay that I was ducking, not only when I passed in front of a window but the entire way down. In fact, I'd begun doing the same thing inside the house whenever I moved from one spot to another. True, I'd learned from my experience with the billiard-ball bullet that keeping oneself below window level is of no use when dealing with modern weapons. But even so, I'd got into the habit of ducking whenever I came near a window. It was as if I were bowing, not on account of the bullets themselves but out of respect for bullet logic, as it were. How degrading it feels to go walking around for days and days bent over like a hunchback. Even if peace had returned to this war-torn city of ours, it might have found that we'd forgotten how to walk upright, with a gait more ape-like than human.

Night-time... the time of brutality, of death that conceals itself even beneath one's fingernails. It was the time of destruction.

I reached the garden and turned towards the back of the house.

To begin with I was frightened by being out of doors. The first time I heard the sound of shooting when I was standing outside, I'd been terror-stricken. Whenever it had begun on previous occasions, I'd been sheltered behind walls or furniture, or had at least been standing up against something. But as I stood now in the garden beneath the night sky, my fragile body stripped of any sort of protection, a fearful tremor went coursing through me at the sound of bullets raining down somewhere nearby.

The sound of shooting in the open air was a new experience. It was death itself, unmasked and drawing near. As for me, I was a mere ant in the vast kingdom of the night. I ran towards the nearest tree – which happened to be a date palm – and clung to its trunk. As I buried my face in its bare breast, it seemed I could hear its heart beating, the sap coursing through its veins and fear's drumbeats throbbing inside its wood. As I clung more tightly, together we became two panic-stricken trees, two terrified human beings, two lives in the grip of dread and fear. The tree, however, would remain where it was until such time as it was struck by a bomb or met its end in a more peaceful manner. Unlike me, it didn't have the option of running away. Consequently, it was a source of some consolation to remember that I was a human being rather than a tree, and that at least I could flee if I chose to.

But oh, the sound of gunfire when I was alone in the open air! In the beginning it terrified me no end. It was as if every bullet that went flying came to rest in my own body and as if every shell that exploded shattered me alone. But finally I came to a critical realization – namely, that if a bullet were ever to strike me, I wouldn't be the one to hear it. Likewise if I were hit by a bomb, it wouldn't strike terror in my heart, since by the time I realized there was something to be afraid of, I'd be shredded to pieces. After all, as long as anything capable of harming me was something I wouldn't be able to hear, then anything I was able to hear must be incapable of harming me. This thought bolstered me up a bit. But even so, I continued to tremble whenever I heard an explosion.

I made my way through the darkness towards the back wall of the pet shop. I was familiar with the locations of the various trees and plants in the garden, but even so I lost my footing more than once, despite the fact that it wasn't pitch dark. I looked up into the sky. There was no moon – only the streetlamps that had survived the fighting, most of which were still giving off some light. At last I reached the narrow window. It was at ground level when viewed from the garden. However, I realized that it might be quite high in relation to the storeroom floor. So how was I going to get down from it?

I might have to bring a rope with me. The only problem was that I'd never climbed a rope before. I wondered: Do you suppose it's as easy as it looks in films? Everything that was happening to me these days, I'd seen before in some film or other. But I was discovering what a difference there is between real life and the staged adventures that one sees on the screen. It occurred to me that there might be something under the window for me to land on, like a chair or a box or even one of the animals' cages. But why was I getting ahead of myself? It was better to try to solve the problem one step at a time. And the important thing was to get the window open first. Later I could figure out how to get down from it.

When I ran my hands over the window in the darkness, it felt as if it were covered with dirt and dried mud. I could also feel bugs or tiny worms scurrying over the surface. Apparently they'd been sent into a panic by the touch of my fingers. The window was covered by a screen with a wooden frame. I wondered if I'd find bars behind it. I realized that I'd need to go back to the house and get a pair of scissors to cut through the iron screen, which, judging from the feel of it, was rusty and corroded. However, before doing that, I shook the frame and was amazed to discover how loose it was. I was even more amazed to find that the entire window had come off in my hand. Not only that, but there were no bars behind it. What sort of prison was this anyway? Why hadn't the pet-shop owner taken any precautions against his charges running away? Of course, imprisonment isn't primarily a matter of locking someone away, but, more importantly, of making certain that one has meek, docile subjects. And the fact was that the parrots, cats, mice, dogs, goldfinches and peacocks making up this particular prison population were very little trouble to keep under lock and key, which meant that they could just as easily be exploited as merchandise to be bought and sold.

I stuck my head through the window and took a look inside. The room was enveloped in silence and darkness, and out of it there wafted a powerful stench. Might they all have run away, I wondered? Or had they all died? On the other hand, like everybody else in the neighbourhood, they might have been crouching panic-stricken, speechless, bewildered and exhausted in their darkened hide-outs. Before long my eyes had adjusted to the darkness and I stopped taking much notice of the unpleasant smell. I noted that the storeroom ceiling wasn't as high as I'd imagined it to be, which meant that I could let myself down from the window, then jump on to the floor without any difficulty. Why should there be a high ceiling anyway? After all, what did the pet-shop owner care about providing healthy living conditions for his captives? Apparently his only concern was to keep them alive so as to be able to go on buying and selling them.

My entry into the shop gave rise to a chorus of murmurs, drones and other strange, inarticulate utterances. So they hadn't died and they hadn't run away. However, just like all the other residents of the neighbourhood, they were in a state of terror and dread. They now sensed an alien presence in their midst and, moved by an instinctive apprehension, they began attempting to identify the nature of the intruder. Was it one of their own kind (i.e. a friend) or some other species (i.e. a foe)? And what would be the consequences of its entry into their prison? Perhaps every animal in the entire place was wondering about this strange, unknown entity that had made its way into their abode. Perhaps the parrots were feeling annoyed now, since they'd memorized the pet-shop owner's prattle about sovereignty — that is, *his* sovereignty over *them* — and now, by virtue of a parrot-like extension of logic, were declaring my entry to be a challenge to *their* sovereignty! But what sort of sovereignty was this? That is, what manner of sovereignty can be claimed by someone who considers a cage to be home and who spends his life as a commodity to be bought and sold to the capricious and the well-to-do? What kind of sovereignty can be had by someone whose life is spent in perpetual incarceration?

It was true that the animals being kept in the display window enjoyed the ultimate in modern, luxurious accommodation, which of course served to attract customers as well as to arouse the envy of the animals living nearby. However, the overwhelming majority of the pet-shop residents made their homes here, behind the high tin-plate wall. Ironically, some interior designer had painted marvellous nature scenes on to the wall, including a captivating seashore, with cedar forests and snow-capped mountain peaks towering in the background.

So, what sort of sovereignty was this? The parrots had been the first ones to greet my entrance with hostility. Their voices had sounded angry and defiant at first, but had then grown more subdued. It was true, of course, that, being parrots, they couldn't help but repeat the same lines they'd been taught by their master. However, it was also true that, being miserable and exhausted, they couldn't help but fall silent, or at least cease repeating their memorized lines with the same degree of enthusiasm. One of them kept shouting: 'Welcome, guest! We love you! Please buy me!' (with an accent that would have rivalled that of any French tourist). Then immediately afterwards he'd say: 'Get out of here, you stranger! Sovereignty first!' It kept on repeating the two statements one after the other, as if they were two sides of the same coin.

Then suddenly I burst out laughing. Heard against the background of that dangerous, terrifying night, the sound of the parrots struck me as hilarious. After all, I wasn't numbered among the ranks of well-to-do customers, nor could I see any reason for me to be branded an undesirable alien. Weren't we all suffering the same misery, the same dread? Weren't we all partaking equally of helplessness, apprehension and even a shared destiny?

The parrots had fallen silent. Nothing could be heard now but a collective murmur, like shouts of protest that trail off into silence after a demonstration that's been subdued by the force of policemen's truncheons. It was a peculiar mélange of meows, yelps and whispers. The sounds being made by the sparrows bore more resemblance to the mumblings of a dying man than they did to chirping or singing. They were frightening, dreadful sounds filled with alarm and dismay, like the voices of a tribe approaching in the distance – a tribe of wounded and dying, their bodies bloodied and their garments scorched by the ravages of war.

When the explosions resumed, I actually felt somewhat relieved. The sounds of the animals' sufferings pained my heart even more than those of bullets being heated to melting point in the mouths of rifles...

Then the gunfire died down, while the murmurings in the pet shop increased in volume again. Just then I heard myself speaking out loud to the animals, saying: 'My dear people!' (When I heard myself, it frightened me. I wondered if I'd begun to suffer from a touch of insanity.) Nevertheless, I went on: 'My dear people... Listen now to Decree No. 1. I've come to you bearing salvation!' The animals responded by raising the pitch of their fearful mumblings and murmurings. 'Clap for me!' I shouted. Then I burst into tears. I felt like some miserable, defeated, bit-part actor playing his role alone on an equally miserable, defeated stage.

By this time my eyes had adjusted to the relative darkness. Then I remembered that the reason I'd come was to bring them food and water and to inspect their living conditions, not to fall prey to delusions of grandeur and set myself up as princess over the kingdom of the wretched and miserable. They suffered no lack of masters to rule over them. What they did lack, though, was food and drink.

But when I approached their cages, I was astonished to find that they already had both food and water. They had enough of everything to last them for several days. Do you suppose the shop owner had risked coming to feed them? I suspected not. It was possible that the young man who'd been killed by sniper fire that same morning was one of the owner's devotees who'd put his life on the line to perform this service. It pained me to contemplate the fate that may have been suffered by others like him, who'd lost their lives convinced that they were performing some sort of moral deed and that their deaths had meaning. However, the only meaning resulting from their deaths was that the shop owner's tyranny over their lives would now be that much more powerful and his trade would continue to flourish. It likewise grieved me to ponder the fates of the young people who sat crouched behind their sandbag barricades, convinced by the shop owners to offer up their lives for the sake of ideals which in reality were nothing but so much rhetorical froth. Such froth, however, served well to conceal the vested interests of shop owners who, though locked in bitter competition in times of peace, were ready to join forces at a moment's notice whenever they happened to be threatened by war or civil unrest.

Be that as it may, there was no lack of food in the cages. It was of pitiful quality, of course, but apparently none of the animals had died yet (unless the shop owner's men had taken it upon themselves to carry away the corpses one at a time and throw them into the streets or under bridges). As for the water, it was contaminated. Despite the darkness, I could make out its dull grey hue and smell its foul odour. But at least it was there, at any rate.

Another explosion went off. In the light of the glow produced by the rocket that flashed across the night sky like a bolt of lightning, I saw everything in a single, sweeping glance. Its effects were indelibly imprinted on my memory, like a tattoo etched with burning embers. It was now apparent that some of the animals were wounded, as if they'd been spending half their time in abject terror and the other half fighting among themselves. Their appalling, wretched prison had become charged with a spirit of enmity, a spirit which sought a release that had been bound to come. Unfortunately, the release was taking place through internecine fighting rather than a united attack on the shop owner, their jailer. As I watched one of the peacocks spreading its tail feathers, it occurred to me that he probably looked down on the other animals. I imagined the larger dogs lording it over the smaller ones and the grown cats exacting 'tribute' from the kittens. Meanwhile, all of them without exception were so preoccupied with the trivial biological differences between them that they hadn't stopped to notice the one vital thing they all shared in common, namely, that every one of them was a slave and a prisoner. The fools! Couldn't they see the reality of the situation? On the other hand, perhaps they had seen it. In the eyes of every one of these creatures – the red eyes of the rabbits, the brown eyes of the dogs, the green eyes of the cats and the yellow eyes of the birds – I remembered having detected the very same look. Their varied hues notwithstanding, in all of them there was a teary-eyed gaze filled with shame, brokenness and dismay, as well as a touch of restless fury.

As I made the rounds of the shop, the streetlamps flickered with every explosion, while a mournful darkness emanated from the cages of the captive animals with their downcast eyes and broken spirits. And as I wandered about among them, I was transformed momentarily into a mad fairy-tale king whose subjects included no one but the wounded, the maimed and the wretched, the king himself being the most wretched of them all...

Addressing them once more, I said: 'My dear people! We have decided to grant you the most precious thing of all – liberty!' But the sound of my voice seemed to alarm them even more than it did me (my own alarm being caused by the discovery that I really was bordering on madness). With every phrase I blurted out, their chorus of murmurs grew louder: the dogs' dispirited yelps which were actually closer to cats' meows: the cats' meows, which were more reminiscent of groans and moans; and the voices of the sparrows, which sounded less like chirping than like the death rattles of an old man. Then there were the gasps and squeaks of the rabbits and mice, which sounded less like their own kind than like owls screeching in the night. I was grieved beyond words by the miserable plight of these captive creatures. Or was I merely seeing my own face in a mirror, if not my entire neighbourhood or city? It was then that I made a decision: to set them all free. I'd grant them liberty and joy. As for the shop owner, who'd been making his living by selling them like so much merchandise, he'd come the next day only to find that they were no longer here. Yes... I'd deliver them from their misery!

In just a few moments I'd be opening all the cages. Then I'd hear the flutter of sparrows' wings as they flew out through the window and over the trees towards the sea, which they'd no doubt been pining for from inside the walls of their metallic prison. They'd flee from this city of madness and retreat into the forests. Within moments I'd be opening the door to the hunting dogs' prison as well. They'd take off like mad, filling their nostrils with the pure night air and the scent of wild thyme, making their escape from the hellish captivity they'd known. In just a little while the cats would emerge as well, meowing in delight like women celebrating a young couple's wedding day with mirthful ululations. Who knows? I thought. They might be so transported with joy that they would raise themselves up on their hind legs.

Then the white mice would come dashing out, climb up on to the branches of the trees and go to sleep enfolded in their leaves. Within moments the peacock would emerge, able at long last to display his tail in its full glory. He'd let the rain wash his rust-covered feathers, revealing their true colours, then allow the dawn's light to polish them until they glistened once more and the wind to go racing and rustling through them, restoring his vitality and strength. As for the turtles, I'd carry them by hand to the window, then watch them remove their shells and go scampering off with the speed of a rabbit. Within a few short moments this dank, gloomy prison would be transformed by the touch of freedom's hand into a festival of joy.

But who should I begin with? Which cage should I open first? I was afraid to open the cats' cage before that of the mice, lest the cats lie in wait at the window and devour their smaller neighbours the moment they made their escape. And I was afraid to open the dogs' cage before the cats' lest the dogs go chasing after them and harm them. And I'd need to set the birds free before either the dogs or the cats so as to prevent the outbreak of battle both on land and in the air.

At last I decided that the rescue operation should take place as follows: first I'd release the birds, then the mice, followed by the peacocks, the cats and finally the dogs. I realized I had no choice but to carry out the operation in stages. However, this discovery came to me belatedly and was something of a surprise — otherwise I would have spent the entire day planning. My hand trembled as I opened the cages of the various kinds of birds, from goldfinches to nightingales to parrots. What a glorious thing it is to be a giver of freedom! The cage door was rusty, but it wasn't shut tightly. As I opened it, the latch let out a loud creak. The birds seemed to start at the sound, as if it had frightened them. Then I opened the door as far as it would go. But to my astonishment, they made no attempt even to move towards the door, much less to take off in search of the night, the winds, the open skies and paths leading to other galaxies. Instead, they headed mechanically to the spot where their food was normally placed, as if they were either blind or hypnotized. They'd grown accustomed to never having their prison door opened unless it was feeding time, so perhaps they thought someone had already closed it again. Whatever the reason, I was appalled to find that not a single sparrow came flying out. It was as if they'd forgotten what freedom was, or as if there were invisible threads binding them to their prison walls.

I watching them in a bewildered daze. Explosives and the sound of gunfire no longer struck terror into my heart. However, the sight of these birds cowering in their cages in front of an open door filled me with a dismay and dread the likes of which I'd never known. I'd always imagined birds to have an insatiable hunger for freedom — a hunger that might drive them to spend an entire night beating their wings and heads against the bars of their cages. I'd been certain that no sooner had I opened the door for them than they'd take off towards the sun of freedom. But throughout this long night, infused throughout with a spirit of cringing docility, I'd been presented with a new, disturbing image of animal nature. I moved closer to the birds' cage and picked one of them up. I could feel its body pulsating in my hand, warm and perhaps afraid. It was as if I could feel its heart beating. Then I lifted it up and threw it towards the window. It spread its wings, but just barely enough to ensure that when it fell it would come in for a relatively smooth, painless landing. Once it was safely on the ground, it righted itself and walked back in the direction of its cage. Then, with unsteady wings, it lifted itself into the air for a brief second so as to land in the cage door and, once inside, it hid among its fellow inmates.

Stupefied by what I'd just witnessed, I sprang towards the cages like a woman possessed and began opening every door, screaming as I went. The animals' response was to move as far inside as they possibly could and seek refuge in each other's company. It was as if freedom had become some kind of ghoul lying in wait for them, as if they'd forgotten everything they'd ever known about open skies, running, soaring and swimming. They seemed to have become utterly ignorant of anything to do with freedom, gaiety, gathering their daily sustenance in the wild or the pleasures of hunting throughout the changing seasons, contenting themselves instead with rations that just barely kept them alive. All the while they stayed hidden away in their burrows and lairs, in constant dread of gunfire and bullets. They seemed meekly resigned to the life they'd come to know in their insipid, languid prison, having surrendered themselves into the hands of fate, as embodied in their lord, the pet-shop owner. They reminded me of the neighbourhood's human residents, who found themselves in a similar state. Around the beginning of every month the fighting would die down a bit, so everyone would go running to collect his salary – or a half or a quarter of it, depending on what kind of a mood his boss was in. Then they'd all go scurrying back to their houses, or rather their cages, loaded down with as much food as they thought they could reasonably hoard. And there they'd remain for the rest of the month, huddled inside in dread of the storms of wind, fire and madness that raged outside, and asking no more of life than the barest minimum – that is to say, sheer physical survival.

By now, every single cage in the pet-shop prison had its door wide open, yet not a single creature had made its getaway through the window. Some cats had stuck their heads out, but still had the rest of their bodies safely inside. One of the dogs came out and wandered about for a bit, then went straight back to the cage that had been assigned to him. It apparently didn't even occur to him to head towards a cage other than the one he'd just left. The scene I was witnessing was likely to rob me of my sanity, so before it was too late, I decided to leave the premises and make my own getaway. I climbed up on to the window ledge, coming out the same way I'd gone in. I put the frame back in place, but didn't shut it tightly, in the hope that should the animals attempt to come out, they'd be able to do so. Outside, the darkness was waiting for me, frigid and gloomy. Meanwhile, the gunfire continued unabated.

Nightmare 52

I ran across the garden hunched over like an ape (which, I'd concluded, must be the normal human gait during times of civil war). I approached the house and, when I reached the entrance, I could hear someone breathing. It was pitch dark. Listening closely, I was transformed suddenly into a single, huge ear. I detected a distinctive scent in the air – the scent of fear. However, I wasn't sure whether it was coming from me or from the unknown entity crouching in the darkness. Do you suppose 'it' is as terrified as I am, I wondered? Or is it waiting for me with a knife in its hand? Might it be a bullet? And speaking of bullets, do you suppose people who are shot to death experience the bullet that kills them the way they would a person who stands waiting for them in the darkness? Of course, no one has ever made his way back from death to tell us exactly what takes place at that subtle yet intense moment that separates life from death. Had that moment come for me? By this time a scream had taken shape in my chest and had begun making its way towards my throat. But before it had a chance to come out, 'it' screamed instead. I recognized the voice as that of Amm Fu'ad's ageing servant.

'You scared me!'

The words escaped from both our mouths almost simultaneously. As for him, he was about to faint. Then the light came on in the house and Amm Fu'ad appeared on the doorstep.

'Where have you been?' he asked. 'We were worried about you!'

Not wanting to get into a conversation, I said: 'Well, I got back safely and that's all that matters.'

It was obvious that they'd been looking for me for some time and that they had truly been concerned. It was also obvious that they were anxious to tell me about it in great detail. After all, it at least provided a topic of conversation in the sea of worry, grief and fear we'd all been floating in. However, my curt reply, like that of someone who's just returned from a burial ceremony for his best-loved friend, cut them off before they could pursue the subject any further.

I knew that I'd have no choice but to spend the night in their flat. The ground floor would be safer than my third-floor flat on a night when rockets were flying.

'Good night,' I said with difficulty as I headed towards the room where I'd slept the night before.

Speaking to me in French, Amin asked: 'Won't you have something to eat with us?'

I made no reply.

Nightmare 53

I've been destined to live my life as an alien, homeless and homesick...

I've been destined to inhale the odour of unfamiliar rooms and to stare at gloomy-looking furniture which I can feel rejecting me, spurning me...

Surrounded by the funereal decor of the room where I was obliged to spend the night, I felt an ominous sort of melancholy descending upon me. After all, this was the room where Amm Fu'ad's wife had died in my arms.

I was coming down the stairs on my way out to see Yousif. As I passed by Amm Fu'ad's flat, Amin opened the door. He was trembling and helplessness was written all over his face.

'My mother,' he said in a plaintive voice.

I went in immediately. Amm Fu'ad was holding her in his arms and calling out to her, saying: 'Layla! What's wrong?'

I went over to where she lay. She was motionless, her hands were cold and a slight blueness had crept into her fingernails. But in her eyes there was a look that I'll never forget as long as I live. There was a radiance in them which had now receded and was no longer directed outward, towards our world. Instead, it was as if it had turned inward, towards a world of which we know nothing. What I'd seen in her eyes confirmed to me in a flash that she was dead.

But I didn't dare announce my discovery. Perhaps they also knew what I knew, yet simply weren't facing up to it.

'Have you called a doctor?' I asked.

They looked at me as if they were hearing the word 'doctor' for the first time in their lives. They refused to believe that her condition might require them even to entertain the notion of calling one.

Then, addressing Amin, I shouted: 'Call an ambulance!'

Amm Fu'ad got up, leaving a lifeless corpse in my arms. I was as terrorized as if they'd buried me alive beneath her cadaver. Nevertheless, I didn't move a muscle until someone came to take her away.

Afterwards I ran to Yousif's house. I was late. He looked peeved, but I didn't explain. I made no attempt to apologize or justify myself. Instead, I shut the door behind me and, without further ado, began to undress. It would be the first time I'd ever been completely naked in his presence. I put my clothes in a pile, lay down on the tile floor in the hallway with my head pointed towards the door and called out to him, 'Come here!'

But why was I blaming this memory – as miserable as it made me – for the fear I was feeling now? Why should I be making accusations against the past for no reason? Was I trying to escape from the torments of the present by fleeing into a past which seemed less shocking and odious?

Why couldn't I just admit that I felt lonely and fearful in the face of the infernal night that surrounded me on every side? And why didn't I own up to the fact that I was inconsolably miserable about Yousif's absence, a loss that no one could possibly make up to me? Besides that, I was anxious and upset about my brother's imprisonment. I felt both furious with him and sorry for him at the same time. Also, why couldn't I admit that I was in a state of grief and shock? After all, right before my very eyes the civil war had exposed the falsehood of my society's pretensions of stability – a lie that I'd nearly fallen for.

I'd always been a loner, a homeless refugee wandering back

and forth among continents, cities, streets and friends. In fact, this had caused a near-complete estrangement between me and my maternal uncles in Syria. I'd always been the 'citified gypsy': no sooner had I settled in one European city than I'd be on my way to another, having left behind a house, a profession, a library, and a small circle of intimates and enemies. I was in a state of incessant peregrination, leaving off one path to take up another, with my hair for a pillow and my body for a travelling bag. It was only my encounter with Yousif that made me feel a need at times to find myself a cave where I could give birth to his child. But I didn't conceive. And Yousif went away. In spite of it all, I was doing my best to carry on with my life, aided by the inward stability in my soul that had been Yousif's legacy to me. I also wanted to live out the new commitment I felt to my homeland, a commitment which had come as a conscious reaction against what I'd discovered to be a mere pseudo-attachment to Europe.

But what a cruel joke! The day I made my move from the 'house of the absurd' to the 'house of stability', as it were, the civil war had come along, making it apparent that I'd built my house at the epicentre of an earthquake. Was it mere coincidence that on the day I decided to put my library in order and hold on to it to my dying day, the war broke out in my very own house, with the first bullet coming to rest – of all places – in one of my bookshelves? Was it a coincidence or did fate want to remind me of a lesson I'd nearly forgotten – namely, that the basic human condition is one of homelessness, alienation and non-belonging? As for stability, it's nothing more than a kind of way station, made possible by fleeting experiences of familiarity and intimacy. Not only that, but stability is an impossibility in an unstable homeland.

Nightmare 54

It's true... Given sufficient time, a person *can* get used to the sound of gunfire. In fact, one can even learn to fall asleep while the bullets are flying.

Despite the machine-gun battle that was raging on Hourani Street – so close as to be virtually next to my pillow – I found myself dozing off. However, rather than soaring into clouds of dreams, I made a slippery descent into the abyss of nightmares.

During the first few days of my entrapment in the midst of this insane battle, I hadn't slept a wink. In fact, I'd started to wonder whether there would ever come a time when I'd be able to sleep in spite of the shooting.

But finally that time did come. I discovered that this body of mine, which I'd imagined to be so fragile, possessed an astounding capacity for adaptation. However, adapting oneself to the sound of gunfire is something like a sick person's adjusting to being afflicted with cancer. And the sleep one experiences on a night filled with shooting might be likened to the sleep of a wounded person in agonizing pain who's been sated with morphine.

It was a night of nightmares...

I couldn't feel a bed under me. Instead, it was as if I were suspended in midair, surrounded on all sides by the winds of the night and of the unknown. They picked me up and carried me across forests and jungles whose 'trees' were human bodies – mangled, bloodied, screaming. Then they took me flying over charred grasslands where children were running along like rapacious kittens baring their tiny, sharp fangs. They transported me over seas whose black waters were bubbling with sulphur, salt and arsenic, and whose islands were inhabited by entire tribes afflicted with leprosy. Meanwhile, I continued to float through the infinite expanse of nightmares.

Then the tribespeople reached out with their leprosy-gnawed fingers and clutched at my hair. They pulled me to the ground and began devouring me. I screamed. But then I resumed my airborne journey, floating once more through the void of the night into the unknown, into nightmares...

Nightmare 55

A sniper sat on the roof of a building facing the sea. He had a single, huge eye in the middle of his face.

For months he'd sat in the same spot, carrying out the mission assigned to him. He no longer even remembered how or why he'd begun practising his present profession. All he knew was that he was to kill as many people as he possibly could.

At first he'd imagined that his task would be far more difficult and that he'd be obliged to go running from one edge of the roof to another in order to hunt people down. He'd assumed that hunting human beings would be more taxing than hunting sparrows. However, he'd found to his amazement that people were coming to him of their own accord. He'd expected, of course, that once the building became known as a site of frequent sniper fire, people would begin avoiding it and he'd have to move elsewhere. But the astounding thing was that, under no outward compulsion, people were turning out in record numbers to stand within his shooting range and let him have his way with them! They would come to him every day, one family after another. A family would come with all its members, from the elderly to the newborn, and all he had to do was gun them down. Then once they'd all been shot, they would wave to him as if to say: 'Thank you!' Whereupon they'd take a few steps towards the sea and fall down dead. A few moments later, a wave would come along to sweep them off the beach and clear the area for the next family. And so on and so on...

He could see that since people kept coming to him of their own free will, they must be engaging in some sort of deliberate, collective suicide. And as a consequence, they'd robbed him of the pleasure of hunting, transforming him from a sniper who kills when the mood strikes to an overworked executioner. He craved the thrill of stalking someone, of striking terror and dread into his victim's heart. He liked first to plant a bullet in front of the person's feet, then wound him in the hand so that he could keep on running. Then finally he'd shoot him in the stomach so as to let him die a long, slow, painful death. But the people of Beirut had taken him by surprise with their seemingly insatiable appetite for death and their intriguing bent for collective self-destruction.

They would come to him carrying their sick on stretchers made from tattered rags, on crutches and on their backs. Then they'd cast them at his feet as if he possessed some magical healing touch. They'd lift their nursing infants on to their backs, then come and stand within his range of vision so as to make his work as effortless as possible. As they stood there waiting they wouldn't move a muscle. All he had to do was pull the trigger.

In fact, they now even had a backdrop for the 'shooting range' similar to the ones used by photographers in amusement parks. They set up a colourful piece of cardboard decorated with a badly executed drawing of a date palm and a cedar tree. Then they'd stand in front of it as if they were posing to have their picture taken – their last picture. And as they posed, they would never smile or cry. Their features were always stiff and expressionless, like someone posing for a mug shot – first from the front, then from the side – before being taken away to jail.

The mass suicide they were undertaking was truly mind-boggling. As for the sniper, he was furious. He felt that he'd got the raw end of the deal. After all, he'd turned into nothing more than a petty civil servant. Once he'd been deprived of the thrill of the hunt, he ceased finding any pleasure or enjoyment in his work. Things went on this way until one day he got downright annoyed with all these families that kept crowding in on him in their zeal to end their earthly existences. He was sick and tired of shooting at targets that never moved or ran away or even so much as complained. So he aimed his rifle at the sky in pursuit of a white bird that was soaring rapturously towards the vast blue sea. He shot at the bird and missed. It was the first time in his entire life that he'd missed a live target. He noticed that his hand had begun to tremble, his fingers had lost their nimbleness and dexterity, and that his big eye kept blinking nervously as it stared through the sight on his gun. The ecstatic high he'd once got from hunting had been his entire life. Now it was gone. He hadn't killed his victims – they'd killed him. After all, they'd been consciously, willingly ending their own lives, as if he were doing them a service!

Just then another family came along. They lined up in front of him and he fired. Each one received a bullet in the forehead, then thanked him with a bow and headed towards the sea to die. But then an odd thing happened: several hours passed without a single person coming along to be shot. He no longer heard a sound. Everything had come to a complete standstill. Everything had died, even the wind. All sound had died, and the corpses of the winds lay sprawled out on the pavements. The sky's lifeless body lay draped over the horizon, with a dark grey blueness flowing through its inward parts. As for the colours, their cadavers were piled beneath the trees like autumn leaves. There was no sound, no movement – not even a bird in flight or an aeroplane traversing the sky. Even the corpse of death itself lay forgotten somewhere. The fishing boats along the shore had been overturned, their bellies face down and their bottoms, normally submerged in water, facing upward, like a dead man sprawled out on his stomach with his face in the dust.

Then he saw a man approaching warily from the end of the alley. He looked panic-stricken – as timorous and agitated as a hunted animal. For all he knew, this might be the last man left in the city. If so, he thought, it would be best to spare his life. That way, the two of them could chat and he wouldn't be left alone. However, the sniper's blood in him began to flow hot in his veins. He forgot his fear and was possessed once more by his bloodthirsty passion. He picked up his rifle and, after mustering every ounce of strength and bloodlust in his body, he fired a shot. It was right on the mark. The bullet hit the ground one step away from the man, which was exactly what he had intended. He'd wanted to intimidate the man and he'd succeeded. A second bullet hit the man in his hand, which began to bleed. As for the sniper, he was so overjoyed, he didn't notice that blood was flowing from the very same spot on his own hand as well. Then there came a third shot aimed straight at the man's thigh. As he fell to the ground, the sniper took no notice of the fact that his own thigh was bleeding from the same spot. A fourth and final shot wounded the man in the stomach, who now ceased trying to creep forward and instead resigned himself to the slow death that awaited him. Again, the sniper failed to notice that his own stomach was bleeding just like that of his victim. He felt so fatigued, he almost decided to finish the man off and put him out of his misery. However, he had a sudden urge to see the man's face. So he ran over to where his victim lay dying. When he turned him over on his back, he discovered that the man's face was his own, exactly as if he'd been looking into a mirror. It was only then that he became aware of the excruciating pain in his bowels and he knew that a long, slow, agonizing death awaited him as well. He didn't have the option of shooting himself in the head so as to abbreviate his torment. After all, his rifle was too long for him to simultaneously put the barrel to his head and reach the trigger.

Nightmare 56

It's true – over time a person *can* adjust to the sound of shooting. She can even learn to sleep through it, in fact. As for the sound of missiles and bombs, that's another matter, especially if they happen to be hitting the ground only ten metres away...

I was awakened by a horrific, thunderous bang. I jumped up. I suppose I should have dived under the bed, but instead I found myself in front of the window. Apparently my sense of curiosity was at least as well developed as my sense of danger. A fire had broken out in the Holiday Inn across the street and a series of explosions could be heard, one after another. Meanwhile, the area engulfed in fire and smoke was steadily expanding, causing the pale greyness of the dawn to penetrate more and more deeply into everything in sight. Outside the window that opened on to the garden, the jasmine bush was still in full bloom, its white blossoms looking like tiny points of light in the midst of a bleak, smoke-coloured world.

I'd held a sort of grudge against the hotel ever since it was built. There'd been a time when I could see the ocean and the white fishing boats on the water directly from my house.

Then all of a sudden they dumped this monstrosity in front of me – this mountain of cement and steel. And from that day on the neighbourhood 'flourished'. That is to say, its prices went up, traffic increased several times over and I could no longer find a parking spot in the afternoon when I got home from work exhausted, feeling like a ball of dough that's been at the receiving end of a good kneading by a farmer's wife. And now the place had turned into a flashpoint of smoke and fire...

A faint voice inside me would come to the hotel's defence. After all, scores of families were making their living there. So what right did I have to feel resentful towards a building simply because it blocked my view of the sun and the ocean, or merely because it was being bombed and striking terror into my heart? However, in the wee hours of the morning, with fear gnawing away at my bones, I was in no mood for long-winded logical defences. Besides, there were other, more immediate problems demanding my attention. Of these, the most pressing was that we were about to run out of bread in the house. Add to this the fact that I was incapable of eating even a single piece of meat after all the corpses I'd seen and all the stories I'd heard about them. In fact, I'd become nearly convinced that all the meat we'd been eating lately was actually human flesh. In any case, we were out of meat now too. So I decided to go up to my flat on the third floor and check out its supplies.

Then the bombing stopped, causing a tense silence to reign once more. It was the silence of the battlefield, a silence different from any other. It's a silence you can listen to. And if you listen closely enough, you'll hear many things. I could hear the murmurings of the creatures in the pet shop. So then, they hadn't escaped yet. I wondered if the rest of the neighbourhood's residents had fled. The windows of all the houses were shut tight, just as mine were, and on one of the balconies there was some baby clothing that had been hanging out to dry ever since the neighbourhood had turned into a war zone. Apparently the child's mother didn't dare bring them in. Or had the entire family abandoned the house by now?

There was a large white shirt hanging on the line among the baby clothes (perhaps it belonged to the father). For some reason it looked to me like a large white flag that someone had raised in the smoke-filled dawn. Just then the door leading out to the balcony slowly opened a crack. A head peeped out fearfully, then disappeared. Then a hand appeared from inside and felt the clothes, to see whether they were dry yet. Finally a woman slipped out, her large belly preceding her, and began hurriedly taking them down. She looked frightened. Her hand was trembling, and now and then she would drop the clothes pegs. Nevertheless, she kept gathering in the clothes, looking around furtively as if she were stealing them. Then suddenly a shot was fired. Had it landed in her stomach – in the foetus's heart, or in her own heart? She fell to the balcony floor and out of sight. This was apparently the sniper's way of saying 'Good morning!' to his neighbours. No one came out on to the balcony. No doubt her husband didn't dare even to drag her in. I could hear a small child wailing bitterly from inside. Perhaps it was the baby boy whose clothes she would never wash again.

When the incident occurred, Amm Fu'ad and the rest of his household were still asleep. I crept upstairs to my own flat, ducking all the way, trembling. One would have thought I was a thief on my way to commit a robbery, not some law-abiding citizen heading home! I was so weighed down with grief, I felt nauseous.

Nightmare 57

I wondered why it was that stray bullets so consistently chose the bookshelves in my study as their target? What was the secret behind this mysterious enmity between the book and the bullet? I went to inspect all the rooms in the house and found that the walls had made it through the previous night without suffering any harm – that is, except for four bullets that had lodged themselves in the shelf where I kept my 'revolutionary books'. The amusing thing was that as long as the sun was shining, I'd sit at home feeling safe. Then as soon as darkness fell, I'd flee to Amm Fu'ad's house! It was as if I thought the only time a bullet might do me mortal harm was at night. Maybe this was just further evidence of the way my thinking had been corrupted by cheap adventure flicks, where the actors are killed only at night, where crimes are committed only in the dark.

I needed to contact a lawyer to get my brother out of jail. But it was still too early to call...

This was my fourth day of total isolation from the outside world. No newspapers. No pedlars. Not a soul on the street. And not a sound except for the unintelligible shouts of armed men somewhere in the vicinity. I even felt a bit of nostalgic longing for the sound of the earthdigger that in bygone days had been the bane of my life. Despite the horrendous racket it had made, at least it had meant that some sort of constructive work was being done. It had been a sign of 'normal' life. And I even missed the voice of our neighbour Jacques, who used to laugh as if he were quarrelling and quarrel as if some sort of massacre had just taken place. I missed his daughters' music and the stereo with eight loudspeakers that used to blast out day and night. In fact, I missed all the things that I'd once loathed and detested.

Anything was better than this dreadful stillness and deadly isolation.

I wished that any creature at all would come along – that the door would open at that very moment and a gang would come in to rob the house. If such a thing were to happen, I'd be sure to give them a hearty welcome and invite them to sit down with me for a while. At least that way we could have a chat and I could enjoy their company before they went on their way again. Before long I could see the whole thing as if it were actually happening: the door would open and in would come three burglars with pistols – no, machine-guns – in their hands. Then again, make that one pistol and two machine-guns. Anyway, they'd come in with their masks on and shout: 'Up with your hands!'

I'd greet them with a handshake and say: 'Welcome! I've been waiting for you for days. In any case, it's still quite early, so I don't suppose you've had your morning cup of coffee yet!' As I fixed the coffee, I'd ask them how they liked it – medium sweet, extra sweet? One would say he preferred it extra sweet, another that he wanted it medium sweet, while the third would say he wanted it with only a little sugar. Laughing, I'd say: 'If you can't even agree on how much sugar you want in your morning coffee, how will you ever agree on anything else!'

When I brought them the coffee, they'd be obliged to take off their masks in order to drink it. Their faces would be careworn and pallid, as if they were suffering from anaemia. We'd chat a bit about the weather, the rising prices, the stench of burning garbage in the streets and the threat of spreading epidemics. I'd alert them to the necessity of having their children vaccinated, then I'd help them pack up the things they'd decided to pilfer. As far as I was concerned, they could take anything they liked, as long as they didn't touch my books. But I'd never heard of anyone being tried on charges of book theft. After all, books are heavy, not to mention the fact that there's no market for them. So no one would be stealing my books and that was all that mattered to me. When they left, I'd stand on the balcony waving goodbye with a white handkerchief. They might even write down their addresses for me — that is, if they had addresses — in case we had the chance to visit each other in the future...

I was roused out of my nightmare by the ringing of the telephone. Who would be calling me this early in the morning? I wondered. Was it more bad news? As it turned out, it was Salwa wanting to know whether Professor Sabri had agreed to let her join his dance troupe! She said she'd been so worried about it, she hadn't slept the night before. And her sister Maryam? Oh, Salwa had forgotten to inform me that she'd been killed...

Nightmare 58

I took out a cigarette and placed it in a holder designed to filter out the nicotine. Then suddenly I burst out laughing. Who was I trying to save my lungs for anyway? For the bullets? I was like someone on Death Row who refuses to smoke a cigarette because its bad for his health! I felt scattered and unfocused, but I knew I mustn't forget to contact a lawyer to have my brother released. It wasn't his being in jail that bothered me, though. After all, prison had become about the safest place in the entire city. At least there, no one had ever been kidnapped or killed by sniper fire. Kidnappers had even made their way into mental institutions. As for the prisons, though, no one had thought yet to snatch anyone from there.

When some patients in a mental hospital were abducted

once, I couldn't understand why people reacted with such shock and amazement. After all, hadn't Beirut itself turned into one big madhouse? If so, then why all this discrimination between residents of mental institutions and people who'd made their homes behind barricades and bolted doors?

I read for a while from the pile of old newspapers, then decided to stop, since they were just stirring up more nightmares in my head. Amassing the horrors of the previous months before my very eyes, the newspapers transformed them into a film strip that went gliding through my head filled with savage brawls and a raucous, nightmarish din.

However, there was no way to avoid listening to our 'honourable' radio station, which was something I hadn't done for quite a while. At six-thirty I began listening to a song that went something like this: 'What a beautiful morning! Together with our neighbours, our hearts full of joy, we live a life of ease and bliss.' The song left me utterly bewildered. How could this 'honourable' radio station of ours be playing songs about 'a life of ease and bliss' when the only 'neighbours' left to us were misery and wretchedness?

Little did I know what other surprises awaited me. I'd awakened at dawn to the roar of explosives ripping through our paralysed city. But the song I heard next said: 'With the dawning of the morning light, work's wheels keep on turning.' The fact was that the only things 'turning' any more were the cartridge clips inside artillery pieces!

At seven-thirty the strains of 'Love Story' wafted over the air, though the only 'love story' taking place in Beirut was between between daggers and wounds, as it were...

At a quarter to eight some disc jockey had the audacity to play a song which said: 'Oh my country, oh dance of brooks and streams, oh playground of sparrows, its paths flanked by ears of grain and grapevines of gold... Her highways and byways are paved with stories and tales, her roofs and terraces mirrors...' Then the singer repeated the refrain, which said: 'Built and peopled by glory, power and might, she's girded with renown and honour, lifted on high like the winds...' It was truly horrifying.

Was the radio station just another parrot, like the ones I'd heard in the pet shop? What was this nonsense about 'glory', when the country was on the verge of collapse? And this senseless drivel about 'grapevines of gold' when the poor and unemployed were bathing the land's vineyards and orchards in their tears of wrath? Then there was the line about the 'playground of sparrows'... What sparrows? With scorched wings, we'd been driven from our homes, our fury released and our claws unsheathed. Even the rats had emerged from their abodes, gnawing away hungrily at the eyes of the corpses that lay blanketing the pavements.

But the real catastrophe hit when the radio announcer began reading the news report. He assured us that calm prevailed in the city, with no disturbances other than a bit of 'scattered gunfire'!

Who do they think they're fooling? I thought. The news reports must be prepared specially to please some 'big daddy' perched on top of the pyramid. But wasn't this radio station, which we were supporting with our own money, under an obligation to give us the facts?

After the sham news report brought to us under the pretext of calming public opinion – as if public opinion were some sort of underaged youth in need of protection – the same old records and bogus songs came back. One of them declared: 'Lebanon is a cedar's breath, bliss to the world, and a hymn to might, honour and renown. A land whose very thorns are blossoms, Lebanon is a world of love, its every season ripe for harvest, filled with marvels of light. Lebanon – oh, Lebanon!'

For your information, Mr Radio Announcer (who, I'd noted, hadn't put a gun to his head before agreeing to broadcast this nonsense), songs like these make Lebanon look as ludicrous as false eyelashes on a one-eyed monster! With deadly battles raging all over our homeland, they sound downright comical, if not absurd. They're about as ridiculous and pathetic as the sight of a roomful of people dancing to a recording of romantic tango music, where suddenly all the people in the room stop dancing and get into a huge brawl, exchanging blows with knives and axes, their screams drowning out the music and blood nearly up to their knees. Meanwhile, the same mindless tune just keeps on playing simply because nobody has the courage to reach out and shut it off. Don't you realize that you won't be able to drown out the voices of the revolution with these vacuous, schmaltzy songs of yours?

At ten o'clock when they put on the song 'Lebanon Land of Bliss', I switched from the official station with its lies and deceit to the unofficial, banned station – that is, to short wave. Only then did I begin hearing about what was really going on: 'Tariq to Number One, over... the National Library is on fire...'

What people were doing all over the country was typical of what anyone might do if he found himself under siege: instead of bothering to scream 'Police!' he might just go and buy himself a gun...

The gap between what was taking place behind the scenes and what was being presented to us on the official 'stage' was truly frightening. So who could blame the 'audience' if they stormed the stage, set it on fire and hanged the actors, thereby exposing the wretchedness behind the curtain to the light of truth?

Nightmare 59

Anis, the lawyer, had a long laugh over my account of how my brother was arrested on charges of carrying an unlicensed weapon. His laughter was out of proportion to the joke, in my opinion. In vain I tried to get him to understand that although it might be a good joke, the fact remained that my brother was in jail. But he insisted on just laughing.

What sort of madness had swept over this city? It had become difficult to carry on a logical, coherent conversation with anyone at all. It was as if the previous few months of civil war had given us all a touch of insanity, or as if we'd all taken a sip from a spring of madness. Some of us were leaving, some of us were laughing, some of us were committing suicide, some of us wanted to dance the *dabka,* and some of us were still upset about events because of their effect on tourism!

A deep sadness came over me. As I saw it, the tragic thing wasn't that I was neutral. On the contrary, I was quite partial. My personal tragedy was that I was unable to give myself over to the use of weapons. I loathed violence. I would have given anything to be able to turn all of my books into fire extinguishers, cotton wool and sterilized gauze. And if all the letters I'd received from my readers had been written on loaves of bread, at least I would have had something to eat!

Nightmare 60

I heard a shrill scream. Even through cascades of bullets and explosives, one can never mistake the sound of a human voice, no matter how faint...
I ran to the window and peered cautiously out at the street that lay between me and the Holiday Inn. On the pavement

directly in front of the hotel, I saw a man who'd been shot. He was holding on to a bag.

As I stood there staring at him, the five metres that went to make up the width of the street suddenly became an eternity – nay, several eternities – separating me from the wounded man. As he cried out in pain, I stood there looking on helplessly, unable even to stick my head out of the window. I knew that he'd go on screaming until he died, exactly like the car whose horn had blasted out into the night. It had kept up its wailing for hours, its voice growing gradually fainter and fainter until at last its battery died. Likewise, this wounded man would go on howling, loudly at first, as he was doing right now, then more and more faintly. Meanwhile, he'd sink little by little into the pavement, which had become that pit of quicksand that we call death. Then once the battery of life inside him had been exhausted, his voice would be extinguished once and for all.

It was dreadful to watch someone die without having the power to do a thing for him other than look on from behind a window. I myself was in pain. Yet at the same time I felt a sort of wicked glee because it was he who was dying and not me! His voice was beginning to grow less audible now. Knowing him to be in pain, I wished him a speedy death. I remembered having said to Yousif once: 'I know what I want you to give me for my birthday. I want you to bring some of that poison that you can put on your tongue and die instantly. It's the greatest gift a lover could present to his sweetheart – the ability to end her life whenever she chooses.'

He had a good laugh at my request. He thought of it as nothing but a bad joke! Why is it that lovers fail to notice how close they stand to death and pain? If this poor man had been carrying some of that same poison in his pocket, his screams would have been extinguished and he would have found relief. He also would have brought relief to others. After all, everyone else in the neighbourhood might also have been watching him through the window, dying with him, agonizing with him. Whenever any living creature expires before our eyes, we all die with him.

Ever since Yousif's death, I'd been enticed by the idea of suicide. All right, then, I thought... All I'd have to do would be cross the street in front of my house, from one pavement to the other. It would be a sure way to die that wouldn't cost me a thing. Scores of grenades would be certain to lodge in my head before I reached the other side. It was as if the pavement on the other side of the street had become the hereafter, while the street had become the grey river of death, the river of no return. So why didn't I take the remaining steps, calmly and without hesitation? Why didn't I go ahead and die with this man whose face I'd never seen before? Our journeys towards death would at least be less lonely that way. I'd take him into my arms and say: 'I've come to you, Yousif. Take me away!' At the moment of death, any man could become my beloved, since at that instant he would embody all the men of the world.

But – I admit – I wasn't really serious about it. The idea of ending my own life was alluring to me, but no more than that. Consequently, I enjoyed the luxury of being able to treat it with a bit of levity.

No. I wasn't going to cross the street. I had no intention of going over to the other side. I wanted to live. I was determined to survive this hellish time. Then afterwards I'd reconsider the question of whether the hand grenade is a more powerful weapon than an inkwell, the bullet than the pen.

I found myself scanning the street in search of my car and trying to estimate the likelihood of being able to escape in it. However, it was covered with broken glass. Who knows?

Maybe the car whose horn had filled the neighbourhood with its screeches that night had been my own!

Nightmare 61

I'd finally decided to flee from this infernal place.

I wasn't a fighter (so far, at least) – I didn't even know how to use a weapon, for that matter. Besides, as long as I was living in a house full of windows and not a fall-out shelter, and as long as the only vehicle in my possession was an ordinary automobile and not an armoured car, then I had to try to leave this battlefield alive.

The telephone rang.

It was Amm Fu'ad. He said they were worried, since they hadn't found me anywhere in their flat when they woke up. So now they wanted me to come down and have lunch with them. I wondered, why is he using the telephone to talk to me when the only thing separating our houses is a short staircase? I knew, of course, that none of them dared to come up to my house because it was so vulnerable to attack. At the same time, they didn't want me to die so they wouldn't have to smell my rotting corpse. The two cadavers lying in the middle of the street were quite sufficient, thank you! No one had dared go near them yet. Even the cat that had sat down the day before in front of one of the two bodies as if she were lamenting the deceased had finally been driven away by the stench!

When I got downstairs, Amin was in a state of turmoil over the flies that had invaded their flat. He'd always been an obedient young man – the model of the dutiful, devoted son. Consequently, his wild indignation about the flies seemed to be out of all proportion, as if it were his way of venting his rebellion against the present state of affairs, or the only way he knew to affirm his existence.

He was swooping down on the flies, which looked particularly huge and ferocious. By the time I arrived he'd killed five of them, and was still bouncing all over the house, which was being rocked by explosions even as he continued to stalk his prey. The fly-killing operation was a never-ending one, since all the windows were open (it being dangerous to close them since, in the event of an explosion, the glass would shatter and go flying in all directions). As a result, he could go on indefinitely with his Quixotic battle.

As for me, I sat with Amm Fu'ad. He pressed me to share some arrack with him, but I declined.

'You'll regret it!' he warned. 'Just like Al-Kas'i!'

I didn't ask him to explain who Al-Kas'i was or what it was that he'd regretted so much. Instead, I just began drinking with him. We sat together in a wordless silence which was interrupted only by his intermittent yawns. After a little while he tried once again to remember a line of poetry that he'd forgotten and began saying over and over: 'He whom death overtakes... he whom death overtakes...' Then, as usual, he was overtaken by drowsiness and sank into a deep slumber. Meanwhile, Amin remained engrossed in the war he'd been waging on the flies.

As for me, I felt myself being overwhelmed by a loneliness that knew no bounds, a loneliness that mingled with the sounds of the bombs that threatened me with every passing moment. I made up my mind that whatever it cost me, I'd find a way out of this hellish place. I wouldn't necessarily be killed. After all, my brother had managed to get out in one piece. On one of the walls there hung an antique Arab sword – a sort of good-luck charm. I took it down, unsheathed it and opened the door. The servant stared at me in alarm, while the expression in his eyes said: 'You're drunk!'

I remembered then that I'd had quite a bit of arrack. However, I was certain that I was perfectly sober (just as all drunk people are!).

As I went out into the garden, I could hear Amm Fu'ad's voice calling after me: 'You'll regret it, just like Al-Kas'i!'

We were surrounded on all sides by towering buildings, one of which was the Holiday Inn. It stood out like a monstrous ogre as I brandished my antique sword in its face. Remembering ancient Arabic legends, I imagined that my sword was an enchanted sabre that could chop the hotel right in two. I kept moving forward towards the garden gate, with the intention of stepping through it on to the pavement and then out into the street. I decided first to try starting my car. If it worked, I'd use it to make my getaway. If it let me down, then I'd have no choice but to walk down the street brandishing my sword! Neither Amin nor the servant came out after me. No one tried to stop me. I was right within the sniper's shooting range, which meant that it would have been a risky venture to come anywhere near me! I could hear Amm Fu'ad's voice ringing in my ears, saying: 'You'll regret it, just like Al-Kas'i!' Cackling out loud like a demented old hag, I picked up my rusty sword and walked with it towards the garden gate.

I had a hunch that the sniper wouldn't kill me immediately. My ludicrous appearance would at least pique his curiosity. He'd seen people carrying white flags, bags of bread and even children, and had killed them all without the slightest hesitation. But I was willing to bet that he'd never seen a lunatic carrying a sword around! Hence, I was pinning hopes of survival on whether or not the sniper had a sense of humour! Despite my uneasy preoccupation with the danger at hand, I noticed the fragrance of the jasmine bush nearby. Looking over at it, I saw a number of spent grenades that had landed underneath it. Even so, it was a delight to feel the sting of the sun's rays on my skin. This was the first time I'd stood beneath a clear blue sky for four days – or had it been longer than that?

I managed to reach the garden's iron gate without getting a bullet lodged in my head. That alone was a major victory. With one hand I kept my Quixotic sword raised in the air, while with the other I tried to open the gate. But to my surprise, I found it locked with an iron chain.

It was only then that a spray of bullets began raining down around me – coming, of course, from the direction of the cursed Holiday Inn. I sought shelter behind a nearby post, clinging to it for dear life. Once the shooting had stopped, I decided to go back to the house to get the key. However, hardly had I taken a step before another spray of bullets was sent my way. I retreated to the spot where I'd been standing near the post. Then, after a few minutes which seemed like an eternity, I made another attempt. But once again bullets began bouncing off the ground in all directions. So now I understood the game. The sniper perched on top of the Holiday Inn wanted to amuse himself. As for me, I was his prisoner, trapped between the post and the locked gate. A single step in either direction would be punished with instant death. The sun was gazing at me across the cloudless sky. And as I stood there, the situation suddenly struck me as laughable. Here I was a prisoner, yet without being enclosed behind bars or shackled with chains. I was being held captive by a vast expanse of sky, by light, trees and soil. No one had bound me to the post, yet I was cleaving to it as if I'd been glued on.

I felt humiliated and degraded – like someone held captive without chains or fetters, imprisoned in an invisible chamber called fear. Its transparent walls let in the rays of the sun, the blueness of the sky and the autumn winds, yet, once they've passed through the prison's walls, they lose their 'flavour'. Instead, they take on the taste of ignominy and abasement – the marks of a prison whose bars and shackles are invisible to the naked eye!

Then suddenly I had a terrible thought: if I wasn't killed on the spot, I'd have to wait till sunset before I could sneak into the house without being in danger of snipers' bullets. I also became aware of how intoxicated I was – and what a buffoon I was being. With this thought, I bathed my Arab sword in tears, pressing my head up against its dull edge like someone weeping on her aged, paralysed father's chest. Indeed, I regretted what I'd done 'just like Al-Kas'i', whose story still remained a mystery to me.

I wouldn't be able to wait until nightfall. I was too agitated, tense and distraught. So I took off running in the direction of the house, like a wild animal whose instinct has won out over its better judgement. And not a single bullet came my way! Perhaps the sniper had decided not to kill me just yet, so as to be able to continue making sport of me in the weeks to come.

By the time I reached the door to Amm Fu'ad's house, I'd recovered completely from the effects of what I'd drunk. Without saying a word to anyone, I went straight upstairs to my flat. I swore to myself that I wouldn't take another drop of alcohol, knowing full well that I'd break my promise the very next day.

Nightmare 62

I paced around the house like an animal that's fallen into a deadly trap. As I moaned and groaned, I could hear my voice mingling with the groans of the creatures in the pet shop. All of us were together in the same trap. As for the pet-shop owner, no doubt he was somewhere safe. Who knows? I thought – at this very moment he might be watching us from afar through his binoculars.

The phone rang. On the other end I heard the voice of Sharif, the radio announcer. I'd been hoping he would call. He told me he'd informed the liaison office of my situation. I was to be rescued that night with the help of the Jumblatt family, whose house was only about 200 metres from ours. And since it was located at a bend in the road in the opposite direction from the Holiday Inn, it lay outside the shooting range of the hotel snipers. An armoured car was to come and pick me up, along with the family of Husayn, Sharif's brother, who lived in the Idriss Building, across the street from the Jumblatt clan.

'When?' I asked.

'After sunset.'

He promised to call again. I gave him Amm Fu'ad's number and told him that I'd be waiting for them there on the ground floor.

Hope... Like a green plant whose tendrils suddenly burst forth, making their way up through frost and ice, hope likewise finds its way into the human heart, penetrating the accretions of grief and sorrow that seek to block its entrance.

Sharif warned me that there wouldn't be room inside the armoured car for suitcases or anything else. I replied that I'd be coming out like a pilgrim on her way to Mecca – wrapped in nothing but her burial shroud!

Nightmare 63

I sat waiting... but the silver-blue sand in my hourglass didn't want to flow downward through its ethereal spheres.

Waiting... like a field of clocks and watches with broken hands. I glanced at my wristwatch only to find that its second and hour hands had died and that their corpses had disappeared. Inside the watch there were numbers – just numbers, nothing more. But no hands...

Waiting... like a rubber heart suspended in space, growing heavier and heavier and inclining further and further downward with every passing moment...

Waiting... like being cast into a minefield tied to a horse that goes galloping aimlessly to and fro ...

I went back to Amm Fu'ad's house to tell him my good news. But to my surprise, he said with disgust: 'You'll regret it, just like Al-Kas'i!'

I didn't ask him who this ill-fated Al-Kas'i was. Nor did I ask him to tell me what Al-Kas'i had done or not done which gave him such cause for remorse. And he for his part made no attempt to explain the sad story to me. Instead he just kept repeating over and over: 'You'll regret it, just like Al-Kas'i!'

As for Amin, I saw a glimmer of envy flash across his eyes. He was envious of my freedom. After all, in some sense I'd taken on the role of the free 'young man' in my family, whereas he, despite being a male, played the role of the traditional Eastern 'female' in his father's household. All the men in tribal societies unwittingly play the role of the 'Eastern female' in relation to their fathers!

I knew he wished he could make a getaway too. However, he was obliged to adopt the same attitude as his father, who was determined to die surrounded by his treasured *objets d'art,* his decorations and badges of honour, and his house of stone. Or do you suppose Amin himself wanted the chance to die with his promised inheritance of expensive rarities, sumptuous furniture and gold-plated china? Was it possible that he'd been so thoroughly brainwashed that he'd lost even his love of life, that 'life' for him had become synonymous with material possessions?

Nightmare 64

The telephone... It was Captain Fathi this time. Sharif had given him my telephone number. He told me that the armoured car would be arriving within minutes.

Before long the phone was ringing again. It was Husayn, Sharif's brother, wanting to know how many people would be with me.

'I'll be alone,' I replied.

The other person would have been Yousif, but he no longer needed to occupy a space in the armoured car. He occupied me instead.

Determined not to repeat the mistake I'd made that afternoon, I asked Amin to give me the key to the garden gate, intending to take it with me when I went out. He resisted at first, mumbling some sort of complaint in French. But he relented when I agreed to leave the key in the lock (provided, of course, that I wasn't killed by the Holiday Inn sniper on my way across the garden, where there was an unroofed walkway between the outside gate and the door to the house).

Waiting...

At last there was the sound of an armoured car. I could hear it roaring in the distance, still some way away. The green shoot in my heart grew a bit more, breaking through the ice and popping its head out. Then I went out into the night, into the unknown, to wait for them as we'd agreed. Despite the intermittent gunfire I could still hear the armoured car. However, it was neither fainter nor louder, as if the vehicle were standing still. What had happened? I peered out into the darkness, but couldn't see a thing. I concluded that it must have stopped to pick up members of the Jumblatt clan and their neighbours before coming to get me.

But that didn't seem possible. My house was located in the

centre of a danger zone, exactly midway between fighters on either side of the conflict. So the most logical approach would have been for them to pick me up first, rather than exposing the others to even more danger.

This was how my thoughts went as I stood there listening and trying to imagine what was going on. Meanwhile, I clung all the more tightly to the post that I was standing beside for protection.

Then suddenly all hell broke loose. Frightful explosions lacerated the young seedling that had begun to sprout in my heart. I found myself glued to the post, a mass of dejection and despair, like someone who's been stranded alone on an island after being left behind by the last lifeboat. Bullets poured down around me on all sides like raindrops in a thunderstorm, while explosions shook me from head to toe. The night seemed darker and eerier than ever before. As for me, I felt terrified, alone, abandoned and too helpless even to scream. My mouth was filled with ashes, blood, gunpowder... and tears.

But then I noticed that the darkness was no longer as pitch-black as it had been. There was something burning at the bend in the road near the Jumblatt mansion, about 200 metres away from where I was standing. I could see the fire's white heat reflected on the pavement on the other side of the street, while the wind blowing towards me bore the scent of charred rubble, covering my face with a layer of fine black dust.

Then all at once my mind was inundated with images from all the civil wars I'd ever read about, including the fire scene in the novel *Gone With the Wind*. Then I found myself falling to the ground in a half-kneeling position and praying to the God of this vast universe. I felt able to call upon the divine from this burning wasteland without any need of minarets or church altars.

Could all this destruction have come about merely on account of a disagreement between those who prefer to call upon God from a mosque and those who prefer to do so from a church?

No, no, no!

Talk about religion was nothing but a smokescreen to conceal the real nature of the dispute. Why couldn't people face up to the truth, rather than accusing Muhammad and Jesus of quarrelling? Why couldn't they just admit that the conflict at hand wasn't over ownership of some mansion of clouds in the heavens? Rather, it was over claims to skyscrapers on earth that seek to reach to the heavens!

Nightmare 65

I realized intuitively that no rescue awaited me, at least not immediately, and that something dreadful had happened.

When I got back to Amm Fu'ad's house, I went in without saying a word. No one asked me a thing. However, Amm Fu'ad's glances were practically screaming at me, as if to say: 'Here you are, regretting what you did, just like Al-Kas'i. Didn't I tell you?'

As for Amin, he shot me a glance that seemed to ooze with malicious glee over my rotten luck. I took a seat near the television where the two of them were watching a programme of some sort. I flung my exhausted body into the chair, but it was no use trying to keep my mind on the programme or even to focus my eyes on the screen. All I could see when I looked at it was an image of myself waiting in front of the garden gate. All I could hear was the sound of the armoured car, and of the gates of hell as they opened up all around me, and the explosions, and the fire, and the armoured car that had disappeared, and...

The news broadcast came on. The announcer began

speaking and the picture on the screen started coming into focus. The armoured car had reached my neighbourhood – I hadn't just been imagining things. However, shells that had been fired at it had set it on fire along with the adjacent gas station, which had belonged to the Jumblatt family.

As I sat there, I found myself yielding at last to the flaming mousetrap in which I'd been writhing and twisting for days – just as the creatures in the pet shop had resigned themselves to their own entrapment. And I wondered: How long do you suppose it will take me to become like them? When will it happen? When will it happen that the door to freedom stands open before me, yet I fail to go through it? When will cowardice and servile submission become second nature to me? When will my valleys and fields be so overrun by the weeds of despair that hope's green shoots can no longer spring up in their arid, barren soil? Could such a thing really happen to me? When will this civil war succeed in domesticating me? And the rest of the city's inhabitants? Has this vicious war managed to tame their spirits? No doubt it's had greater success with some than with others. However, we're all travelling the same road – or are we? It seems to me that even a few years ago, we were already like the creatures in the pet shop – servile, browbeaten, fearful – the only difference between us and them being that we'd deceived ourselves into thinking that we were free simply because we were capable of geographical movement. But what about historical movement? If an animal's freedom depends on its ability to move from place to place, then doesn't human freedom depend on our ability both to move from one place to another, and to progress from one era to another? To what extent have we had a part in creating our own and others' destinies?

As apprehensions and concerns like these assailed me in merciless succession, I wondered bitterly: How many failed experiments of this sort will I have to go through before I either succumb to despair and refuse any attempt to rescue me, or surrender to the call to revolution, even one that requires me to resort to violence after having relied for so long on the pen alone? Would it really be possible to tame me – this wild, headstrong filly, this gypsy woman raised on freedom, remote villages and sunrises breaking over distant mountain peaks? Is it possible that the sniper on top of the Holiday Inn might succeed in breaking my spirit?

Nightmare 66

I sat waiting for the familiar sound of Amm Fu'ad's snores. That would be my green light to head over for another visit to my comrades-in-destiny ... my neighbours in the pet shop.

I didn't dare leave the house right in front of him since, after the shake-ups of the previous day, he, Amin and the servant were bound to think I'd lost my mind (or, perhaps, discover that I really had lost it!). And in that event, they could bring some ropes and tie me down without the slightest compunction, convinced that they were saving my life and doing both me and my family a favour!

At last, everyone was sound asleep...

I slipped out of my miserable bed, the bed where Amm Fu'ad's wife had died in my very arms. Before long, I found myself standing once more in front of the back window of the pet shop. It was in the same position as the day before. I tried to prise it loose, but met with some resistance. I noticed that it had been closed tightly. So then, someone had come along after me and secured it again. I pounded on it several times, taking care not to make too much noise lest I wake someone up. But whenever the sound of the shooting got louder, I beat on it with a rock, knowing that the thunderous din produced by the shooting – which by now had become such a familiar sound that it aroused no one's suspicions – would drown out whatever racket I happened to be making.

Finally the metal screen came loose from its frame. I let myself down inside the window, then took a leap as I'd done the night before. Burning with impatience and apprehension, I wondered: Have they escaped?

I'd left them yesterday with their cage doors open – open to freedom, to wide open spaces and the stars above. I'd broken the storeroom window open for them. So had they made their getaway? True... all day long I'd been hearing sounds like their voices. But for all I knew those sounds might have been coming from the other – human – prisoners residing in the neighbourhood.

My jump was painful this time. Maybe I was more distraught than I had been the day before and as a result had misjudged the elevation of the window in the darkness. Feeling some pain in my right foot, I sat down on the floor while my eyes adjusted to the darkness enough for me to see my surroundings...

But the voices I was hearing now left me in no doubt as to the truth of the situation. Perhaps the sound of my fall had wakened those of them who'd been asleep, since I could hear their fearful, plaintive cries growing louder again, coiling about me like the branches of a sinister, bewitched tree. I felt as if I'd fallen inside a wild, man-eating flower – half-plant and half-animal – which had dug its thorns into my veins and was about to suck my blood. In the light coming from the street I could see that the locks on their cages had been secured once more. Might the animals have done it themselves? That, of course, wouldn't have made any sense. It was far more likely that the shop owner – or one of his proxies – had come as usual to check on them and feed them their paltry rations (lest they die and thereby deprive him of some of his potential profit). Then, seeing their cage doors open and the window off its hinges, he must have relocked the doors and shut the window securely. Perhaps he thought a thief had tried to steal the animals, but at the last moment had failed to go through with it for some reason – for fear that a bomb would hit the place unexpectedly, for example, or that another thief would come along with a more deadly weapon in his hand.

This was the only logical explanation. Even so, I wasn't entirely satisfied with it. In my mind's eye I could see the animals after my departure the night before: the parrot was preaching a sermon, decrying the act of sabotage that had been perpetrated by the 'alien' – by me, that is – and declaring that it was necessary to expel me from their midst if they were to ensure their well-being, peace of mind and tranquil coexistence – not to mention the satisfaction of the shop owner and their 'clientele'. I could hear some of them shouting: 'Down with the alien!' – that is, down with me. Then I could see them marching out of their cages and making their way heroically to the window to close it in my face lest my subversive ideas succeed in penetrating their ranks. Finally, they all went back to their cages and shut the doors behind them.

I roamed about among the cages in bewildered amazement. Not a single animal had fled. In fact, the looks in their eyes made me suspect that they'd forgotten all about their experience of the night before. They'd resumed their pained moaning and groaning as if all they really wanted to do was voice their complaints, not stage an insurrection. Their masters hadn't extinguished their ability to feel pain. However, they'd apparently managed to rob them of their instinctive desire to change a painful situation. They were clearly full of rage. However, they'd forgotten their way back to the jungle.

Then suddenly I found myself running from one cage to another as I'd done before. Only this time I didn't content myself with just opening the doors. Instead, I drove the animals out. I expelled them forcibly. By now it had become obvious that the cats weren't going to eat the mice, and nor would the dogs be biting the cats. Rather, they'd all been brought together by a single common denominator – namely, their shared wretchedness and misery. They were no longer rabbits, cats, sparrows and dogs. They were nothing now but one single species whose distinctive features had been eaten away by ignominy and shame. Leaving them outside their cages, I climbed up to the window. Then I crawled out and sat down just outside, and looked in on them stealthily from my concealed perch. What do you suppose they'd do?

Then, as in a nightmare that takes place in utter silence, I looked on aghast as every one of them, down to the last animal, padded calmly and silently back to its cage. It was as if some elusive, wicked sorcerer were commanding their destinies by remote control! With that, I jumped back down into the shop and locked the cage doors again, not to imprison the animals – since they were already prisoners of their own invisible cages – but rather so that when the store owner came back to check on them the next day, he wouldn't notice that an alien hand had been trying to rescue them. If he did notice, he'd be sure to respond by locking the window, thereby robbing me of a chance to make another attempt. The fate of these creatures had gone beyond the point of being a mere curiosity and had taken full possession of my thoughts and attention. We were one people!

Nightmare 67

Here I was moving about within my new little routine – my civil war routine. I would spend my nights in Amm Fu'ad's ground-floor flat, fearful of the perils I might encounter if I ventured upstairs. Then at dawn I'd ascend to my own flat, as if death could come only by night, or as if rockets could be fired only in the dark! I spent my days alone in the house, wandering about aimlessly like a lost soul: reading old newspapers, writing in my diary, giving myself over to nightmarish day-dreams and answering phone calls from friends. Among them there were both those who were genuinely concerned about my welfare and others who were secretly gloating over my misfortune. Whenever the shelling intensified, I'd run for cover to the hallway, where I'd sit listening to the short-wave band (the forbidden station). The real facts about what was taking place would come pouring out in what seemed like a torrential black stream. And whenever I heard a cry of distress, I'd go racing to the window.

Sometimes I'd head down to Amm Fu'ad's place, laden with whatever remained of the food in our flat and in search of whatever starchy foods might be left in his. At other times I'd contact friends in the hope of locating someone who might be able to extricate me from my hellish predicament. I'd try, I'd fail, I'd think about Yousif and agonize, then think about my brother and agonize some more. I'd wait for nightfall to come so that I could visit my neighbours in the pet shop, then return once again to my sarcophagus on the first floor to try to get some sleep. And so on...

This particular morning marked the beginning of my fifth day in captivity – or was it the sixth? I'd lost track. All I knew for certain was that there hadn't been a single break in my routine. Even the Holiday Inn was still in flames, just as it had been. The jasmine bush was also still blooming, in spite of the fact that the heaps of grenade shells lying beneath it had multiplied several times over and were mingled now with the corpses of some of its white blossoms. I could see rats marching back and forth in front of it every morning at dawn, as if fear had driven them out of their nests...

As usual, I was greeted by the ringing of the telephone. It was the lawyer. He'd called to tell me that there had been no new developments. Since all the relevant offices were closed, my brother would remain in prison until further notice!

Then the phone rang again. This time it was a friend calling to ask if I was all right. In his voice I thought I detected a bit of barely concealed glee over my plight. So, not wanting to ruin his fun, I assured him that I couldn't be in worse shape – and I wasn't lying!

Nightmare 68

As I stood on the dividing line between life and death, I felt a kind of mysterious tranquillity enveloping my spirit – the kind of tranquillity that I suspect must be experienced by those who've crossed over from the realm of sanity to that of madness. It was the inward peace that lies beyond pain. It was the same sensation that always came over me whenever I sat down to write, to record what was to become *Beirut Nightmares*.

The sounds of gunfire from the battle raging in the street below were growing steadily louder. They'd come to sound like the banging of sticks on copper pots and pans. As I sat listening to the din, I pictured a city whose entire population had come out together, clanging and banging with all their might to keep the whale from swallowing the sun. Then it started to sound as if everything was happening right on top of my head. I was dying to see what was going on outside, but I didn't dare move near any of the windows. It was the only adventure film I'd ever had to listen to without being able to look at the screen.

The mere act of getting up off the floor (where I lay writing, stretched out on my stomach) and approaching the window assumed the proportions of a frightful undertaking. Meanwhile, the metallic-sounding clanging and banging were about to split my skull in two. Just then the electricity was cut off. I got up from where I lay, gathered my papers and lit my black candle, which I carried with me into the corridor to resume my writing session. Lying on the floor again, I continued with my writing by the light of the candle. As I wrote I wondered: Is it mere coincidence that the colour of the candle is black? Or is it that light can be born only out of darkness and that the sun rises only after having passed through the lightless passageways of pain and suffering? If the black-out was permanent, it could mean very frightening things indeed. However, with the cacophonous roar of the shooting tearing at my insides, I couldn't begin to calculate all the dreadful consequences that might be in store for us. Nor did I even know whether I'd live to suffer through them...

Nightmare 69

The battle continued to rage...

No doubt there were many slain lying on the roads surrounding my house, while others were still in torment, not yet having been relieved by death's arrival. There wasn't a single ambulance that would dare come near this accursed place. The wounded, lying only a stone's throw away from me, would have to suffer for a long time, since I was helpless to do so much as even moisten their brows with a drop of water or reach out with a touch of gentleness and compassion. I was feeling pain in my eye, in the spot that had been grazed by the bullet. Whenever the battle heated up, the pain would come back, as if it weren't my own wound, but the wound of the entire city...

I took a tour of the house in search of the quietest room – relatively speaking, of course. But wherever I happened to go, it sounded as if the explosions and gunshots were coming from the very room I was standing in.

Then suddenly everything was utterly still. And perhaps for the first time I understood the meaning of the phrase 'the silence of the grave.' It was a hostile silence, full of dangerous foreboding – not like the silence of a tranquil village or of a school playground after all the children have left. I felt tremendous fear, fear of a different sort from what I'd felt even while gunfire had been strafing the city. Through the silence I could hear the voices of the creatures in the pet shop. This time, though, I detected a tone of fury that hadn't been there before, like the rhythm of drumbeats growing louder and louder in a symphony of confusion, brokenness and despair. And I wondered: Do you suppose they've begun to get hungry – like me?

I could hear an armoured car coming down the street, so I stuck out my thumb like a hitchhiker as if to ask it to stop for me. Who knows? I thought. Maybe it could get me out of this inferno. So even though all the windows were shut tight and innumerable walls blocked its view of me, I kept sticking my thumb out as if I actually thought it would do some good. Then finally I burst out laughing at myself. But my voice frightened me. Might this be a sign of impending insanity?

Then I heard an ambulance. The sound of an ambulance is the

sound of leavetaking, of parting – the sound of a body parting with one of its limbs. The sound of someone bidding farewell to himself. I could hear it growing louder, then fainter, as if it were making circles around our neighbourhood without being able to come any closer. As it kept up its loud lament, for some reason I thought of women ululating at a wedding. I tended towards the opinion that most weddings accompanied by loud trilling of this sort are nothing but pseudo-celebrations – as if ululations of joy are really nothing more than a mask to conceal secret tears of refusal. In fact, both ululation and wailing are sounds that I detest. Perhaps it's because I hate all loud noises – that is, except those that occur in nature, like the sounds of thunder and wind. As for those produced by human beings, they've always been associated in my mind with evil, with masks of deception, with preaching to the masses, with monstrous historic lies. Faint sounds, on the other hand, are associated in my mind with prayer, love and tranquillity.

There was an argument going on in a house nearby. I could hear a man shouting at the top of his voice and a woman doing the same. Still, by comparison with the symphony of explosions to which I'd just been treated, their voices sounded anaemic and fragile. It was as if the spouses' altercation was a comic interlude between the acts of a play fraught with violence and rage.

I kept on roaming aimlessly around the house, which was being convulsed with shudders and rumblings as if about to collapse in an earthquake. Then suddenly I tripped over a tiny lamp. It was a special lamp for killing mosquitoes that I'd been in the habit of turning on every night before I went to bed in the hope of fending off their attacks. Seeing it reminded me that I hadn't used it for some time – since the bite of bullets had become a greater threat to my slumber than that of any mosquito. I turned it on with a chuckle. It didn't work, of course, since the electricity was still off...

The anti-mosquito lamp, and for that matter all our familiar household gadgets and other creature comforts – like clocks, nutcrackers, cigarette filters, glasses, rose water, Kleenex, house slippers, ashtrays, hairpins and hundreds of other things the likes of which fill our houses to the brim – now struck me as ridiculous, laughable and useless. Even the broad, high windows in the house now seemed like nothing but sources of danger. I thought of the way ancient fortresses used to be constructed, with narrow windows cut into their walls at an oblique angle. I wished that whoever had built our house had thought to imitate the style of the fortresses in Sidon or Husn, for example. If he'd only designed one room the old-fashioned way so that I could run to it for shelter!

It saddened me to think that there had been a time when I wouldn't have hesitated to hitch a ride with any family I saw in a car, and I'd be taken free of charge to some new land. I'd always been an impoverished tourist in love with making new discoveries. And it gave me cause to rejoice that the loveliest things in life all come free of charge – sunshine, the sea, the night-time, the moon, laughter, freedom and the delights of sexual love and expression. I used to dream of making my home in a tent on a vast sandy beach in the summertime, while in the winter I'd take up residence in a room with glass walls set on top of high boulders overlooking the towering waves. Yet now, as my diaphanous dreams of yesteryear were battered by bombs and bullets, they were being transmuted into dreams of impregnable stone fortresses...

A voice inside my head screamed: How detestable war is!

And another voice replied: Rather, how detestable are those who make war into the only way left to live – the only way to reclaim the shores of joy and gladness where we can set up our tents of freedom and build our glass-walled houses of serenity without fearing the sticks and stones of those who seek to hoard the sunlight, claiming that life itself is their own exclusive property...

Nightmare 70

I'd had enough of this wandering around the house from room to room, like a tormented spirit hovering about a grave. I was also tired of busying myself to avoid dealing with the task that I'd come upstairs to accomplish on this particular morning – namely, to collect Yousif's photos, letters and other memorabilia and pack them up, along with what I'd managed to write of *Beirut Nightmares*. I'd decided to do it in the hope that, if a miracle occurred and an armoured car actually came to lift me out of my 'combat position' (defenceless, unarmed civilian that I was!), I'd be ready to whisk them away with me at a moment's notice. With every word I penned in my diary I wondered: Do you suppose I'll live to see these words in print? Or will I be incinerated along with them beneath the ruins of this house? In that case, no one would ever hear the cries of distress that I'd uttered as I lived through my nightmares, as fragile and isolated as a lone tear on an orphan's cheek.

I was also tired of trying to distract myself from thinking about Yousif's papers, his possessions and the days we'd shared together. I had no choice but to face up to the acute suffering it caused me to be reminded of him in any concrete way. It was as if the material remains of our days together robbed them of their amorphous, dream-like character – which at least brought with it a measure of consolation – restoring to them their immediacy, their reality, their ordinariness. And it was a reality that might have continued if... if... if he hadn't been murdered by others who, like him, were needy and poverty-stricken. They'd been duped into believing that he was their enemy merely because what was written in the 'religion' box on his identity card was different from what was written on theirs. In place of the word identifying his religion, couldn't they have read the word 'poverty' that had been branded there?

I'd made up my mind that if a tank did come to my rescue, I'd take my papers with me, as well as some of Yousif's things. I'd put them all in a small shoulder bag, and if the officer objected that there was no room for luggage, I'd just tell him to think of my bag and me as equivalent to one fat lady. After all, being rather on the skinny side, I knew that even with my bag I wouldn't take up any more room than some overweight woman would have done. Supposing I *had* been fat, they surely wouldn't have asked me to leave part of my body behind, or to cut off some of my extra flesh since it wouldn't all fit inside the tank! And Yousif's pictures and letters were as much a part of my 'flesh' as if they were my own body. Which meant, of course, that I had no choice but to bring them along...

But... where *were* his things?

Like someone recalling a painful dream, I remembered that on the night he died I'd come back home and, in a dreadful, tense silence unmitigated by even a tear, gathered up his pictures, his letters and a glass ball that he'd asked me to look into whenever I missed him — like a sorceress gazing into her crystal ball, certain to conjure up the image she seeks. Along with these I gathered together the little things that we'd shared in common: a half-burned candle that had witnessed some of our sweet moments together, a match that we'd used to light a farewell cigarette once upon a lovers' quarrel, the pipe that he'd kept continuously between his lips until he gave up smoking (to save his pocket more than his lungs), some educational books, his music... Along with these there were innumerable other little things that wouldn't have meant anything to anyone but the two of us. To me, though, they bore the scent of a distant star in whose luminous orbit we'd made our life together – that is, until the days had thrust me violently back into my old familiar world, into the ordinary, mundane death that I'd grown accustomed to dying day in and day out.

I remembered gathering up as many of his things as I could. Too numerous for me to able to pick them all up, they'd surrounded me on every side – small, yet painful, like pins pricking my skin without mercy. Even so, I'd carried them away and hidden them somewhere. The strange thing now was that I could no longer recall exactly where... I'd forgotten, but not forgotten. I knew just where they were, yet I couldn't picture the spot! Where on earth had I gone with them? I could see myself picking them up roughly and carrying them away like a mother cat who's decided to prey on her own young. But where had I absconded with them before delivering them up to be torn apart by the fangs of oblivion? Where? And then I began to remember... I'd left my room and headed towards the hallway that opened on to the kitchen, the roof, the study and the balcony. Then where had I gone? At this point I saw myself disappearing into a thick white fog, beyond which I had no idea where I'd ended up.

I decided to look in the study...

But after an hour of exhausting, frenzied searching, during which time I was tied in knots with fright, I still hadn't found a thing. As I searched I was obliged to open all the windows so as to let in the light of day (since the electricity was still off). In the process I became the target of both a rain shower descending from above and a spray of hot lead from below, along with the howling winter winds that had begun announcing their arrival at this gloomy outpost of ours. For a solid hour I turned drawers inside-out and upside-down. My papers went flying every which way, as did my senses and my ability to concentrate. Still, I couldn't find a thing.

I sat down in the middle of the room, encircled by the sounds of renewed battles and by the winter that seemed to be peering in villainously through the windows that surrounded me on all sides of the room but one. Staring blankly at the walls, I wondered: Where do you suppose I hid them? Did I burn them? Only one possibility remained – namely, that I'd hidden them behind the books on one of the shelves that lined the walls of the room and the adjacent hallway.

So I resumed my miserable search, hurling books off the shelves and on to the floor, emptying one shelf after the other. Within half an hour I was tripping over monstrous heaps of books strewn all over the place. But there was still no trace of Yousif's things. I didn't have a clue as to their whereabouts – not even so much as a whiff of his special scent. His image didn't appear in the crystal ball, his voice didn't come wafting out of his phonograph records, nor did the smiling face in his pictures burst out laughing. O Yousif, my dear one, where did I take your things?

When I left my study, it looked as if a flood had swept through it, first picking up everything in sight, then depositing it all over the floor in a chaotic heap before finally receding.

However, I didn't forget to shut the windows tight. I loved my books the way a fighter loves his weapon and knew them with the same intimacy. Aside from my papers, they were the only things that I hoped would never come to harm. In fact, I was already grieving over them. Like the human body, they could go up in flames – either water or fire could be the death of them. Not having been made for the battlefield, they were fragile and vulnerable. It's true, of course, that burning a book can't destroy the ideas it contains, any more than killing a human being can destroy humanity. Still, every human being's death is a kind of mini-drama – like that of a small home library whose owner has hand-picked every book in it, one at a time.

My only consolation was that thieves don't generally steal books. This being the case, my books were fairly sure to survive in the event of the house being looted. The only thing that posed a genuine threat to them was fire. I thought of how, in ancient times, words had been etched on to fireproof clay tablets or carved into rocks and boulders. Why had people believed the lie of civilization and been content to start using printing presses, paper or even papyrus leaves? Couldn't they at least have waited until these evil days had passed, war had become a shameful disgrace and the use of weapons a scandal meriting a public outcry? Why were words printed on paper's fragile body in an age of fire and iron? I found myself wishing that rough drafts of all my works could be engraved in stone in a cave somewhere rather than being written in ink on leaves as delicate as cigarette paper, rose petals and dragonfly wings.

But where *had* I put Yousif's things? Where on earth could they have disappeared to? Do you suppose that when he died, they'd been gradually transformed into ashes, then blown away in the darkness of the night? Might his things have vanished automatically when he died? If so, it was as if they were trying to say to me: Memories aren't a man's body. Trying to live with memories is like trying to share a home with the corpse of a man who before his death was more precious to you than your very own life. Yet now he's died. And all that death leaves behind is a lifeless body! Sooner or later, a corpse is bound to putrefy and disintegrate, at which point we have no choice but to flee from it.

Just then a bullet stole into the room, hit the wall and ricocheted off it on to a mound of books. As I left the room, I wondered again what might be the secret behind the enmity between bullets and books. Or had this been just another coincidence?

Nightmare 71

Even after searching high and low for Yousif's things, I never found them. I pictured them having flown away by night, floating like a severed head through black oceanic expanses, going far away from me to the depths of the sea – to the place where their possessions go once lovers have bidden each other farewell.

I gathered up my papers. Since everything was written on airmail stationery, this made it possible for me to take the most important ones – in fact, the majority of them – with me without having to deal with the problem of things being too heavy or too large. Papers in hand, I went down to Amm Fu'ad's flat, where I found him and Amin packing all their silverware, *objets d'art* and expensive dishes into large suitcases. What a strange world. One person's treasure is another's burden. My treasures were these flimsy, diaphanous papers, specially designed to be transported from place to place. I'd never been a believer in the myth of permanence. That was why I'd always written my things on 'pilgrims' paper'. In terms of weight and ease of transport, a single silver spoon of theirs would have equalled half of all my papers, with all the treasures and worlds contained therein...

Nightmare 72

After a while Amm Fu'ad and Amin got tired of packing up the silverware, so they came and sat down with me to rest from their labours.

Jokingly I said: 'When the thieves come and find all your valuables neatly packed up in expensive leather bags, they'll thank you for all the trouble you've gone to. All they need now is for someone to pick them up and take off with them!'

Apparently my joke didn't go over very well, since Amin glowered and said: 'Do you mean to say that we might be robbed?'

'Why not?' I replied.

With a lump in my throat I remembered my books, then comforted myself with the thought that no thief in his right mind would take them if that meant leaving Amin Fu'ad's silverware and other riches behind!

Amin got up and disappeared for a while into one of the side rooms, then came out carrying several black velvet boxes covered with a thick layer of dust. Before long I'd figured out that they weren't boxes after all, but family photograph albums. Amin was from a well-to-do family that had passed down its wealth from one generation to the next. My own family, by contrast, was of fairly modest means. My deceased father, who'd been a scrupulous, impartial judge (and consequently an impoverished one as well), had begun renting the third floor of this building many years back. As time went on we decided to stay, as the rent was a mere pittance considering the frightfully expensive times we were living in.

Amin began leafing through an album containing photos of the daughters of a prominent Lebanese figure, all of whom had married Arab princes! In one of the wedding photos, Amm Fu'ad's late wife appeared beside the newlyweds, since the two families were connected by a long-standing friendship. But as I looked at the pictures, I didn't pause over the faces of the brides and other women, who were no doubt society ladies whose pictures occupied the diary pages of newspapers and magazines. Instead, my attention was drawn to the jewels that dangled from their necks like the limp bodies of so many dead birds. From the bride's neck there hung a huge jewelled necklace that reminded me of the albatross in Coleridge's, 'The Rime of the Ancient Mariner'. All that wasted money! All those red velvet couches and all the obscene wealth that betrayed itself even in the gold-plated drinking glasses in their hands... The sight of it all gave me a vague feeling of distress. However, I noticed Amin looking at the photos with a sort of affection, as if he were taking refuge in them from his dark, gloomy present. When he suggested that I might 'enjoy' looking at one of the albums, I declined. I had a powerful suspicion that this upper-class past of his was what had helped to create the bloody, explosive present which we were now witnessing.

Nightmare 73

Amin handed me my third glass of beer as if it were some sort of magical 'cup of forgetfulness', saying: 'This is from the last bottle in the house!'

It was a bit warm – another reminder that the electricity had bitten the dust. Which meant, of course, that the food in the refrigerator would spoil. It also meant hunger, real hunger.

Thinking of hunger brought back memories of one night in London, after my brother and I had just spent our last penny on university tuition fees. We decided to pay his girlfriend a visit at dinner time in the hope that she might feed us something.

When we arrived, she received us with typical British 'warmth'. She poured each of us a few drops of rum. Then when the critical moment arrived – when dinner was to start – she served herself two pieces of pork, a carrot and half a potato, then proceeded to devour them in front of us without feeling the slightest guilt or obligation to offer us hospitality – something that was second nature to us. And so we had to suffer twice – the first time from our gnawing hunger and the second from having to watch her sate herself, oblivious to our plight...

Then, two days later, the 'miracle' occurred, in true Egyptian movie style, and it became apparent that such things really do happen sometimes, since that morning I was offered a job as a translator in one of the Arab embassies in London. In fact, they were so anxious to hire me that they offered to pay me an advance salary of £100. As I accepted the offer, my voice was barely audible. At first they interpreted this as a refusal on my part, not realizing that the reason for the faintness in my voice was that I was famished!

And now here I was, in my very own house, in danger of perishing from either starvation or gunfire. The choice was mine!

Just then there was a series of explosions. Mingled with the sounds of the explosions I thought I heard glass shattering. As I sat there listening, I pictured the façade of the odious Holiday Inn, which no doubt contained enough glass to cover a football pitch. I imagined it as a huge, transparent pane towering up towards the clouds. And now here it was falling on top of our neighbourhood and shattering over our roofs.

Then suddenly everything grew calm...

It was a truce of the sort that ordinarily didn't last for more than fifteen minutes but would always be accompanied by a frightful, solemn, tomb-like silence, charged with tension and foreboding.

A fly buzzed past my face, then tried to land on my glass of beer. Under the circumstances, it sounded louder than a machine-gun, and it was to drive me out of my mind with its stubborn insistence on flying back and forth in front of my face. Monstrous and fat, it looked as if it had just drunk from someone's wounds.

I finally got up and went to the window. As I stood there gazing out at the wild cats in the garden, I began to see them with new eyes. Were they well fed? How many days would their meat last us if we were forced to slaughter them for food? And what would cat meat taste like anyway?

I was roused out of my reverie by Amin telling me a joke in French. The fact was, this was the first time I'd heard him tell a joke in any language. He related it as if it were a Shakespearian tragedy and consequently it depressed me so much I wanted to cry instead of laugh. Then he handed me an ancient-looking notebook full of French jokes. But when he noticed that I was staring at it rather unenthusiastically, he got up to carry on with his campaign against the seemingly infinite fly population.

Attempting to humour him, I said: 'Killing flies is a crime. But not killing them is a greater crime.' He didn't get the point.

When we got up to eat, the cook donned a white jacket with gold buttons and, put silverware on the table, then began serving what was nothing but a poor excuse for food and wouldn't have sufficed to satisfy even a small child. However, at least it had been served 'according to proper etiquette'.

As miserable and hungry as I was, I couldn't keep myself from laughing. There were scores of silver utensils and gold-plated spoons glistening on the red velvet tablecloth, yet there was barely enough food on the table to keep us alive! However, the important thing is to eat 'according to proper etiquette' and, if one must starve, one ought to do so 'according to proper etiquette.'

Nightmare 74

In spite of the storm raging outside, I could hear the voices of the creatures in the pet shop. But in their fearful, bewildered moans there was a rage that hadn't been there before – like my own rage over being hungry. I wondered if they'd begun to go hungry too.

I put on a raincoat, then took it off again when I remembered that although it might be water-proof, it wasn't bullet-proof. Then I descended the stairs, the darkness enveloping me like a light drawing me on towards another of my nocturnal visits.

Once again I found myself in the darkened garden. I tried taking a breath of fresh air the way prisoners do during the brief moments when they're allowed out into the prison yard. But even the night air wasn't fresh any more. Instead, the wind was laden with the stench of rotting corpses. The odour might have been coming from the bodies of the man and the dog that had been gunned down by our local sniper, or from the innumerable other cadavers lying in the surrounding streets and in hotel rooms that had now become battlefields. The stench of death mingled with smoke from the horrific conflagration that had broken out across the street in the monstrosity that we called the Holiday Inn. The nights were no longer pitch black, since tongues of fire had transformed the darkness that once enveloped the neighbourhood into a kind of never-ending, flaming sunset. It was as if the sun had come to a halt on the horizon joining sea and sky and at the upper edge of the forests, and had then proceeded to reduce the trees to ashes and send the waves up in clouds of steam. The rain paused for a short while, but the bullets continued to pour down unabated. Lightning came flashing out of my hair, which flowed loosely over the shoulders of the night in a kind of timeless, fervent entreaty, while the thunder kept up its wrathful intimidation.

Feeling as alone and insignificant as a butterfly wandering about lost in a vast unknown, I ran over and clung to the chest of the towering palm tree, then continued on my way towards the back window of the pet shop. I found it partially unhinged, just as I'd left it the day before. I removed it as usual and a fierce wind came blowing in. Meanwhile, the animals' cries and conversation grew steadily louder as they picked up the scents of smoke and fire, winter and rain.

As soon as I jumped inside, I was assaulted by a disgusting odour. Despite the cold, the smell was more pungent than usual. I sat down on the floor while my eyes adjusted to the darkness, then took a look around me. The cages were closed, just as they had been when I'd left the day before, but they were completely out of water and even the trifling amounts of food they normally contained were nowhere to be seen. It was obvious that the shop owner, or whoever had been coming in his stead, hadn't managed to get to the shop that day. Things had begun slipping out of his control.

Hunger has its own distinctive odour, its own special aura. I knew it well, just as they did. I'd learned to recognize it both by its smell and by its sound. As for its sound, it concentrates first in the throat, beginning with muttering and complaining, after which it takes the form of extra fangs that grow in the hungry creature's mouth.

At first I decided to run and get them some food. At least that was my initial, spontaneous reaction. But then I remembered that there wasn't enough food left in the house to last me for more than a single day. So by dint of cold logic, I convinced myself that I'd have to let them go hungry at least long enough for their survival instinct to kick in again, in which case they'd leave their cages and go out hunting for something to keep them alive. But then it occurred to me that their refusal to flee might be based on some hidden wisdom to which I wasn't privy. I thought of the dog that had been killed by the sniper just two days earlier. It was possible that they'd been staying in their cages in response to the sound of the shooting, as if they realized that going out now would mean certain death. In other words, perhaps it wasn't that they resisted going out on principle, as it were, but simply that the timing wasn't right. On the other hand, how would they have figured out that there was a sniper outside? Maybe all they had was a vague sense that it wasn't safe out there. In any case, I'd never know exactly what was going through their heads. The dogs were the most ravenous of all, or at least they were the most vocal. So I decided to open their cages and see whether they'd come out or not. As I unlatched the door of a cage with five enormous dogs in it, they came up to me, then started hovering around me, howling and yelping in a fierce, hungry rage. I began to be afraid that if I set them loose, I'd be attacked. My fears were confirmed when the largest of the bunch struck me with its paw. Its pointed claws sank into my flesh like knives, leaving four deep gashes on my hand. With that I fled to the window and climbed out. Only then did I remember that I hadn't closed the latch again. It was true that I hadn't opened the cage door. However, sooner or later they were bound to discover that they could get out. I decided not to be concerned about it, though, since they posed no threat to me as long as I was able to shut the window securely, thereby keeping them imprisoned inside.

I was trembling with fright as I very carefully put the

window frame back in place. As an extra precaution, I rolled a large rock over the iron screen. Meanwhile, the wound on my hand was hurting me with growing urgency.

Aided by the ghostly light of the streetlamp, I looked inside again through the tiny openings in the screen. I saw the cage door open, then watched as the first dog emerged, storming with rage. In its voice I detected the same new tone – frightful, yet lovely, like a painting etched in blood. It moved with the gestures of a man who's come out brandishing his sword in the face of everyone he meets, because he hasn't been able to find enough food at home to keep his children from starvation.

Just then several explosions went off, shattering the streetlamp and immersing the shop in utter darkness. However, I could still hear the dogs coming out of the cage one after another. Not long afterwards, during a quick flash of lightning, I caught a glimpse of them as they roamed about the shop like five angry giants.

The rain was coming down in torrents and by now I was chilled to the bone. Then suddenly I wondered: Am I bringing about a massacre? After all, it was possible that the dogs would attack and devour the rest of the hungry creatures in the shop.

I really did need to bring them some food...

With this thought, I took off running towards the house. However, I knew full well that as there wasn't enough food left inside to keep even us humans alive, I was helpless either to feed the dogs or to force them back into their prison cells!

Nightmare 75

Through the windows that lined the stairwell, I could see reflections of the red light emanating from the fire still ablaze in the gargantuan hotel across the street. Yet it was a frightening kind of light – more frightening than darkness itself. I went in through the first door I came to, which happened to be the door to Amm Fu'ad's flat.

He and Amin were listening to the radio and had turned the volume up as far as it would go. I ran towards the telephone, which by now was suspended in a state somewhere between life and death. I had to wait nearly half an hour before I managed to dial out. First I called my friend Yemen, wife of Sharif, the radio announcer, who'd been staying night and day in the operations room of the military liaison office. I told her I was in danger, not because the shelling was any worse than it had been in previous days (it couldn't have been any worse, unless they'd decided to throw in an atom bomb for good measure!). However, my nerves had begun to fray and were beginning to feel as fragile and worn as the threads of an old fisherman's net, not to mention the spectre of hunger that had begun haunting me night and day.

Then I called Amal, Huda, Bilqis and all the close friends I could think of. As for my friend Fatimah, I didn't try calling her since I knew she was suffering the same way I was and that her house in Ra's Al-Nab' was as much of a battle front as ours. Like a ship on the verge of going under, I was sending out distress signals in all directions at once. At the same time, though, I had to endure a wait of more than half an hour between calls.

It seemed like ages before the telephone rang again. The voice on the other end told me that Captain Ayyoubi wanted me to describe the location of our house to him so that he could arrange for a tank to come to my rescue.

After listening to my description, he said: 'The place is extremely dangerous, but we'll try...'

I could tell from his tone of voice that the words 'I'll try' were just a nice way of saying: 'Impossible.' Desperate to convince him to come, I told him I'd wait for them on the side-street behind our house – on Hourani Street, that is – in front of the pet shop. He replied that the tank wouldn't be able to come down that street. It was too narrow and steep, he said, and there was a danger that the tank would lose traction on the wet pavement. And, he added, one tank had nearly got stuck there just the day before. I knew he was telling me the truth, since the night before, when I'd been half-asleep and half-awake, I'd heard the sound of a tank going back and forth outside. However, at the time I thought I was imagining things, like a thirsty man who imagines an oasis in the desert or a lover who sees an apparition of her beloved. Under the circumstances, it would have been quite natural for me to find myself dreaming of tanks, but it hadn't been a dream after all. A tank nearly stuck in the mire had been struggling to get off the steep, rain-drenched incline.

However, I wasn't ready to give up yet. I told him that I could wait for the tank on the street that led down from Clemenceau Street to the Fortress Harbour police station. Yousif and I had named it 'Sigh Street'. Whenever we drove down it as he was taking me home, we'd begin heaving lovers' sighs, knowing we were soon to part and wouldn't be seeing each other again for another whole hour (or some such thing). Of course, I didn't tell Captain Ayyoubi that I'd wait for him on 'Sigh Street'. Instead I called it by its regular name – that is, 'Makhfar Street' – and told him I'd be waiting for them in front of the police station.

He replied irritably: 'It's a location that's impossible to get to! We haven't even been able to get bread to our men stationed there!'

In an attempt to keep him from cutting off the conversation – and with it my last thread of hope – I said: 'Would you like me to take some bread to your men in the police station? I can slip out through our back garden after dark.'

Of course, I didn't mean a word of it, since I knew we didn't have a single piece of bread to spare in the entire house. But then, as if he understood what I was aiming at, he said: 'Here's a number for you to take down. The person you need to contact is a man by the name of Haydar. He's the officer who'll be driving the tank. Maybe the two of you can figure out a street that he can get to or arrange a place to meet.'

And that was the end of the conversation. Once again a deep gloom descended over me. Even though I'd taken the number down, I didn't try to call officer Haydar. After all, I knew in advance that he'd refuse to venture into the heart of the hotel war zone! Besides which, the telephone was about to bite the dust for good.

I felt as if my chest had been ripped to shreds, while the evening weighed heavily upon me as if a steamroller had just passed back and forth over my body. I sat there motionless, with my body flung across the chair next to the telephone, while the candle next to me flickered in the cold wind coming in through the windows. We didn't dare close them for fear that glass would go flying in all directions if there were an explosion. And now here was 'Lord Winter' roaming the streets and entering our houses at will.

I could hear the screeching of Amm Fu'ad's radio, but I wasn't making any effort to understand what was being said. I'd arrived at the conclusion that the only news broadcast I could take at face value was what reached me borne on the winds. And as for the winds, they brought me nothing but shrieks of perdition and the mournful, wintry scent of destruction mingled with smoke and the stench of the rotting cadavers that blanketed the pavements.

Nightmare 76

The phone was ringing again. So then... we could still receive calls, but just couldn't make them any more. On the other end I heard the voice of our neighbour Hussein, who was living in the Idriss Building across the street from the Jumblatt mansion.

'Are you ready to leave?' he asked.

'Of course,' I replied. 'Who wouldn't be ready to get out of this hell-hole?'

'A tank will be there shortly. Wait for us at the door.'

So then, no one had escaped the day before. The tanks had been hit without rescuing a soul.

Once again I emerged into the dreadful night. Once again I sat clinging to the frigid post, listening furtively for the sound of that huge, metal life buoy more commonly known as an armoured car. And once again I cursed Amm Fu'ad's loud-mouthed radio, which was putting so much static in the air that I could hardly listen for my rescuers. Then it began to rain and the excruciating pain in my hand reminded me once more of the furious, hungry dog that had taken a swipe at me with its claws. In happier lands, people would have gone to a doctor for a rabies vaccination if something like that had happened to them. But I'd forgotten even to wash my wound. Here, surrounded on all sides by death's gloom, I might be shot and bleed to death without anyone so much as reaching out to lift me off the ground. I opened the iron gate leading out of the garden, removing the chain that was wrapped around the lock. The mournful, cold sound of the metal conjured visions in my mind of prisoners on a sinking ship having the shackles removed from their legs.

Then at last I heard it approaching in the distance. It was a sound that had become synonymous in my mind with life, with escape from danger. It continued to draw nearer and nearer until suddenly the roar of its engine came to a halt. I stuck my head out a bit, trying to catch a glimpse of it at the end of the street. But I couldn't see a thing. The streetlights were all either turned off or shot full of holes. Even the fiery red light coming from the Holiday Inn couldn't penetrate the veil of darkness that now enveloped the bend in the road where the Jumblatt mansion and the Idriss Building stood.

Closing my eyes and relying on nothing but what I could hear, I tried to construct a mental picture of what was happening. I could see people coming down out of their flats, overjoyed to have survived their ordeal, then disappearing with a sigh of relief into the tank's metallic womb. As for me, I was still 'in the belly of the whale' as it were: the whale of fear and loneliness. Once again I could hear the tank, whose rumbling came a bit closer this time. Meanwhile, the showers of bullets heading my way from the direction of the Holiday Inn began coming thicker and faster, now mingled with infernal-sounding, thunderous explosions – the thunder of bombs. I couldn't hear a thing any more.

Not long afterwards, everything fell silent and I knew that the tank had retreated. Even so, I kept waiting, hoping against hope that it would turn around and come back to get me. I don't know how long I waited. But I could feel the rain soaking me to the bone, dripping down off my hair on to my face and blending with my tears. By now the pain in my ear and hand had become so unendurable that I too retreated. Heading back towards Amm Fu'ad's flat, I was too weary and weak to relock the iron gate with the chain. What was the use of locking it anyway? Who would have the nerve to venture in our direction when even army tanks fled from this inferno?

When I came in, I looked over at Amm Fu'ad and Amin, who just sat there gaping at me. Only then did I realize that I must look like a drowned rat. And I was trembling like a ghost who's just emerged from a grave at the bottom of the sea. After staring at me for a few moments, they turned their attention back to the news broadcast. I thought I'd detected a trace of malicious glee in Amin's eye. He'd capitulated to his father's wishes and ways of looking at things and now every passing day – so far, at least – was confirming to him that he'd chosen the path of prudence and wisdom. After all, he was sitting high and dry in his comfy armchair, while I was spending night after moonless night falling to pieces on hope's tenebrous ladder. And in spite of it all, I refused to stop trying...

Nightmare 77

I woke up feeling fatigued and oppressed, having just been through a number of miserable, disturbing dreams. For some time I lay limp as a rag in my strange, unfamiliar bed, my mind shifting back and forth between wakefulness and nightmares – or rather, between one kind of sleep and another. After all, aren't bad dreams just an expression of an elevated level of perception? Don't nightmares take place in a state of heightened alertness? And isn't what we call madness in actual fact a kind of complete 'unfiltered' awareness?

Just then I heard a rocket blast, followed by the sound of glass shattering and falling to the ground. The sound of the glass as it fell seemed to stretch on and on, as if it were echoing the explosion, while the sound of its shattering reminded me for some unknown reason of the bluish-white colour of modern hospital walls. It was as if the strange bed where I'd been spending my nights of late had become a kind of medium, dispatching warning signals to me across unseen wires from the realm of exile and homeless wandering.

According to my watch it was 3.48 a.m. I got up and went to the window. The sky was clear as clear could be and dotted with brilliant stars. It looked like a page out of a modern atlas illustrated with gorgeous if overblown colours. As I stood there, the heavenly dome seemed truly awesome, immense and eternal, and it grieved me to know that it wasn't as it appeared. After all, I thought, half the sun's life has already been spent, which means that it has only 4 billion years left before its fire goes out and the nuclear reactions in its core come to an end! Consequently, ultimate annihilation looks like a foregone conclusion – that is, unless the inhabitants of planet Earth join forces to head off the tragedy of the sun's death by migrating to some other planet whose sun is still in the prime of life, and unless human beings cease their flirtation with war and self-destruction.

However, people go on being so engrossed in their own petty hatreds and quarrels that they have neither time nor energy to spare for the challenges of transcending self, overcoming gravity or breaking barriers of sound and light. If people broke down the walls of hatred, then science in turn would manage to crash through the light barrier, make death a thing of the past and send us galloping back and forth between different universes of time and space. And as for me, I'd be able to meet Yousif on some other planet – on a planet where we'd taken up residence after breaking through the 'life barrier'.

'Yousif...' I whispered his name, mustering all the power in my being in the hope of merging with an infinite, cosmic cloud.

'Yousif...' Repeating his name in a kind of prayerful reverence, I could feel unseen doors and obscure, darkened walls opening up before me. I was certain that somehow or other, he could hear my voice. Then I went back to bed – to my bed of exile and estrangement – and slipped once more on to slumber's hidden shores.

Nightmare 78

The night train came to a halt and its only passenger disembarked, stepping down on to a platform awash with blood.

No sooner had the traveller arrived than he was accosted by a horde of creatures – birds of the night, cats, mice – who gathered about and eyed him with curiosity. The newcomer's body was the trunk of an aged, gnarled olive tree and his hair was seaweed from the ocean depths. Whoever looked into his eyes would find himself lost in tortuous passageways with countless, mirror-lined walls and on his lips one could detect a half-innocent, half-bemused smile.

Astonished to find that no one was there to meet him, he cried sorrowfully: 'Where are you, my people? Where are you, my children, my poor, my innocent, guileless ones? Where has everyone gone?'

Just then he was approached by a courteous, affable owl. 'What's your name, sir?' he inquired of the visitor.

'My name is Holiday,' said the old man.

The creatures who'd gathered around him burst into peals of laughter at this strange reply, since to them life itself was a daily, ongoing celebration. They didn't have to wait for the 'holiday train' to pass by, since they were living on board. A silky-tailed grey squirrel among them declared that human beings must be laughable, silly creatures indeed, since they wait for Old Man Holiday to pay them a visit without stopping to notice that the daily rising of the sun, the dance of the tide's ebb and flow, and the joyful choruses sung by the rain and the changing seasons are all holidays. In their mad preoccupation with the manufacture of ugliness and destruction, people have all but forgotten what holidays are.

The old man set off, walking towards Beirut, and on the way there he was stopped at an armed checkpoint.

'What's your name?' he was asked.

'Holiday,' he replied.

None of the men seemed to have heard the name before, although one of them looked as if he was trying to retrieve a coloured image that lay hidden in the recesses of his mind. However, his efforts were to no avail, since the sounds of gunfire for weeks on end had shattered his 'memory screen'.

So the old man repeated himself, saying: 'Holiday...'

'Pleased to meet you,' they replied, 'Where's your ID?'

Pointing skyward with his gnarled hand towards a gaunt-looking new moon, he said: 'That's my ID.'

They didn't even lift their heads, since apparently they'd got out of the habit of using them for anything but hunting. Then one of them took aim at the moon and fired, shattering the delicate crescent and bringing its corpse tumbling to the ground in a heap of ashes. That got a laugh from his cronies, who let the crazy old man go, since they didn't figure he was worth wasting another bullet on.

'My lady, my lady, what have you done to your braids?'

She was a woman whom the old man had known and loved for a long, long time. She'd been beautiful and elegant, and always wore gloves.

'I cut them off,' she replied, 'and then I used them to strangle my children, one after another.'

'My lady, my lady,' he asked, 'what have you done to your beloved?'

'He betrayed me, so I hanged him on the walls of my heart.'

'My lady, my lady, what have you done to the walls of your heart?'

'I've hung the corpses of my days upon them, then left them there for vultures soaring through cloudless skies to devour their eyes and their livers.'

'My lady, my lady, what have you done to your smooth, translucent skin?'

'I married it to the soil, then cleansed it with thorns and perfumed it with the scent of gunpowder.'

'My lady, my lady, why didn't you wait for my night train to come in, as you've done every other year?'

'Because I've lost the ability to numb myself to the pain.'

'But I'm the "Holiday"!'

'Yes, but you're nothing but a passer-by. And I've grown weary of passers-by, just as I have of the prostitutes that frequent our ports by night.'

'My lady, my lady Beirut, have you lost your senses?'

'Perhaps so. And then again, perhaps not. It may actually be the first time I've ever thought clearly.'

'My lady, my lady, your lips are cracked and parched as dried meat, your face is as scorched as the desert sands, and your neck looks as gaunt and lean as a bird whose nest has gone up in flames. How can you endure?'

She then took him by the hand and led him to a hill made up of seven tiers. The first tier was of salt, the second of cadavers and the third of blood. These were topped by layers of sin, regret, repentance and finally understanding. And in the soil that had been created by this curious, enigmatic blend, a green shoot was forcing its way tenaciously upward amid the darkness, the wind, the moans of the dying and the gasps of those giving birth to new life...

'My lady, my lady, how do you spend your nights now?'

'I've shattered my bottles of nocturnal potion on the

seashore and left them to disintegrate like rusted, empty sardine cans. I'm ready to stake a claim to a different, better future.'

'My lady, my lady, I fear this may be the end. For you've ceased to be beautiful.'

'I was never beautiful to begin with. There can be no beauty without justice or truth. I was nothing but a beautiful mask – and now the mask is gone. Along with it I'm also taking off my jewels, my furs and my gloves. And I'm going to cleanse this face of mine, even if I have to wash it in blood.'

'My lady, my lady, it's too late now. Your chance has been lost!'

'True – I turned down my chance to be first dancer in the Middle East cabaret! But I may still rise from my ashes. I may still manage to purge myself of this river of blood. It's my only chance to be, to survive.'

'My lady, my lady, where is that hotel of yours with the grand, luxurious couches? I'd like to get some sleep.'

'One's homeland, sir, isn't a hotel. On your next visit, I hope you'll come to stay. I hope you'll decide to take up permanent residence in the kingdom of joy – my kingdom.'

'My lady, my lady, where are you going?'

'To where I can find deliverance – or die!'

Then the old man gathered up his suitcases, his old, worn-out toys, his silly-sounding horns and his funny-looking party hats and headed back to the station.

Meanwhile, the green shoot glowed in the darkness, as the young, the poor and the pure of heart planted its roots in their veins where it could grow and flourish...

As the old man stood waiting for the train, he was hailed once more by the congenial owl, who tried to ease his loneliness and cheer him up by telling him a few light-hearted jokes. But Old Man Holiday, still bewildered and perplexed, was wondering to himself: This lady named Beirut... do you suppose she's bringing about her own demise? Or could it be that if she takes off her masks, she'll manage to rise out of her ashes like the legendary phoenix?

And might he actually become a citizen of her empire? Or when he made his next visit, would he shoot himself in the head on one of its darkened railway platforms?

All this raging, clamouring and bitter violence – was it a sign of imminent death or of new birth?

Nightmare 79

Sprawled out motionless on my bed of exile, I tried to reconstruct my fractured dreams and nightmares.

As I lay there, Amin peeked in and asked me if I'd slept well. It was obvious from looking at his face that he hadn't slept a wink and that he was hoping I'd ask him the same thing. I didn't. However, he'd made up his mind to pour out his tale of woe to me whether I asked him or not.

'I took five Valiums,' he said all of a sudden, 'and I still couldn't sleep.'

'The nights are long and gloomy,' I replied, 'and Valium has only a limited effect. So you can expect that, in a time of civil war, any sedatives you happen to swallow will dissipate into empty space. They'll never make it into your bloodstream!'

It was the longest conversation we'd had in years. After he left the room, I stared out at the pouring rain and was aware of how fortunate I was to be in a bed rather than lying wounded in the open air. Just then I felt a painful twinge of hunger and, as it happened, it was as if the atmosphere had altered the frequency of my brainwaves, transporting me to another plane of consciousness and causing my inner radar to begin picking up the sounds being made by the creatures in the pet shop.

Their voices sounded to my ears like a symphony of rage that nearly drowned out the sounds of the thunder and the rain. I wasn't able to pick out any voice in particular. Instead, it felt as if I were listening to some sort of dissonant, macabre choir shrieking out an anthem to hunger. It was then that I remembered they'd been hungry when I left them the night before, since the recent escalation in the fighting had prevented their master (or whoever had been standing in for him) from coming to give them their daily rations.

It was truly amazing, but even as I lay there in bed feeling torn and limp as a rag, I could hear the voices of the creatures in the pet shop over the roar of bullets and explosives, isolating each sound down to the faintest whisper. It was as if my body had been transformed into a sophisticated, high-precision instrument capable of identifying and classifying even the most elusive of sounds. And if I closed my eyes, I could see clearly everything that was taking place in the back room of the pet shop, thereby completing the sounds with images.

The five hunting dogs, as lithe and nimble as Arab stallions, emerged from their cage and went roaming through the storeroom prison. For some time they continued butting their heads up against the walls in search of a way out and leaping up towards the window that I'd been crawling in through every night. Hunger was making every leap a bit higher and every gasp a bit louder than the one that had preceded it. Meanwhile, a sense of dread and panic, now mingled with growing hunger, was steadily creeping into the hearts of the other imprisoned animals. The wrath-charged electrons being emitted by the hunting dogs were coming thicker and faster and had taken on an increasing radiance. Meanwhile, they were being picked up by the other animals, who in turn added to them as their cries of terror, hunger and fury grew to a fever's pitch. A bird that hadn't exercised its wings since the day of its imprisonment began trying to fly off. Instead, all it managed to do was collide with the birds around it, rousing them from their fitful slumber, and bang up violently against the bars of the cage. As for the parrot who'd been trained to chatter for hours on end, it had fallen as silent as the minister of information under a dictatorial regime. It had forgotten the line it used to repeat in three different languages – 'Buy me! Buy me! Buy me!' – and had gone back to the screeching and cawing of its jungle days – the screeching of freedom, hunger, rage and honesty.

They were also screeches of terror – terror of the dogs which had now gone in search of something to devour. Their bared fangs had begun reaching aimlessly through the iron bars of the cages. However, most of the cages were enclosed with wire screens as fine as sieves, so almost no one came to harm. As for the other animals, once they'd been roused out of their state of semi-unconsciousness by hunger and a sense of danger, they seemed to regain their physical fitness and dexterity, since they deftly evaded the dogs' fangs and claws, turning the place into a veritable witch's cauldron, bubbling over with contradictions and a spirit of dark savagery. I could see the fish speeding through their now-darkened aquarium in search of whatever leftover morsels might still be lingering in the water. At the same time, the small fish would pile on top of each other, with each one measuring itself against its neighbour to see who was biggest and who would be most likely to devour the other.

One of the dogs had managed to wound a rabbit with its claws. Being ill, it wasn't able to move quickly enough to get away from the side of the cage from which the blow had come. It sought refuge in a far corner of the cage, bleeding along the way. As the smell of the blood diffused through the room, the prison was convulsed as if by an earthquake. It was as if blood possessed some magical power that called for more of the same, or as if it had the capacity to reproduce itself. Perhaps it was because the wizards and witches of the Middle Ages recognized this unnamed force – a force concealed in blood's very fragrance and colour – that none of their rites or ceremonies ever took place without it.

The wounded rabbit sent a wave of madness through the entire place, an inexplicable, all-encompassing turmoil that left no creature untouched. It was as if the rabbit's blood were a warning cry which, in the world of the jungle, served the same function as an air-raid siren does in the city. And just as human beings have their own particular ways of responding to such portents, some animals fell into an anxious, apprehensive silence, while some of the birds got looks of such profound grief in their eyes, one would have thought they were children who'd just been orphaned. Even the self-assured peacock froze in his tracks, his brilliantly coloured tail unfurled and erect without the slightest showmanship or narcissism, like someone so terrified that his hair is standing on end!

As for the sleek, nimble hunting dogs, they let out piercing cries and took off running through the shop in a mad, furious dash. They leapt into the 'tourist section', with its huge murals designed to impress all the foreign customers who used to come to buy the shop owner's imprisoned charges, and from whose eyes he'd ingeniously concealed all evidence of the animals' appalling misery. With every angry, desperate leap, another piece of the decor would come tumbling down. Digging their claws into the posh leather armchairs, they proceeded to rip the upholstery to shreds, then mangle their cotton stuffing and strew it about like so many cadavers. Following this they went on to demolish the paintings on the walls and relieve themselves on the shop owners' armchair, all the while frothing at the mouth and spewing the white foam of their saliva on everything in sight.

Nightmare 80

I was still sprawled out on my bed, feeling ragged and lonely. As I lay there, I thought:

Even if your body were a wave on the sea which bullets could penetrate without doing it harm... Even if your heart were an electric pump which couldn't be paralysed by fear and anxiety and whose rhythm was unfazed by human emotions ... Even if your nerves were made of steel, or compounds primed to withstand the stresses of outer space... Even if your heartbeat were as predictable as a Swiss-made watch straight off the production line... Even if your sleep patterns were as constant as the Earth's orbit around the sun... And even if you had a capacity for joy and celebration as irresistible and overpowering as the waters pouring down Niagara Falls...

Even if all these things were true of you, you'd still find after eight months of civil war that chaos had begun to penetrate the very depths of your spirit. You'd find it gradually infiltrating your thoughts, your most deeply held values, your feelings, your disposition, your relationships.

After eight months of civil war, you'd feel the need for an internal ceasefire that would allow you to stop thinking – to stop thinking about all the bullets that had missed you, about the missile that had sent your house up in flames, about the sniper who'd shot the cap off your head, about your bitter, grey, daily bread, kneaded at dawn to the roar of missiles and blistering conflagrations. You could cease thinking about your long nights plagued by the cold, the unknown and the screams of the helpless and wounded, about the mournful wailing of ambulances which, unable to reach the wounded until it was too late, had been transmuted into hearses, and about fire engines incapable of doing anything but offer consolation to the fire's victims, having been prevented by the shooting from reaching their destination before the flames had consumed everything there was to consume.

After eight months of life in a city whose streets remain darkened and eerie night after night, eight months of gruesome nightmares whose sounds seem to take up residence in your pillow, ringing in your ears like a tape recording that plays nonstop, you'd feel that you needed to be able to encounter yourself, if only just once, without at the same time either being in flight under a barrage of gunfire, hiding behind a barricade or kneeling at the epicentre of an earthquake.

And like me, you'd slip away while no one was looking and flee to the seashore.

Once you were safely there, you'd fling your body nonchalantly on to a boulder, the same body which in moments of dread you'd been in the habit of rolling up into a ball so tight that it occupied as little space as possible – the way some animals do when danger comes upon them unawares.

You'd spread your body out on the shore like a cloud, then leave it there to disperse little by little until it had expanded to the size of your dreams at a time when your ability to dream was a possession you'd nearly forgotten you had.

Like me, you'd choose a huge boulder jutting out into the water so that when you stretched out on top of it and turned your back towards the city, you'd imagine yourself sailing out to sea in a boat made of stone.

After eight months of civil war, you become conscious of

how the frightful chaos around you has taken possession of your inner being, and you feel the need to reorder the world inside you, including your values and your ways of understanding things. Everything looks different in the light of the surprises that have come your way and the discoveries which, whether they've come as painful blows or sources of intense joy, have in either case left you both baffled and astounded.

You find yourself re-examining everything, and the place it's occupied in your life: your friends, your work, your place of residence, your heart and your spirit's ability to gauge which direction you're heading in as you speed along in your boat of stone over the vast, dispassionate sea. Down is now up, and up is down. Ceilings have become walls and walls have become roads leading to who knows where. And you? Just exactly who are you anyway?

How very alone you are...

In a time of famine, those you love can steal you something to eat, but they can't digest it for you.

They can provide you with a bed, but they can't sleep on your behalf.

They can give you their own blood as a gift, yet the unhealed wound remains yours and yours alone.

They can even offer apologies for the ways in which they've ill-treated you, yet they can't suffer in your stead the pain they have caused.

How alone you are indeed... And civil war will remind you of this fact with unsurpassed eloquence. Like a masterfully crafted mirror, it reveals to those who dare to gaze into it the flimsiness of what we call the 'bond of human fellowship'.

Rather than being the thickness of an umbilical cord, it's finer than the legendary hair of Caliph Mu'awiyah![3] But if you aren't consumed by civil war's inferno, you'll emerge from it having had your eyes opened to the realities of existence, if even for no more than a split second. The important thing is not to forget... Civil war offers a rare opportunity to the artist who goes through it and survives, since he comes out alive not just once but twice!

You close your eyes with me for a bit, then sail on in your boat of stone amid the waves over an endless sea of blue...

Then suddenly you feel blissfully happy, for no other reason than that you're alive. What a miracle it is that your heart is still beating! You're still capable of dispersing like a cloud till you're as vast and wide as your dreams. And you still have the ability to restore order to your world in a sea of chaos, destruction and new birth.

Life continues to be a marvel as long as the inquisitive child living inside you still knows how to laugh, sing and explore!

You hear an explosion, but you aren't afraid. It's just the dynamite used by the fishermen. As on land so also at sea, they kill. Isn't that so?

But even after this journey of the mind, I found myself right back where I had been before, sprawled out on my bed like a worn-out garment, feeling ragged and lonely. Meanwhile, the sea was still far, far away, as inaccessible and remote as ever.

Nightmare 81

As the women sat waiting in reverent submission, Khatoun the fortune-teller sat down before her crystal ball, then proceeded to gaze at it for a long time. During her days as a seamstress, she'd grown accustomed to staring for hours on end at one single spot since, as she sewed, her eyes would follow the needle's tiny steps. However, times had changed and the ladies had begun flocking to shops that sold ready-made clothes. One after another, they'd all abandoned her, the only reason being that she happened to charge moderate prices. And, like their husbands, Beirut's 'velvet' society ladies held moderate prices in contempt, preferring instead to wear outrageously expensive designer fashions complete with the signatures of Pierre Cardin, Jean Bateaux and the like.

Consequently, Khatoun had decided to turn herself into a fortune-teller, an expert in such arts as breaking magic spells and making 'binding knots' that would keep husbands and sweethearts from straying. She could 'bring back the one who's strayed and foretell both the present and the future'. This, at least, was how she'd described herself in the newspaper ad that her out-of-work husband had suggested to her. She put the ad in the newspaper along with her address, and the response was no less than astounding.

Ladies began coming to her in droves, bringing her questions about both the dead and the living, the past and the future, breaking the power of charms and talismans, and preparing a special type of knot that was guaranteed to keep one's beloved in tow for ever. And what astounded her even more was that men – politicians for the most part – also began seeking out her services. And at that point, of course, she had no choice but to make a suitable adjustment in her prices.

Spirits such as 'Shamhursh', 'Tas'ira', 'Hafshit', 'A'war Al-Dajjan', 'Atlamis', 'Zaghbibaz' and others were among the jinn she'd had previous dealings with. As for the crystal ball, she'd acquired it when she first began her new trade without ever expecting to actually see anything in it. The only reason she'd bought it was to have something to help her avoid making eye contact with her clients, lest any of them discover that she was making it all up!

However, in recent days she'd begun experiencing

something peculiar. It happened whenever she received a visit from a certain influential bey, who always arrived surrounded by bodyguards who would stand waiting for him outside the door. The minute he entered the room, she would feel a heavy 'presence' weighing on her chest. She'd also find herself yawning tensely, as if she were in need of more air. She wasn't certain if it was because of a rumour she'd heard to the effect that he'd murdered several people in a local place of worship without batting an eyelid, or whether it was simply because he had a kind of inexplicable, sinister aura about him. Whenever he came around, her joints would start to ache and she'd fall into a painful stupor, like someone who's undergoing brain surgery with nothing but a local anaesthetic. She was beginning to suffer the types of symptoms which at first she'd only been faking!

'What do you see?' the bey asked her as she sat staring into her crystal ball.

She felt as if his voice were gagging her, suffocating her. She just wanted to admit to him that she didn't see a thing, then throw his filthy money in his face and be rid of him for ever. However, she remained rigid and motionless, her glance fixed on the globe before her. It was as if he were emitting foul-smelling, electrically charged particles that had left her frozen, incapacitated. Then suddenly she found to her amazement that the ball was no longer empty. In it she saw the bey himself, his bloodied, bullet-riddled corpse flung onto the pavement.

'What do you see?' he asked her once more.

The bullet wounds that dotted the corpse were bleeding profusely. As for the face – his face – it was undergoing a kind of transformation. Instead of being just one face, it had become the faces of numerous other men. She couldn't make them out clearly and most of them she didn't recognize, although she'd seen pictures of some of them in the newspaper before.

Finally she said: 'I see blood... much blood... more and more blood...' Looking dazed and perplexed, Khatoun went on staring absently into the glass ball. Meanwhile, the scene before her was suddenly transformed into a vast field strewn with ashes and human remains. And as the field was convulsed by a colossal earthquake, a tiny green shoot could be seen forcing its way up through the surface of the ground.

'What do you see?' he insisted.

She replied: 'I see a man with two heads, each of them cursing the other, and a scorpion stinging itself in a field of smouldering embers. I see a funeral procession in which an influential figure is being escorted to his final resting place and I see people running alongside the bier playing reed pipes.'

'What else?' he prodded.

But this time she didn't hear him. Her glass ball had taken on a luminous, fiery glow, while the images inside it had begun appearing and disappearing, blending into one another in rapid succession. First she saw snow-capped mountains whose sides were blanketed with oaks, cedars and the remains of the slain. Then there appeared vast, sandy shores and blood flowing towards the sea in torrential streams. Then the land was rocked by an earthquake which split it into two massive ridges, between which there opened up a vast, unfathomable abyss. Out of its depths there emerged tongues of fire, which climbed steadily upward until they began licking at the clouds. The first earthquake was then followed by another, which shattered the land into fragments too numerous to count. This was followed by still more earthquakes, which struck in rapid, uninterrupted succession.

By now the land had been rent totally asunder. Springs of blood came bubbling up out of the ground, while blistering conflagrations billowed out of the ever-growing number of cracks and fissures, spewing forth foam-like dross in towering geysers of flame. By this time the earth had swallowed up the entire funeral procession with its sheep, its musicians and their musical instruments, as well as the surrounding houses and trees. Meanwhile, a storm of fire and loud shrieks had blown up, turning the eyes of the weeping women into darkened hollows filled with blood and smouldering embers.

'What do you see?' he asked her again.

Then, repeating his question over and over, he began slapping her in the face in a desperate attempt to rouse her from her maddening, silent trance.

She tried to answer him but couldn't. Her tongue was tied. She was vaguely aware that she'd been struck dumb by a force beyond her control. It was as if, at the moment her eyes were opened to the unseen world of the supernatural, she'd been struck by a thunderbolt that had burned her vocal cords to a crisp, reducing them to mere ashes.

Nightmare 82

As I lay in bed, limp and motionless, I could smell the nearby conflagration, its odour laden with particles of rainy cold. After having cleared somewhat before dawn, the sky had once again turned into a grey, steely dome. From where I lay, I could see the Holiday Inn continuing to burn. I tried to get up, but my hand began to hurt, reminding me once more of the wound I'd received from that hunger-crazed dog. Its claws had left their marks on my hand in the form of four gashes, two of them longer than the others, and my skin had become slightly inflamed in the area around the wound. Four slash marks, like the tracks left by a plough in the soil...

As for the ear that had been grazed by a bullet, it was also still hurting me, although the wound had stopped festering. Before long all the dried blood would fall off and everything would go back to normal. But was it really possible (as some people were hoping) for the wounds of this city's people – their inner, unseen wounds – to heal over without even so much as a scar and for everything to go back to the way it had been? (What a tragedy it would be if everything really did go back to the way it had been!)

An explosion went off, followed as usual by the sound of breaking glass. I jumped out of bed almost effortlessly. In fact, despite the hunger, the terror, the isolation and the wounds I'd suffered, I was feeling relatively rested and refreshed.

Everything around me made it seem like a veritable miracle that I could still carry on. However, the fact was that I kept on going without considerable effort. I might sink into the depths of despair, but before I knew it I'd be floating to the surface again. It was as if life itself were proving its determination to win out in the end.

As I headed upstairs to check on my flat, and my library in particular, I was surprised to find Amin and the servant hurling heated accusations at each other. As for the bone of contention, it was... the monkey.

The monkey – I'd forgotten all about her. Of course, she wasn't *my* monkey. Amin had bought her two years earlier for some unknown reason. What had struck me at the time was that he happened to buy her on the same night that his latest engagement (to some university student, as I recall) had been called off. Do you suppose it was a mere coincidence?

In any case, he'd brought her home and built a cage for her in a remote corner of the garden. At first it had grieved me just to look at her or to think of her being held captive that way. In fact, I'd even made up my mind to sneak out into the garden one night and let her go. But then my brother talked me out of it by helping me to see that setting her free would actually mean dooming her to destruction. After all, either she wouldn't be able to find anything to eat in the jungle of stone and asphalt that surrounded us on all sides, or somebody would capture her and try to sell her or make his living from her by putting her to work as a clown or a dancer to entertain the masses in the marketplace!

Whenever I looked at her, a vague feeling of distress came over me. The sight of a creature being robbed of its freedom has always caused me pain – whatever kind of freedom it happens to be, and even if the captive party happens to belong to some species other than my own. Of course, Amin's monkey was in a situation not altogether different from that of some of the wives in our society. Like them, she was basically a prisoner, though she also provided Amin with moments of enjoyment and entertainment whenever he so desired in exchange for being fed, cared for and protected from any sort of outward harm – as well as from any kind of emotional contact with other monkeys, of course!

'How could you have forgotten to feed her!' Amin shouted.

'I don't know!' retorted the servant. 'The fact is, I didn't forget. But I didn't dare.'

Pounding himself on the head, Amin kept repeating over and over: 'It's your responsibility, so do something about it!'

To which the servant replied: 'She's *your* monkey, not mine! And I'm not about to go out into that garden now.'

There was no choice but to wait until nightfall. The hungry monkey's shrieks had begun to take their toll on our nerves, yet no one had set foot outside the house since the day our neighbourhood was turned into a war zone. I could feel both of them looking in my direction, as if to say: *'You* go out and feed her!'

After all, I was the only one who'd ventured out into the garden even once during daylight hours.

Before they'd had a chance to utter a word I said: 'It's true – I did go out there once, but you'll also recall that I happened to be drunk at the time!'

Still, neither of them said a thing. Instead they just kept staring at me with a look of obstinate resolve in their eyes.

Finally I said: 'Look – I'm not going to help set the stage for the revolution. I won't be the one to do it!'

They didn't have the slightest idea what I meant and I didn't explain. Instead, I just continued on my way up to my flat. As usual, I took the stairs running. As usual, I ducked whenever I came to a window. And as usual, I escaped being hit by a sniper's bullet – for the time being, at least.

Once upstairs, I followed my usual wartime routine. I began by going in to inspect my library, where I reshelved the books that I'd piled on the floor during my frenzied search for Yousif's 'remains'. My library contained the only things in our whole house that I considered to be real treasures. My father had been a man of learning and piety. I'd inherited the first of these two qualities, if not the second, along with a library brimming with rare Arabic manuscripts to which I'd added a number of modern works in other languages. The library had also come to house my personal papers and archives, as well as everything I'd written over a period of ten years. Included among these were the 'radical' books whose translations I'd overseen during my five years at a publishing house held in such disfavour by officialdom.

As bullets whizzed through the air, devouring the world around me, I stood gazing at the shelf full of books without feeling the slightest bit of fear or regret. After all, the words I'd helped to bring into existence were now leaping off the page and into the world of concrete reality. Every word had become a fighter, every comma a bullet, and together they'd gone racing through the city to fulfil the ideals I held so dear. So why should I be afraid? And what sense would it make for me to have spent half my life working for transformation, liberation and social justice, then cry for an entire week because I couldn't bear the thought of bloodshed? What outrageous contradictions lurk in the human heart.

If I couldn't reconcile myself to the inevitability of death, weapons, violence and bloodshed, there would never be any peace for me.

But... was such a reconciliation possible?

Nightmare 83

Whenever the shelling intensified, I'd flee to the hallway for shelter, having concluded, based on what little I knew about warfare, that it was the safest place in the house. But as I sat crouched there on this particular occasion, a strange feeling came over me. I sat staring morosely at my books and at the words that had now turned into fighters in the streets. The terror I felt made me think of what Pygmalion's creator must have experienced when the sculpture he'd fashioned uttered its first word.

I closed my eyes and a multitude of corridors and passageways opened up deep inside me. I remembered the dream I'd had the night before, and Yousif's things, and I marvelled at the world of mystery to which we're transported when we shut our eyes and sail away to the land of Nod. But is it really *another* world? And what sort of waves were they that had borne me aloft and deposited me in the upper room beneath the tile roof – a room I hadn't set foot in since I was a young child – then suggested to me in such compelling, lifelike detail that I'd hidden something there? And why *there* of all places, in that forbidden, unapproachable region?

But as I recalled my peculiar dream, it seemed so palpable and real I could almost taste it. So, like someone in a hypnotic trance, I climbed the ageing staircase. As I ascended, I could hear wild, explosive music ringing in my ears and mingling with the frightful explosions going off outside. When I reached the attic, the room was enveloped in near-darkness. I didn't know where the light switch was or even whether there was one. However, I remembered the path I'd taken in the dream. So I followed it again, and as I did so I was astonished to find everything exactly as it had been in the dream, including the old chest of drawers and the cradle I'd slept in as a baby. Rocked by the force of explosions and gunfire, the cradle shuddered and quaked as if my childhood itself still lay sleeping inside it. Then I removed the ancient-looking blanket that I'd seen in the dream, only to discover to my amazement that Yousif's things were resting underneath!

Nightmare 84

In a small leather bag I deposited his pictures, his letters and various small memorabilia. I didn't dare read a single line of his letters. It would have been more painful than having to stare into the open coffin of the person dearest to me in all the world. And I didn't have the courage to look at his pictures. Even so, I was determined to carry them away with me, although I did ask myself: What's the use of taking them along when I don't even have the strength to look at them? I was like a mother so beside herself with grief that she's determined to carry away the body of her dead child – whom she knows quite well to have died – as she flees from beneath the rubble of a building whose walls are collapsing around her.

On top of Yousif's things I placed the manuscripts of some short stories and notebooks filled with memoirs that I'd written over the previous seven years. Along with them I put the rough draft of *Beirut Nightmares*, which I'd been recording day by day and moment by moment, all the while tottering on that fine line that separates life from death (or does it merely separate one kind of life from another?).

As I shut the suitcase, I got a painful lump in my throat. No doubt all those who'd later become refugees had gathered up a few belongings in small suitcases on a gloomy morning just like this one, assuming that they'd be coming back in just a few days. Then they departed, never to return...

As I unplugged the refrigerator, I was gripped by a feeling of misery and angst. I was afraid that the electricity might come back on without me! I recalled the innumerable accounts I'd heard of people who, when they fled their homes, had left their refrigerators running and full of food in a vain attempt to convince themselves that they'd be gone for only a few hours. Yet they never came back to eat the food they'd left behind.

With the same miserable lump in my throat, I decided to shut off the house's main breaker switch. I pressed down on a red lever, thereby causing a small square-shaped light on the panel to black out. As I stared at the tiny darkened square, I imagined it growing larger and larger until it had covered the face of the earth.

Then all of a sudden I was struck by a vague sense of foreboding. Somehow I knew that never again would I see a light come on in this house of ours.

Just then there began a new round of explosions that sent me scurrying back to my main 'combat position' in the hallway, alone and afraid.

Nightmare 85

I was thrown to the floor by what seemed like the tremors of an earthquake. It was only afterwards that I heard the sound of the explosion. Showers of splintered glass were falling on top of me and I found it unusually difficult to breathe, as if invisible fingers had gripped my chest and were squeezing all the air out of me. I lay motionless on the tile floor in front of the door, still holding on to the small suitcase that had been on its way out of the house with me.

At first I felt as if I'd been torn limb from limb, with nothing remaining attached to anything else except for the suitcase that still clung to my hand. However, it wasn't long before I'd regained a sense of being all in one piece, as it were. In fact, I felt that I'd been transformed into a tightly sealed vessel, filled to capacity with blood that had been heated to boiling point. I leapt towards one of the walls of my bedroom, which was where the explosion had originated from. The wall had all but disappeared, while what remained of it was in the process of collapsing. My bed was dangling off the edge of what looked like a bottomless pit, while everything around it was engulfed in a cloud of black smoke.

Then the wind began invading the room and I noticed that half of the opposite wall, which contained the door opening on to the balcony, had collapsed as well. As for the balcony door itself, it had been damaged beyond recognition. I stood frozen in the doorway, not daring to go in. Meanwhile, the wind was blowing rain into the room, sweeping away the dust, the papers strewn here and there, and the sawdust that had resulted from the splintering of wooden objects.

I don't know how long I stood there outside the room, unable to move a muscle, yet clinging all the while to my little suitcase as if it were a life raft. But as I stood there I finally became aware that the room had been invaded by a missile.

Eventually, the dust began to settle. And when it did, it became apparent that nothing in the room had stayed in its place. Only my nightgown remained draped over the bed – which was still teetering on the brink of the abyss – its sleeves dangling in midair like the arms of a dead man. The sight of it filled me with sheer terror, as if I were still inside it! The message I was being sent from the land of exiles and fugitives had come through loud and clear. Consequently, I determined that I would never again sleep in this room, which was no longer a room. On that day I drove the first tent peg into the ground in preparation for what promised to be my next nomadic sojourn.

Nightmare 86

Shakir was a shopkeeper who sold household goods. He wasn't rich and he wasn't poor. He wasn't handsome and he wasn't ugly. He wasn't terribly smart and he wasn't stupid. He wasn't a saint and he wasn't a criminal.

Shakir's shop was located in one of Beirut's many marketplaces, where he managed to make a moderate profit, cheating just a bit now and then so as to be able to pay his seven children's school fees. Whenever tuition increased, he was obliged to cheat a bit more, and whenever prices went up he had to cheat still a bit more, begging forgiveness of his Lord and calling down curses on his miserable plight.

One day in the early dawn hours as he was on his way to the market, he stopped at a checkpoint, where he was informed by the police that the market had caught fire and that all the shops had burned to the ground. He asked them where they'd been when the fire started and why they hadn't been there to keep the shops from burning down, rather than keeping the shop owners from getting to them now. However, he got no reply. So he spent that entire day consumed by fears and apprehensions. Had his shop been among those that had burned to the ground? It was his only means of livelihood...

He bought every newspaper he could get his hands on, then pored over the pictures of the marketplace and the charred shops. Looking at one of them, he imagined that it was his. But no... The shop in the picture had two windows, whereas his had only one. Then he saw another one that he thought looked like his. But no... His shop had an ornate, antique-looking frieze around the edge of the roof, whereas there was no sign of such a thing in the photo.

He tried to get some sleep that night, but all his anxious fretting seemed to keep his eyelids propped wide open. He'd got into a loud, angry quarrel with his wife and children without knowing why. Then she and the kids had all run off to bed to get away from him. He felt resentful and bitter because sleep seemed to come so easily to them, and because he was responsible for feeding all these mouths whose snores and calm, monotonous breathing now filled the house.

The next morning he rose at the crack of dawn, having made up his mind to go and check on his shop even if it became his grave. So he left the house, prepared to face any contingency. But when he arrived at the market, he was surprised to find it swarming with shopkeepers and camera-toting journalists. At first he wasn't able to locate his shop. After all, it was difficult to distinguish one from another now that the place looked more like an ancient ruin than a modern thoroughfare. The shops had virtually all been marred beyond recognition, having been reduced to heaps of rubble topped by layers of fine black dust and charred, half-collapsed walls.

When at last he did find it, he couldn't believe his eyes. And when he carried away what was left of his shop, he couldn't believe his hands. Then he drove off in his old banger with what little remained of his ephemeral worldly possessions, which had proved to be ephemeral indeed.

Nightmare 87

The next day, forced into action by the need to put something in his hungry children's mouths, Shakir went out with what was left of his merchandise to try selling it on the street. He put everything in his car and headed for Hamra Street. When he arrived, he spread out what he'd brought by way of saucepans, spoons, plates and kitchen utensils on top of his little car and on the pavement. Then he stood there waiting. The street was terribly crowded, but no one bought a thing.

Although he'd been here many times before, somehow the pavements now seemed alien and hostile to him. In the past he'd enjoyed coming to Hamra Street and stealing glances at slender girls with their pretty legs. Then he'd sigh with regret as he recalled his wife's legs, which had grown as thick and veinous as a couple of ageing, gnarled tree trunks. He'd also been in the habit of coming here on holidays to bring as many of his children as he could to the cinema. He'd gaze at the holiday decorations and the passers-by, the succession of colours and sounds, and take in the rhythm of 'life in the fast lane', so full of youthful vigour. Every now and then, when he came on such outings, he'd notice beggars sitting at the roadside who would try to extract donations from passers-by by means of deformities and physical impairments, most of which were faked.

He remembered in particular a blind beggar who'd always insisted on singing in a loud, funereal voice and whom he would always give some money to in the hope of shutting him up, or at least getting him to screech a little less vociferously. But oh, the irony of fate! Here he was now, spreading out his merchandise in the very same spot where that beggar used to sit. Unlike the beggar, however, he remained silent. In fact, in contrast to his fellow vendors who, like him, had been banished to the streets, he couldn't even bring himself to call out to people to draw their attention to his wares.

He didn't sell much all day. He heard one woman say to another that all the things being sold on the pavements were stolen goods. And as if that weren't enough, a little boy tripped over an expensive vase and broke it, after which the child's mother berated him mercilessly for having made her son fall down!

But in spite of everything, he spent the entire day pinned to the pavement on Hamra Street. He'd sold very little and suffered a great deal, pining away for the comfortable chair in his shop and his ledger of credits and debits. Then that evening as he approached the corner of the alleyway leading to his house, he was waylaid by a man carrying a gun.

In a harsh, commanding tone, the man said to him: 'Whatever you've got on you, hand it over.'

So he did. He hadn't made much, but the money he handed over was, literally, his children's bread for the next day.

Bewildered and alarmed, Shakir asked the thief: 'Who are you?'

'I'm a hunter,' said the man with the gun.

'Whatever you say, hunter,' Shakir replied.

Nightmare 88

The next day, Shakir and his fellow sufferers were forbidden by the police to peddle their wares on Hamra Street. So he headed instead for the Qantari district, where he set up shop once more.

When he arrived, the rain fell, the winds blew and all his would-be customers fled. All of them, at least, except for a jaded woman who stood haggling with him for an entire hour over the price of a kitchen knife and a few spoons, after which she bought the spoons and left the kitchen knife behind.

As he was on his way home that night, he was detained by the same armed man (the 'hunter'), who once again told him to hand over whatever money he had with him.

He hadn't made much, but this money was, without exaggeration, the price of his children's bread for the next day. Even so, he handed it over without hesitation. He was too weary and fearful to do otherwise.

'Whatever you say, hunter,' he said as he gave him the money.

On the third day, Shakir picked up his wares and carried them back to the Qantari district. But when he got there, he found it had been taken over by bullets and battles, wind and rain. So he kept on walking until he came to the Rawsheh district, then set up shop there instead. The pavements had become his marketplace, the cold winds his customers and the rain his executioner. He wept much and sold little, and on his way home that evening he was halted by the same armed man at the alleyway entrance. Before the armed man had said a word, he handed him his day's earnings, saying: 'Whatever you say, hunter.'

On the fourth day, Shakir didn't go to work. He didn't set up his vendor's stall anywhere and he didn't sell a thing. Instead, he slept all day. But as evening approached, he picked up the kitchen knife that he hadn't managed to sell, then went and stood at the entrance to a nearby alleyway. And there he waited for the arrival of the street vendors as they returned home after their day's work.

He'd decided to become a 'hunter'…

Nightmare 89

I don't know how long I stood petrified outside my bedroom door after the missile had passed through it. The winds accompanying the autumn thunderstorm had picked up my clothes, my papers and the splinters of wood scattered here and there, then deposited them in the 'bottomless pit' that had opened up on one side of the room. They even managed to strip the pillow and blanket off the bed, leaving it as bare as a cockroach whose body has been hollowed out by ants.

No one called. No one came up to check on me. No one dared show concern for anyone else's fate. After all, civil war lays human relationships bare, stripping them of their façades and turning them into nothing more than a worm-eaten skeleton. Amm Fu'ad and everyone else in our neighbourhood had always done their utmost to keep up social traditions, no matter how small or trivial they might seem. So much so that buying a new chair, for example, had been an occasion that merited someone's receiving visits and congratulations for seven days straight. And here was a missile that had landed in my house, but not a single soul had had the courage even so much as to stick his head round my door to find out whether I was dead or alive. Civil war loosens false attachments and in so doing it exposes the heart all the more to estrangement and loneliness. So perhaps violence is just a means people resort to in the hope of breaking out of their orbits of alienation and estrangement at times when they sense the absence of love and justice (in other words, when they lack the human intimacy and connectedness they crave). Civil war creates greater alienation, which is then shattered in a brutal yet fleeting and temporary way. The brutality leaves in its wake still more alienation, which leads in turn to further violence. And thus the infernal vicious circles repeat themselves over and over in continual, never-ending succession.

But most insufferable of all is to have to live through a time of civil war deprived not only of tenderness but of violence as well (which is what happens to most artists, who spurn the thought of bearing arms). This was exactly the situation I found myself in. The fault lay to a large extent in my location. After all, I was living in a neighbourhood which I didn't belong to by way of either social class or lifestyle. Consequently, I wasn't prepared to take up arms in its defence, nor was I able to relate in any meaningful way to any of my neighbours. But... what fault was it of mine if I'd inherited the lease to my father's old house the way I'd inherited his library? Perhaps my guilt was no different from that of all the other 'innocent criminals' who had accepted at face value what was written in their passports and identity cards and had then proceeded to live accordingly. As a result, their houses had become little more than 'landing pads' and their religion a mere accident of fate. And these things in turn had made their entire existence – whether they survived or whether they died as victims of the civil war's violence – little more than a bad joke at the hands of fate!

So for the first time I found myself wondering: How many of my female friends do you suppose are *really* my friends? And how many of my male friends are true soulmates?

The wind was still toying with the pages of my address book, which was lying on the floor. I picked it up. It was stuffed with the names of acquaintances and friends that I'd made over the years. I began reading through them, one name at a time, and was astounded to find that I could no longer recall more than the tiniest fraction of them. It was as if their faces had all been blown away by the 'missile' of painful reality. Yousif's name alone conjured an image so vivid that I could see him standing before my very eyes. His number was the only one I hadn't recorded along with the rest. After all, I'd had no need to be reminded of it. And now I needed someone to help me forget it.

Sitting on a nearby chair, I felt a sharp pain shoot through my ear, thanks to the shell that had come flying from the direction of the Holiday Inn a few days earlier. However, I'd decided to monitor my telephone. I wanted to see who would try calling me to find out whether I was dead or alive. To that end, I also made up my mind not to call anyone else, but instead just to watch and wait... Who would call me anyway? I laughed out loud at the attack of paranoia that seemed to have suddenly come over me. But I kept on waiting all the same.

When at last the phone hadn't rung even once all day, I felt the need to dial Yousif's number – knowing ahead of time, of course, that I wouldn't hear his voice. This was a bad habit I'd got into lately. I lifted the receiver, only to discover that the phone was dead. Ah... I'd forgotten that it had stopped working altogether. When had it gone dead? The day before? I couldn't remember. Everything had become a blur to me – even the passing of the days.

Nightmare 90

As I headed down the stairs to Amm Fu'ad's flat, I was making promises to myself and to time, saying: If I get out of here alive, I'll do such and such... I'll go and see all the cities of the world that I haven't visited yet. I'll resign from my job and try to set myself up in some sort of freelance work. I'll take a new look at my values, my attitudes, my location, my friends...

When I was a schoolgirl, I'd always make promises to myself during the critical period leading up to exams. I'd resolve that if I passed, I'd do certain things during the summer. I'd go on a diet, I'd keep on getting up at the crack of dawn, I'd exercise, I'd go swimming, I'd reread all my textbooks from preceding years to get a better grasp of what I'd learned. And so on and so forth... But when exams were safely behind me, I'd spend the following days sleeping, eating and reading detective novels!

When I got downstairs, Amm Fu'ad was wandering about the flat like some sort of deranged fool, humming a romantic tune from Chopin to the rhythm of a military march. Meanwhile, Amin was carrying on an anti-cockroach campaign, laughing a hysterical laugh that sounded more like the rumbling innards of a dysentery victim!

They asked me what had caused the racket upstairs.

'A missile,' I replied.

But no more questions were forthcoming, as if a missile attack were a perfectly ordinary, humdrum event. So all I got was silence. Utter silence.

Finally I said to Amin: 'Surely you've exterminated all the flies and cockroaches by now.'

'Yep,' he replied as he baited an old-fashioned mousetrap, 'so now it's time to declare war on the mice.'

And he was right. Perhaps the sound of the explosions had driven them out of their holes, since all of a sudden our flats seemed to be crawling with them. This made them an attractive target for Amin, who, after keeping his aggressive inclinations under wraps for so long, was looking for a good fight. I urged him on in the pursuit of his 'unholy war' against the mouse occupation, since I could see that it was a war borne of tedium and monotony, and I had harrowing memories of a neighbour of ours who'd been driven by boredom to go to work as a sniper! He'd been a skilled physician and a not-so-skilled husband. Then his European mistress skipped town when her clientele dropped off. After that even his patients started to disappear and he found himself obliged to stay at home more and more, until he'd become a virtual prisoner in his own house. Then one early morning his wife was startled to find that he'd got up and headed for the roof with a rifle in his hand. It was said that he'd started shooting at anything that moved, even cats, mice and an occasional bird flying overhead.

As for me, I was still being haunted by the voices of the creatures in the pet shop. I genuinely looked forward to my nightly visits to them, and I wondered what was happening now that their once placid prison had been stricken by hunger and terror. But no – it was madness to be thinking this way... Maybe it would be wiser to pay a visit instead to our neighbours living above the pet shop. I thought of the lady of the house, who'd always given me the impression of being made of the insides of a loaf of bread. As for her husband, he made me think of a wooden puppet – like Pinocchio, only fitted out with an internal tape recording that played the same words over and over and over...

Despite the dangers, I decided to go ahead and pay another visit to the pet shop. I could at least peek in through the window to see what effects hunger had had on the place. If I found it still in a violent uproar, I wouldn't go in. Instead I'd content myself with spying on them from the outside. Hunger. Ah, hunger... I'd truly started to feel it now. In fact, I'd begun imagining what it might be like to trap the cat in the garden and devour it on the spot. Then I remembered Amin's monkey. I'd heard that monkey meat was a lot tastier than cat meat. On my first day of hunger, I'm sure I couldn't have brought myself to eat either. However, on the seventh day – by which time I was about to perish – I strongly suspect that I would have been capable of devouring even human flesh.

So, this was hunger, Lord of history, whose logic remains incomprehensible to the philosopher or writer sitting in his cosy office, eating pickles and spinning out theories to explain the fates of the world's peoples. Those who weave their theories of war rarely compose their works in bomb shelters, on military bases, under gunfire or in the face of actual blood and carnage. Rather, hunger remains the philosopher of history *par excellence*, its true leader and commander.

Amm Fu'ad kept wandering about the house, which was almost completely dark thanks to the thunderstorm and the recent power failure, all the while shrieking out his romantic Chopin ditty to the beat of a military march. Amin for his part kept up his campaign against the mice, while I for mine fled to the telephone to dial Yousif's number – knowing, of course, that he wouldn't answer.

Nightmare 91

I lay down once more on my 'fugitive's bed'.

There hadn't been any attempts to rescue me that evening except for a call from Captain Fathi, who'd promised that someone would be sent for me tomorrow. The word 'tomorrow' in war time becomes synonymous with 'never'. However, I made no objections. I knew that in the mad inferno that surrounded us on all sides, it would have taken more than a tank to rescue me. It would have required digging an underground tunnel like the ones that used to be dug in ancient cities under siege.

So this would be one more night of misery and lonely exile. I shut my eyes and a wave of drowsiness came over me, seeking in vain to sweep me off the shores of consciousness into slumber's ocean depths.

There'd been a brief respite in the man-made thunder. However, the deafening booms emanating from the heavens were still at a blazing peak. Meanwhile, over the roar of the storm I began to pick up the most extraordinary sound – the sound of someone playing an accordion! Whoever it was was playing the French tune 'The Rose is What Matters'. Heard against the backdrop of the night's eerie gloom and the destruction being wrought all around me, the song sounded full of sorrow and bitter lament, as if all the roses in the entire world had been encased in a film of fine black dust. But even so, I felt that what I was hearing was a rallying song for all the fighters who had taken up arms in order that life might remain as sweet and unblemished as a rose that never withers or fades...

Nightmare 92

Weary and famished, I kept trying in vain to get to sleep. I'd been intending to slip out for a visit to the pet shop, but then realized that I was too exhausted to go outside in the stormy, frigid darkness. Under the circumstances, I didn't see how I'd be able to steal back into the shop again to see what was happening there. But as I lay in bed thinking, suddenly I found that the shop had made its way to me. When I closed my eyes, I could see clearly and hear.

Throughout the back room of the shop, hunger's refrain was being echoed to a variety of rhythms and cadences. The dogs now on the loose were making raids on the aquarium, while in one corner of the tank a larger fish had begun devouring a smaller one. The birds were squabbling, the cats were casting long, voracious glances at the mice's cage and one of the larger cats lunged over and over at the mice, seemingly oblivious of the fact that with each successive leap its head collided with the iron bars of its own cage. The parrot had given up speaking in French and had gone back to the loud, hungry squawks of its jungle days. The sleek, nimble hunting dogs had succeeded in demolishing the shop's smart entrance and tearing apart its touristic façade, while the rabbits which had been mating with such frequency and enthusiasm in the early days of their captivity had now desisted from such pastimes. A mother cat was giving birth to a litter of kittens and no sooner would she bear one of them than it would be devoured by the other cats in the cage. As a result, the sounds of new life were mingled with the savage, untamed shrieks of starvation and death.

Then when the mother cat had given birth to the last kitten she devoured it herself.

Ah, hunger... Before it all masks come tumbling off. Under its influence, even love falls away like an adder's skin that's been shed and cast aside.

Nightmare 93

The alley was terribly cold and dark. But he wasn't about to go back. The little boy had slipped out of the house, intending to run away from home. After all, this was the eighth straight month that he'd been held as a virtual prisoner in his house, forbidden to play in the alleyway with his friends. Even going to school had become a coveted aspiration, not to mention playing in the dirt, the mud and the snow, riding his bicycle and other such unattainable wishes. Whenever he insisted on going out to play, his mother would scold him and say: 'The adults are playing now and you might be hit by a stray bullet.'

But it seemed to him that the adults had been playing for altogether too long. They'd been playing day and night, summer and winter, without anyone making them wash their hands and faces or go to bed on time.

Besides, he was sick and tired of hiding in the hallway. He was tired of living like a frightened mouse. He was tired of hearing his mother and father argue whenever his father came home armed to the teeth, carrying nothing but a few meagre morsels in his hands and what his mother called 'stolen merchandise' and 'tainted money'.

So he'd decide to emigrate and nothing was going to stand in his way. He'd travel to Australia the way his older brother had. Ever since he was a baby, he'd been hearing stories about his clever brother who had emigrated as a stowaway on board a ship bound for Australia, thus managing to get there without paying the fare. The whole family waxed eloquent over how 'clever' he was and the boy intended to show them that he was no less of a genius.

The alley was cold and dark indeed. But he wouldn't go back.

The bundle of food that he'd brought along felt heavier than it had when he'd left the house and the rain that had begun as nothing but drizzle was now a veritable downpour. He was shivering with cold and fright, and the darkness was much more gloomy than he'd realized it would be. But he wasn't going back. His foot slipped, which sent him falling into the dirt and mud. And before he'd tried to get up, he saw someone leaning up against a tree who, like him, was spattered with dirt and mud. He didn't feel afraid of the stranger, since he was an elderly man who looked quite a bit like his grandfather. In fact, the old man seemed too weary and sick even to reach out to help him up. So rather than trying to get up by himself, the little boy dragged his body through the mud and leaned his back up against the tree next to the old man.

'Sorry I didn't help you, son,' said the old man. 'But I'm so tired I could just die. Besides that, my joints ache, my blood pressure is high and I'm bound to have a heart attack one of these days. This damned city is about to kill me.'

'What's your name, sir?' the boy asked him.

'My name is Death,' replied the old man.

The boy recognized the name, though only vaguely. It didn't arouse any particular emotions in him. However, the sick, weary old man's appearance made him feel sad.

'What kind of work do you do, sir?' he asked.

'I'm the hardest-working person in this whole city,' the old man replied. 'For the past eight months I've been working night and day without a moment's rest.'

'Are you a doctor, sir?' asked the boy.

'Well, yes, in a manner of speaking. In fact, when it comes right down to it, you might say I'm the most important doctor there is.'

'Why don't you emigrate with me?' the boy asked him. 'I've decided to leave this city forever. I can't bear to live here any longer. All the toy stores are closed, there's not much to eat and it's too cold. And not only that, but I can't even sleep any more, because every night my mother wakes me up, along with my brothers and sisters, then drags us out of bed and piles us on to the tile floor in the hallway for fear that the house will be hit by a bomb.'

'You're right, my little one,' said the old man, 'life here has become intolerable even for me.'

'Why don't you emigrate, then?' the boy asked.

'Because they haven't given me even a single moment to pack up my coffins – I mean, er, my suitcases – and get out of here! How exhausted I am ... My back hurts me, and my arms, and my legs... Take a look at my scythe. How they've dulled its blade and chewed up its handle. Like I said, I'm the only one in this whole city who's been working his fingers to the bone. They're showing me no mercy in my old age and they don't give me a single moment's rest. I tell you, they'll be the death of me!'

The child had become so engrossed in listening to the old man's tale of woe, he didn't notice the bitter cold that had begun to nip at his feet.

Then he asked the old man: 'Why do they hate you in this city?'

'Hate me?' the old man asked with a laugh. 'I didn't say they hated me. In fact, they love me in a way I've never been loved in any other country in the whole world. They even name their streets, their rivers and their bridges after me. Haven't you ever heard of 'Death River', 'Death Bridge' and 'Death Street'? As a matter of fact, all the streets in this city are named after me now. They've made me king over them and every day they offer me their choicest young men. Oh no, I didn't say they hated me! On the contrary, they love me like I've never been loved before in my life. And their love is going to be the death of me! I really do need a doctor...'

The biting cold continued to overtake the child's body. But he was so concerned about Old Man Death's tragedy, he didn't notice that his lower half had grown completely stiff.

Leaning his head on Death's shoulder, he asked him: 'Why don't you run away from the place where you've been working?'

'They've closed off all my escape routes,' replied the old man. 'Besides, there's even more work to be done in the areas surrounding Beirut than there is the centre of the city.'

Now frozen stiff all the way up to his chest, the child said: 'I'm tired like you and I need to go to sleep. So could you open up a book and read me a bedtime story?'

'Come here, little one,' said Death. 'Unfortunately, I don't have any children's books with me and frankly I prefer dealing with older people. But I'll show you my invoices and tell you the stories that go along with them. I'm afraid they're the closest thing to a picture book I can come up with.'

'That's OK,' replied the little boy. 'Tell me any story you like. Then after that you can go and see your doctor, though actually I think it would be better for you to sleep here with me until morning, then come with me on my trip to Australia once you've had some rest.'

'To be perfectly honest,' the old man replied, 'it looks as if I won't be able to emigrate anywhere. I've got so much work to do here and my clients never let up for a minute. In fact, they've founded an organization in my name. It's called the "Long Live Death!" organization. The damned fools. They're about to kill me with all this "love" of theirs.'

Then he opened up the notebook where he kept his accounts and invoices. To the little boy, the huge book looked like a book of fairy tales. Then Death began reading his 'invoices', and complaining about all the work he had to do:

Invoice: Khalil Abu Faris is standing at the entrance to the Electricity Authority in the Mar Mikhail quarter. Before long he'll be fatally wounded in the head by an armed man. You are requested to come and 'collect' immediately.

Invoice: Two managers of the Phoenicia Hotel have been trapped by smoke inside the hotel building. One of them will manage to slip out of the window, whereas the other, being rather portly, will get stuck on his way out and suffocate. Please be apprised of the situation and take the necessary measures.

Invoice: An Italian man who specializes in robbing disaster-stricken neighbourhoods recently stole a tape recorder from one of his neighbours. It so happened that the same apparatus had once belonged to a family of seven, all of whom were found murdered in their house. When he listened that night to a tape that was still inside the machine, he heard a live recording of the fighting that had taken place and the atrocities that had been committed in the house, as well as the screams of the seven family members as they were being tortured and killed. After listening to the tape, the robber jumped out of the window and is now in the process of dying a slow death. You are requested to proceed towards the site of the robbery. And on your way there, you'll find other assignments awaiting you.

Invoice: An ambulance carrying ten live armed men stops at a checkpoint. The driver declares that he has ten corpses with him that he's taking to the cemetery. The people manning the checkpoint don't believe him, but let him pass through anyway. The driver has hardly gone any distance at all before the men at the checkpoint open fire on the ambulance, killing the ten armed men inside. The driver keeps on going. Now, however, he really is carrying ten corpses, so he heads for the cemetery as he had claimed he was about to do. Please take stock of the situation immediately and proceed to do whatever is required.

Invoice: Scores of cars will be passing over 'Death Bridge' (your namesake) and snipers will open fire on them, killing the passengers inside. One of them will be a Mercedes-Benz carrying two journalists by the names of Fatimah and Mary. Both of them will be spared this time, so you aren't requested to take any action in their case. However, you are requested to take care of all the others who'll be crossing your bridge this morning.

Invoice: Hajji Shabbour's son was shot accidentally as a result of having tampered with machine-gun together with three of his friends and is now in the hospital in a critical condition. Hajji Shabbour has sworn that if his son dies, then three other funeral processions will take place along with his son's. Proceed without delay to the hospital to 'collect' and while you're at it pass by to see his three friends.

Invoice: A man by the name of of Zayn Al-Hayy has been killed and his funeral procession will take place this afternoon. As is the custom in this city, neighbourhood youths will shoot into the air. However, young men from the adjacent quarter will think the shots are being fired at them and will respond in kind. The result will be a delectable massacre. We request the honour of your company at the site of the clash, where your duties await you.

Invoice: Somewhere on Umar Ibn Al-Khattab Street, a man by the name of Shihab will be fatally shot as he sits watching television. You are kindly requested to pay him a visit.

Invoice: Before last leaving his house, a man by the name of Karim wrote up his will and testament. His premonition had been well-founded. You are requested to meet him on the street where the Sudiko neighbourhood's local sniper is stationed.

Old Man Death kept turning the pages of his gargantuan book of invoices. Meanwhile, the cold continued to take over more and more of the little boy's body and it was becoming difficult for him to keep his eyelids from closing. Even so, never in his entire life had he heard such exciting bedtime stories. When he came home after his adventures abroad, he planned to tell his mother that she didn't know how to tell a proper bedtime story. He'd tell her all about the old man who knew how to spin such wonderful yarns and whose name was Old Man Death. Noticing that the child's eyelids had grown heavy, Death went thumbing through his notebook in the hope of finding a story that would rouse his interest. He was so weary after all his back-breaking labour, he felt the need to chatter away to someone.

Hoping to arouse more of the child's sympathy, the old man said: 'And as if it weren't enough for them to establish the "Long Live Death" society in my honour and name streets, rivers, bridges and valleys after me, they even started passing laws that would make it easier for me to carry out my assignments and make me a joint ruler of the country along with the king!

'You see, people had started refusing to go out into the streets for fear of being killed. So what did the authorities do? Instead of ordering a curfew, they made it mandatory for people to go walking around in the streets. Not going out became a crime punishable by death by electrocution. Ever since these orders were issued, my work has been hard labour. They think they're making things easier on me by passing this sort of a law. But the fact is, they're killing me! Now I have to go running through the streets like some postman with a pack of hungry dogs snapping at his heels! How tired I am, my little one...'

'I'm sorry, Uncle,' whispered the little boy.

Death was so moved that he started to get teary-eyed. Then he went on, saying: 'They make me work whether it makes sense or not. Listen to this story about the crazy taxi driver. Here, let me read you his invoice...'

Invoice: A 'strongman' doubling as a taxi driver manages to get his seven passengers safely through all the checkpoints they come to – the Muslim ones, the Christian ones, the Druze ones, you name it. This leaves him feeling quite powerful and full of himself. So when he finally gets his passengers to a relatively safe area, he suddenly has the urge to do something that will make him feel more powerful than all the checkpoints put together. Consequently, he's making plans to kill them with a machine-gun that he's hidden under his seat. Yet he won't be taken either to an insane asylum or to prison. You are requested to proceed post-haste to the scene of the crime, 'collect' the passengers and leave the driver alive.

It had now begun to snow and the cold continued to creep slowly upward till it reached the boy's neck. He could no longer move so much as a finger, nor did he feel any need to. As for Old Man Death, he was coughing violently and cursing his luck, saying: 'And to top it all, I'll bet I get a chest infection. They wouldn't even let me take a vacation for the holidays this year!'

Then he resumed his story-telling.

'Listen to this one,' he said to the boy. 'I think you'll like it. There was a naughty little boy who put one of his mother's nylon stockings over his head. Then he took his toy machine-gun and went and knocked on the door of the neighbours' house as a joke. Everyone's nerves are on edge these days. So as soon as the neighbour lady laid eyes on him, she screamed, and before long her children were screaming along with her. The little boy was delighted at the reaction he'd managed to get out of them. But just as he was about to take the stocking off his head, out came the woman's husband with a machine-gun in his hand and shot the boy before he had a chance to see who it was or what was going on. After all, his nerves were shot too. The little boy died on the spot. Besides that, the man had mistakenly shot the members of his family, who now were breathing their last. Realizing too late what he had done, the man put a bullet through his own head. I was sound asleep when the "family committee" summoned me to the scene of the accident to "collect".'

The little boy smiled faintly. The cold had begun spreading through his face, where his muscles had begun twitching uncontrollably.

Meanwhile, Death went on, saying: 'Listen to this one, will you!'

Invoice: Armed men came knocking one day at a certain man's house. The man came to the door and no sooner had he opened it than they opened fire and killed him. Hearing the shots, his wife came to the door, screaming hysterically.

'What's your husband's name?' they asked her.

'Samir...' she replied.

'Oh, pardon us,' one of them said. 'We're looking for somebody by the name of Sammara – not Samir. I'm afraid we've made a mistake. We really apologize. So sorry...'

And off they went in search of their man, leaving *her* man as nothing but a lifeless corpse. When they were gone, the woman drenched herself in petrol and set herself on fire.

'I had to get over there right away to "collect," ' Death added, 'and the smell was truly awful.'

By this time the snow was coming down thick and fast. The boy was still listening to the old man's captivating stories, the likes of which he'd never heard before, and he was leaning back on to Lord Death's chest in calm, trusting repose.

He went on plaintively, saying: 'I told you the people of

this city would be the death of me! I've been looking for a doctor for weeks on end. But they've all disappeared, God damn 'em! They gathered up their money, their wives, their mistresses and their children and ran off. I haven't met up with a single doctor, even in hospital corridors or among the countless wounded that I've had to go checking on at the request of the National Committee on Death. And speaking of hospitals, listen to this story... Let's see if I can find that invoice for you...'

As they sat there, the wind began ruffling the pages of the monstrous notebook which the old man held in his lap. Then he began reading again in a raspy voice, coughing wearily like someone who's been smoking for years on end: 'Hospital Invoice No. 1,015... That's right. I received a call from a hospital and, as usual, I got there in a flash. When I arrived, I found the place horribly crowded, with the wounded piled up in the waiting rooms, the corridors and even at the entrance. There had been a massacre and most of the wounded were dying because the hospital and the surrounding neighbourhood had been targeted for a bombing raid. As I made my way from one victim to the next, their agonized shrieks and moans kept getting louder and louder. Some of them had lost entire limbs and most of them were calling out to me to deliver them from their misery: "O Death, come closer! Have mercy on me and save me!" It was tearing me up inside to listen to them. But to be perfectly honest, I was so busy looking for a doctor for myself, I couldn't give them my undivided attention. As I told you before, I'm the only one in this entire city who's been working his fingers to the bone for the past eight months. For eight straight months, I'm the only one who's even gone to work! I go rushing around collecting the spirits from the bodies of the dying that lie strewn all over the city, like some garbage collector who has to run around picking up the refuse off the streets!

'In any case, I finally found a doctor and began complaining to him of my aching joints, my cough, my congested lung, my high blood pressure and this heart of mine that's on the verge of being stricken with angina pectoris. I said to him, "To be perfectly honest, I'm afraid I'm going to die."

'Then he asked me what my name was, so I told him the truth. "My name is Death," I said. But instead of shaking my hand and saying. "Pleased to meet you," the fool just gasped and fainted! So I wrote up an invoice for him too, then went on looking for another doctor. Meanwhile, the gasps of the dying and wounded were tugging at my heartstrings in a dreadful way. The fact was, they were calling for me more than they were calling for the runaway doctors! So I decided to write a letter of protest to the medical union, since they hadn't kept the agreement we'd made to divide people equally among us and instead were leaving all the work to me.

'Then suddenly in walked a handsome, bearded, long-haired young man who reminded me of pictures I'd seen of Christ in church icons. At the sight of his five half-mutilated brothers and sisters who were all calling out to me at once, he let out a bloodcurdling scream. At the time of the bomb attack they had all been in school. But before I'd had a chance to do my job, the young man suddenly took something that looked like a pomegranate out of his pocket and removed its stem. Then there was a dreadful explosion. Oh, if you only knew how much work I had to do that evening! I had to make out more than fifty invoices in one corridor alone, not counting the one I'd already written up for the doctor!'

As he listened to Old Man Death, a look of grief appeared in the little boy's eyes. He was so paralysed from the cold, he could neither laugh nor cry any more. Even the muscles in his mouth were stiff, as if he'd been immersed in a frozen puddle.

However, his eyes still shone with curiosity, like stars on a cloudless summer night.

So Death went on with his tales of woe, saying: 'Now I'll tell you a story about an artist named Ibrahim... Ibrahim. Hold on just a minute while I find his invoice. Yes, here it is – Ibrahim Marzuq.[4] Ibrahim Marzuq had begun to get very hungry. So on the first day he drew a loaf of bread and ate it. On the second day he drew another loaf of bread and ate that too. On the third day he did the same thing. However, he was still hungry. So off he went to a nearby bakery to buy some "real" bread. When he arrived, the sky was raining molten iron and I was up to my ears in work. Then all of a sudden I had to concentrate my efforts in front of the bakery, where someone had sent down a "loaf of fire". Ibrahim Marzuq's lacerated corpse mingled with the bodies of the men, women and children who had come out that day in the hope of buying a bit of nourishment and contentment. There were torn-off limbs and other body parts clinging to the bakery walls. And what with the melted plastic shoes of the poverty-stricken, their tattered clothing and severed limbs scattered here and there, it was one of the most true-to-life depictions of cruelty and violence I'd ever seen in my life. And the artist Ibrahim Marzuq was at its very heart. After all, this time he'd created a painting with his own body and with the bodies of his people. Oh, what a lot of work I had to do that morning. I really wore myself out!'

Death kept chattering away, overjoyed to at last have found someone who could listen to him without fainting or obliging him to make out another invoice.

'Just listen to this one, will you!' he said. Then once again the wind began turning the pages for him as he read once more from his notebook.

Invoice: Nadine was an artist whom people described as eccentric. She bought herself a coffin to sleep in every night because, as she put it, she wanted always to remember that ultimately she would never be truly married to anyone but me. Over and over she used to say: 'Death is my true beloved. Death is my true beloved...' Of course, when the civil war broke out, there wasn't a single thing around her that didn't remind her of me. But one morning she decided that instead of sleeping in her coffin that night, she'd sleep in her bed. At noon the same day, she was struck by a sniper's bullet. So that night I had to lay her out in a coffin once again. Only this time, she'd have to stay there for good.

Invoice: Salima is a twenty-year-old expectant mother living in Beirut's Khunduq Amiq neighbourhood. She's planning a birthday party for her little girl, who's turning one year old, though the only visible evidence that a celebration is about to take place is the single candle on the table. Then all of a sudden shots ring out, the electricity is cut off and Salima falls down dead. You are requested to pay a visit to her home at the specified time.

Invoice: Amira has forbidden her fiancé to come and visit for fear that he might be kidnapped on the way. So in accordance with her wishes, he's stayed at home this evening. However, as he sits in his flat, he is visited by a piece of shrapnel which takes his life. You are requested to take note of the situation and do whatever is needed.

Invoice: Amal was driving her car through the city when she noticed to her surprise that it was beginning to get dark before 5.00 p.m. She was frightened. She spotted a traffic policeman whom she hoped might escort her home or at least give her some reassurance. So, intending to attract his attention, she honked her horn and sped in his direction. As she approached, the terror-charged particles that had been floating freely in the atmosphere suddenly collected in the policeman's head and he was frightened too. At that moment, the only thing he was conscious of was that he started firing at the car he saw charging in his direction. As for Amal, she received a bullet between the eyes. Please be apprised of the situation and act accordingly.

Invoice: A number of young men in a refugee camp between the ages of seventeen and twenty-five years old are being trained in the use of artillery. A minor technical error occurs and a shell is accidentally set off. Twenty-five of the youths are seriously injured. Please take stock of the situation and take the required action.

Invoice: There is a two-car collision in which four people are killed and the remaining passengers are injured. Another car passes by driven by an armed man whose nerves are on edge. When he sees the two cars joined in battle, as it were, he mistakes them for an armed checkpoint, and opens fire on them with his machine-gun, thereby killing the passengers who had survived the accident. Please take the required action.

Invoice: Three vigilantes manage to kidnap the man they were after. However, they then get into an argument over how to kill him and who will be the one to 'do the honours'. This is followed by name-calling and mutual recriminations. Finally, they cock their rifles and open fire on each other. As a result, all three meet their end. You are requested to pay them a visit and take whatever action is required. And please release their hostage unharmed... until further notice.

Invoice: Mona used to go everywhere on her motorcycle. At first, she was irritated by the traffic and the way some people would try to harass her. Now, though, she's terrified by the emptiness of the streets. She goes racing along at top speed, her heart beating wildly. And she's constantly wondering: Which do you suppose is better – to speed up or slow down? If I speed up, I might reach my destination just as it's being rocked by an explosion, whereas if I slow down the explosion might take place before I get there. On the other hand, the exact opposite might be the case. Well, one evening Mona is especially weary. The streets are deserted and, as usual, she is at odds with herself over whether she should speed up or slow down. Then all of a sudden, she stops her motorcycle and sits down on the pavement. She's decided neither to speed up nor to slow down. Instead, she isn't going to budge even an inch. Within minutes, an explosion goes off in the very spot where she's seated. Who knows? The explosive might have been in the motorcycle itself. You are requested to take the required action.

The cold continued to make its way through the child's tiny frame, taking possession of the nerves and muscles in one part of his body after another. Even the twinkle in his eyes, which had once glowed like the stars on a summer's night, had begun to fade away and he let himself sink peacefully into Mr Death's embrace. The old man drew his arms tenderly about the little boy and continued to pour out to him his tales of woe.

'You know, son,' he said, 'they've become real experts around here. They know how to serve up death on a platter in a thousand and one different ways. Just listen to this one ... 'In the flea-market of the village of Itroun, a certain man shot his own brother dead. And as if that weren't gruesome enough, he sawed off his head, his arms and his legs, then disposed of the body by throwing it on to some out-of-the-way boulders. And why? All because of a dispute over the title to a piece of land! Everywhere else in the world people die once and that's that.

Here, though, they insist on declaring their allegiance to me by dying several times over. The first time, someone might be shot dead; the second time, have his throat slit; and the third time, who knows what? Didn't I tell you how much they loved me? And their king loves me too! Ever since we signed a contract agreeing to rule the country together, I've been doing all the ruling on my own and all the burdens have fallen on my shoulders...'

> **Invoice:** Walid and Nada are a married couple who left their village in south Lebanon and went to live in the Shiyah district of Beirut to get away from Israeli gunfire. Then they fled from the shooting in their new home and returned to their house in the south. But they arrived back home in their village only to be received by an Israeli bomb. You are requested to pay them a visit at the right time.

Death went on pouring out his bitter complaints in a tone so sad it would have tugged at anybody's heartstrings: 'Didn't I tell you, son, that they'd worn me out? I've even got arthritis now from all this running back and forth: from the Israeli border in the south to Tripoli in the north, from the Beka Valley in the west to Zahleh in the east. In fact, the assignments they've given me haven't just been on land but in the air as well! Just look at this invoice: "Lebanese plane crashes, killing eighty-eight Lebanese citizens on board..."

'What this means is that in order to do my work, I have to go up to an elevation of more than 33,000 feet in this frigid, snowy weather! O my little one, I'm so very weary. That's not to deny, of course, all the honour they've shown me or all the ways they've tried to make my work easier. But no matter how "convenient" one's work conditions are, nobody can go on slaving away night and day, especially if he has to work in the air and on land at the same time! All the newspapers talk about any more are my "accomplishments". They devote every single inch of space to me – the headlines, the photos, you name it. In the past, all I got was a modest little column stuck inconspicuously at the bottom of one of the inside pages. It had a black border around it and was called the "Obituaries". Now, though, there isn't a single page that isn't devoted to my endless, varied feats. Even my "partner" the king never gets mentioned any more unless it's in connection with one of my accomplishments. But to speak frankly, the man has tired me out and broken the agreement we made. And to top it all, he keeps me so busy I can't even stop working long enough to pull out of our partnership. As for the ordinary residents of the city, they certainly don't help matters. After all, they worship me without realizing it. If you don't believe me, just look at the way they've stopped celebrating births and weddings, whereas they hold funerals as if they were going out of style!

'Just listen to this invoice. One of the obituaries reads: "It pains us to inform you of the death of our son. The funeral procession will take place on Taqseem Street, located between the Shiyah and Ayn Al-Rummaneh districts." The funeral will be attended not only by the family of the deceased but by hordes of people who were mere acquaintances, despite the fact that his house is located in a neighbourhood plagued by shooting and unrest – or, as Beirut residents would say, in a really "hot" part of town. Yet in spite of the danger, a huge crowd will turn out. During the wake a missile will explode in the house, turning most of those who've come to offer their condolences into still more "deceased". You are requested to pass by the house at the time of the wake to collect approximately forty invoices, one of which will be for the priest.

'So, little one, don't you see how easy they make my work for me?'

But the child made no reply. He lay asleep and motionless in Mr Death's lap. His eyes were open, but the two glowing summer stars that had once shown in them had gone out.

Trying to rouse the child in the hope of recounting more of his woes to him, Death said: 'Listen to this story, little one. This is an exciting one. On the day before 'Id Al-Adha,[5] ten men went out with a flock of more than 100 sheep. But as they were herding the animals along, they were accosted by a group of wartime vigilantes, who let the sheep go free but "slaughtered" the shepherds. (Imagine – I even have to help prepare the holiday sacrifices!) As their wives came out on to their doorsteps the following morning, each one found not a holiday sheep slaughtered and waiting to be prepared, but her own husband's body with his throat slit from ear to ear.

The child still didn't answer. His eyes were open, but his breathing had come to a halt. The old man realized that his young companion wasn't listening to him any more and that he had departed for a place very far away – somewhere more remote than Australia by far. He'd emigrated to another planet, perhaps never to return.

As the old man made out an invoice for the child, a coughing spell came over him suddenly and his hand began to tremble. He was truly saddened to see him go. Then he got up and continued on his way. Despite the memories of the glory days he'd enjoyed over the past months, he'd made up his mind to take leave of the city without another moment's delay.

By this time the sun had come up and fierce, violent winds were buffeting him this way and that. Even so, he kept on walking. As he passed by the cemetery wall, he heard what sounded like a huge blast and the wall came tumbling down. The storm winds were so violent, they were unearthing the contents of the graves and scattering them hither and yon, then depositing some of them on the pavement that ran alongside the cemetery's collapsed wall. The winds had also flung the contents of some the tombs on to the street outside the cemetery, turning the immediate vicinity into a vast, open grave.

Then, to Old Man Death's surprise, the gravedigger came running towards him, shouting: 'Aren't most people buried just once? But in this damned city, I have to bury the dead several times over! Come quickly, Death, and deliver me from this torment!'

Shouting back at the gravedigger, Death retorted: 'Instead, why don't you bury me and deliver me from *my* torment! I want to die myself! I want to die!'

The next morning, the child's frozen body was found beside a tree at the end of the alley leading to his house. The corpse showed no signs of having been abused. Others came upon the body of the ageing gravedigger, who'd been known to be quite overworked of late.

Nightmare 94

I woke up feeling unspeakably weary, more weary than if I'd stayed up all night digging graves.

Oh, nightmares, nightmares… They would sprout inside my head, then climb up the walls of my spirit like malevolent, bewitched plants that one reads about in fairy tales.

I'd endured so many nightmares about Mr Death, it was almost as if he'd passed right through the house and my throat was as dry as if he'd run his hand over my chest. Even so, I got up and headed towards the kitchen. The dawn was still emerging from among the night's shadows and diaphanous threads of ashen light coiled themselves about everything as far as the eye could see. It was as if the intermittent yet ongoing gunfire had bathed everything in a sombre, greyish hue. Or as if grey were the colour of the time about to come upon us once the dawn had broken.

I gulped down some water that we'd boiled once all the drinking water had run out. Floating on the surface there was a film of lime with a particularly revolting taste and it took some effort to keep my body from rejecting what I'd just put into it. I was normally in radiant health, but I'd reached a state of such utter exhaustion that hunger had begun to take its toll on my body.

So I decided to return to bed. I wasn't feeling energetic enough to go up to my flat and inspect the traces left behind by the latest round of bullets and shells – or, to be more exact, to check on the library, my most precious possession. Nor was I up to the risk of standing near the window in the hope of catching a whiff of the jasmine bush. Meanwhile, the odour of something burning remained in the air, from which I concluded that the Holiday Inn must still be ablaze.

On my way back from the kitchen, I noticed Amm Fu'ad sitting in his chair in the living room. He was surrounded on all sides by piles of painstakingly wrapped silverware and *objets d'art*, not to mention a number of expensive flower vases, each one of which – as hard as it was for me to fathom – would have fetched a sum exceeding the cost of an entire library!

I was too tired even to say: 'Good morning.' Nevertheless, I was drawn to him in spite of myself by a subtle, mysterious presence. It wasn't on account of the way he was sitting with his head resting limply on the back of the chair, nor was it the rigidity of his body. Rather, it was a kind of scent which my spirit picked up without the aid of my senses. At the same time, there was a shadowy light emanating from him which I saw not with my eyes, but with my pores. I saw it with those veiled hidden senses which modern science has yet to discover – senses experienced and understood by the guileless and simple, while those steeped in the pursuit of knowledge fail even to acknowledge their existence.

Like someone under a magic spell, I began walking towards him. When I finally reached where he was sitting, it was no surprise to find him dead. The fact is, I'd realized it when I was still in the other room. I'd sensed it even before touching his icy, bluish hand and before I'd experienced the horror of seeing the opaque, faraway look in his eyes. Something in me had picked up the signals, making me conscious of what had happened without knowing exactly how. As I pondered the sight of him encircled by his expensive rarities, he made me think of a scarecrow keeping watch over a field of ashes.

He was wearing his antique Ottoman robe and had covered his chest with his old military decorations, as if he were anticipating the arrival of a distinguished visitor. And his guest hadn't kept him waiting in vain.

I sank into the chair facing him. I wasn't afraid. I wasn't even sad. In fact, I felt just the way I normally did whenever I sat with him, or for that matter with any of the people whom I considered to be more or less strangers to my soul, or who'd estranged themselves from me after once having been trusted companions. Even so, it was rather a cosy session. He didn't say anything and consequently I wasn't obliged to say anything in return. He didn't come out with any of the conventional, worn-out platitudes which, though they communicate virtually nothing of any significance, one is expected to use in the interests of 'polite conversation'. And, as a result, there was no need for me to reply in the same language, which I generally find to be both painful and somewhat nauseating.

At last I could sit with him without having to put on even a single mask in the face of the countless masks which he was so accustomed to wearing. It was the first time I'd ever felt at ease with him. In the past, we'd managed to endure one another's company by bribing each other with a few standard clichés or snippets of polite jargon. But now I could talk to him without being afraid that he'd either misunderstand me or not understand me at all, that he'd come back at me with some sarcastic, bigoted remark, lose his temper or merely respond with cool indifference.

As we sat there facing each other, the peculiar thought occurred to me that we'd begun to look a bit alike. Perhaps the only difference between us now was that, unlike me, he wasn't hungry any more and was no longer in a position to learn anything new. In any case, it wasn't the comparison that mattered. The important thing was the truce that we'd concluded for the first time since we'd known each other – a genuine armistice rather than a mere ceasefire. I actually felt more comfortable with him now than I did with a lot of other people I knew! So here I was, chattering away with utter abandon – I, the woman who'd always remained a loner despite the crowds around her, the one who'd always kept her heart's wounds safely hidden from view no matter how many people happened to be standing by ready with gauze bandages.

When Yousif's life was snuffed out, my own life seemed suddenly to be emptied of all meaningful exchange. Like a glowing, live coal, he'd been the sole source of warmth and tenderness in my otherwise frigid, isolated existence. Gradually, he'd coaxed the 'turtle' of my spirit out of its shell until I was able to cast it aside completely. So as I sat there with Amm Fu'ad, I began baring my soul. I laid before him my fears, my hopes and my sorrows without holding back even my deepest, darkest secrets.

I said to him: 'Lots of people have asked about me and been worried on my account. But none of them has been genuinely concerned about my well-being – at least, not in the sense of being willing to share directly in my life or concerns, or to stand by me when I'm caught in a whirlwind of bullets that threatens to sweep me away. It seems that even the most profound communion of spirits can never penetrate the inner walls that keep us forever isolated from one another. All civil war does is make the walls visible, stripping off the usual veneer of courtesy and social niceties. You know, Amm Fu'ad … it isn't just the shooting that scares me. It's this terrible inward isolation that I feel sometimes. It's as if all the ties that once bound me to others had been hopelessly, irreparably broken. You know what I mean? I'm sure you must. After all, your own earthly ties have been severed once and for all...'

Then, without waiting for him to reply, I went on: 'At one time I was actually prepared to take up arms on a certain side of the conflict. In fact, I was about to join the people who've been busy shooting at each other right outside my house. That was the only time I'd ever affiliated myself with any of their parties, even briefly. I still sympathize with that particular party's aims and philosophy. But it didn't take me long to realize that I wasn't cut out for party work. The reason is that, first and foremost, I'm a writer, which means that the pen – rather than the gun – is the only tool I really know how to use in trying to bring about change. The party member's basic working principle states: Act, then discuss. For the thinker, however, the principle is reversed: Discuss, then act – and with as little violence as possible! You might compare the writer to an autonomous republic or an independent party. Or you might say he's a sort of "hustler" for the truth! That is, once he's got hold of what he understands to be "truth", he'll resort to any means at his disposal to promote his "commodity" and bring in "clientele". But for this very reason, he isn't free to marry "her" himself, even in secret!

'So the writer is faced with a choice: Will his primary allegiance be to his art or to the party? Theoretically speaking, there may be no conflict between the two. However, sooner or later he's bound to pass through a moment of indecision, a moment of confusion and uncertainty, of conscious rejection, of conflict and contradiction. Consequently, it's also a moment of betrayal – and that one moment may be sufficient to nip his creative gift in the bud for ever.

'Even so, as I see it, there's still something ludicrous about the whole thing. I mean – on the one hand, I might be shot dead by "the enemy". But on the other hand, the bullet that does me in could just as easily have been fired by the very people whose aims I've devoted my life to serving. After all, bullets don't bother to look at what's written in people's identity cards! The tragedy of war lies not only in the heinousness of the crimes to which it always leads, but in its utter stupidity. The bullets come pouring down like a cloudburst that makes no distinction between the wheatfields that lie parched and in need of moisture and the cotton fields for which the very same rains pose a life-threatening danger.

'Where the party is concerned, I find myself up against a painful reality – namely, that this party – like any other party would in similar circumstances – sees no alternative but to sanction violence as a legitimate means of changing the status quo. And even though at times I'm convinced that violence really is the only choice we have left, at the same time I refuse to try to justify it to anyone on philosophical grounds.

'So you think I'm inconsistent? Well, you're right! And that's my personal tragedy. I want the sun to come up, but I don't want to have to slaughter the rooster in order to prove to him that dawn will break with or without his help! That may in fact be the only way to prove such a thing. But if it is, then I have no choice but to devote my life to the search for other means. As I've said before, in my view, any loss of life is a cosmic disaster of sorts. However, I'm not convinced that preaching is the way either to win ideological battles or to raise people's awareness. And parties dearly love to preach. They prefer a demagogue who can deliver a second-rate speech to the masses over a first-rate artist who's sworn himself to silence until he knows what to say. The artist may choose to say nothing at all rather than risk uttering blasphemy, even if it means remaining silent for an entire lifetime. He doesn't concern himself with the release of party communiqués, but with the birth of his creations.

'Of course, neutrality in a world reigned by violence is no less of a crime than violence itself, since in effect it just helps one party to liquidate the other. Besides, joining one side over the other robs death of some of its sting. After all, it's easier to confront death *en masse* than as isolated individuals, deprived of the moral support to be found in collective rituals, peer approval, mounting hysteria and heroic sacrifice. But wait – I can't condone violence simply because I don't want to die alone! What about the thousands of other defenceless people who are suffering just as I am and whose lives are in constant danger? As they cower in silence with bullets raining down all around them, they're probably wondering to themselves: Is spurning violence such a terrible crime that one deserves to die for it – and violently at that?

'Why couldn't the travail leading to the birth of joy be a conscious humanitarian effort rather than a whirlwind of violence? On the other hand, perhaps the sheer ferocity of the tempest will be enough to bring about the contentment we seek...

'As a writer whose primary allegiance is to truth, I have no choice but to take a stand against "injustice" wherever I see it, whether it's committed by those in my own "camp" or by those I've had to part company with on both intellectual and humanitarian grounds. After all, "injustice" as I understand it may not be "injustice" in the view of others, including even those who are supposedly on my "team". This is true especially in time of war, when words like injustice are stretched and distorted as if they'd turned to rubber. As far as I'm concerned, though, moral values are never negotiable. No matter what the circumstances, I'll always maintain that, as the Qur'an itself says: "... if any one [slays] a person − unless it be for murder or for spreading mischief in the land − it would be as if he slew the whole people ..."[6]

As I talked on and on, Amm Fu'ad listened with a serene detachment that seemed to lie somewhere between goodwill and apathy.

I continued: 'And what good would my death do anyway? Who would benefit if a bullet were to come in through the window by accident and then on into my skull? If I were going to die to prove something, maybe I could accept it. But then again, why should I die to prove anything at all? If I really wanted to prove something, I could do it much better by staying alive. This, of course, goes against the whole notion of "martyrdom" − a principle most likely thought up by the "culture of death" to make one's demise more palatable and to dull people's instinctive urge to live. No... I'm not ashamed of my love of life and I'm not going to justify my refusal to die as if the desire to live were some sort of sin or crime. Of course, it *is* a crime and a sin in a society that's come to be dominated by a veritable "death cult". I abhor the notion of death for death's sake, so if I had to choose, I'd die for life's sake (though I'd prefer, of course, to *live* for life's sake).

'Yousif used to hate it when I'd say: "I love you to death!" Instead he'd insist that I say: "I love you to life!" And now that we're on the subject... you know, Amm Fu'ad, I still love Yousif.

I still perform pagan death rituals where I gather up his papers, his pictures and other keepsakes from our days together, then hide them away somewhere and guard them as if my very life depended on it. All of which, of course, is entirely inconsistent with my reasoned, thought-out convictions. Inconsistency seems to be part and parcel of human nature. But surely there isn't anyone who doesn't long deep down to reach a point of self-understanding, inner harmony and a sense of oneness with all that exists. I may still be just a novice on the path, but at least I'm aware that it exists and that I need to keep heading down it wherever it leads...'

I was still sitting in my chair across from Amm Fu'ad, who hadn't moved a muscle. Meanwhile, he kept staring in my direction – and then straight through me! After resting for a while I got up and thanked him for being such a good listener. I told him that since it was still so early, I was heading back to bed for a while and advised him to do the same.

Once I was buried under the covers, I felt a strange mixture of relief and exhaustion – like what a believer must experience when he's just come away from confessing to his priest with a notice of absolution in his hand. Then I was overtaken by waves of drowsiness. They raised me up, bathing me in that delightful sense of near-annihilation that comes right before one falls fast asleep. With high tide they washed me on to the shores of awareness, then with low tide they bore me out into the murky waters of oblivion until at last I was deposited on the other shore – the shore of dreams and nightmares...

Nightmare 95

'This bottleneck's getting to be more than I can take.' Saber kept saying this over and over to himself as he received the latest truckload of corpses. 'I can't take it any more,' he thought to himself again as he stared at the pile of bodies that had just been dumped in front of him.

In his capacity as supervisor of the government-run cold-storage locker, or 'the frozen graveyard' as it was sometimes referred to, Saber was responsible for finding a place for all the new corpses that were brought in day after day.

'This is getting out of hand...' Hemmed in on all sides by mangled, dismembered bodies, he stumbled over two or three of them whichever way he turned.

He wasn't normally bothered by how crowded the locker was. In fact, he generally liked to have the places he supervised filled to capacity. But what was he supposed to do when the vault was only large enough to hold thirty-six bodies?

During his days as a ticket vendor at a local cinema, he used to get a sense of satisfaction from seeing the seats filled with filmgoers and from having to apologize to people, saying: 'Sorry, no more seats. We're all sold out.' It made him feel that all was well with his work, with the cinema, and with the whole world...

However, the problem he now faced was that the cold-storage vault had become so full that there wasn't a single 'seat' left – neither in the main section, nor on the 'balcony', nor even in the seats normally reserved for VIPs. Meanwhile, the corpses kept coming in droves and demanding that he give them 'seats'.

Not only that, but when he'd apologize to them saying: 'Sorry, we're all filled up,' they wouldn't leave quietly the way would-be filmgoers do. Instead, they'd just stick around with their entrails hanging out, insisting on being allowed to come inside before they began to rot, and shouting in his face with voices that sounded like the howling of a winter wind.

So what on earth was he supposed to do when, morning after morning, the city would fling a new heap of corpses on to his doorstep? What was he supposed to do when there were dead bodies screaming at him from all sides, demanding to be rescued from the microbes that had begun reproducing inside them and threatening them with putrefaction and disintegration? How did they expect him to cope with hordes of cadavers that pleaded and threatened night and day in the hope of being allowed into the vault?

One of the bodies shouted: 'I'm the nephew of the Sunni Muslim minister. If you don't let me in, my uncle will relieve you of your job!'

Another cried out: 'And I'm the nephew of the Christian Maronite minister. If you don't let me in, you'll be violating the principle of equal representation among the sects and of allowing corpses to be seated along sectarian lines! Besides that, my uncle will have your head!'

'I'm a Shi'ite!' cried another.

'I'm a Druze,' shouted still another, 'and my reincarnated spirit will make certain that none of your offspring survive!'

'I'm an Orthodox Christian!' shouted out another.

Then a fourth chimed in, saying: 'I'm a Jew from Wadi Jumayyal – a member of a "persecuted minority". And I'll zap you with a guilt complex if you don't let me in. By the way, I also want a flat next door to the synagogue!'

'I belong to the huge—clan,' bellowed a fifth, 'so if you don't reserve me a seat in the VIP section, my brothers and cousins will come after you to avenge me. And if you're stupid enough to turn me down, the feud will be carried on into the next generation.'

'My father is a member of parliament!' shrieked a sixth, 'and he has a blue licence plate on his car. So clear these filthy corpses of yours out of my way or I'll have every one of you killed all over again by my father's personal militia. You'd better get me into this place right away or else ... and you know what "or else" means!'

Then a seventh body with a rasping voice sobbed—'I'm the famous singer —. If you don't let me in and preserve this silky voicebox of mine, people will start saying that Lebanon isn't the "land of stars" after all and that it even persecutes the brilliant and the gifted!'

After this, an eighth body the size of a dinosaur howled: 'I used to be the bodyguard for the well-known political leader —Bey, son of—Bey, son of—Bey, son of—Bey, son of Adam, peace be upon him. If I don't get a seat, the Mafia I belong to will attack and loot your vault, then sell the flesh from all the corpses both wholesale and retail – that is, after they've plucked out their eyes and left them hanging for three days on the telephone poles that haven't been pulled up yet.'

'Let *me* in,' cried a ninth body, 'and I'll pay you off royally!'

'And I'm an election key,' declared a tenth, 'so I'd advise you to let me in, or we'll arrange for you to be hit by a "stray" bullet!'

'I'm an American,' screamed another, 'and my mighty embassy with its atom bombs will make you send me back.'

'As for me,' said another corpse dejectedly, 'I'm a poor man with no family. So please, just let me go...'

'That's it! I'm a goner!' Saber said over and over to himself, shuddering with dread and revulsion at the litany of threats he'd just been subjected to.

He opened up the vault and began chasing out all the unidentified corpses. Then, as a new group of cadavers came parading into the vault, uttering threats and warnings, he stood at the door shouting: 'Tickets! Tickets, please! Show me your tickets – that is, your identity cards! If you're poor, come this way, please. Those who don't have "connections", come this way. As for those who don't have anything to verify their ancestry and religious affiliation, they need to come this way... This is a government-run locker, mind you, so everything has to be done the proper way!'

Nightmare 96

She sat waiting anxiously for the telephone to ring. Meanwhile, she busied herself by making a clay statue in the shape of a baby, knowing she might be summoned at any moment to 'make' a real live one.

Her fingers fussed with the clay, rounding the head, drawing eyes, ears and lips, and forming a delicate body the size of an infant's at the moment of birth.

She'd reached the legs now and still the telephone hadn't rung.

The day she'd chosen to go into the medical profession, or, to be more exact, into obstetrics and gynaecology, her choice had been considered a kind of 'feminist revolution' in the family. Was their bashful, diffident daughter actually going to break free and become a doctor? No one knew that in so doing, she was giving sanction to her instinctive shyness around men. She'd always become so flustered and confused in their presence that she found herself unable to release all her creative powers. No one knew that she'd chosen to specialize in obstretrics so that her fingers would never have to touch a man's body. For the 'patient' would always be male as far as she was concerned. That was something she'd never be able to put out of her mind. She simply wasn't able to wipe out 2000 years of ignorance (an ignorance which was still as profound as it had been in pre-Islamic times) with a university degree completed in seven years. She'd chosen to become an obstetrician so that her dealings would be limited to women. That way, she'd be sparing both herself and others discomfort which they'd all prefer to avoid. She practised her profession with masterly precision and skill, but also with the mechanical efficiency of a conductor on a crowded bus.

That is, until civil war broke out in Lebanon. Oh, how the war had changed her.

That damned phone, she thought. Why doesn't it ring? Isn't there a single woman in this whole city who wants to create life tonight, to make up for all the death being manufactured by male society?

She went back to busying herself with the tiny clay baby she was making. Ever since she'd begun seeing corpses piled in the streets and in hospital corridors, or dangling from trees, from signs on department stores, from balconies and telephone poles, she'd come to see birth in a new way.

She no longer saw her profession as an escape from contact with males. Instead, she'd come to see the event of giving birth as something splendid and marvellous, a source of luminous brightness, as a kind of sacred rite by which she could compensate women for the brutality of male society. She'd begun waiting impatiently for the ringing of the telephone that would call her to assist some woman in labour. Then she'd run to the hospital, oblivious of the snipers in the streets, the mines planted under the asphalt, the checkpoints that had become the sites of kidnappings and murders, and the death that hovered everywhere like an ominous, low cloud. She saw bringing a child out of its mother's womb and into the world as a dazzling achievement, an act of beauty. In fact, she found it the only thing of any value in this time of madness and brutality.

She felt as if she were a priestess in life's temple, performing rites of the utmost splendour, magnificence and perfection. She herself gave birth with every woman that she attended, creating life along with every womb that delivered its offspring into the world. All these children were her own. She no longer felt shy or flustered around men. However, she didn't feel contempt for them either. Instead, she felt a kind of complementarity and equality with them. At times they would kill and she would create, while at other times she would kill and they would create. It was the natural law of the universe which applied to all without exception. When it comes to people's capacity either to stumble and fall or to rise to great heights, she could see that there was no real difference between male and female.

But the telephone didn't ring that night. Meanwhile, her fingers continued making the statue of the baby with skill and precision, and as she worked she began to feel something like labour pains in her stomach. As the pains accelerated, her fingers responded by working all the more rapidly. Then the pains started coming faster and faster, growing stronger and more intense as she struggled fiercely to form the child perfectly. Then she screamed and cut the umbilical cord.

The statue started moving about, screaming and crying as it gulped down its first breath of life.

'Thank you!' it said to her as it opened the door and went out to proceed with its new life.

'No, but I thank you!' she whispered, 'You've made me a mother!'

Nightmare 97

I was suddenly jarred awake by the sound of someone

screaming. It was Amin.

It seemed like the first time in ages that I'd woken up to the sound of a human voice rather than the roaring of missiles and bombs. At the same time, though, his voice wasn't entirely human. Rather, it sounded more like the bellowing of a panic-stricken animal. I leapt out of bed, fearful at first that he might have been shot. But then I remembered Amm Fu'ad dead in his chair and realized that Amin must have discovered his father's corpse.

Amin was in tears and the servant was sobbing along with him. But it seemed to me that they were weeping more out of fear than out of grief. It was as if Amm Fu'ad's death had been a message from the realm of the spirit, warning us all of the death that none of us can ultimately escape, yet which we're obliged to overlook (for the time being, at least) so as to keep on playing life's game. Amin was lamenting his father in a voice full of dread and anguish. It was almost as if he were mourning his own death as he wailed: 'They've murdered him! Somebody's murdered him!'

Then, to my astonishment, I saw him get up and start searching the house, which we'd sealed up as tight as a can of sardines.

I said to him: 'Isn't it obvious to you that he died of a heart attack or some other natural cause? It's plain to see that whatever he died of didn't come from outside.'

Even so, Amin continued to insist that his father had been murdered.

In view of the countless murders that were taking place all around us, it had become difficult for any of us to imagine that someone might actually die of natural causes.

'There isn't a single trace of a bullet or piece of shrapnel in his whole body. And I dare say that fright and exhaustion are more likely to have killed him than a bomb. Can't you see that his body hasn't been struck by anything?'

'Maybe he was strangled, then,' Amin replied.

'But there are no marks on his neck. In fact, there isn't a scratch on his entire body! Besides which, all the doors and windows are shut, just the way we left them last night. The man died a natural death, the way most creatures do.'

But he still wasn't convinced. With all we'd been through over the past few days, he thought it extremely peculiar that anyone should die a 'normal' death. And it was obvious that the elderly servant shared his opinion, for soon they'd both gone searching everywhere for the tell-tale signs of the alleged murderer, with the sounds of the surrounding gunfire close on their heels.

Meanwhile, I sat back down in the chair facing Amm Fu'ad and said to him: 'The murderer is inside you. He came out, committed his dastardly deed, then went back into hiding. It was love that murdered you – your love for these endangered "treasures" of yours.'

And as I said it, I thought I could see a glimmer of tacit acknowledgement in his eyes!

Then finally I said: 'Thanks for listening to me so attentively a while ago!'

Nightmare 98

Amin and the servant kept running around in a frenzy, looking for the supposed murderer. The initial shock had apparently charged them with nervous energy which they could only get out of their systems by moving around, so I left them to get on with it.

As for me, I was facing a difficult practical problem. I'd been stuck in the same house with three men who were all in a state of collapse. And now here I was with two men (still in a state of collapse) plus a dead body. The problem was the body. There was no way for us to bury it, unless, of course, we wanted to be gunned down by the sniper while we were digging a hole out in the garden. In that case we would literally be digging our own graves. Nor was there anyone who could get close enough to our house to smuggle us out, or even gather up the dead bodies that had begun accumulating in the neighbourhood.

So then, the corpse would stay with us. And before long it would begin to decompose and stink. As a consequence, we'd soon have a new catastrophe on our hands far exceeding the lack of electricity, the bullets raining down on all sides... and hunger.

About an hour later Amin came back. Collapsing into the chair next to me, he wailed: 'Oh, my father!'

'He's no longer your father,' I told him. "He" is now a corpse. And we've got to do something to keep ourselves from being asphyxiated by the stench once it begins to rot. We have to think of a suitable place to store it before it's so stiff that we have difficulty moving it.'

He seemed utterly mystified by what I'd just said. It was obvious that what he saw in the bluish, rigid body before us wasn't a lifeless corpse but a man whom he loved – namely, his father. He hadn't yet noticed what a predicament it put us in to have a cadaver on our hands in circumstances such as ours. Nor had he grasped the reality that nothing was left of his father but a dead body. However, I decided to keep quiet and let the next few hours make clear to him what I'd meant. I told him I was going up to the third floor to check on my flat, trusting that time, with its wordless eloquence, would eventually enable him to understand the difference between a living father and a lifeless body now stripped of what had once made it a unique, cherished human being.

Nightmare 99

As I proceeded with my morning inspection tour of what remained of my flat, I found myself unable to get terribly worked up over anything. It was as if hunger had dulled my usual sensitivities and at the same time had released other hidden powers of perception, including my receptivity to horrific, overwhelming nightmares. In the sitting room, which had sustained considerable damage, there were chairs which had been literally torn to shreds. But by what? Bullets? Knives? I had no idea. The fact was, though, that none of this really mattered much to me. What did matter was my library, which alone had succeeded in convincing me to give up my life of ceaseless wandering. After all, libraries can't survive on the wings of aeroplanes or in transit lounges any more than grass can grow on a perpetually rolling stone.

I wasn't worried about the house being robbed, since there was nothing of any value in it apart from my books and a marble inkwell that Yousif had given me one day. Thieves generally turn up their noses at books, since they are a big bother to lug around and they don't even fetch a decent price. (But go ahead and steal them, you fools! For all you know, times might change and books could become more precious than gold. But if you don't believe me, then at the very least don't set them on fire!)

I knew that if a thief did set foot in my house, he'd probably throw a fit once he discovered that it was devoid of valuable silverware, furs and rare carpets. But I hoped that no matter how furious he became, he wouldn't go so far as to torch the place.

Then suddenly my grand library, which covered no less than six whole walls, was rocked by a series of blasts. The fighters' morning break had come to an end and another fierce battle was underway.

I withdrew into the hallway, which I'd chosen as my personal bomb shelter. If I died here, at least I could be buried under an avalanche of my beloved books!

Nightmare 100

With no electricity, the hallway was black as pitch and it seemed to be growing narrower by the minute. Then I felt something nibbling around the edges of my hand. I recoiled in terror. Might it be a rat? I wondered. Or was it just my imagination? If it *was* a rat, do you suppose it thought I was dead?

Just then I felt myself plummeting into an inky abyss...

In my mind's eye I saw twenty-six people on Beirut's Ghazzal Street. They'd fled from the fighting to a shelter with their children. There was no light in the shelter, so they just sat on the floor, trembling with cold and fright. They hadn't been in the shelter very long before they were attacked by rats, who concentrated their attentions on the children's tender flesh. They were wounded, yet due to the heavy shelling outside it was impossible for them to come out.

As if the vision had lit a fire under me, I jumped up and shot like an arrow out of the darkened corridor.

The wound on my hand was bleeding slightly, so I hadn't been imagining things after all. Rats had begun trying to feast on my corpse even before I'd had a chance to die.

In civil war, as in any other, the strong devour the weak at every available opportunity. As for 'revolution', it contains within it the seeds of a certain tragic complication – namely, that large numbers of the very people it intended to deliver from harm end up being its victims.

Nightmare 101

Bullets. Bullets.
Thinking is an impossibility. The brain wasn't made to be used while nails are being driven into it.
I'm a frightened animal...
I whine and I howl...
I don't meditate or cogitate...
I bellow and I shriek...
I don't ponder or deliberate...
I bark and I whimper...
I whine and I howl...

Nightmare 102

I whine and I howl...
. . . .
. . . .
. . . .
. . . .
... and I howl...

Nightmare 103

Yousif came to me, the bullet holes in his body growing steadily larger. He'd been bleeding for months now and still his wounds hadn't closed. He would always come to me when death was close at hand and when the roar of the explosions was at a deafening peak. I was feeling as fragile and insignificant as a teardrop. As I'd done on all his previous visits, I groped for him, then took him into my arms. But my fingers passed through his rarefied, ethereal body and he vanished once again into nothingness.

I felt angry as I ran my fingers over my own body, which was *not* rarefied or ethereal. The wound in my hand, which was crying out with pain, was at the same time crying out with life. I was hurting. Therefore I was alive. But I wasn't going to allow pain to be the only sign of life left in me.

I had to accept the fact that Yousif had truly died. He'd departed, never to return. Yet I'd been trying to live with the lifeless 'corpse' of his memory, just exactly the way Amin had been insisting on living with his father's dead body as if it were his father himself.

I ran to look for the little tape recorder that Yousif had given me along with his music, whose strains had been the accompaniment to our sweetest days together. The battery was still working, so I put in one of his tapes, turned up the volume full blast, and began listening to the music of our memories against the background of the gunfire outside – the sound of present reality. Then, little by little, the sound of the music began to grow faint and sluggish as the batteries ran out. Meanwhile, like an old tape that's erased when something new is recorded over it, Yousif's music was being drowned out more and more completely by the crackling and whizzing of bullets and bombs – the voices of the here and now. As the music steadily lost volume and speed, it took on a mournful, gloomy air and its rich resonance and lively beat were transformed into a hollow, nasal twang. Then at last it faded out entirely, evaporating into total silence. And at that moment I experienced a relief akin to what an adder must feel when she's just shed her old skin!

Nightmare 104

It was just like a nightmare...

Winds laden with poisoned rain were whistling through shuttered windows whose glass portions had been left open, the result being that the light remained outside while the biting, wintry cold came streaming in. Just the way it happens in nightmares...

Visibility was virtually nil and I couldn't imagine how bullets managed to see their way to their targets or shells to their victims' heads. This purgatory, with its grim, bitter cold, was harrowing indeed, a place where one would dream of hellfire as a warm, cosy respite!

Just like an overdone horror film...

Amin, the servant and I all sat gaping at the cadaver that lay sprawled out on the chair in front of us. By this time it had become completely rigid, while its features had begun swelling and undergoing subtle mutations. The jaw hung open slightly and what looked like a condescending smile had spread over the bluish lips, which had parted to reveal a set of false teeth. It was the Mona Lisa! The Mona Lisa, civil-war style! The Mona Lisa, vintage 1975!

Suddenly I burst out laughing. Pretty soon the servant was laughing along with me and then even Amin joined in. But just as suddenly we all fell silent and nothing remained of our laughter but gasps which before long had turned into muffled sobs in Amin's throat.

Night was rapidly falling. It probably was no later than 4.00 p.m., yet on a ghostly winter evening such as this one, the sun might seem to have disappeared in a hurry for the simple reason that it had never appeared in the first place! So despite the earliness of the hour, the frigid wind was already suffused with ashen particles which gave notice of the dismal evening that lay ahead.

It was either a Saturday or a Sunday. I didn't know for sure. I turned on the radio in hopes of hearing someone announce the date. But instead I heard a voice singing.

> He went and presented his grievances to the wind,
> Then struck himself on the cheeks and wept...

I turned it right back off.

No, it had to be either Saturday or Sunday, which meant that people ought to be occupying themselves with simple, mundane problems such as where to spend the weekend or whether to make the cheese sandwiches with radishes or tomatoes. As for me, though, I had to spend this Saturday or Sunday evening pondering conundrums of a very different sort – namely, what to do about the dead body that lay collapsed in a heap before me, and how to deal with thirst when the water had run out and with hunger when there was no more food.

In countries whose populations are starving, the weekend – like the rest of the week – is a time of mass annihilation, a time to be spent not planning outings but burying the dead. How is it that the people who go cruising on yachts at Hotel St George or ice-skating at the Cedars Hotel could have failed to notice the tents of the hungry scattered along the sides of the roads as they headed for their resorts and places of entertainment? How could they have seen, yet not seen?

Amin was the first one to speak. 'We'll carry him to his bed,' he announced.

'But we'll be needing his bedroom,' I objected. 'It's the safest room in the house. Since it's right up against the garden wall, it has a double layer of protection.'

But Amin insisted, saying: 'We'll carry him to his bed and wrap him in a sheet.'

'The stench will end up spreading to both your bedroom and mine,' I told him.

However, he was adamant. 'We're going to do things the proper way and carry him to his bed!' he said emphatically.

So we carried him to his bed and stretched him out on top of it. He was heavier than one would have expected from looking at his frail, shrivelled frame. When I pulled the pillow out from under the bedspread in order to lay his head on top of it, I found four loaves of bread that he'd stashed there. Under the other pillow I came upon two apples and a bag of roasted chickpeas. Too ravenous to be shocked or angered by my discovery, I started gobbling down one of the loaves of bread without even stopping to think that I ought to wash my hands first.

But after taking the first few bites, I felt even more ravenous than before. It was as if food had restored my ability to experience how famished I really was. Amin glared at me angrily as if to say: How dare you eat in the presence of my father's remains? But I just kept on feasting, and finally, overcome by temptation and need, Amin too picked up a loaf and started munching away...

Nightmare 105

I lay down in the hope of getting some sleep. I didn't feel drowsy, but ever since the electricity had been cut off we'd found ourselves obliged to go to bed with the setting of the sun to conserve candles – of which we had very few left – and as a way of fleeing from the eerie, frightening darkness. As I lay there, I could hear the sounds of the creatures in the pet shop as if they were all around me.

Then my thoughts turned for a while to my brother and I

wondered how he was doing in jail. I wasn't worried that he might be 'ruined' by the company of criminals. After all, the only criminals who ended up in our prisons were the 'little guys', so to speak. As for the 'big guys', they were still out carousing in the cages of an illusory freedom, or occupying positions of power and influence.

Then once again I was assailed by the voices of the creatures in the pet shop. They came to me with the shrill whistle of the ice-cold winds, on which I thought I could detect the odour of Amm Fu'ad's decomposing body. But no... In this kind of weather, it wasn't possible for his corpse to have started fermenting yet, nor for thousands of microbial organisms to have already come to life and begun multiplying inside him. However, the cold was causing my hunger pangs to come back with a vengeance. It was also exacerbating the pain in my hand where I'd been bitten by the rat and in the wounds left by the claws of that hungry hunting dog, as nimble and sleek as a pure-bred Arab stallion...

. I don't know why, but it seems it's always at night that pain intensifies and old wounds are set on fire. Just like my emotions, everything on this otherwise arctic night seemed to be ablaze.

That's right! Even my wounded ear, which had nearly healed over, was pricking me like needles. It made me think of the countless numbers of people who lay wounded on the pavements of our grief-stricken city, or those among them who'd been fortunate enough to be placed in hospital beds – the thousands who at that very moment lay bleeding in dark alleys, while merciless winds cut through their wounds like knives.

Do you suppose it was just a dream? Or did I really go spying on the creatures in the pet shop that night? But what's the difference between dream and reality anyway? The important thing is certainty and awareness. And I knew for certain that I'd seen them...

I'd seen famished dogs in combat. I'd heard their barks and howls. I'd seen how they inspired dread in the other captive creatures, who withdrew fearfully into the far corners of their cages. The only creature which seemed undaunted was the large fish that was now devouring a smaller one at the bottom of the silent aquarium. Meanwhile, the hungry dogs went on with their internecine warfare. Their prolonged, involuntary fast had made it virtually inevitable that they would begin preying on one another. Such is the order of life. The first dog to be wounded would be the first to be eaten, either after it had died or while it was still struggling for its last breath. That would depend on just how ravenous the others had become.

By this time the dogs' violent confrontation had utterly demolished the shop's tourist façade. The battle-weary rabbit opened its red eyes in horror. The Siamese cat meowed frantically, exhaling puffs of air in a belligerent, snake-like hiss. The parrot was going berserk in its cage as it watched the dogs engage in their repeated attack and retreat manoeuvres. Meanwhile, it was persisting in its boycott of French – that decadent, coquettish-sounding language – preferring instead to screech and squawk after the manner of its jungle forebears.

Then there was the dust and the spreading stench – a foul odour born of bodily waste, of sweat exuded in moments of terror and of saliva dribbling from the mouths of hunger-crazed animals. Eventually the five canines ran out of steam and each of them quietly retreated to a far corner of the shop. One of them was injured and bleeding. And although it attempted to conceal this fact by furtively licking the wound clean, it knew that its 'secret' was out and that the extraordinary canine sense of smell had exposed the truth of the matter.

Now that they'd got a whiff of newly spilt blood, the dogs' appetites were reawakened. Soon the battle was on again, so the injured dog plucked up courage and began fighting for his life. After all, he knew that if he didn't rise to the occasion, he'd be killed and eaten instantly. But as long as he was still alive and able to join the fray, he was determined to retain his right to bark, bite and multiply for as long as possible.

By the end of the second round, all the dogs were exhausted and a second one had been wounded. Too spent to go on, they lay down and went to sleep, at which point the other animals breathed a sigh of relief. After all, they had been looking on in consternation and horror as the dogs did battle, absorbing what seemed like death-charged ions that had been emanating from the bloody fray. As a result, they were as enervated as if they themselves had been locked in mortal combat.

Then, one by one, all the animals in the shop nodded off – to be greeted by the same miserable, fitful sleep that awaited their human neighbours.

Nightmare 106

I found myself stark naked in a freezing, empty room. Pacing around in tears, I wondered: Where's my brother? Where's my brother? Where's Shadi? I decided to try calling out to someone for help, so I went to open the window. But the 'window' was nothing but coloured lines drawn on to the wall.

I ran to the wardrobe to look for something to put on. But it too was nothing but lines etched on to a wall.

So I rushed over to the door, hoping to flee. However, the 'door' likewise wasn't a door but a mere drawing. And so were the knob and the lock.

I screamed and screamed, but no words came out of my

mouth. Instead, all that emerged was a sound that bore a vague resemblance to the meow of a cat having its throat slit.

It had now become apparent that the room was a cement box with no way in or out. Meanwhile, the cold was piercing me like a knife. Oh, where is my brother? I wondered in desperation. Do you suppose he's still in jail? And how am I ever going to get out of this bizarre sepulchre?

I went rushing from wall to wall and from one window latch to another. My fingernails broke on the hard, stony walls. There were no windows. There was no door.

'Where is my brother?' I screamed.

Then, all of a sudden, the roof opened upward, as if it were the lid to a tightly sealed box.

As I gazed through the opening, I saw five bearded men staring down at me. I noted with alarm that they all had the same face and were wearing the same clothes. It was as if they were a single man surrounded by four huge mirrors.

Then one of them hurled a burlap bag at me. It landed on top of me, knocking me over, and split open to reveal an ice-cold cadaver. I got up from underneath the body and turned it face up, only to discover to my horror that its face was that of my brother.

I let out a long, bloodcurdling scream, like a jackal on a yellow-mooned night, and all five men leapt into the room, surrounding me on all sides. Sobbing, I ran my hand over the bloodied bullet hole in my brother's temple.

'Who murdered him?' I cried.

In reply, one of the men pointed menacingly at me with the iron hook that he now wore in place of one of his hands and said: '*You* murdered him!'

As if I hadn't heard him, I repeated: 'Who murdered him?'

'You did,' he said again. 'Aren't you his older sister? Don't the two of you have a deceased mother? If so, then you're the one who killed him.'

'Who killed him?' I persisted.

'As he was coming out of the jail, he was hit by a stray bullet.'

'Who killed him?'

'We were firing into the air in mourning for a friend of ours, when all of a sudden your brother was hit by a stray bullet that killed him. It's *your* fault that we've had to go to all this trouble on his account and that a perfectly good bullet went to waste.'

Then without the least warning all five men lunged at me, tied me up with a rope that smelt of dried blood, took out whips and started lashing me.

As they flogged me, they said: 'We've decided to try you on charges of inciting your brother to walk around in the street unarmed and defenceless. For goodness' sake, you'd think the pavements had been made to be walked on by unarmed pedestrians, who should have stayed at home or in the shelters, leaving the streets empty for us! So it's been decided that you deserve to be executed for the crime of causing your brother's death, and of bothering us and wasting our precious time.'

If it hadn't been for the excruciating stings of the whips on my back, I would have thought it was some sort of practical joke. But then they wrapped the whip around my neck, suspended me from a metal hook which they'd driven into the wall and left me for dead. When the men finally left, I was bleeding so profusely that the rope which they'd used to tie me up was soaked with blood. And I was choking to death.

I tried to shout at my brother: 'You idiot! Why in hell did you have to go running away from prison, where the worst you'd have had to contend with was a bunch of petty criminals? Didn't you know you'd just land in the street where the "big boys" play?'

But the voice that came out of me was nothing but an anaemic meow. And the room where I was held prisoner was nothing but a painted cement box. Through its open lid I could see the sky, which looked like a massive slab of hard granite.

Nightmare 107

I dare say there isn't anyone alive who could sleep through the blast produced by the sorts of shells we were being treated to, no matter how exhausted he was. As I lay in bed, I shrank back in terror as if my body were trying to hide inside my skin.

I didn't get up.

I could hear Amin's panic-stricken voice calling to me through the door, but I played dead. He persisted. I persisted in ignoring him. Then he began weeping in a barely audible voice. Feeling sorry both for him and for myself, I asked him what he wanted.

'I was hoping you could help me move my father. I'll sleep in his place and he'll sleep in mine. After all, his is the safest room in the flat. And these missiles...'

'Didn't I tell you that in the beginning?' I yelled back at him. 'But no – you were determined to do things "the proper way"!'

He didn't reply. Seeing that he'd already woken the servant, I went ahead and got up. The body seemed to have grown heavier since the last time we lifted it, and in the dim light of the candle, its features seemed to glow with radiant health. In fact, I thought I detected a jovial smile on its face. It was as if Amm Fu'ad enjoyed having us cart him around from one bed to the next – and he seemed to be getting quite a kick out of this new 'game'.

Seeing our shadows on the wall frightened me. They loomed up large and inky black, three spectres carrying a fourth. Somehow they didn't look quite human to me, as if we were members of some other species – apes, say, or dogs, or ghouls coming out by night to carry away the bodies of the dead.

Once the task had been completed, everyone went back to bed without exchanging a word.

Nightmare 108

This time Amin woke me up without there having been an explosion.

God! I thought. Will I ever see an end to this night?

The freezing winds continued to huff and puff, blowing up a veritable hurricane of hail and bullets.

'What is it, Amin?' I asked.

'My father has to be moved.'

'You mean his corpse?'

Ignoring the hint, he repeated: 'My father has to be moved.'

'Why?'

'Because of the smell.'

'But it hasn't begun to spread yet.'

'Frankly,' he confessed, 'I'm really scared. Every time I close my eyes, he calls out to me and asks me to come stay with him. His room is right next to mine, you know. Please, let's move him to the living room!'

So the three of us – the servant, Amin and I – gathered round the body. As we braced ourselves for the task before us, the servant had a look of numb resignation on his face. As for Amm Fu'ad, he seemed to be staring straight ahead with a spiteful, piercing gleam in his eyes. I stepped forward to take hold of his head and shoulders. I tried to close his eyes for him, but the eyelids resisted more obstinately than I'd expected. Instead of closing, they just kept gazing into space. His smile seemed to have become brighter and his face looked healthier than ever (or was it just more swollen?).

At last we laid him out on the sofa in the parlour, which was fairly remote from the bedrooms.

I looked up at Amin and could see that he wasn't entirely satisfied, which meant that he'd be waking me up again soon. So I asked him: 'What do you say we move him somewhere else?'

'Like where, for example?'

'Well, we could put him in the big freezer. It's true that there isn't any electricity, but at least it closes tightly, so you wouldn't be able to hear him or smell him!'

'Do you mean we'll have to cut him up into pieces?' asked the servant.

'No,' I said. 'What I mean is that we could take the shelves and drawers out of the freezer, remove some of his clothes and medals, then stuff him inside in one piece. He wouldn't be terribly comfortable, of course, but he'd at least be able to sleep!'

Nobody laughed at my joke. Nor did Amin agree to my suggestion. As a result, we all withdrew once more to try to get some sleep. However, as expected, before long Amin woke me.

This time he was sobbing. As for me, I was trembling with rage. Catching a few winks in such circumstances was turning out to be about as easy as hunting down the legendary griffon! And here he was getting me up again, just at the moment when I was about to close my hand over slumber's elusive butterfly. In any case, I understood: he wanted us to move his 'father'.

'Honestly, now,' I shouted, 'what *do* you want to do with the body? Listen... you've got to face up to the fact that this is a cadaver we're dealing with here – a dead body! As for the three of us, we're still alive, and that's also a fact we have to accept. So tell me, what exactly is upsetting you so much?'

As I listened to myself, my voice sounded commanding, harsh, cold. It was as if it weren't my voice at all – not the voice of the woman who, with Yousif, had been the epitome of gentleness and sensitivity.

'The fact is,' he said through his tears, 'I'm scared to death. I don't have the guts to sleep in the same house with a dead person, with a c... c... c... corpse!'

'Great,' I said. 'At least you recognize now that that's all it is. So then, do you want it out of the house?'

He nodded his head in affirmation.

'Well,' I went on, 'digging a grave in the garden is out of the question, since they'd be sure to think we were planting mines. And the latest models of snipers' rifles can see quite well in the dark.'

He nodded his head again.

'It would also be impossible to throw it into the street, since we're surrounded on all sides by the garden.'

He nodded in agreement once more.

'So,' I said, 'the only option left is to put him outside the building's main entrance – which, of course, is the "proper" way to treat someone of his importance – then look into the problem again in the morning – that is, if we're still alive then.'

We went to wake up the servant, who still looked as if he were asleep even as he helped us pick up the body. As for Amm Fu'ad, his grin was broader than ever. For all we knew, it might have been the most enjoyable night of his entire 'life', bed-hopping, as it were, with the help of three 'living dead' straining under his weight every step of the way. How long do you suppose it had been since he'd been carried, or dandled on someone's knees? Perhaps not since he was a little boy – in other words, not for nearly 100 years. Ah, time...

Prior to this crisis, I hadn't realized how much muscular strength I had stored up inside my skinny body, or that I had the capacity to be so relentless and callous.

In any case, by this time Amin was in an alarming state of collapse and I was the one in charge of the 'cadaver transport operation'. As for the servant, he seemed a bit flustered. I figured out why when I noticed that some gold medals were missing from the breast of the deceased! Perhaps he'd slipped in through the darkness to where the body lay, managing to keep his shudders of horror and revulsion under control long enough to take what he'd come for and slip out again. I didn't blame him. After all, such is the logic of hunger and poverty.

At long last we reached the door, looking like a ragtag procession of lunatics amusing themselves by playing with a cadaver. When we leaned him up against the outside wall, he looked like a weary beggar crouched at the entrance, unable to reach the doorbell above him. Then without another word, we went back inside and headed for our respective beds. Yet in Amin's eyes I could still see a thinly disguised look of dissatisfaction, and I knew he hadn't got me up for the last time. With this in mind, I lay down in bed but didn't go to sleep, so that when he came for me the next time I'd already be awake. Meanwhile, I began listening again to the panting of the creatures in the pet shop and to their groans of hunger and pain. Where had their owner run off to? How dare he run away like that, leaving them to die in their cages? During those six years that he spent buying and selling them to earn his daily bread, didn't he become bonded to them by a single thread of fondness or camaraderie, or even by some sense of responsibility or duty? Do you suppose he's in Paris now, or London?

I couldn't take the animals anything to eat, since we hardly had any food left in the house. And even if there'd been enough to share with them, I wouldn't have had the guts to go into the shop again. After all, I knew full well that the hungry hunting dogs were on the loose, their fangs bared, ready to fight to the death at the slightest provocation with no eye to the distinction between friend and foe.

When Amin came back once more to wake me, I was expecting him.

'I can't sleep,' he said. 'He keeps ringing the doorbell.'

'But that's impossible,' I replied. 'Have you forgotten that there's no electricity? Besides, a corpse... I mean, you know, he's stopped ringing any sort of doorbell.'

'But I can hear him. And after he rings the bell, he beats on the door with both hands and starts shouting at me, asking to come in. He says he's afraid and that it's cold out there.'

'All right then,' I relented, 'so what do you want to do with him? Would it be better for us to bring him inside and have a nice, long chat with him?'

But it was no use. He was in such a state of hysteria that any kind of humour or sarcasm was bound to be lost on him.

So I began puzzling over our dilemma. There was a corpse that we had to dispose of somehow. It had to be disposed of in such a way that it stayed neither inside the house, since this was too terrifying for Amin, nor outside the house, since this terrified him just as much. Hence, what was required was a place which was neither inside *nor* outside. And then it came to me – the roof!

'We'll carry him up to the roof,' I told him.

But then I began thinking about the ninety-five steps that led up to the roof and the heavy corpse that kept getting heavier as the night progressed. As I pictured the three of us alternately dragging and carrying it, stumbling under and over it, at the mercy of the cold, the whistling wind, the driving rain, our exhaustion and hunger, I realized what an impossible task it was. Fortunately, Amin reached the same conclusion and said so.

'So then,' I asked, 'what can we do to reconcile your feelings towards death on the one hand and your reverence for 'propriety' and tradition on the other?'

He replied instantly, as if inspired, saying: 'We'll put him in front of the garden gate where there isn't any bell.'

'But he'll beat on the door with both hands. Or, I mean, you'll *hear* him beating on the door.'

However, his mind was made up, and he replied: 'We'll put him inside the rubbish bin near the back door to the house. Then we'll close the lid tight.'

When we tried getting the servant up this time, he declared himself on strike. He said he was worn out and that if he absolutely *had* to exert some effort, then he'd prefer to exert it feeding the monkey in the garden. For now, though, he just wanted to be left in peace. Then, in a final declaration of headstrong resolve, he closed his eyes without even waiting for us to reply!

This time, I let Amin carry the upper torso while I pretended to be carrying the lower half. I was so exhausted, I'd started cheating a bit. I let him drag it along the floor until we reached the back door leading out of the kitchen. But no sooner had we opened the door than we were assaulted by a violent gust of wind. It was as if unseen powers beyond nature were delivering us a cryptic, wordless rebuke.

But – I said to myself – what we're dragging out of the house is nothing but a corpse. As for us, though, we're still alive and we're in circumstances that leave us no choice but to act in a way that seems cruel and heartless. The dressy robe he's wearing, the metals and the badges of honour harking back to some time in the past won't keep his body from rotting. In fact, that's exactly what his body is: a disintegrating, putrefying past. And it's this past that we have no choice but to bury.

I had to keep talking to myself this way as we put the body in the rubbish bin. The sheer physical aspect of the operation also proved more taxing than I'd expected. After all, what we were dealing with by this time wasn't so much a body as a marble statue. It took a superhuman effort to bend its limbs enough to get it to fit into the bin and more than once I thought of seeking the aid of a hammer. Meanwhile, bullets were raining down all around us and the longer it took us to complete the task, the more danger we exposed ourselves to. There are few things more odious than to be hungry, terrified, cold and sleepy and then, as if that weren't enough, to find oneself lumbered with a dead body to boot!

When we'd finally managed to deposit Amm Fu'ad's remains in their cylindrical, metal coffin, Amin startled me by slamming down the lid as if he were afraid his father would try to escape!

I didn't wash my hands before I went to sleep. Instead, I decided to save what little water remained for drinking. What I really needed to do was wash my memory – to purge it of the last vestiges of this horrific night. Yet it wasn't the dead body that had frightened me. Rather, it was myself. What had truly unsettled me – indeed, had struck terror in my heart – was the image I'd seen of my own soul in the mirror of events.

Prior to this, I would never have imagined that I had it in me to be so callous or confrontational. Of course, it's possible that anyone caught in a similar whirlwind of distressing events would have responded much as I had.

Shrill, violent blasts were going off outside. Yet, in spite of them, I found myself sinking steadily downward into slumber's abyss. It was the first time I'd ever been able to fall asleep with missiles exploding all around me. Yet it was an unrestful, troubled sleep, sullied as it was by an obscure ache somewhere deep in my gut (or was it in my spirit?)...

Nightmare 109

Responding to a plea for blood donors that he'd heard on the radio, Nadim went down to the hospital one morning to donate some of his blood. He was proud of the fact that his blood type was O positive, which meant that it could be given to anyone, no matter what the recipient's blood type happened to be. And within just minutes of making the donation, his blood was flowing in the veins of a wounded man named Salim.

But when Nadim came back home feeling weary and drained, what should he find on his way into the house but the dead body of his brother, who'd been missing for some time after being kidnapped.

Meanwhile, thanks to Nadim's gift of blood, Salim had begun to feel life stirring in him once again. Soon he'd recovered enough to vacate his bed to make room for another of the countless wounded that filled the hospital corridors. Before long, he'd left the hospital and was heading for home.

At around the same time, Nadim set out in search of someone belonging to the 'other' religion with the intention of killing him. With this in mind, he set up an independent checkpoint to serve his own ends rather than those of the cause.

Who should happen to come driving through the checkpoint but Salim himself. As soon as Nadim discovered that Salim belonged to the 'other' team's religion, he pulled the trigger and shot him dead.

Salim's bullet wound continued to bleed copiously as if it would never stop. As for Nadim, little did he know that the blood he had shed was his very own. Nor did he know that his boss, who hadn't paid him his salary for months, was a business partner of Salim's boss, who likewise hadn't paid Salim for months, or that at that very moment the two business partners were downing shots of whisky at the Monte Carlo Hotel and gambling away outrageous sums of money, which happened to be the salaries of hundreds of company workers who, like Nadim and Salim, also hadn't been paid in months.

Nightmare 110

Maron hadn't sold a thing all day. The wind was blowing savagely and the pouring rain had driven people off the streets. Seeing that he wasn't going to get any business that day, Maron decided to go home early. Though he couldn't tell just why, he suddenly had the oddest feeling that he didn't quite know the way home, or even which house was his. But he set off all the same. The first checkpoint he came to was manned by a fellow named Husnayn, who, when he heard Maron's name, killed him on the spot.[7] After he'd died, Maron got up again and continued on his way home.

At the second checkpoint, he was stopped by a man named Joseph.[8] When Joseph discovered that Maron hadn't joined Joseph's 'team', he killed him twice over.

Although by now he'd died three times, Maron got up and continued on his way. However, this time he didn't head for his house. Considering what he'd just been through, he was feeling extraordinarily energetic and that he now knew exactly how to get 'home'.

Nightmare 111

When Amin woke me up this time, he wasn't sobbing. And he wasn't calling out my name. Instead, he was shaking me violently by the arm.

Knowing Amin, I felt sure he must have exhausted all other possible means of rousing me before finally resorting in desperation to this sort of manhandling. I'd probably sunk to such depths of nightmarish slumber that I seemed like little more than a lifeless corpse, weighed down beneath stones of fatigue and helplessness. Perhaps he thought I really *was* a corpse. Perhaps he thought I'd died, which must have terrified him all the more.

'What's going on?' I asked groggily. 'Has your dad climbed out of the barrel?'

The sun hadn't come up yet and I didn't know whether I'd slept for two seconds or two hours. Amin had a lit candle in his hand and in its dim light I could see huge beads of sweat bleeding through the pores in his face. Would he have a heart attack too? I wondered. My God! The last thing I need tonight is another dead body in the house!

'Please,' said Amin, 'I'm scared. Would you mind if I slept in here with you?'

'Why don't you sleep in the servant's room?' I asked. 'Oh, I know – it wouldn't be "proper", right? OK, then. You can sleep wherever you please. But I beg you, don't wake me up again tonight! If you don't let me get some sleep, I don't know if I'll be able to handle the catastrophes that tomorrow sends our way.'

That was all he needed. Without further ado, he collapsed on to the couch, wrapped himself in a woollen cloak and blew out the candle.

As for me, though, I wasn't able to get back to sleep right away.

Then suddenly I got the giggles. For some reason the situation reminded me of the maudlin Arabic films that people flock to see. In a situation like ours, the hero and the heroine would be expected to fall in love, then exchange amorous attentions under the pretext of fear. The title of the film might be something like *A Woman and Three Men*. The men would, of course, be expected to fight over the woman, who in turn would spend all her time crooning in front of a shuttered window, or beseeching the Almighty to let her true beloved triumph over the evil machinations of his foes.

As for us, here we were... a woman, two men and a cadaver, with me playing all the parts except for that of the female. After all, who but I had been leading the 'cadaver transport operation', comforting the afflicted and encouraging the faint-hearted?

In the films that are so popular with the masses, the only reason a man might sneak into a woman's room would be to ravish her, or for the two of them to exchange impassioned tokens of their affection. The scene would inevitably lead to the shedding of tears and the rending of various articles of clothing.

Yet here we were in the 'theatre of life', where the man goes stealing into the woman's room because he's frightened. As for overpowering her with his passionate advances, he'd need at least six months of bedrest before he could even contemplate such a feat! True, some tears had flowed, but they'd been his, not hers...

What a frightful injustice is done to women by cheap so-called 'art'! And even more tragic is the fact that women are far and away the most dedicated fans of these travesties, ensuring their continued success by coming in droves to see them, then weeping into their hankies from beginning to end. When will women ever open their eyes to who they really are?

And when will the makers of such films cease to prostitute life, presenting distorted images of its realities which serve only to keep their coffers full and the masses pacified?

'Can you hear him?' Amin whispered. 'He's pounding on the inside of the lid.'

'It's just the wind,' I replied reproachfully.

'It's the body...'

'It's the wind...'

Nightmare 112

My brother Shadi sat in the corner of his prison cell. He hadn't budged since the time he arrived. He hadn't engaged anyone in conversation. He hadn't answered anyone's questions. Consequently, everyone had mistakenly concluded that he was a deaf mute.

He felt a loathing and disgust that knew no bounds. It was incomprehensible to him that anyone could be stuck behind bars without being guilty of a crime and he couldn't think of any reason for him to have been thrown into such a vile, filthy place. He didn't understand how the other prisoners could put up with the miserable rations they were served, or how at times they could joke among themselves and form friendships, then at other times argue and fight even to the point of coming to blows. Fighting was utterly abhorrent to him, as was anything that bore the remotest connection to violence. At night, some would seek each other out for sexual gratification, apparently oblivious to the rotten stench that seemed to grow constantly worse.

He loathed where he was and had begun dreaming of another country, another 'homeland'. Feeling as limp as a plant that's been savagely uprooted, he sat in his accustomed spot, leaning against the fetid, moss-covered wall. He imagined himself emigrating to Australia, or the North Pole, or Mars, or to some other planet where violence was still unknown. If it hadn't been for this dream, he would have died of despair.

Then, as usual, someone came up and cuffed him. He didn't care enough to return the blow. In fact, he didn't even care enough to complain.

'I swear, this guy's got something wrong with his brain,' said the prisoner who had hit him. 'What he needs is a shrink, not a jail sentence!'

And of course, judged by the standards of a city that had gone out of its senses, the rejection of violence really *was* a 'defect'!

When the other inmates made an escape attempt, Shadi paid no attention. And even when the attempt was successful, he remained unfazed. They broke down the prison wall and set the place on fire, but he just sat there immobilized until he was about to be asphyxiated by the smoke. Even then, all he did was move over from one cell to another. Finally the guard came and drove him out, saying: 'Come on, get out of here, you bum! If you don't, they'll come and rebuild the jail and it'll be all your fault. And if they do that, they'll bring me back to keep guard over you! So beat it, harebrain!'

Shadi got up heavily and left the jail, moving so slowly it was as if he'd forgotten how to walk. After all, he'd grown accustomed to not moving from one spot except to 'take care of nature' in the far corner of the cell (which was jokingly referred to as 'Honeysuckle').

Shots were fired at the fleeing prisoners. But while everyone else was running for his life, Shadi just kept dragging his feet, as if the whole thing were nothing more than an irritating inconvenience. He felt the need to say goodbye to his sister, or to somebody at least. At the same time, he felt pained and repulsed by what was commonly referred to as his 'homeland'. His sole aspiration in life was to set out for the horizon, never to return. His one and only desire was to flee far, far away, to a new 'homeland', to a tranquil, kind, humane land made for peaceable citizens like him — for people who had no stomach for violence, chaos and loud noises, but instead craved an ordinary, routine existence complete with children and cooking odours wafting from the necks of plump, contented wives.

It so happened that as the prisoners fled, there was a ship approaching a nearby harbour. It was only when Shadi looked up and saw the ship that he started to feel life surging through his limbs again. He decided straight away to sneak on board and head off to some other part of the world. After all, anywhere else, as far as he was concerned, was preferable to this miserable 'homeland' of his. He didn't want to struggle. He didn't want to fight and kill. He didn't care about the battle between 'truth' and 'falsehood'. All he cared about was to be able to live and die in peace.

What mattered to him was for there to be somewhere in the world where he could let down his guard, even if that place happened to be Israel! He'd been hearing a lot lately about Israel's 'kind' treatment of the residents of Lebanese villages along the Lebanese–Israeli border.

Like a frightened mouse in a field strewn with mines, all he cared about now was his own personal safety...

As he crouched hidden behind a barrel on the ship's crowded deck, he kept repeating to himself over and over, 'I'll run away — as far away as I can get!'

Then he heard the droning of the ship's horns and the sounds of frantic footsteps and frightened whispers sweeping up and down the deck. Before long, several warships had approached and he knew then that the liner was being commandeered by Israeli forces.

He remembered his sister once saying to him: 'You'll never be able to live and die in peace as long as there's injustice in the world. Any human being who's been wronged, in any corner of the globe, is you yourself! So actually you owe it to yourself to combat injustice. Any attempt at solitary escape is doomed to fail.'

At the time, he hadn't believed her. His would-be philosopher sister, up to her ears in the translation of 'revolutionary' books, irritated him and frankly made him downright nervous. He wanted to get as far away as he possibly could from her and everything else.

So then, he thought, we'll see if it's really impossible for anyone to pull off a 'solitary escape'. God, his sister was so ridiculous! As for him, though, he wasn't going to be afraid of Israel any more. He'd been told that people living in villages in south Lebanon were being treated well by the Israelis, who'd even been buying their crops. At least, that was what one of the other inmates had reported to him. So he intended to take him at his word and to live in peace, even if it meant taking up residence in Israel. He'd show that revolutionary, sophistic sister of his that a single person *can* get away from it all if he sets his mind to it and...

Just then he thought he felt his head bump up against something. Someone had discovered his hiding place and had hit him with the butt of a revolver.

When he came to again, he heard an Israeli investigator saying in broken Arabic: 'He's one of the terrorists we've been looking for. Take him away and get rid of him. There'll be no need for a trial or for anyone to know about it. After all, he's not listed among the passengers, so he won't be missed...'

Nightmare 113

By the time the radio announcer reached the station, he was in a pitiful state...

On his way he'd had to pass as usual through the Sanaai district, where he'd been shot at by a sniper who missed his head but managed to shatter the front windscreen of his car. Add to this the bomb that had gone off just half a minute's distance behind him on Shaykh Bishara Khouri Street and the heavy shelling that had gone on all night around his house, which was located midway between the Shiyah and Ayn Al-Rummaneh districts.

He'd had to go through this sort of miserable ordeal in one form or another every morning for months on end.

Once he reached his workplace, he composed himself in preparation to read the morning news broadcast. He was well aware that hundreds of thousands of Beirut residents who'd been kept awake all night by the constant heavy fighting in their neighbourhoods would be gathered around their radios to hear what he had to say. They'd base their comings and goings on the information he gave them concerning road conditions – which roads could be travelled safely and which ones had become snares where death lay in wait for unsuspecting passers-by.

As happened every morning, he was taken aback by the report he'd been given to read. According to the report, 'calm' had prevailed throughout the capital city the night before and all the streets were described as 'safe and passable'. In fact, the report even contained an invitation to merchants to go downtown and carry on with their businesses.

He began to read. He knew that if he refused, his sole means of livelihood would be cut off and that his head would soon follow. Not long after that, his widow's water and electricity would be cut off as well, and his children would be consigned to lives of despair. So he kept on reading...

Meanwhile, there passed before his eyes image after image of people coming out of their houses based on his instructions and of those who'd been slain in the streets for no other 'crime' than that they had believed what he told them. He continued to read...

But as he did so, he could feel that same unnameable illness in his throat growing worse than ever. He remembered how the first day he was asked to read such a report, he got into an argument with his supervisor. In fact, he'd simply refused to read it. However, the station head had justified it to him by saying that reports like these were necessary to keep up people's spirits. But what about the spirit itself? What sense did to make to destroy people's very lives under the pretext of preserving their morale?

He argued with his boss the next day as well and didn't read the report. On the third day, though, he'd begun to feel the pinch from having his pay docked, so he read it. From that day on, he'd begun to notice the symptoms of a peculiar ailment in the region of his throat. He began detecting changes in his voice, until finally it started sounding remarkably similar to the bleating of a lamb. It was as if some damage had been done to his vocal cords or the muscles in his neck, and with every passing day his voice seemed to become less like that of a human and more like that of a sheep.

Not a day passed without the inexplicable malady growing still more severe. Finally he took himself to the doctor, who spent a long time poking around in his throat with a probe, then examining it under various sorts of lighting and multicoloured rays – white rays, red rays and blue rays. When he'd finished, the doctor told him that his throat was fine. However, he said that the nerves in his head might need to be examined, and he advised him to take a vacation.

A vacation! As if he were rich! How were working-class people like him supposed to take a vacation! Would his children's stomachs agree to take a vacation from being hungry?

So he went back to work and he read the report just as it was. But that same day, he started to observe new symptoms. Besides the disturbing changes in his voice, for example, he noticed that the hair on his face and body was growing thicker than usual. And when he ran his hand over his head, he discovered that two small protrusions like a sheep's horns were sprouting under his hair.

He kept these things a secret from everyone, including his wife. However, he kept asking her whether she'd noticed any change in his voice.

'Nothing about you has changed at all,' she replied. 'Your nerves are shot, that's all.'

He kept on reading the report.

The only part that remained now was the line in which he assured his listeners that all the roads were safe and passable.

He felt as if he were some bloodthirsty murderer setting death traps in the streets for innocent victims. But no – he wasn't that exactly. He might be the instrument of the crime, but he was no more guilty than the revolver used to commit a murder. After all, it's the murderer who's imprisoned, not the revolver. Rather, he felt like some sort of rare songbird that's been placed by the hunter inside a trap to lure other birds to their death.

He stopped reading for a moment. He felt he couldn't go on. But then he remembered the hunger that awaited him, and the reprisals, and the homelessness. So he read some more...

Then, all of a sudden, he was astonished to hear himself bleating: 'Baaa! Baaa!'

Before the sound engineer managed to regain his presence of mind and cut the broadcast, thousands of listeners heard their favourite radio announcer go from a description of road conditions to a plaintive: 'Baaa! Baaa!'

And the rest of the sheep understood.

Nightmare 114

The shop quaked from the force of the surrounding blasts.

Whispering into the darkness, she said: 'There's something strange going on around here – not an earthquake, perhaps, but something just as scary and no less of a disaster.'

'You're right,' he said, taking her into his arms.

'I've been telling you so for months now,' she said, still in a whisper, 'but you wouldn't believe me. Instead you kept trying to find simple, mundane explanations for all the confusing, awful things that have been happening.'

'You were right all along,' he confessed.

'I'm scared,' she said. 'In fact, I'm terrified.'

'So am I.'

'I feel like running away.'

'So do I.'

'But, of course, as long as the shop door is locked, we don't have that option.'

'The proprietor hasn't come by for a long time,' he mused. 'Neither have the sales assistants. I can't quite figure it out.'

The wind was whistling up and down a lightless Hamra Street, while a fierce downpour pummelled the night, beating mercilessly against the display window through the metal grating that had been lowered over the front of the shop. There were no cars passing by. No aeroplanes flying overhead. No customers. No beggars. There wasn't a living soul in the street

– not even a cat. The only creatures that dared to blaze a trail through the silence and darkness were armoured police cars, which would trundle past, leaving behind them a street devoid of everything but the echoes of gunfire and explosives.

Clad in silk bikinis with leopard-skin designs, they were both still dressed in summerwear even as winter's icy hand tapped at the city's doors.

She whispered: 'When the tree outside took off its leaves but the shop attendant didn't change me out of this swimsuit, I knew something mysterious was going on in this town.'

He replied: 'I just thought we were being neglected because the proprietor was too busy flirting with the shop attendant who usually changes our clothes. It never occurred to me that it might be anything more serious than that.'

'Oh, I knew it was,' she said. 'When I used to sneak off on my nightly expeditions, I found out all sorts of things that no one else knows about.'

They drew their plastic bodies up next to each other in a futile attempt to get warm. However, the cold wasn't the only thing bothering them.

'The cold I can stand,' she murmured, 'but what really kills me is being deprived of people's admiring glances. I need people to stand outside and gaze at me, and to hear the ladies gasping over the expensive clothes draped over this phenomenal body of mine. They used to come in and buy things under the illusion that they'd look as good on their flabby bodies as they do on my trim physique, and that by paying the price displayed on my bosom, they'd look just like me. I miss standing under the display-window spotlight, knowing that there isn't a single passer-by who can keep his eyes off me.'

'I miss all that too,' he said. 'When they turned off all the lights, I had a feeling something bad was in the offing. But I just figured the owner had taken off with his salesgirl sweetheart. Little did I know what sorts of bewildering changes the future held in store for us!'

A soft dawn light had begun stealing over the horizon. And as she did every morning, the mannequin slipped out of her companion's arms and resumed her motionless stance a few steps away.

She'd been standing in the very same position for two years now. During that time she'd watched the passing of two winters, two springs, two summers and two autumns. Although she didn't know the names of the days or the months, she'd learned to recognize the changes in the seasons by observing the periodic transformations that would take place in the tree that grew up out of the pavement in front of the display window. She'd also learned to pay attention to what clothes were being worn by passers-by and by the people who frequented the big coffee-shop on the street corner opposite her window, as well as the fashions in which she was dressed by the shop attendants. (When they'd pin the price tags on, it would sting a bit, but she never complained.) Mink coats meant it was winter. Bikinis meant summer was approaching. And woollen dresses signalled autumn's arrival. Sometimes the shop attendant would be in a bad mood, in which case she might end up pulling one of her hands off as she tried to get her arm through a sleeve. But like most mannequins, she would have endured nearly anything for the chance to appear in public decked out in some sort of dazzling apparel.

She was particularly happy with her location right in the centre of the fashionable Hamra shopping district, where thousands of admirers would pass by daily and linger unhurriedly in front of her window. In fact, she was probably more content than the young women she saw sitting in the coffee-shop across the street. The 'coffee-shop girls' were doing nearly the same kind of 'work' that she was. In her case, though, she was just doing her job as a shop-window mannequin, which meant all she had to do was stand there stiff and motionless, showing off her charms day and night. But as for the coffee-shop girls, they were obliged to sit around for long hours pretending to be drinking coffee and smoking cigarettes. Another advantage she had over them was that the price tag for the dress she was wearing was tacked right on to her chest, whereas her less fortunate sisters had to whisper their prices into their customers' ears. She wondered why they didn't make life easier for themselves by doing as she did. In other words, why couldn't each of them just hang a price tag directly on her body?

She'd grown accustomed to spending her days basking in people's admiring gazes, all the while taking in what was happening on Hamra Street with her glassy, absent-looking eyes. Her attention was especially drawn to the nearby coffee shop and to its spacious glass front that reminded her of own display window.

After she'd slipped out of her companion's embrace to resume her daytime pose, he asked: 'Why did you run away?'

'The sun's coming up,' she said.

'But nobody will be coming around to see us. No one's passed by our window for days now – except for ambulances with their sirens screeching.'

She didn't reply. She was, after all, a conservative, traditional girl who insisted on conducting herself with proper decorum.

What the city's human residents didn't know was that once darkness fell, the majority of its mannequins and statues would spring to life. In fact, when the human population departed each night for the land of Nod, the city's 'other' residents would regularly take over the entire metropolis. Then with the first touch of dawn, each one would resume his post in this or that display window or on top of a glass pedestal before people had come back from the land of slumber to retake the city.

The mannequin's hair was made of glossy, black silk and her long lashes framed huge green eyes of glass. Keeping to her corner of the display window, she stood poised with one hand raised and the other lowered to her side, while her companion stood nearby with his hands on his waist.

'Get back to your usual spot!' she said to him reproachfully. 'The shop owner could come back when we're least expecting him!'

But no one came.

The day began with an air of gloom and before long processions of weary women and men whose faces were the very picture of grief came marching past them on the pavement outside. She revived a bit at the sight of them, since it was neither the cold nor the darkness that terrified her, but rather the prospect of being forever deprived of people's looks of approval and admiration. But no one even gave her a passing glance. They seemed to be in quite a hurry, as if they'd just left the funeral of an infamous outlaw. They kept looking around apprehensively and from time to time they gazed upward as if they were fearful of something lurking on the balconies or behind the windowpanes.

'What's got into people around here?' he asked.

'Don't forget our traditions!' she scolded him. 'Not a word during the day! Your comments can wait till after sunset.'

'Nobody's going to hear us,' he objected, speaking even more loudly than before. 'Can't you hear the explosions going off all around us?'

She didn't reply.

The first time she'd heard the blasts, she thought that maybe people were just setting off fireworks. At the same time, though, she'd sensed from the very beginning that something was amiss. She'd realized it from the time when beggars began to appear in increasing numbers in front of her display window, from the time she'd seen some men and women standing on the pavement outside and glaring furiously at her and her companion. After reading the price tags hanging from their chests, they shook their fists menacingly, then ran off, their feet unshod and their faces careworn and livid.

Indeed! Not everyone was happy to see her. Even the sales attendants would sigh longingly every now and then as they were dressing her up in her new, outrageously expensive attire. She'd also noticed that some of their clothes were tattered and torn.

Even so, there were some ladies who were still overjoyed to see her. In fact, there was one customer who used to make special trips from some other Arab country just to buy up whatever they happened to be displaying on her body. But ladies of her ilk had begun coming less and less frequently of late.

From where she stood in the display window, she could see that something had begun to go awry and that what was happening in the coffee shop had taken on a new, different rhythm. Over time she'd learned to read people's lips and most of the conversations in the coffee shop lately revolved around travel to London or Paris, how to enrol one's children in schools there, laws governing emigration to Australia, Canada and Venezuela, etc. There was also talk about the two rounds of fighting that had taken place thus far, and about people who'd met their deaths in places other than ski resorts or dance floors!

One night in particular stood out vividly in her memory.

The owner of the shop had been anticipating the arrival of

a certain big client who always made purchases amounting to hundreds of thousands of Lebanese pounds. Consequently, the owner considered him worth waiting for till the small hours of the morning if need be! As it turned out, the customer was delayed, so he called the shop saying that he was in the middle of an important meeting. However, he promised to pass by immediately afterwards to buy gifts for his family, since he'd be leaving the country early the next morning.

At least, that was what she'd heard the owner tell his wife over the phone, adding that this would be a rare opportunity to recoup the losses he'd suffered from three months of slow business.

When the client continued to be delayed, the merchant laid his head down on the counter and fell fast asleep. The lights in the shop were off, since they'd stopped leaving them on all night several weeks earlier. She didn't know the reason for the change, but in any case she decided to take advantage of the opportunity to sneak out and see what was happening in the streets. True, she was a conservative mannequin, but after all, who can resist the temptation to go spying out the truth, even if he happens not to be Prometheus but a mere department store mannequin?

So, after throwing on a simple dress, she left her place in the window and slipped outside. Actually, this wasn't the first time she'd gone out to roam through the city or sit in the front windows of coffee shops the way most young women did. But thanks to the striking resemblance she bore to most of the coffee-shop girls on Hamra Street, no one noticed that she was just a mannequin. Besides which, it would never even occur to most people that a mannequin might leave her post, whether in the daytime or at any other hour. Consequently, the sales attendants never bothered to check to see if she was keeping regular hours the way they always did to each other, with each one making sure to 'tell' on any of the others if she got to work late or was remiss in her duties. So, being a mere mannequin whom no one would ever expect to budge from her place, she was in a perfect position to disappear without anyone even noticing.

Yes, indeed, she remembered it well.

She'd heard the shop owner reminding one of the sales attendants to change her out of her bikini into an autumn dress. From this she'd gathered that summer must be drawing to a close. She could also tell from the cool sting in the air that struck her cheeks as she left her place under the warm spotlights in the display window and ventured out into the relative darkness of the street.

From the moment she came out, she sensed that something about Hamra Street had changed. For one thing, the lights in most of the shop windows were out. But despite the darkness, she noticed that her fellow mannequins were weeping tears of frustration and grief. They were pining away for the looks of admiration which had once been their daily fare. Pained by what she was seeing, she wondered to herself whether mannequins weren't really just 'society ladies' in disguise. After all, she couldn't see much difference between herself and most of the women in Beirut. The only thing that distinguished her from them was the fact that, unlike her, 'real' women would get pregnant and have babies now and then. In every other respect, though, they seemed no different at all. All she was, then, was a society lady who never had children. But no – another difference was that she was a 'working girl'. She had to be on her feet night and day showing off this garment or that, whereas society ladies lounged around in bed most of the time. At least, that was what she heard the shop attendants whispering to each other when they gossiped about the customers.

She took a seat near the front window of a coffee shop and began eavesdropping on the conversations going on around her. People were talking about going on trips, about emigration and about fleeing the danger of stray bullets (and non-stray ones). They talked about the schools that wouldn't be open during the coming year, about the fighting, and about the wounded and dying.

Meanwhile, the coffee shop clientele were being beleaguered by flower vendors trying to sell them garlands of jasmine blossoms. No one seemed interested in buying one, not even for his sweetheart. Instead, all they did was scold the flower vendors and try to drive them off. As for the poverty-stricken vendors, it appeared that they weren't so much selling anything as trying to intimidate passers-by. A necklace of jasmine flowers had been transmuted into a scream of rage, a reminder of poverty's curse. Each blossom looked crimson red to her, as if it had been dipped in the blood of some unsung vendor's kinsman.

When the waiter came by, she ordered a cup of coffee. She knew, of course, that she wouldn't drink it, since display-window girls get all the sustenance they need from being looked at and admired. When the waiter brought the coffee, the table was wobbling, as was the chair. The waiter apologized, explaining that one of the table legs was a bit shorter than the others, and tried to rectify the situation by stuffing an empty cigarette packet underneath the short leg. But even after he'd steadied it, it seemed shaky to her. In fact, it wasn't only the table or even the entire coffee shop that seemed unsteady. The whole street looked as if it were swaying from side to side without anyone taking any notice or rushing to brace it against a boulder or some such thing. Virtually everything was rocking to and fro. The ground didn't seem completely firm either. She felt that it was beginning to collapse from beneath and that at any moment everything in sight might plunge into a bottomless abyss. She noticed that most of the women in the street were dressed in black and that the prevailing aroma on Hamra Street of late had been that of burning refuse. An ashen, pungent-smelling cloud cast a gloomy pall over everything in sight, as if the street itself were heaving visible sighs of distress. Come to think of it, it had been several weeks since she'd seen a garbage truck pass in front of her window.

Just then, three women garbed in black passed by. It reminded her of the fact that most of the women's clothing they'd sold at the store lately had been black. It was as if dressing in mourning was the latest summer fad.

As she sat pondering this peculiar phenomenon, a young man came up to her and invited her to spend the evening with him.

'I can't,' she replied.

As if he hadn't noticed that she'd turned him down, he pulled up a chair and took a seat at her table.

Then, in a tone the likes of which she'd never heard used by any of the fellows who'd flirted with her on her previous nocturnal excursions, he said: 'Listen. The city is on fire and we could die at any moment. So there's no need for long introductions. You're pretty and I want you to share my bed with me tonight. So, what's your price?'

She was so stunned, she didn't even reply. She wouldn't have minded accompanying him to his bed. But once he discovered that she was nothing but a display-window girl rather than a real female, he'd probably set a match to her! True – there wasn't much difference between the girls that frequented the Hamra district and the mannequins that filled its display windows. That was something she became more convinced of with every passing day. However, she wanted to get back to the shop as fast as she could, before the owner left and noticed that she wasn't in the window.

He went on, saying: 'You're a knock-out. A real doll. So your prices have got to be sky-high. But you know as well as anybody else what kind of shape the city's been in lately. The company I work for hasn't paid me for more than two months now. But I'll do my best to satisfy you.'

She didn't reply.

He got up, muttering execrations.

'You slut!' he fumed. 'The city's burning to the ground, and you want to sit here and bargain as if you think you're the hottest thing since the Queen of Sheba!'

Everybody else was on edge too. At the next table, a lady was berating the waiter because he'd forgotten to put the olive in her dry Martini.

The waiter shot back in a surly tone that she'd never heard him use before.

'Listen,' he growled, 'two of our other waiters have been kidnapped. So if you're planning on ordering dinner, you'd better do it now, since we'll be closing at ten o'clock sharp.'

A man came into the coffee shop and started making the rounds of all the tables, asking for donations to the Blind Society. Following this, the adjoining pavement café was besieged by hordes of young beggars, and before long the beggars, the donation collectors and the vendors of jasmine, Chiclets and lottery tickets had outnumbered the customers by far.

As she sat there observing these goings-on, she heard someone at a nearby table saying: 'I'll bet you this is the last jasmine season Hamra Street will ever see. Beirut's *dolce vita* days are over. Its golden veneer is wearing thin and it won't be long before it shows its true colours.'

As the prophet of doom spoke, the dissatisfied customer

started pestering the waiter again to bring her an olive to float in her dry Martini.

Frightened, she got up and left the coffee shop.

As she watched people hurrying down the pavements, they looked as if they were floating through the air like so many balloons... She also noticed for the first time that the trees lining the street on either side were really nothing but fake plants placed there for decoration, and she saw men climbing up and attaching yellow, autumnal-looking leaves to their branches. She heard a woman laugh, but the sound of the laughter made her think of a faded, artificial rose pinned to a tattered, ageing garment. She ran off in a hurry, anxious to get back to her spot in the display window. When she arrived, the shop owner was still asleep, and the VIP customer still hadn't shown up.

The following day, the shop owner didn't show up at all. Then a long time passed before he finally appeared one day in a big truck accompanied by a number of other men. As she looked on in amazement, they emptied the shop of most of its contents and hurriedly loaded things on to the truck. Before she knew it, they'd rushed off without even giving a second thought to her or her companion. From that day on, not a soul had come to the shop. No one had even gazed at her through the window. She'd been forgotten by the whole world. Even the few passers-by who did appear didn't so much as give her a nod of recognition. Everyone was in a constant rush, exchanging looks of fear and suspicion. But no one looked her way at all...

Then there came the day when even the streetlights were turned off. It was then that she began hearing the sounds of shots and horrific explosions. But there was nothing she and her companion could do but wait.

And now it was raining, which meant a further decrease in

the number of passers-by. Even the trucks whose visits had given her some measure of comfort no longer came around to haul off the contents of the neighbouring shops. Talk about rotten luck! Why couldn't she have been a display-window girl in a place like London or Paris – or any place, for that matter, where the lights didn't all get turned off, and where the stream of shoppers roaming the pavements didn't dry up at the drop of a hat?

Meanwhile, it kept raining.

And that, of course, meant the entire day would go by without her getting even a morsel of admiration. If things kept up this way, sooner or later she'd wither up and die of starvation, so hungry was she to be wrapped in the embrace of someone's eyes.

'I hear the roar of a truck,' whispered her companion.

Hope's flame was rekindled in her heart, if only for a few moments. Might the shop owner be coming back at last? Having been quite a contented mannequin, she still hoped things would go back to the way they'd been before.

The truck which they'd heard approaching in the distance stopped in front of the shop. However, the shop owner was nowhere to be seen. Instead, there appeared a group of armed men who, after getting out of the truck, inserted something into the lock in the door, lit it, then moved away in a hurry. She was startled by their movements. Then she heard a tremendous blast and for a few minutes there was so much dust flying through the air she couldn't see a thing. Meanwhile, she'd been flung by the force of the explosion to she knew not where.

At last she opened her glassy eyes, only to find her companion being consumed by tongues of fire. She saw the men rush inside the shop, then flee through clouds of smoke carrying the iron safe in which the shop's money was kept.

And then they disappeared. The whole thing had taken place in a matter of moments, with the speed of lightning.

Then just as rapidly she got up, rushed out of the shop, and went racing down the street. She stopped at the first coffee shop she came to. It was closed, so she kept on running. The streets were utterly deserted except for bundles of trees that had been stacked on either side. Soon they'd be taken away and 'transplanted' elsewhere. As she paused to look at them, she heard a voice saying: 'This play has run long enough here. It's time to move the stage set so we can put on the same performance in some other city.'

She looked around for the person who'd been speaking, but she couldn't pick him out of the crowd. She wanted to ask him the name of the city where they were planning to take their play so that she could join them there. She imagined for a moment that it was the chairs in the abandoned coffee shops that had been speaking. Or might it have been one of the café proprietors?

Next she passed by the bakery, where at last she came upon real, live human beings waiting in line for bread. They were all dressed in black garments and dark sunglasses and had long white canes in their hands. Only when she saw the canes did she realize that she'd come upon a procession of the blind.

Apart from the blind people, she hadn't laid eyes on a soul. However, everything around her had an air of gloom about it. Everything seemed different from the way it had been, as if somehow or other death had reached out and touched her with its powerful sceptre.

It seemed that the street's only regular 'visitor' any more was the ubiquitous garbage. It loomed up in huge mounds and, despite the recent rains, its stench pervaded the atmosphere. As for the flies, each of which had become gargantuan, they'd now taken over the streets and swarmed in huge masses around the mountains of refuse. The outer walls of most of the buildings bore scars left by bullets and shells, and were covered with posters showing pictures of the slain who were now remembered as martyrs. Posters such as these had taken the place of flyers announcing forthcoming dance parties and wrestling matches and titillating photos of the 'stars' of Beirut's nightlife. She gazed pensively at the martyrs' youthful faces, which looked just like pictures one might see in a university yearbook.

When at last she came upon a lone coffee shop that was still welcoming customers, she quickly went in and sat down. But once she'd taken a seat, she discovered to her dismay that she was surrounded on all sides by creatures with men's bodies and rats' heads. They chattered nonstop, their long, scrawny necks swaying back and forth inside their neckties and white starched collars.

One of them screeched: 'So this is the price we pay for letting the Palestinians into the land of "the descendants of the giants"!'

Then along came the waiter, who was mere skin and bones – or, to be more exact, an outright skeleton. Pointing over at a man whose body was a gargantuan corpse with the head of a long-whiskered rat, he said to her: 'The bey is willing to pay one pound.'

She was nonplussed. Apparently, she'd been taken for some sort of foreign hooker. But no one had ever offered her less than several hundred pounds for her services.

Then the waiter went on, saying: 'As you're probably aware, a head of cabbage costs six pounds these days, while a man's head goes for a half a pound – that is, the price of a bullet! So, as you can see, the bey's offer is really quite reasonable and you'd be well advised to accept!'

With that, she decided to let it be known to all that she was *not* a coffee shop girl, but rather a display-window girl. So she stood up, climbed on top of the table and positioned herself the way she did while she was on duty. She raised her right hand with her fingers spread and let the other hand fall to her side, the way a dancer does before she begins her performance. And thus she stood, without moving a muscle.

The other customers found her such a hilarious sight, they all burst out laughing.

'The whores in this city have lost their marbles! With all the young men getting killed off, their business must be going to pot. Who knows? One of these days, groups of ten women might have to marry one man – that is, if even one is still alive at the end of all this madness!'

'Listen,' another replied, 'the fact is, we're all in the same boat. No income. No cash. They spend their nights alone and we spend them with our wives!'

She left the coffee shop. When she got outside, she noticed deep grooves in the asphalt where army tanks had passed. Then, before she knew what was happening, she was grabbed by several armed men. She'd heard about kidnappings from conversations she'd overheard in her shop and in the coffee shops. And now here it was happening to her! How exciting! she thought, though she wondered how they'd known just from looking at her that she was a display-window girl.

One of them said: 'This mannequin would make a good decoy for catching snipers. We'll make her into a battlefield scarecrow that can dupe the 'fire birds'. Come on now – let's try out this novel idea.'

By this time, she didn't have a clue as to what was going on.

In the midst of gunfire that was growing steadily louder, they drove her to a place she'd never seen before. When they stopped the car, the ground was shaking as if they were in the middle of an earthquake. But she was in too much of a daze even to feel afraid. She didn't know exactly what they were going to do with her. But they did...

First they dressed her up like a soldier, complete with an army jacket. Then they nailed her feet to a wooden platform on wheels which had a long rope attached to it. One of the men pushed her out from behind a barricade into the street, which was devoid of anything but wreckage and debris.

'This dummy will save a lot of lives,' he said as he gave her a final shove. 'This way, we'll be able to pinpoint just exactly where that damned sniper is hiding himself. Then we'll do him in!'

Hardly had the platform carried her to the middle of the street before someone fired a shot that struck her right in the head. She didn't feel any pain and of course she didn't bleed. But she heard someone shooting from behind the barricade in the direction of the person who had fired at her. Then she saw a man tumble off a high roof and she could hear voices coming from behind the barricade saying: 'We got him, the bastard! It's about time, after all the innocent folks he's done in.'

At that moment she felt a kind of joy she'd never known before. She felt that she'd accomplished something, something different from her work in the display window, and it gave her a sense of inner peace. Even when she discovered that she'd caught fire, she didn't grieve over what had become of her once-spectacular body. Instead, she realized that inside her there was something precious that she'd never been aware of throughout her entire career as a display-window girl. And it was something that couldn't go up in flames...

Nightmare 115

Even as the prison was going up in flames, Shadi wasn't afraid.

In fact, to his amazement and consternation, he felt a kind of euphoric exhilaration. And when he was passed by a man whose body was literally being consumed by tongues of fire, he experienced a frightfully intense 'high' like the physical rush one gets at the moment of orgasm. He felt the same thing when he saw some of his fellow inmates being trampled underfoot by their fleeing companions. In fact, he nearly stopped in his tracks so as to be able to watch them perish. It was as if he wanted to maximize the pleasure of seeing them as they teetered on the brink of death.

He didn't know what had come over him...

Ever since he'd been slapped behind bars in what seemed like an act of tyrannical aggression, he'd felt loathing and revulsion towards everything around him and he was possessed by a desire to destroy anything he could get his hands on. A fellow inmate whom he'd kept close company with ever since entering prison was a bodyguard for a certain bey and Shadi had actually gone so far as to agree to work with him and his gang once they were both released. According to his new friend, the bey was only too happy to have 'cultured' types join his retinue.

He *really* didn't know what had got into him. He felt as if anything he touched would go up in flames, anything he threw would turn into a hand-grenade. He was 'Midas of Lebanon'! The grass was sure to die wherever his feet trod, the women he touched would turn to mounds of ashes and singing children would fall silent whenever he came along. Even the stray cats and dogs that roamed the streets seemed to avoid coming too close to him, as if he were some sort of horrifying apparition.

At one point he'd decided that maybe it was all in his head. Perhaps if he just had a woman in his life, her presence would help to quell the storms of madness that beset him on all sides.

Perhaps it would dissipate the air of bitterness and violence which he seemed to exude wherever he turned.

Then he remembered his sister. He decided to write her a letter and deliver it by throwing it into her bedroom in their flat across from the Holiday Inn.

He knew she could be exceedingly 'stupid' whenever she loved someone. He also knew that she was quite emotional, which meant, of course, that she was 'stupid' most of the time. That, in fact, was what he loved most about her. It was also what he felt he most needed in his own life.

So he wrote the letter, crumpled it up into a tight ball, then flung it into her bedroom one night.

But to his untold dismay, it exploded as if it were a handgrenade, sending his sister's dismembered remains flying out through the windows and into the inky, nocturnal void.

He stood gaping at his hands in horror. Everything he touched turned to ruins. He was, indeed, the 'Midas of Lebanon' – wretched and disconsolate!!

Nightmare 116

All at once I was roused from my horrific nightmares. But considering that my room had just been invaded by a missile, the blast I'd heard wasn't nearly as dreadful as I might have expected. I had a suspicion that it wasn't the missile itself that had wakened me, but rather some sort of cryptic sixth sense (one might call it 'the sense of danger', I suppose).

One of the bedroom windows – or rather, its ageing wooden shutter – had a gaping hole in it. The window was located between the bed where I'd been sleeping and the sofa where Amin lay collapsed in a heap. At first, the room was filled with thick, blinding clouds of dust. And when at last the air cleared enough for us to be able to see again, what should appear before our eyes but... a missile!

Although the missile had managed to force its way into the room, it hadn't exploded. Instead, it had settled 'peacefully' on top of a velvet-upholstered armchair. When it had first stormed in, we heard the sound of wood splintering and scattering in all directions. I didn't scream and neither did Amin. Instead, we just jumped up and stood staring wide-eyed and bewildered into the face of death, which had just paid us a visit encased inside a metal cylinder. It was approximately a metre long and dark green. How ironic that death should come decked out in the same hue as the trees – those peaceable, eloquent symbols of life and growth!

We bolted out of the room as fast as our legs would carry us and headed for the furthest corner of the flat. As for the thought of fleeing the house altogether, it was out of the question. After all, trigger-happy snipers lying in wait not far away continued to hold us captive inside the building, which had now been turned into a veritable deathtrap. Once we'd made it to the other end of the flat, we waited for the blast. But nothing happened. We kept on waiting for quite a long time, until at last Amin called out to his servant. There was no reply. So on we waited. I can't say I felt afraid exactly. At such moments the body is possessed not so much by fear as by an intense, almost passionate sense of anticipation and readiness.

The minutes crept slowly by and the missile continued not to explode. I looked at my watch, only to find that it no longer had either hands or numbers. I'd lost track of the hours, the days and even the months. The phone was out of commission, the batteries in the radio were dying a slow death and, one by one, all bridges linking me to the outside world were collapsing.

So here I was: famished, exhausted and catapulted

somewhere outside time and space. There was an unexploded missile just metres away from me and a cadaver in a rubbish bin in the garden outside. I had a brother languishing in prison, a father in the grave and agonizing memories of experiences I'd shared with someone who'd been closer to me than my own heartbeat. And to top it all, I had friends who, for all I knew, might be suffering torture and death at that very moment.

I reached for a cigarette. But when I struck a match to light up, it flew out of my hand and on to my clothes. The incident disturbed me to a disproportionate degree, as if it were an omen of other conflagrations to come. Then a biscuit-tin lid slipped out of Amin's hand and on to the tile floor, and we both jumped with fright. With our nerves frayed as they were, the racket it made sounded as loud as if a bomb had gone off in the room.

I took another look at my watch, which truly seemed to have no hands and no numbers. It looked like nothing but a small, white circle enclosed in glass with a black dot in the middle. I felt that I was like that black dot, a captive of vacuous time, imprisoned within its inscrutable, never-ending circle.

Then suddenly Amin spoke up, saying: 'It didn't explode.'

I thought to myself, since it still hasn't gone off after all this time, it probably never will. However, I couldn't be entirely sure of it and I regretted never having read any military manuals or made any independent inquiries into the workings of modern explosives. If I had, I might not have found myself perched on top of a (potentially) live missile, repeating my own version of Hamlet's famous line: 'To explode or not to explode? That is the question!'

Yet in spite of it all, I wasn't nearly as miserable as I would have expected myself to be had I known that one day I'd find myself hungry, alone, terrified and faced with the prospect of dying either of hunger and thirst or by being burned to a crisp – not to mention having a wounded hand and a wounded ear. On the contrary, the situation even struck me as amusing somehow and I felt a deep serenity that almost bordered on euphoria. It was as if I'd been equipped with some sort of psychological 'righting mechanism' designed to overcome the effects of outward events. Or perhaps it was only natural that after having sunk the day before into oceanic depths of sorrow and madness, I'd now find myself floating on the water's calm surface. Perhaps it was to be expected that, if only for a few brief moments, I'd be raised aloft on spirits' wings and go soaring high above this land of sorrow. It was as if somewhere in the deepest recesses of my being there lay a store of hidden power, such that whenever I began truly to collapse, a mysterious force would be activated and come to my rescue, if only for a short while.

I said to Amin: 'I'm going up to check on my flat and then I'll be back.'

In an attempt to detain me, he replied: 'And the missile?'

Indignant, I asked, 'Do you expect me to take it off the chair for you, then go and throw it into the sea?'

'And do you expect *me* to feel like joking with you just now?' he retorted.

There was no point in *us* trying to carry on a conversation. The best we seemed to be able to do was exchange meaningless chatter. That, of course, was nothing new, since as long as I'd known Amin, we'd never had any sort of mutual understanding. I'd looked upon him as someone who, in his heart of hearts, was nothing but a stereotypical 'Eastern girl' whose mental capacities had been put on hold. And he in turn had seen me as the female version of a Western young man who'd cut himself loose from all the traditions that he (Amin) most revered. But lo and behold, upon his very first exposure to life's harsh realities, what should he do but toss his father's dead body into the rubbish bin! I felt an urge to cause him pain – to say to him, for example: 'All right then. I'll go check out the missile in the armchair and *you* go and check out your father's cadaver in the rubbish bin.'

But I held my tongue, if only for selfish reasons. After all, had he kicked me out of his flat, I would have faced certain death. First of all, my own flat on the top floor was exposed to more danger than his was. Besides which, by this time my phone had bitten the dust once and for all, whereas his still worked at least part of the time – depending on which way the wind was blowing, or whether it happened to be raining at the moment, or perhaps on other factors unknown to us. Apart from this, virtually all the food we had left, along with the few remaining candles, was being hoarded in his 'cave'. So, practically speaking, it looked as I had no choice but to make peace with him.

Without saying another word, I went on up to my flat. As I climbed the stairs, I thought back on the nightmares I'd been having about my brother and wished I could hear just one piece of reassuring news about him – or even *un*reassuring news, for that matter. Even having my worst fears confirmed would have been better than staying locked in my world of nightmares, dreaming up one frightful scenario after another.

Most of the windows had bullet holes in them, and the floor was littered with iron scraps of various shapes and sizes, including untold numbers of spent shells. I picked up a handful and began scrutinizing them in disbelief. Any one of them could have ended up somewhere inside my body, a blistering, cauterizing fragment of semi-molten metal. Yet here they were now in the palm of my hand, cold and half-oxidized. As I pondered my 'miraculous' escape, I felt a rush of euphoria. Not a moment passed when I wasn't snatching life from fate's iron grasp. I'd been wresting it by force from the powers of death that pressed in on me from all sides, stalking it anew with every sunrise like an unarmed hunter in a jungle where perils beset him at every turn.

As I inspected my library, running my hands affectionately over the shelves and their contents, I realized that here alone lay the source of all my unrest and that, in a time of civil war, one can count poverty a blessing rather than a curse. After all, apart from these books, I didn't have a single possession that I feared losing. I comforted myself with the thought that practically nobody goes around stealing books. They have only one true enemy: fire.

I had two small fire extinguishers. However, after my experience with modern-day billiard-ball bullets, I wasn't so sure any more just how much good these puny red cylinders would do me. I reread the instructions written on one of them. I was supposed to break the plastic seal around the top, then press a button that would cause some sort of magical fire-dousing substance to come gushing forth. And what might this substance be? I wondered. Was it bubbly like soapsuds? Did it come out as a blue cloud? Or was it nothing but a single teardrop shed by a true-blue soul?

As I made the rounds of the flat, I smelt an exceedingly unpleasant odour coming from the direction of the kitchen. It was the rank smell of unwashed pots and pans and of the leftover food that still clung to them. There was also a stench escaping from the refrigerator. No sooner had I opened it than I was nearly bowled over by a swarm of tiny mosquitoes and a gust of foul odours. The primary reason I hadn't been able to stay in my 'headquarters' in the hallway after the shelling intensified was that the odour wafting out of the kitchen had simply become more than I could take.

I picked up a small, orange-coloured bag decorated with

the initials of some airline company and went back down to the ground floor. I didn't go near the window. I didn't feel like looking out into the street to see what had become of my old banger. In fact, I felt apathetic about everything. All lines to the outside world had been severed, all bridges had come tumbling down. Yet despite everything – or rather, *because* of it – I knew there had to be a green bud sprouting somewhere not far away. Even when my thoughts turned towards my brother, I could only think of him at that moment with an apathy bordering on indifference. Practically the only entity whose fate was a source of genuine *angst* for me was my library. Apart from that, the only thing I cared about trying to rescue was the contents of my little orange bag. Inside it were the pages on which I'd recorded blow-by-blow accounts of my 'nightmares' as fighting raged all about me.

Oh, writing – that peculiar strain of madness that pulsates in one's fingers, one's cells, one's very nerves. This was the 'malady' to which I'd succumbed from the time I was a child (though it didn't appear to have been catching). Through it I'd sought to escape from my tears and to compensate for the absence of the mother I'd never known, of tenderness and affection, and at times even love itself.

The small orange bag contained a large yellow envelope on which I'd scrawled in large letters, 'Manuscript for *Beirut Nightmares*'. Beneath it I'd placed my memoirs and other personal documents, along with various things that had been Yousif's: papers, photos, matches, memorabilia and a few of his other possessions. These were the only things I intended to take with me from this infernal place – that is, if I were destined to get out alive. From the moment the orange bag became the repository for these treasures of mine, I'd been holding on to it for dear life, not letting it out of my sight for a moment.

Just then I thought I heard Amin scream. The sound had made its way to where I was despite the storm of gunpowder raging outside. As for the storm originating in the heavens, it had abated somewhat and a feeble ray of sunlight had made its way inside through the stained glass of the skylights. Ah, the sun! What joy! With the sunrise came memories of woods, the sea, the moon, wild flowers, dew-covered meadows, trees, grass – and Yousif. Oh, Yousif... When he'd been swallowed up by the abyss never to return, had he really taken everything with him?

Nightmare 117

I was right. Amin really had been calling me. I came out of my flat and found him standing half-way up the stairs. I knew something utterly catastrophic must have taken place, since this was literally the first time he'd set foot outside his flat since the fighting had confined us to the building.

'What's happened?' I asked.

Instead of replying, he just kept on calling to me as if he hadn't heard my question. Then he took off running down the stairs, with me close behind. When we reached his flat, we both went in and he scurried over to the window that opened out on to the garden behind the house.

Through a small crack in the shutter, we could see the servant sprawled out on the ground with his face in the dirt, as if he'd been suckling at Mother Earth's breasts. If it hadn't been for the pool of blood that had reddened some small pebbles near where he lay before disappearing into the dark brown soil, I would have thought he was sleeping.

'Maybe he stole something, then tried to escape,' said Amin.

I didn't reply. Instead, my eyes had been drawn to an object that the slain man was clutching tightly in his hand. It was a yellow 'something' – it was a banana!

It was then that I knew why this noble soul had lost his life. But I didn't say a word. I didn't tell Amin that his servant had been murdered for trying to feed another living creature – namely, a monkey! After all, the kindness and compassion that had led to the servant's demise were sentiments that someone like Amin would never understand, and which no one but the poor and the pure in heart would be courageous enough to act upon.

Nightmare 118

It's hell...
It's hell to be living with someone to whom you feel no more bond than you would to some locust in a nearby field.

It's hell... for the two of you to be like a couple of hotel guests who've been forced to share the same room and to talk to each other without any meaningful exchange taking place, since each one is 'broadcasting' on a totally different wave-length.

It's hell.

And here were Amin and I, obliged to stay together in a single room at one end of the flat for fear that a missile sitting on a chair at the other end of the house might explode!

At first I'd been able to stay by myself most of the time. Now, there was a corpse in the garden and another in the rubbish bin. In addition, I had a third 'cadaver' sharing the same room with me – namely, Amin – only he, unlike the other two bodies, was a chatterbox!

Having finally decided to get some use out of the family treasures, Amin had opened a bottle of aged wine. The wine in turn had loosened his tongue, causing him to let forth torrents of what had been pent up in his inanity-sated breast.

He had an old joke book which he insisted on reading to me. Meanwhile, I was trying to concentrate on the book I'd brought down from my flat, *The Arab Mind* by John Levine. From the opening lines of the book, the author began launching verbal assaults on the Arabs. As I leafed through its pages, I found it to be nothing more than an ode to ridicule. My God, I thought. Everybody's against us! And then we go forming alliances with our enemies against ourselves! Horrors...

It was hell...

Amin kept on reading out of his ancient joke book, every now and then letting out a frightening, hysterical laugh. As for me, I kept having the insistent thought: I've got to get out of here. I've got to escape. I sat with my elbows resting on my orange airline bag, which contained everything that mattered to me in this ugly, wicked world.

I wondered whether it was mere coincidence that this bag was orange and not some other colour. When I was a little girl, I used to draw the sun as a circle with spokes coming out of it. And in spite of the art teacher's instructions to colour it yellow, I always insisted on colouring it orange instead. Once I stared at it to see whether it was orange or yellow. The result, of course, was that my eyes hurt terribly and, rather than appearing either orange or yellow, the sun just looked black. Whichever way I looked for some time after that, I was haunted by the image of that black sun. Even so, I continued to insist that it was orange.

Amin was determined to read me one of the jokes a second time, since I didn't laugh at it the first!

It was hell...

I tried to avoid interacting with him by reading newspapers left over from the days before we'd been cut off from the outside world. They were filled with pictures of the bodies of the slain, some of whom had been tortured. As I sat pondering them, I noticed that the features of the dead are always relaxed, as if they've just woken up from a long sleep.

Amin snatched the newspapers out of my hand, still determined to 'amuse' me by reading me some more jokes. I tried to be polite to him. I did my best to smile. All the while, though, I was cogitating, scheming, planning my escape. That's it! I thought. The telephone is my only hope.

The phone lines hadn't been severed. However, there was no dialling tone. At least, during the entire half-hour that I'd spent sitting with the receiver in my hand, not a drop of 'juice' had flowed through it. But as long as the telephone was the only way left for me to send out my cry for help, I was prepared to sit like this for a whole hour, or all day if need be.

It was hell...

Feeling hungry and lonely, I thought of the hundreds of nameless individuals in various Arab cities and countries who for so long had sympathized with the things I'd written and who had made their way to my heart over the bridges laid through my words. I remembered the letters I'd received from women who had found in my torment a mirror of their own sufferings. If they'd only penned their letters to me on bread instead of paper, I would never have known hunger.

But I *was* hungry.

Amin continued to sip his wine and tell his jokes. The telephone was in the room right next to the one where the unexploded missile was sitting and I was undecided as to whether to risk my life by going to the phone or to stay put and end up dying of exasperation with Amin. This man was sure to be the death of me. He'd slay me with the one weapon of which no mention is made in the penal code: offensiveness!

It was hell...

My eyes darted to and fro, looking aimlessly at this and that, all the while scrupulously avoiding eye contact with Amin. Through the open door I could see the chair where Amm Fu'ad had died with his treasures all about him. Amin would most likely expire in the same chair, surrounded by the very same treasures. For so long people have been prepared to die for their idols. Wealth is merely one of the most recent fads in this regard – wealth in all its varied shapes and forms, including silver, china and gold containers.

Oh, how I yearned for sunshine, joy, freedom, the sea, forests, the moon, the stars. Oh, Yousif... what is it that makes people outdo themselves trying to amass idols, even to be ready to die on their account?

I could hear Yousif's voice saying: 'It's emptiness – a hunger for love.'

Yes, exactly, I thought. And here was Amin sitting in front of me feeling unspeakably empty, like a huge jar filled with nothing but holes. Oh, Yousif...

So this is what makes people fight like dogs over affluence and power, then go on to commit the most heinous of atrocities – that is, war...

As for those who've learned to love, they have no desire to surfeit themselves on morsels snatched out of others' mouths. After all, they crave no more than what the earth can provide. Lovers are in full possession of themselves and consequently feel no need to establish their existence by making material reality into a kind of outward embodiment of their souls.

Those who seek to replace love with the desire to possess are the very people who also make wars. They perish in terror, surrounded by their earthly treasures, and afflict their progeny with 'the curse of Midas'.

It was hell...

The shelling still hadn't let up enough for me to go and try the phone. In fact, the entire house was dancing as if an earthquake had shaken it loose from its foundations and then gone running with it through the streets of a village on the verge of collapse.

I decided to wait till the shelling had abated, and then head for the phone. That way, there would be less likelihood of the missile's exploding in the room right next to me.

However, the fighting didn't let up in the least, and I thought about the hundreds of people who must have been dying at that moment.

'Every affliction comes to an end,' pronounced Amin sanguinely. 'Soon everything will go back to the way it was and you can repair your flat.'

The fool! Did he really believe that *anything* could go back to the way it had been? And the people who were perishing – did he think of them as nothing but chess pieces that merchants could import replacements for?

With this thought, I found myself jumping up and running to the telephone. I lifted the receiver, only to find to my surprise that at that very same moment there was someone on the other end who'd been trying to call me. A familiar-sounding voice, it turned out to be that of my friend Amal. So, like a sinking ship that sends out distress signals in every direction, I started talking as fast as I could for fear that either the phone or I would die at any moment.

'Listen,' I said, 'one way or another, I've got to get out of this place. Contact everybody you can think of – all the people who would be likely to write long, flowery elegies on my behalf if I died, and everybody who would want to see my talent and youth spared. Tell them I'm not interested in being eulogized, and curses on anyone who would write me an elegy or commemorative poem! Tell them that I want to live and that I'm ready to risk anything for the sake of getting out. The fact is, I'd just as soon die as go on living in this situation. I need a tank and I'm willing to come out to meet it even if I have to run through a storm of bullets to get there.'

Then the line was cut off. But I knew she wouldn't do a thing.

It was hell...

I said to Amin: 'There's a possibility that a tank will be coming to rescue me. Do you want to come too?'

Astonished, he asked: 'How could I do that? What about the house? It would be looted by thieves!'

It was hell indeed! And how could it have been otherwise in a place where even walls had been made into idols to be worshipped and revered?

When I voiced this thought to Amin, his reply caught me off guard.

'But you're just like us,' he said. 'You may happen to worship a different idol, but it's an idol just the same. That orange bag of yours and the papers you keep inside it, aren't they idols too? And your constant dread that your library will go up in smoke – well, it's no different from the way we fear for the safety of our gold and silver. If I'm an idol-worshipper, so are you, even if the things we worship happen to be different.'

I made no reply. On the one hand, what he'd said seemed to be true, at least to a certain extent. But, I thought, if we assumed for the sake of argument that he was right, then wasn't there at least some difference – quantitative if not qualitative – between someone who worships gold and someone who worships books?

One voice inside me cried out: No! There's no difference at all! Both are worship and that's that. A book should be treated merely as a means of discovering new knowledge, not of clinging to what one's already learned. A book is nothing but a present moment, as it were, to be followed by another, then still another. And what this means is that every book I finish reading should be allowed to pass away, to 'breathe its last', so to speak. I should let go of it in anticipation of the next book that will come my way.

On the other hand, my library wasn't a mere collection of books, at least as far as I was concerned. It was a dialogue. Every book it contained represented a human being with whom I'd engaged in a conversation, an exchange of ideas that had now been recorded in its margins. It was there that I'd scribbled cries of approval or rage, queries or comments. I seem unable to read a book without doing so as if I were in some way rewriting it. I participate with the author in his or her perplexity, explorations and questionings. So one could never say that my books were just for decoration. Rather, they were the minutes of meetings which had been convened between me and each of their authors.

It was hell...

I couldn't say all this to Amin, since I knew he wouldn't understand. The silver and gold trays in his house could be replaced with a mere stroke of the pen in a chequebook. As for my library, its contents couldn't have been bought in their present form anywhere in the whole world. I could have replaced the books themselves, of course, but not the intimate conversations I'd had with their contents. The marginal glosses which now filled them revealed my own personal interactions with each book, which went far beyond the contents of the book alone. And such human interchanges can't be bought or sold.

If I *had* told Amin these things, he could simply have responded by talking about the scratches on various gold-plated dishes, bowls and trays, what the memory of each scratch meant to him personally, as well as the things that were said at the moment the scratches were made and the particular occasion recorded by each one. And he could have claimed accordingly that every dish or plate was now a sort of 'phonograph record' whose scratches preserved cherished – indeed, priceless – encounters and gatherings. And in this respect they were essentially no different from the marginal notes in my books.

It was hell...

It's hell to find that you have nothing left but silence – to find that you have no choice but to withdraw into your shell like a panic-stricken turtle lest your words be trampled underfoot.

It was hell...

It was an unfriendly silence, the silence borne of the inability to meet half-way on the bridge of exchange and understanding. It was the silence of the ages prior to the invention of language. The silence of the caves. The silence of strangers. The silence of bank managers listening to a financial report, who look on unfazed and indifferent as the speaker keels over dead from a heart attack.

It was hell... a torment that called for the endurance and fortitude of a Robinson Crusoe.

It was a wordless stillness enclosed within the rock of a greater, more immense silence, the silence of death and detachment – the silence of aliens and alienation.

It was the silence of those for whom all bridges have been burnt except for the bridge of hope itself. Unlike the pregnant, eloquent silence that rested upon Yousif's bullet-ridden breast, it was the silence of ashes.

Oh, Yousif... Yousif... Yousif!

Nightmare 119

It was hell...

And I was truly famished. It was a frightful, involuntary hunger, not that of someone who's fasting and whose hunger is of his own making, as it were. It was the hunger of the oppressed and persecuted, not that of ascetic, otherworldly penitents whose physical senses work in tacit cooperation with their inner worlds as they walk the path of self-denial, where hunger is transmuted into a source of serenity and inner rest.

It was the 'hunger of revolution' – the very hunger that had helped trigger the social conflagration which had now broken forth. The pangs I felt in the pit of my stomach weren't so much signs of emptiness as signs of a bomb ready to go off at any moment. Forgiven are the sins of the hungry. Forgiven are their transgressions. Forgiven are their resentments and their fiery outbursts of rage.

A little while earlier, Amin had left the room without announcing where he was going. When he reappeared, I thought I detected a slight rosiness in his cheeks. He'd had something to eat – the sneak! Now I was convinced that, like his father before him, he'd stashed away some extra rations just for himself. I'd committed a serious error when, from the very beginning of our present crisis, I'd brought all the food left in my flat down to theirs. That hadn't been terribly clever. But as I'd never known this kind of fierce hunger before, I'd not learned what precautions I needed to take should I be faced with it in the future.

But *now* I was hungry. And I'd learned...

When I got the chance, I stole up to the loft above the kitchen where the servant used to sleep. I recalled that when we came upon his dead body in the garden, he'd been holding a banana that he'd pilfered with the intention of feeding it to

Amin's monkey. And seeing how the bananas had all been 'missing' since the third day of our captivity, I figured that he must have had a cache of bananas at the very least.

Once my eyes had grown accustomed to the darkness, I began my search in earnest. I turned his pillow over, but didn't find anything. I turned back the covers on his threadbare cot, with similar results. Then I got down on my hands and knees to take a look under the cot. Being bone-weary, I found it restful to go crawling around on all fours. (Like a jungle creature, I'd come out in search of a morsel to sustain me.) There was nothing there, either. But finally, after inspecting every nook and cranny in the room, I ended up at a narrow window where I came upon a veritable hoard of treasure: four bananas, an orange, three apples, two biscuits, seven olives and several pieces of dry bread. It was a feast I shall never forget.

Some of my find I devoured immediately, before I could be 'caught' by Amin, and the rest I carefully concealed under a pile of old newspapers. As I headed back from the servant's quarters, Amin was shrieking in alarm: 'Where have you been?'

If he'd taken a closer look at me as I came into the room, he would have seen the same half-guilty look in my eyes that I'd seen in his when he'd just returned from his secret supper. However, I was still hungry. So hungry, in fact, that I made up my mind to slip out after dark and eat the banana that the servant's cadaver was still clinging to with such tenacity. On the other hand, I thought, perhaps I really ought to feed it to the monkey, since this, after all, was what that noble human being had been intending to do with it when he lost his life so suddenly and cruelly.

It was hell...

And I was ravenous. In fact, I was even more ravenous than I had been before I'd gobbled down my delicious but meagre repast. Everything around me seemed to be crying out with hunger: for food, for sunshine, for freedom, for happiness.

Yes, this was hunger.

I could hear voracious howls and yelps coming from the direction of the pet shop, where the animals' cries of distress were mingled with plaintive moaning. They were the bitter, agonized cries of hunger which no one but those numbed by surfeit could fail to recognize.

Still, it seemed that the wounded dog was alive and capable of defending itself. Perhaps at that very moment it was fighting off sleep lest it be eaten by the others.

With this thought, I became aware that I myself was waging a losing battle against drowsiness. Vexed and fatigued, I said to Amin: 'I'm going to sleep now.'

'And me?' he asked inanely, sounding like a senile old man.

'I hope some gregarious "thieves in the night" will come round to keep you company!' I retorted.

Little did I know at the time that the words I'd uttered in a fit of exasperation would turn out to be a prophecy.

Of course, as long as there was an unexploded missile resting near my bed, I'd have to sleep right where I was. So I made my orange travel bag into a pillow and, despite the roar of explosions all about, I fell fast asleep. After all, if sufficient doses of them are taken for long enough, one can develop a tolerance for even the most deafening blasts.

Nightmare 120

Shadi was seated at his desk in a room the shape of an immense tube. It looked something like an outsize sewer drainage pipe and emitted a stench like that of a sewer as well. The floor of the room was covered with black rubber and the walls with rust.

Flanking Shadi on either side were hookers with obese, flaccid bodies and faces that looked as if they were made of coloured wax.

After leaving prison, Shadi had arrived at the conclusion that the war was really nothing but a great opportunity to amass a fortune and he intended to do just that, so that later on he could escape from the inferno to which his country had been reduced. Then he'd make his home in Geneva, Switzerland, and replace the map of his homeland with a chequebook. Until then, he was prepared to do anything that would further him on the road to becoming a rich man.

The suffering that he had witnessed and experienced in prison had taught him that the big-time outlaws were still on the loose, carousing, feasting and otherwise indulging themselves outside the prison walls, while the ones languishing behind bars were nothing but small-time crooks. So, after his own release, he'd made up his mind to join the ranks of the big-timers, and was already well on his way towards fulfilling this aspiration.

On this particular day he was expecting a visit from the leader of a Beirut weapons ring, one of the many of his kind who'd managed to infiltrate the ranks of the honest, respectable insurgents. Shadi had invited the warlord to spend what he promised would be an enjoyable evening at his place. However, even after having all his 'girls' pass in review before him, he hadn't found a single one who would 'do' for the occasion.

Besides which, he had a lot of other hassles to contend with as well. Just the day before, for example, he'd got into an argument with one of the co-founders of what they'd decided to call the 'War Profiteers' Mafia'. In the course of the altercation, he'd committed a serious blunder by threatening to kill the man. What he ought to have done was simply to humour him, then send someone out later to kill him with a 'stray' bullet.

Someone else had been sent to see him by the leader of an operation also dealing in arms, yet which posed as a gathering place for the intelligentsia. In this case he'd had to convince the man from the outset of his goodwill towards him, so as to be able to liquidate him at the appropriate time without unnecessary complications.

And as if these troubles weren't enough, all the whores left in Beirut were as unsightly as the war itself. Something else to keep him awake at night...

He'd formed several gangs devoted to breaking into people's homes and to robbing pedestrians at gunpoint. However, he was certain that the gang leaders were trying to dupe him, skimming off more than their fair share of the loot. His whole life seemed to be just one problem after another.

What he needed was someone who still had some of the freshness and youthfulness of women whose bodies haven't become common currency, so to speak.

Then he remembered a woman who fulfilled his specifications perfectly. Without batting an eyelid, he gave his men a detailed description of her, adding: 'She lives in a flat across the street from the Holiday Inn and is alone at present. She's to be abducted without delay.'

And, of course, he didn't bother to tell them that she was his sister!

Nightmare 121

I woke up screaming: 'Where's my brother? Where's Shadi?'

The darkness around me was still total, though shadowy grey strands of pre-dawn light had gradually begun coiling themselves about the cosmos.

Meanwhile, voracious-sounding yelps and howls from the pet shop had begun sending tremors through the nearby trees and earth. I decided to take another look inside the shop before sunrise so as not to be spotted by some sniper lurking in the vicinity. As for Amin, he was in a deep sleep, though his muted, uneven snores made it seem as if he were still trembling with fright even as he slept.

I left the room, passed through the kitchen, then left the house through the kitchen door that opened out on to the garden, leaving the door open behind me.

I passed by the rubbish bin where we'd stashed Amm Fu'ad's body. A powerful stench was emanating from it, or so it seemed to me. Yet I felt no remorse about what we'd done with his remains. After all, I see very little difference between a rubbish bin on the one hand and a coffin or grave on the other. Or between leaving a cadaver to be preyed upon by vultures and having it embalmed or cremated, then spreading its ashes over the ocean.

From there I headed towards where the servant's corpse lay. Everything around me was still blanketed in darkness. But I hadn't been that anxious to cast him a parting glance anyway. As I tried to extricate the banana from his hand, I still hadn't decided whether to feed it to the monkey, to split it with her or to wolf down the entire thing myself – though the last of the three possibilities was the most likely! By this time his fingers were so stony and rigid, they might as well have belonged to a statue. In the end, the banana imploded with a sickening 'squish'. In the darkness it had the feel of something slimy and alive, and it caused my skin to crawl.

From there I headed towards the pet shop's back window so as to look into the storeroom where the animals were kept. As I peeked in, the pallid rays of the early-morning sun had begun reaching into the room's darkened corners. By this time, I'd become quite adept at seeing in the dark, like a lone owl in a forest of ashes.

I closed my eyes for a few seconds to let them get accustomed to the semi-darkness. Then I pressed my face up against the window's metal screen and cupped my hands around the sides of my face, creating a kind of 'binocular' effect by shutting out all light that might intrude from outside.

I didn't see much. Nevertheless, what I did see was just as I'd left it and just as I'd imagined it would be.

Daybreak's misty rays had roused the animals out of their troubled sleep. They'd never fallen completely silent even during their sleep-like torpor, but now the hungry cries of protest coming from their 'cells' began growing steadily louder.

Though I couldn't see it clearly, there was one dog which I suspected was wounded. Unlike the others, it stayed crouched in one spot, growling and muttering. Meanwhile, the other dogs went roaming among the cages, uttering sounds which, though devoid of words, nevertheless bespoke that peculiar madness to which hunger alone can give birth.

I don't know how long I stood there. However, after some time I heard rather than saw an unusual movement in the lock of the door leading into the storeroom. Or was I just imagining things? No... I wasn't. For shortly thereafter, the door cracked and a patch of bright light fell on to the floor of the inner room.

Who should appear in that flood of light but the owner of the pet shop, in the flesh! I didn't see his face, since he was standing in relative darkness behind a flashlight which he held in one hand. However, I could see that in his other hand he was carrying a large bag.

So, then, he'd finally come to feed them, now that they were about to breathe their last. He'd come to moisten their parched throats lest they die and he lose what little profit he now stood to gain from them. He apparently still held out hopes of being able to land a few more deals, even if he had to sell them dirt cheap. After all, like they say: 'Business is business.'

For a moment I wondered, is he really the pet-shop owner? Or might he just be some burglar who's down on his luck? But then I heard him calling the animals by name, as if in doing so he could fortify himself against his apprehensions. Who knows? It might have been the first time in his life that he'd ever called to them with such heartfelt affection.

'Bobby! Kika! Simo!' he cooed. 'Papa's brought you something to eat!'

Then without warning, the now-uncaged dogs lunged at him in a single, collective leap. The flashlight fell out of his hand and rolled some distance on the floor, but didn't go out. From where I stood, I was able to see the entire scene with frightful clarity.

Having pounced on top of him, the five dogs proceeded to tear him limb from limb. Even the wounded one took part in the gory festivities. Terrified, the man let out a blood-curdling scream, after which I heard a cracking noise as his skull was crushed between the jaws of one of his former charges. They devoured him, ripping his clothes to shreds as they went. As for me, I just stood gaping at them like someone bewitched, unable to move a muscle. It was a spectacle utterly beyond belief, like something lifted straight out of the depths of myth and legend.

By the time the night had come to an end and another dawn had broken, the dogs had virtually consumed him, leaving nothing but the barest remains. Then, one by one, they went outside through the shop's half-opened door. Meanwhile, I stared at what remained of the pet-shop owner's blood, his mangled flesh, his face – which was now nothing but a formless mass out of which jagged bones could be seen protruding here and there – and his neck, which had been stripped to the bone. His head looked as if it had been chopped off under the razor-sharp blade of a guillotine.

However, I felt neither fear nor pity. Nor was I even surprised. On the contrary, I'd known that this very thing had been all but inevitable.

The idiot! Had he really been under the illusion that the animals would just stay in their cages docilely awaiting his return, even if their loyalty to him meant dying of starvation? Couldn't he have predicted that a stranger's hand might have intervened and set them free?

The fool! He appeared to have been totally unaware of the fact that even peaceable domestic creatures can become hungry enough and enraged enough to bare their fangs. He'd come to them defenceless, not even armed with his whip. And why? Apparently it had never occurred to him, even for a single moment, that this might happen.

By now, the sun had come up, which meant that I'd make an ideal target for any sniper who happened to feel like putting a bullet through my head. So I ran back to the house, having ushered in the new day in the company of no fewer than three cadavers: one of them was in the rubbish bin, another lay under the palm tree, while nothing remained of the third but a skeleton and a heap of tattered clothes.

And there was a fourth as well, waiting for me inside. This one happened to be a talking cadaver, whom I could hear bellowing at me, saying: 'Where did you run off to? I'll have you know I was attacked by thieves!'

At first I didn't believe him. He was going on in such a hysterical tone of voice, I was inclined to think he was just trying to get my sympathy so I wouldn't leave the room again.

But then I noticed that the windowpane was broken.

'Did a bullet come through the window?' I asked.

'No,' he said, 'the thieves did it. I swear to God! I woke up to the sound of shattering glass and then what should I see but a bunch of faces staring in at me through this broken window. There was a woman, a little boy and several men. I was so scared, I shouted in their faces and they shouted right back. Then they took off running and so did I!'

So then, our neighbourhood had been pronounced dead, as it were. And sure enough, here were the flocks of starving ravens who had begun descending upon the area to scavenge for treasures among the corpses of the slain. However, they happened upon a survivor, who'd been no less astonished by their appearance than they had been by his.

Forgiven are the sins of the hungry. And blessings be upon everything that they burn or destroy. For now I too know what hungry truly means!

Nightmare 122

I wasn't entirely convinced by Amin's story until I took a stealthy look out of the corner of the window. When I did, I was surprised to see a half-open bag that had been flung on to the ground. Inside it there was a revolver, a fur coat and a few other items that I couldn't quite make out in the dim morning light.

So, then, he hadn't been lying after all.

The flocks of starving ravens had begun sweeping through Beirut's charred neighbourhoods, which by now were little more than open graveyards. However, they apparently hadn't yet dared to approach the living, just as the creatures in the pet shop had been unwilling to devour the wounded dog among them until it expired of its own accord. And it now appeared that in their frenzied flight, the 'ravens' had dropped some of their booty.

I stood staring out of the window at the half-open bag. But as the dreary, joyless day commenced, the only thing I could see glinting in the sunlight was the revolver.

On the revolver alone my glance fixed itself, as if the fur and other costly trinkets which wreathed it simply weren't there.

Prior to that time, I'd had a loathing for weapons of any kind. Even the sight of a slingshot like the ones kids play with and use to hunt birds was more than I could stomach. And never in my life had I given a child a toy pistol or machine-gun, or anything else that might even vaguely be conceived of as an instrument of violence.

Once an officer friend of mine had given me a small, pricy revolver with a gold handle. It was the type that gun-lovers would have considered a choice collector's item. In any case, I turned right around and gave it away again to one of my lady friends, then broke off relations with the officer.

But now, after having passed through the city of hunger, terror, hysteria and violence, I found myself contemplating the gun before me with fascination and even delight. I began dreaming up ways to get at it in its elusive location without exposing myself to the danger of being gunned down by a sniper.

Did I just want to possess it and nothing more? I wondered. Or would I actually be willing to use it if necessary? In other words, did I just want it to satisfy some sort of psychological need, or would I now be prepared to fire it – I, the one who at one time had been terrified of killing a mosquito?

However, at that moment I wasn't up to thinking about such things. I realized, after all, that violence isn't something that can be justified through rational argument. Rather, it's simply engaged in. My sole, unthought-out concern that early morning was to get hold of the revolver that had been tossed out of the window.

Struck suddenly by an idea, I said to Amin: 'Do you have a magnet in the house?'

He looked perplexed, so I rephrased the question. 'Do you have any sewing supplies?' I asked.

I knew that Amin's mother used to bring in a seamstress who would spend the entire day at the house making her clothes. Consequently, I was sure they must still have some sewing gadgets on hand, including the sewing machine that I'd seen on so many occasions, and that among them I might find the magnet that seamstresses have always used to gather up pins from the chairs, pillows, cushions and floors. Sure enough, I came upon the magnet in a sewing box. Around it I tied a piece of twine that I'd found in one of the kitchen drawers, then threw it out of the window so that it landed near the revolver.

I watched the revolver draw closer and closer to the magnet until at last it attached itself. Then, from my post near the window, I tried to rope in the revolver without at the same time providing amusing target practice for some 'early bird' sniper. I began tugging on the string, hoping to draw in both the magnet and the revolver that now clung to it.

The plan started out successfully enough, with both of them sliding along the ground until they were directly under the window. However, when I started to pull on the string so as to lift the objects off the ground, the revolver detached itself from the magnet and fell. Its weight was too great for the attractive force of the magnet – which, after all, had been made for picking up pins, not revolvers. And thus fizzled my very first attempt at military strategy!

Nightmare 123

The electricity was still cut off and the phone had all but expired. There was no dialling tone, it never rang and I couldn't call out on it. Besides which, I'd lost track of how many days I'd been held prisoner in our apartment building, completely cut off from the outside world. However, I was sure that it had to have been more than a week now.

Amin disappeared from the room, so I figured he'd gone to snack on his hidden stockpile of dry bread. Inspired by his example, I stole back up to the loft where I'd hidden the chunks of dry bread that had been 'bequeathed' to me by the servant. As I munched away, I noticed that the mice had helped themselves to part of my stash. Then I descended to the kitchen to force down a few drafts of revolting boiled water. It was saturated with lime, which, as a result of being repeatedly boiled and then cooled, had become like bitter-tasting salt. Then, as I was trying to force myself to swallow just enough of the vile potion to survive, the 'earthquake' struck.

The ageing house seemed to shudder down to the last stone. I heard horrific explosions and the sound of shattered glass striking the ground. Frozen in place, I watched the autumnal sun's frigid rays glint like knife-blades on the jagged, splintered glass.

The old house had received a direct hit. Sometimes one knows things with such certainty and clarity that it's hardly necessary even to verify them with the five senses. It's as if there existed forgotten, unnamed senses which only begin to function when we find ourselves treading that fine line which separates life from death. And when that occurs, all sorts of cryptic, unseen forces kick in, equipping us with power and knowledge, as well as an astounding capacity for ferocity and even ruthlessless.

My initial interpretation of what had happened was that the missile sleeping in the armchair in what had once been my bedroom had at long last woken up. This, at least, was what I wanted to believe. However, the sight of huge chunks of rock plummeting into the garden from the upper storeys of the building forced me to conclude that the situation wasn't quite so simple. Then, even before I'd caught sight of the smoke, the scent of something burning began making its way to my nostrils.

At that moment, in rushed Amin, shouting at the top of his voice: 'Your flat is on fire!'

I bolted towards the kitchen door and opened it. However, I wasn't able to get out to the garden to take a look up, since hunks of rock were raining down in a veritable avalanche. As they landed on the ground, they went scattering in all directions, mingling with unidentified burning objects that would plunge violently on to the grass, then lie there smouldering.

Once I saw what was happening outside, I dashed towards the staircase and, like a woman gone mad, began my ascent. However, I wasn't able to go beyond the second-floor landing. When I got that far, I saw flames billowing out of a gaping hole in the wall that ran along one side of the hallway in my flat. And as if that wouldn't have been catastrophic enough, the flames were licking at the very section of the wall that was covered from floor to ceiling with book-laden shelves. It was obvious that the wall had been penetrated by more than a mere shell. Ironically, the blow had struck the one and only spot that I'd mistakenly imagined to be safe (relatively speaking) – namely, the wall that I'd been accustomed to leaning up against whenever the shelling grew especially intense. This was the haven to which I'd taken myself for refuge so many times that I'd dubbed it my 'military headquarters'!

Emitting an eerie hiss as they went, the flames sounded like a bloodthirsty ogre that had gone munching with its frightful teeth on everything in its path, or like an infernal, disembodied gullet swallowing everything in sight. Oh, my poor library!

With thoughts like these running through my head, I went charging up the stairs again, but then decided instead to make a circuit around the house so as to see whether the flames were coming from my library. I ventured outside, only to find that my worst fears had been realized. Copious flames were surging out of the windows and, in a moment of untold misery, I found myself face to face with what I had dreaded more than anything else on earth: my library was on fire! Then, in a second agonizing moment, I realized something else – namely, that the wall which had collapsed was the same one that faced on to the back garden and that the flaming 'unidentified flying objects' that were hurtling downward into the garden like so many shooting stars were none other than my books!

So, once again I went streaking up the stairs like a mad woman, thinking about the little fire extinguisher I'd discovered earlier in my flat. Like someone who tries to keep a mineshaft from collapsing by propping it open with a piece of firewood... like someone who tries to travel to the moon on a bicycle... like someone adrift on a storm-tossed sea who tries to make it back to shore on a matchstick... this is about as clearly as I was thinking as I headed up the stairs to my incinerating flat. This time, however, I didn't even manage to get as far as the second floor. Everything was enveloped in a thick layer of smoke. My eyes and lungs burned and I began coughing violently. Then suddenly I lost my balance and fell on the stairs, after which I rolled the rest of the way down. Once I'd reached the bottom, I went crawling towards the garden gate in the hope of catching a breath of even semi-fresh air.

Then I picked myself up again, having decided to try

reaching my flat by way of the spiral iron fire escape that ascended the rear wall of the building. The sniper came to mind, of course, but even that thought didn't daunt me. Instead, the image of the fire had fixed itself in my mind's eye, while its aroma had so inundated my senses that it nearly suspended them altogether. Even my sense of fear and caution seemed to have vanished into thin air. So here I was, rushing madly back out to the garden – I, the one who just an hour earlier hadn't dared step out even for the few seconds it would have required to pick up a revolver from the ground.

Rocks and books like flaming orbs continued to cascade into the garden. Meanwhile, the rubbish bin had been knocked over and Amm Fu'ad's corpse was on fire. Despite the dense clouds of smoke engulfing me on all sides, I could smell the distinctive, penetrating odour of burning human flesh. As for the servant's corpse, it was still a fair distance away from the area where the fiery chunks had been hitting the ground – so far, at least.

As I made my way up the fire escape, I knew there was no need to worry about being shot by a sniper, since by now, the smoke was so thick that it cast a protective veil around me, hiding me from view. On the other hand, I started to wonder if the smoke might not be more of a curse than a blessing. In other words, was it protecting me from a sniper's bullet only for me to choke to death instead?

I could hear Amin shouting up at me: 'Get down here, you crazy woman. You're going burn to death!'

However, I just stood there thinking about my papers... and my books. Then, in a single moment, the titles of hundreds of books that I'd collected from all over the globe passed before my inner eye. Among them were books that I'd managed to afford only by going without food and clothes. But no sooner had I reached the top of the staircase than I was met by the fire, which was blazing out through the kitchen door and windows, all the while spitting and crackling in the most dreadful way. Under the circumstances, opening the door would have meant casting myself into a fiery furnace whose tongues of flame were ready to leap out and consume me at a moment's notice.

As I headed back down the stairs, a feeling of dizziness started to come over me and there was a distressing ringing in my ears. It was as if my body were issuing its final warning. When at last I reached the ground, I was obliged to remove myself to the remotest corner of the garden, since the wall of the study had begun to disintegrate completely and, like lava spewing out of a volcano's mouth, the flames which were consuming the wall were being hurled tremendous distances. Some of them landed on the date palm tree and began incinerating its branches, while others settled on the servant's dead body, which was likewise set ablaze.

Everything seemed to be against me on this particular morning. The sun was observing events below with a cool, dispassionate eye and the wind was doing an admirable job of spreading the fire!

'O god of rain!' I pleaded. 'Couldn't you pay a visit just now to my house and my heart? O god of rain, send forth your clouds and have mercy on these humble lines, which were written not with ink (as some have mistakenly imagined), but with tears of sorrow and struggle!'

Then I ran back into the house, having finally been convinced of the futility of playing fireman. Once inside, I sprinted over to the phone, still clinging to the hope that I might be able to get the firemen to come. However, there was still no dialling tone. And as for the idea of going outside to call for help, it would have meant being shot the moment I stepped through the door.

I started to head back again to the inside staircase. This time, though, even so much as stepping into the stairwell would have all but guaranteed death by asphyxiation.

However, I mustered sufficient courage to go out and pick up the revolver that had fallen from the bag of loot left by the 'ravens'. As I went back inside, I planned my next attempt to make contact with the outside world. Even so, I knew full well that even if I did manage to contact the fire department, no one would dare come to where we were, in the very heart of the war zone. I also knew that even if the firemen did come, they'd be shot at before they arrived and as a result wouldn't be able to put out the fire after all.

So I flung myself on to a chair, letting my arms dangle limply at my sides like the oars of an abandoned rowing boat. There was nothing left for me to do but listen to the hiss of the blazing inferno above me. From where I sat I could see it as it gobbled up my precious, irreplaceable books. And along with the books, the flames had begun devouring paintings by Ghassan Kanafani, Rafi' Al-Nasiri and Farouq Al-Baqili. After consuming everything there was to consume on the first wall, it moved on to the other walls, where it proceeded to ravage works by Afif Saydawi, Na'im Isma'il and 'Arif Al-Rayyis. Then finally it migrated to the next room, where it swallowed up paintings by Nouri Al-Rawi, Lu'ay Kayali, Rafiq Sharaf, Nadhir Nab'ah, Mustafa Farroukh, Younis Al-Ibn and, well, that's all I care to remember.

Then suddenly I heard a blast go off somewhere above me, from which I surmised that the container of butane gas in the bathroom had exploded. So, then, the fire had reached that far ... Oh! I thought, if only the cleansing, purging flames could distinguish between that which they ought to reduce to ashes and that which they should leave untouched! If only this fire had eyes, it would weep at the sight of the works of art being destroyed by its flames, every one of which was once a 'piece' of a human being.

How many friends and comrades of mine were having parts of their inner beings now go up in flames, mingled with parts of my own spirit as well?

Why is it that fire has to be like a mother cat who doesn't have sense enough to recognize that the tasty meal she is about to devour is the fruit of her own womb?

As I sat there ruminating, in came a terror-stricken Amin, who announced: 'Your whole flat is going up in smoke! And I'm afraid the fire might spread to the whole building!'

The louse! I thought. He couldn't care less about my library – the only thing he loses any sleep over is his *objets d'art*! Likewise, he doesn't give a damn if an inferno is blazing in *my* house – all that matters is for it not to spread to *his*! I wondered, do you suppose someone might catch sight of the clouds of smoke rising from my flat and rush to my rescue? On the other hand, who would be daring – or foolhardy – enough even to come near the place? Firemen? An ambulance crew? Perhaps it was hoping for too much to think that the fire in my house might become the means of my escape.

The situation made me think of an Alfred Hitchcock novel that I'd read a few months earlier, about an elderly woman living in a secluded house who became the victim of a plot by her son and his wife to murder her for her money. Their plan was to kill her by giving her the wrong amounts of her medicine. But first they disconnected the telephone to prevent her from communicating with the outside world. When the old woman learned of their plans, she was at a loss to know what to do. However, at last she concluded that her only hope lay in setting the house on fire. So that's exactly what she did, with the result that people in a neighbouring village saw the fire and clouds of smoke and came rushing to her rescue.

So, I wondered, was it possible that my library had been set ablaze as an offering on the altar of my continued survival? Would anyone come? Would anything happen?

It was obvious that the fighting going on outside was proceeding as if nothing had happened and that one more fire would do nothing to change either the course of the shells or the movements of the fingers poised on their respective triggers.

Even so, I ventured towards the outside door of the building. I was spurred on in part by a vague, ill-defined hope and in part by a profound urge to blow up everything around me that was capable of being blown up, even if it meant setting off a bomb in the very house that had been giving me shelter.

Pacing around me nervously and staring at his family treasures, Amin said: 'That fire has got to be put out. Otherwise, it'll spread to the whole building. Don't you think so? Or do you think it will go out of its own accord once it's burned up everything in your flat?'

I gave him the answer he was longing to hear.

'Oh,' I said, 'I'm sure it will just go out automatically when it's burned up everything upstairs!'

Then a light went on in my head. By now, the fire surely must have reached the old wooden posts holding up the roof, in which case it had also extended as far as the ten barrels of water located in the same place. If the barrels burst, torrents of water would be sure to come pouring out of them in all directions, which in turn might put out the fire. On the other hand, I realized that since our water supply had been cut off for so long, they might all be empty by now. How woefully ill-informed I was about the workings of our house!

The winds that had initially helped to fan the flames had also blown in a thick layer of cloud. During the first four hours after the fire began, the sun seemed just to gaze down calmly at events below with the aloofness of an impartial observer. Now, however, the dark, opaque clouds that had remained obstinately in place during the previous days began reclaiming their positions and a slow, gloomy drizzle began to fall.

I said to Amin: 'If the water barrels under the roof burst, then they're bound to douse the fire, since the water will come spilling down on top of it. Besides, it's starting to rain now too.'

'Which means that tomorrow we'll die of thirst!' he retorted.

'Well,' I said, 'that's better than burning to death.'

I don't know for certain what was on Amin's mind just then – whether he was worrying about the prospect of either dying of thirst or burning to death, or whether he was contemplating the treasures he'd inherited from his father and the irony of the fact that they were in danger of going up in flames just forty-eight hours after they'd become his!

Be that as it may, the burning-barrel scenario I'd come up with turned out to be a false hope.

The only visible reactions aroused by the fire thus far were the flight of the garden cats to who-knows-where, and an ever-so-slight cracking of the windows by some of our neighbours across the street. No doubt there were inquisitive onlookers peering out and watching the fire with apprehension and concern, yet without daring to throw the windows wide open so as to get a clearer view of what was happening outside. Yet even from behind their windowpanes, they could look on with dismay and alarm at fire's awesome capacity to spread itself abroad, all the while thanking their lucky stars – or God – that the shells hadn't landed in *their* walls and that the flames hadn't gone sticking their tongues out of *their* windows!

In any case, I now knew that everyone else had also stayed meekly in their 'cages'. By this time, even the animals in the pet shop had devoured their jailer and near-executioner. And now what about us? When would we find it in ourselves to follow their example?

Nightmare 124

I held the revolver in my hand, turning it over and over and scrutinizing it from all angles.

I didn't know whether it was loaded or not. I didn't even know whether it worked. And supposing it did work, I didn't know whether I myself would be capable of putting it to use. From somewhere inside me I heard an obscure voice, commanding me to fire a shot at the as-yet-unexploded missile.

I don't how long Amin and I had been sitting there immersed in funereal silence, though it seemed like quite a while.

The sound of the drizzling rain had now turned into the thunderous roar of shelling and gunfire, and the winds began pummelling the city once more with a merciless barrage of raindrops.

'Come on,' I said to Amin, 'let's check things out.'

We opened the door of his flat and approached the staircase. Noticing that the clouds of smoke were thicker than they had been before, I said: 'This means that the fire has begun to die down.'

Our feet were getting wet and when we took a closer look at the spot where we were standing, we discovered that the floor was immersed in water. It was rushing down the stairs in copious torrents, like a waterfall whose voice was being drowned out by the 'symphony' of bullets and rain. Could this all be nothing but rainwater? I wondered. Or had the barrels burst after all? And the fire – had it died down or not? There was no way yet to get clear answers to any of my questions. But one thing at least was certain: there was now a greater chance of our dying of thirst than of our burning to death! As to whether we might die of starvation, that was another question.

The thought of starving to death brought to mind Amin's monkey languishing in her cage. So I asked him: 'Aren't you going to feed your monkey?'

'You want me to put my life on the line just to feed a monkey?' he said.

That was all I needed to convince me. I was hungry and frightened enough by this time that even the flimsiest argument in favour of self-preservation would have won me over in a split second. From now on, I was going to look out for number one!

Then I asked him: 'If you could leave the house, would you take her along with you or abandon her in her cage?'

Irritated, he replied: 'Take her with me? You've got to be kidding!'

Then, pointing to his copious treasures, he went on: 'There's no way I could fit her into my car along with all my stuff. Even if they brought me three trucks, they wouldn't be big enough to hold all my things!'

This time, though, I wasn't satisfied with his answer.

Meanwhile, I kept fidgeting with the revolver in my hand, gazing at it thoughtfully and wondering... and wondering... Then smoke began engulfing me on all sides and I began coughing. Judging from the noticeable increase in the density of the smoke, I concluded that the fire must have gone out.

Nightmare 125

I was no longer obliged to avoid sitting near glass windows. It was true that every one of the windows in the flat had once been a potential dagger, which at any moment could have been plunged into my body in the event of an explosion. However, all the windowpanes in the house were now shattered, which eliminated the danger of any future implosions of splintered glass.

Having planted myself in a corner of the flat as far away as I could get from the unexploded missile, I sat writing. I was making notes on the Beirut nightmares which I'd been living through every waking – and non-waking – moment. They were nightmares which I'd become aware of months before the outbreak of the actual fighting, having more than once received warning signals alerting me to their imminent approach.

On that ever-so-fine line that lies between life and death, I fidgeted, I squirmed, I writhed... and I wrote. I wrote, with the words pouring from me like blood from an open wound.

My hand was hurting. Some of the wounds left by the angry dog's claws had healed over, while others were on their way to becoming infected, the flesh around them having grown puffy and red. Still I kept writing.

As I wrote, Amin stared at me angrily across the room. He was listening to the radio, though the battery was about to go dead. As the war swallowed up everything around us, our distinguished local station was blithely broadcasting some sweet-sounding waltz. After that, an announcer came on and started talking about a group of pacifists and 'non-partisans' who'd taken to the streets in non-violent demonstrations, then held an American-style vigil in one of Beirut's public parks, their signs and slogans all being in English and French.

As I listened to the announcer, I burst out laughing. How naïve and even childish such gatherings seemed when judged by the 'logic' of hunger, terror and fire! To me, such people seemed innocent to the point of being out of touch with reality – in which case their innocence was itself a crime!

When I'd finished writing, I leaned back against my little orange travel bag, then picked up the revolver and began examining it again.

Nightmare 126

Amin brought out another bottle of aged wine from among his treasures.

'I wouldn't advise you to drink wine,' I said to him. 'You'll be thirsty afterwards and you'll end up having to drink huge amounts of revolting water that's full of lime.'

'I don't care,' he said. 'Since I'll be drunk, I won't notice how it tastes.'

I cautioned him, saying: 'Remember that if we each drink two glasses of water a day, our supply will only last us for three more days.'

'It doesn't matter,' he said. 'I'm going to drink it anyway.'

'Oh, yes it does,' I offered defiantly, rotating the revolver in my hand. 'It matters, because I'm not going to let you get drunk and then use up my share of the water. I'm warning you – I don't intend to give you a single drop of my share! And don't get it into your head that just because you're a male, you're entitled to double my share of the "siege water"!'

Then I went back to inspecting the revolver in my hand.

As for Amin, a worried look crossed his face and he said: 'Put that revolver away.'

But rather than complying with his request, I found myself

tightening my grip on the gun and perhaps for the first time, I realized how much I needed it if I was going to survive in the 'jungle' we now found ourselves in. The war had burned away all our masks. It had laid bare the savagery that had once remained hidden behind the city's veneer of civilized urbanity.

Then I said to him: 'Come on, let's put a few containers outside and collect some rainwater. We might need it!'

It amazed me to see myself thinking of all these things, planning for all possible contingencies – all, that is, except suicide. It was hard to believe that I was the same person who, just a few months earlier, had been in the habit of driving through Beirut's perilous streets in the hope that some sniper would relieve her of the burden of having to go on living in this world. That was how little value I'd placed on my life after losing my beloved Yousif. But now I held a gun in my hand and was prepared to aim it at just about anything – anything, that is, except my own head.

'Please,' Amin implored, 'get rid of that thing. After all, you and I are both hoping for the same things: peace and stability.'

I replied: 'When one's own homeland has "emigrated", leaving behind the values of humanity and social justice, how can any of its citizens be "stable"?'

Nightmare 127

I'd been holding the receiver in my hand for about an hour, hoping against hope that it would show some signs of life. As I sat there waiting, a warm sensation came over me. It was like a heightened consciousness of my own aliveness, as it were – the realization that, against all odds, I was still living and breathing. I was wresting life by force out of death's omnipresent grip, inhaling life-giving oxygen despite the clouds of smoke that threatened to engulf me, snatching my daily bread out of the clutched fists of the slain and stealing the moments of sleep I needed to survive out of the talons of nightmares.

I may have sat there with the receiver in my hand for over an hour. However long it was, there continued to be no 'juice', no dialling tone and no sign of the familiar ring which at that particular moment would have been music to my ears.

And thus ended another attempt in failure. However, I decided to try again later on.

Nightmare 128

Another evening approached...
Before long it would be followed by another night laden with bad dreams and screams of terror.

I told Amin that I was going upstairs to see what the fire had done.

'I'll come with you,' he said, no doubt burning with curiosity to see what sort of tragedy had befallen somebody else's home. This way, he could take secret pleasure in destruction without its touching him personally, like a filmgoer slouched down in his cosy, velvet-upholstered seat in a darkened cinema watching some pilot burn to death in his cockpit, enjoying the sight of violence that poses no danger to his own person, of death that poses no threat to his own existence.

As we headed up the staircase, it became clear that even to come near the entrance to my flat would be a life-threatening venture. Dangling from what remained of the ceiling were clumps of rock and cement hanging by iron threads, like macabre chandeliers decorating a vampire's abode.

And from the roof above there dripped muddy, blackish water that looked like the tears of the approaching night.

As for the doors that had once led into the flat, there was nothing left of them. They'd been literally consumed by the flames. However, we weren't able to take even a single step inside. The floor was covered with heaps of rock and ash, from beneath which hot smoke continued to waft upward. There was no furniture left in the entire place, nor had any of the walls been left intact, while the stones that lay beneath the roof looked as if they had been stripped completely bare. I realized that the nondescript heaps I was seeing on the floor must be a mixture of incinerated furniture and rocks that had fallen from the ceiling and the walls.

As for the gaping hole in the wall, I could see when I looked through it that what had once been my 'military headquarters' was now little more than a few iron skewers covered by traces of cement. As for the hundreds of books which had once covered the wall, they'd been transmuted into the black heaps that I'd seen on the floor. Out of them rivulets of thickish smoke were coiling slowly upward, while drops of blackened water trickled down on to them from various hard-to-identify locations. The heaps on the floor were so hot it would have been impossible even to try to walk over them.

I stuck my head in and in a single glance I realized exactly what had become of my library. For as I looked through the opening that had once been a door, I couldn't see a single trace of the room's original features. Most of the walls had collapsed and the furniture had vanished. In fact, there was virtually nothing left but the floor, which was now blanketed with huge mounds of the ghastly concoction that had been left behind by the conflagration. Whatever it was smelt like a mixture of fire and water in a house devoid of everything but thick smoke and fine black dust saturated with moisture.

Why is it that fire can't tell the difference between a wall and a painting, or between Kleenex and papers on which precious manuscripts have been written? Why is it that records, books and paintings – which themselves are living beings in my view – are incapable of defending themselves against fire, or even fleeing? If a fire happened to break out in the Louvre, for example, and no one intervened, you can be sure that the cats that hang out at the museum would make a quick getaway, whereas the Mona Lisa herself would meet a tragic end!

I must have leaned my hand up against the wall, since the next time I looked, it was covered with thick black dust.

Then suddenly I found myself rubbing my face with my grubby hand in unspeakable grief and sorrow. There was no doubt about it – my library, my paintings and my music had all gone up in smoke!

So I went on smudging my face with black dust like a grief-stricken aborigine at a funeral.

Nightmare 129

It was night-time and I was now paying for the foolishness in which I'd indulged earlier in the day. Standing out in the garden in the pouring rain, I scrubbed my face with soap so as to remove the grime and soot, then let the rain wash it all off. I hadn't wanted to make such a spectacle of myself in front of the trees and other plants in the garden. However, there was little else I could do, since the only water we had in the house was being reserved for drinking.

The cold water awakened and revitalized my senses and once again I was inundated with a feeling of joyful exhilaration at the mere fact of still being alive – at the fact that with every passing moment I was wresting life from the powers of death that threatened to close in on me from all sides.

The cold water seemed to have revived not only my senses but everything that was 'me', everything in the deepest part of my being that was authentic and real. At that moment, as I stood there being washed clean by the rain, I found myself deciding with a sense of serenity and even joy that if the flames which consumed my home were the labour pains necessary for the birth of the joy to come, if the fire which destroyed my precious papers was the purgatory agent needed to cleanse the people of this land, and if the bombs which razed the walls of my house serve to open up even a single window in the dungeon of spiritual and material wretchedness in which we've been languishing, then all I can say is: Blessed be the tongues of fire which engulfed my abode! Blessed be the tremors which razed it to its foundations, if by so doing they could at the same time bring down the walls of injustice and alienation! Blessed be the firestorm that caused ten years of my life to go up in smoke, if that same volcano could banish those who had brought such suffering and travail upon this homeland of ours, bringing them out of the depths of darkness into the brilliant light of freedom and justice.

I also decided: If I get out of here in one piece, I'll go and buy myself enough blank paper to equal the volume of all my charred manuscripts. Then I'll start writing, and I'll keep on writing until I've filled up every page. I'll continue crying out for equality, justice, freedom and joy, and I won't let myself be daunted by a burned-down house! After all, houses are nothing but stones piled one on top of another, and planet Earth is at best a temporary home in which we're never more than mere guests, regardless of where we happen to make our dwelling. The only true home I've ever known, the only one

I've inhabited all my life, is my body, and that home, I still occupy to this very day.

Blessed be the fiery lips which swallowed up my dwelling place, if by so doing they could purge this sorrowing homeland of its anguish and distress. The important thing now was for me to remain alive – for only then could I go on writing.

I rushed to the phone again to make one more attempt at getting help. And oddly enough, no sooner had I lifted the receiver than the dialling tone returned. So I quickly dialled the number of my friend Amal. Her voice came over the line, saying: 'At 7.00 a.m., a tank will come to get you out, military conditions permitting.'

'Seven o'clock *tomorrow* morning?' I shouted into the receiver. But before the scores of questions on the tip of my tongue could come tumbling out of my mouth, and before I could ask for clarification as to how and why and who, the phone gave up the ghost.

I tried to call her back, but to no avail. The phone had breathed its last. The time I'd have to wait until the next day's rendezvous seemed more like twelve light-years than a mere twelve hours. But, I wondered, did she really mean 'tomorrow'? What exactly *did* she say? I could feel her words coming unglued from each other in my memory. Then they fell to the floor and scattered in all directions, like a bag of coloured marbles that had just been kicked over by a peevish, contrary little boy! Oh, my peevish, contrary memory!

Nightmare 130

I closed my eyes and could see the scars left by the fire on the sides of the buildings. I looked around at the appalling destruction that had left its mark on entire neighbourhoods and commercial districts, at the rains that were striving in vain to wash the soot off charred, blackened walls, and telephone poles that had snapped, their wires now dangling in the wind like the bodies of lifeless adders.

Everything in Beirut was black and grey – everything, at least, except for the multicoloured mountains of putrid refuse which had taken over the pavements, covered with feverish swarms of mammoth flies each of which was the size of a full-grown man.

Rubble was strewn everywhere, as far as the eye could see – shards of splintered glass, the fragmented remains of doors, ruins that had once been homes and the tattered remnants of cherished memories.

I shut my eyes again and could see Beirut's gaping wound. Open and exposed to the rain, the winds and the freezing night, it ran the length and breadth of the city, up one street and down the next. At the same time, I could hear a voice crying out from somewhere deep inside me: But even before the war, Beirut wasn't as beautiful as people imagined her to be!

She'd worn a lovely, alluring veil, of course. Now, however, her disguise had been burned away by the war and all her infirmities lay open to public gaze. She'd known how to deck herself out in the most bewitching, brightly coloured finery. But beneath it she'd concealed cancerous growths which, once her condition was beyond repair, could be treated only by cauterization with a red-hot iron. Foreseeing the tragic end that awaited her, the wise and discerning had cried out year after year for her to be delivered from her deadly affliction, until at last they'd shouted themselves hoarse.

The neon-lit boulevards filled with raucous, drunken laughter and the frenzied beat of rock-and-roll music represented little more than 5 per cent of all the streets in

Beirut, while on the remaining 95 per cent – streets paved with the dust of hunger and starvation, ignorance and disease, defeatism and privation – copious tears of despair were watering the seeds of bitterness and hatred. This was the 'dynamite soil' whose explosive implications couldn't be missed by anyone familiar with even the most elementary principles of historical causality.

Although it's true that tens of thousands of people were now losing their lives in the throes of this miserable war, it's nevertheless also true that people had been perishing by the thousands prior to the bloodshed as well. They'd been dying of tyranny and inequity, heartsickness and worry, hunger, destitution, rage and ignorance.

And they'd been dying in silence, in the secrecy of anonymity. At the same time, the streets were teeming with people who were still technically alive, although inside something had broken or perished. As a result, their bodies had become little more than 'portable coffins' which served to conceal the fact of their clandestine 'departures'.

Nightmare 131

Was it thunder I was hearing or the screams of our tormented hearts?

Autumn had now arrived. It had returned to the forests, but all it found was charred stumps. It had gone searching out its old familiar paths, only to find them strewn with the corpses of the slain. Then it had gone back to the riverbanks and seashores, where the winds told it the story of Beirut's gruesome, bloodstained summer.

It had returned to its 'family' of kind-hearted, simple souls who loved life and each other with a passion, only to find them wounded and bleeding. Perhaps that was why the sky had done nothing all night but weep and weep and weep. Most people had mistaken its tears for rain. However, what had been falling from the sky this year wasn't rain – but the tears of the four seasons!

I tried to distract myself from the sound of the thunder by listening to the radio. When I turned it on, the announcer was bringing us the glad tidings that the vending booths which had been set up by destitute merchants on Beirut's Hamra Street were now being removed. It was a desperate attempt to restore a tourist-friendly façade to the site which had once been looked upon as the counterpart to such attractions as Paris's Champs-Elysées and London's Oxford Street. So, here they were cleaning up the pavements of Hamra Street by sweeping away the cries of its tragedy-stricken pedlars. They were stocking up on every imaginable sort of food, drink and clothing in an attempt to repel the assault that had been launched on the street by the proletariat masses. Chairs had been set out in the pavement cafés again in anticipation of the return of the 'coffee-shop revolutionaries' (whose favourite pastime was championing the cause of the oppressed masses over cups of Turkish coffee or sticky sweet tea). But... would it really be possible for anything to go back to the way it had been 'before'?

No, never. In this drizzly, gloomy, Beirut autumn, a hot morning cup of coffee at a pavement café would taste less like cardamom and more like an open wound.

The misery of those who had once taken up residence on the pavements of Hamra Street couldn't be so easily swept away from the pavements of our memories. Nor could the sufferings of those who languished in the poverty-infested chimes ringing the city.

Just as no one can treat a wound by keeping it out of sight, neither would they be able to conceal Beirut's maimed, bloodied face behind the 'veil' of Hamra Street.

No one, of course, could object to the idea of turning Hamra Street back into a clean, 'civilized' place. However, the fact that those in positions of responsibility could consider this one step sufficient to solve the problem simply exposed their woeful ignorance of the true nature and import of what had been taking place.

Moving the misery backstage, as it were, wouldn't remove it from existence any more than hiding a patient under the bed would cure him of his illness. And even if it did happen to relieve his suffering for a time, sooner or later he'd be bound to come out of his drugged stupor, at which point he'd find that his pain had grown fiercer and more excruciating than before. Then, in an agonized rage, he'd fling himself at his 'torturer', the hospital warden who'd taken great care to ensure the cleanliness of the corridors and waiting areas, while leaving the patients' rooms to become filthy and infested with vermin!

As the city's wound split open, it was producing a sound like a raging, fiery thunderstorm. It's a phenomenon to which the histories of nations and peoples have borne repeated witness. But in this particular place and time, it seemed that those with the necessary power and influence to benefit from such lessons were unwilling to listen or understand. Even tuning in to their radio broadcasts had become an insufferable nightmare!

Nightmare 132

I woke up screaming: 'Where's my brother?'

At the same time, I sensed that something out of the ordinary had happened to me. I was curled up next to the pillow and the bed was practically empty. My body had grown noticeably smaller and, when I felt myself, I found that I was covered with feathers. I tried to get up and fortunately it was quite easy. Then I tried walking towards the mirror to see what had happened to me, only to discover that instead of walking I was taking tiny hops. I'd sprouted wings as well, so I flew over to the mirror, nearly crashing into it, so astonished was I to find that I'd been transformed into a small owl.

But where's my brother? I kept wondering.

Seeing as how I'd sprouted wings, I decided to fly to the prison to see him. So off I went, soaring through the air over streets and alleys blanketed with the bodies of the slain.

Away I flew into the gloomy night, the night which had now become a minefield sown with dread and ghastly explosives.

Yet since I was now an ethereal being, the bullets passed through me without doing the slightest harm.

I flew in among the lightless prison cells, searching for my brother, and found that I could see quite well in the dark.

I could see the inmates crowded into the cells, each of which was filled with men, rats and all sorts of filth and rubbish. Resisting the urge to fly down and devour a rat, I continued my search for my brother.

Then at last I found him, squeezed into a tiny cell with one other inmate. The two of them were talking, so I pressed up against the window and began to listen.

The other inmate was saying to my brother: 'I wish you could see how I fight. You're invited to come along, Shadi!'

My brother replied: 'I've been invited to all sorts of social occasions in my time, but as for being invited to go to war – well, that's never happened to me before, Abu Tha'ir.'

Abu Tha'ir took off his shirt to reveal a map of Palestine tattooed on to his chest.

'What's that?' Shadi asked. 'A map of Palestine?'

'That's right,' replied the other. 'I'm from Nablus.'

'But what are you doing here? Why did they put you in prison?'

'There isn't a single country I've gone to without ending up behind bars,' he said. 'And my only crime is being Palestinian. I've seen the inside of a cell in most foreign countries, and in most Arab countries as well. I learned German while I was doing time in Munich, then I learned English in jail in London. I learned how to play chess in prison too. If they leave you in here with me tomorrow, I'll teach you. We can draw the squares on the floor, then kill some cockroaches and make them into kings, pawns and bishops. Chess is a great game, though personally speaking I prefer real war.'

It was obvious that Abu Tha'ir had been dying to talk to someone – anyone. He went on and on, letting forth a continuous stream of incoherent chatter.

'I have five kids,' he said. 'My wife is my paternal cousin and in ten years of marriage I haven't seen her legs even once – all I know is how they feel in the dark.'

My brother replied: 'They've decided to put me in solitary confinement, because this morning I slugged one of the other inmates – though I can't remember any more why I did it. It was the first time I'd ever hit anybody in my life. But the guard – who happens to be in on the same hashish-supply network as the inmate that I hit – decided to throw me into solitary confinement. But there weren't any empty cells available at the time, so they put me in with you for the night. They said you'd beat me up – that you beat up anybody who sets foot in your cell.'

'That's not true,' protested Abu Tha'ir. 'Just because I'm Palestinian, they either accuse me of the most heinous crimes or credit me with the most glorious virtues. They either deify me or treat me as if I were the vilest of malefactors. No one bothers to look at what I really am – an ordinary human being who feels pain and rage, a refugee without a land to call "home".'

Interrupting him, Shadi said: 'I never imagined that I'd see such atrocities in prison! I honestly believed that our country was "the land of glorious splendour", and I was taken aback when some of my friends decided to take up arms.'

Abu Tha'ir made no reply. Even the things he *had* been saying weren't so much 'replies' as continuations of the conversation he was having with himself. The same was true of the things my brother had been saying. Both of them would speak at the same time, as if they were merely taking solace in each other's voices.

Abu Tha'ir: 'I don't read and I don't write. But even so, I learned foreign languages in European prisons, just as I learned to play chess. In most Arab prisons, though, it was a different story. In one of them, they hung me from the ceiling and beat me for God knows how long. My hands were broken in several places, and I've got an iron rod in my back now where my crushed spine used to be.'

Shadi: 'I had no idea what agony the Lebanese people were going through till I heard the stories that some of my cellmates had to tell. The situation is appalling. In the past I used to be revolted by the mere sight of a weapon, whereas now I'm revolted by anyone who refuses to carry one!'

Abu Tha'ir: 'One time I was with a delegation that had been sent to represent our cause at the United Nations. As the helicopter was lowering us on to the roof of the UN building, we were surrounded by CIA agents who'd been sent out to "protect" us. So we in turn gathered around one of our men in order to protect *him*. Then I turned to one of the CIA guards and said: 'I'd like you all to buy us a little hash if you can.'

'Well, one of my pals started berating me for what I'd said.

So I yelled right back at him: "What the hell's wrong with what I said? I mean, isn't the US the biggest hash factory in the world?"

'Then after I got locked up here in Beirut, I met a Lebanese journalist by the name of Sami who'd been slapped behind bars simply because he'd had the audacity to tell the facts "straight" – without beating around the bush, you know. He was punished for demanding that justice be done for his suffering people!

'...When I was at the military training camp in Zarqa, we kept being attacked by Israeli planes. I'd been exploding enemy shells before they hit the ground by shooting them down with my automatic rifle. One day I destroyed more than ten of them with an Israeli plane hovering right over me. Then, all of a sudden, I heard my little boy calling out to me from a nearby trench. I was nonplussed: What could have brought him all the way here? I wondered. Anyway, I'd barely reached the trench when a bomb went off and demolished my car and with it my automatic rifle, which I'd left inside. I didn't find my little boy in the trench. But at least I got out of there alive.

'If I do get out of prison, I'll never forget. I've changed completely, once and for all. I used to hear people say: Whoever opens a school, closes down a prison. Well, I regret the fact that I ever even attended school. All it did was distract me from seeing the tragedy that Lebanon was living through. As for prison, it's the only true "school" I've ever known!

'And then there was "Operation Green Belt" – that was unforgettable. I remember seeing our men advance, then join battle with the Israelis. I was still recovering from wounds I'd suffered in a previous confrontation, so I had to stay in the observation tower. And from there I could see everyone dying, Palestinians and Israelis alike.

'Oh, all the fighting I've done. Everything in my body is worn out and out of commission – that is, except for one certain part.'

'And it isn't your head, of course!' Shadi commented wryly, at which they both broke out into loud guffaws.

It delighted me to see my brother laughing.

'Shadi!' I called out to him, trying to get his attention. 'Look at that owl!' Abu Tha'ir exclaimed. 'You know, I consider owls to be good omens. Or at least, they bring a lot less bad luck than most Arab leaders do! Who knows? Maybe its visit is a sign that the prison is going to be destroyed.'

The prison was ablaze. Meanwhile, together with Abu Tha'ir and a huge cavalcade of fleeing prisoners, my brother was sprinting along as fast as his legs would carry him. They were being shot at, but they kept on running. All Abu Tha'ir had carried out of the prison with him was the map of Palestine tattooed on his chest. Likewise, Shadi had nothing in his hands. But I wondered what new images had now been burned into his heart.

As he ran, he flapped his arms in the wind, like the wings of a bird making its way towards the safe havens that lie hidden in the sun.

In a military training camp, my brother stood with a machine-gun in his hands. Abu Tha'ir was standing beside him.

'Fire!' said Abu Tha'ir. 'Is this really the first time you've done this?'

'It sure is,' replied Shadi, 'but I'm convinced now that it's the only way.'

Then he fired.

But I couldn't make out clearly what happened next, since the sun was quite bright and I was an owl!

Nightmare 133

I lay stretched out on the floor, with my back to the wall and my head resting on my orange travel bag. In the hand that was nearest the floor I clutched the revolver, with my finger on the trigger. The stillness was broken intermittently by Amin's snores, which from time to time were drowned out by the deafening clamour of bombs and other explosives.

As for me, I'd known from the start that I would neither sleep through the night nor be able to stay completely awake. Instead, I'd spend the night being preyed on by nightmares as I awaited the appearance of the sun. And with the sunrise I'd begin awaiting the arrival of the tank which I'd heard might come to rescue me the next morning.

It was possible that Amal had said 'tomorrow', but maybe I hadn't been paying close enough attention. Perhaps she *hadn't* said it, assuming that I'd understand automatically that this was what she meant. One thing she *had* stated clearly was '7.00 a.m.' But why not 6.00, or 5.00 for that matter? At 5.00 a.m., for example, it would still be dark, in which case it would be easier to carry out the operation without being detected by snipers.

I wondered which direction the tank would be coming from. Would it approach along Hourani Street, Makhfar Street or the main thoroughfare that passed in front of the Holiday Inn? Would I be able to run out to meet it without being injured? And if I did happen to be injured, would they take me to hospital in the tank or leave me to die and beat a hasty retreat? If I were carried to the tank, would someone suddenly barrage us with shells in an attempt to put the tank out of commission? And if so, would the shells actually hit us? Would the tank burst into flames? Would it catch on fire from the inside or would we manage to escape?

Would they come the next day or not for another month or another year? Would they arrive on time?

Should I wait outside, thereby exposing myself to further danger from the snipers? Or should I wait inside, thereby running the risk that they might come by and not see me, then conclude that I'd decided not to come after all for fear of losing my 'treasures' (not realizing, of course, that, being poor, I had no worldly treasures to lose) and leave without me? Would they know where I lived or would they get lost and end up waiting for me in front of some other house, then finally give up and leave? Would they let me bring my orange bag with me or would they make me leave it behind, saying that there wasn't enough room for both of us in the tank?

Once inside the tank, would I find scores of other suffering souls who, like me, were fleeing from the fighting and conflagrations? Would there be so many of us that we'd die of asphyxiation and overcrowding or would I be alone? What would the tank look like on the inside? Where would its door be – on the top or on the side? And if I'd been wounded on my way to the tank, would I be able to climb in?

And so the questions went on, as I sought to cope with what seemed like an endless number of frightening unknowns.

Nightmare 134

Oh... how long the night can be when nothing stands between life and death but hours of dread-filled anticipation.

How sluggishly the black sands of darkness make their descent through the hourglass when the extent of one's ambitions has been reduced to surviving the final watches of the night and seeing the break of dawn.

What brutal desolation awaits someone who, having been

stripped of all means of self-defence, finds that the inferno that now engulfs her is her only hope of survival.

And as if all this weren't enough, I was being obliged to listen to Amin snore!

Then it occurred to me to get up and do something. Moving around might help me throw off the listlessness that had come over my body, perhaps due to the feeling that time had come to a near-standstill. Picking up my body and moving it somewhere could protect me from the cold in all its varieties: the uncomfortable nip in the air, the icy chill of loneliness and the shudders that went up my spine as I felt time sliding over my flesh at the pace of a cold, clammy snail.

Hunger and cold – they were like the pincers of a crab assaulting every square inch of my body at once...

Yes – it would definitely be better for me to do something, to get up and move my body, which had become weighed down beneath burdens of hunger, darkness and bitter cold. But where could I go?

I thought of paying a visit to the creatures in the pet shop. From where I lay in the darkness, I could hear their shrieks and whimpers. In my mind's eye I saw a large, bullish-looking fish that had just finished devouring a smaller fish with colourful fins that looked like the wings of a butterfly. I could also see the cats as they awaited the demise of a wounded one among them so that they could make a meal of him. The parrot had lost consciousness, while the rabbits were jumping about madly in their cramped cage and banging their heads against the iron bars.

Why don't I let them loose? I thought to myself.

If I did that, I'd be placing them in danger of either starving or being shot in a city which was in the process of burning to the ground. No, it would be better to leave them where they were, in relative safety. After all, there was still the possibility that someone might come to their rescue at the last minute.

Then I thought: Why not just admit that I'm scared and that the only reason for my hesitation is fear of being attacked?

I knew, of course, that the strongest and most intrepid of the bunch had already taken leave of the place after the 'liberty feast' in which they'd devoured their jailer. On the other hand, what did I know about how cats, rabbits, birds, turtles and mice were likely to behave following a period of starvation? Wasn't it possible that a famished cat might turn into a tiger? Might not a starving rabbit be transformed into a cheetah or a panther? And a voracious sparrow into the fearsome roc? And a turtle into a dinosaur? And a mouse into a fox?

During the first few nights of the animals' ordeal, the shop had been a cavern reverberating with the echoes of their agonized laments. But now that it had been touched by hunger's magic wand, it might well have been transformed into a veritable lion's den of bared fangs and unbridled fury.

I pictured myself opening the turtle's cages, whereupon they gobbled up my feet. Then I let out the rabbits, who proceeded to devour me up to my chest. After that I released the cats, who ate up as far as my neck, followed by the mice, who finished off my cheeks, then leapt inside my skull and started coming out through my ears. Then finally I uncaged the birds, who pecked out my eyes, after which they all went on their way, leaving my bones to be chewed over by the dogs.

A shudder went through my body as if these things had actually happened! Oh, the merciless forebodings that can haunt the mind during the sleepless hours when nothing stands between life and death but a single night of dread-filled anticipation!

If only I could have dozed off for a while and let the nightmares come. *Anything* would have been preferable to this excruciating wait.

Nightmare 135

After escorting the young man who hadn't yet died to the hospital in a solemn funeral procession, bemoaning his departure with bitter tears as they committed him to the dust and concrete of the land of the living, the community of the deceased returned to the graveyard...
When they got back home early in the evening, they found that there had been quite an influx of new residents that day, whose stories they hadn't yet had a chance to hear.

'Come, let's knock on their doors,' said their leader.

So they rapped on the first fresh grave, whereupon a new neighbour emerged from his tomb. They gave him a hearty welcome.

'And who are you?' they inquired.

'I used to be a government employee. I'd spent my entire life in people's service. Then I was killed by a sniper, who shot me simply because I happened to be alive!'

All together, they replied: 'What a nice thing to do – may God reward him richly! These snipers grant people peace free of charge. So apparently there are still some people left in your world who know how to do good!'

'Well,' said the newcomer somewhat indignantly, 'I used to do good too! The day Beirut went crazy with a wave of killing, with people being murdered right, left and centre at armed checkpoints just because of what happened to be written on their identity cards, someone could lose his life for no reason other than that he'd been born to a Muslim or a Christian father. So I came up with the idea of "flower checkpoints." At this type of checkpoint, you're stopped by a group of young men and women holding flowers in their hands. Instead of asking you about your religion, then killing you (or sparing you) according to the law of chance, they give you a flower simply for being alive and for being a fellow citizen. In fact, sometimes they plant flowers in soldiers' gunbarrels in the hope that their rifles might be transformed some day from "trees of fire" into "trees of blessing". But then I was killed by one of those "trees of fire", even though I hadn't done a thing wrong!'

The newcomer had expected his story to arouse some sympathy on the part of his fellow deceased. However, this only showed that he was still a stranger among them. He hadn't yet learned their ways, or the by-laws and principles that operated in this land of theirs. Consequently, he was surprised to find that instead of showing admiration and approval for the accomplishments in which he'd taken such pride, they simply turned away from him.

'Tell me, for God's sake,' he pleaded with them, 'what did I do to deserve such treatment? What was my crime?'

'Your crime,' replied one of their sages, 'was that you turned a blind eye to the truth. Did you actually believe that you could treat the wound by merely planting a flower in it?'

Nightmare 136

Mansour hadn't actually been intending to do what he did. It was as if fate had deliberately aided and abetted him in committing the act and he just hadn't been able to resist the temptation any longer.

Every night for ten years he'd dreamed of doing this very thing. However, he'd never actually intended to carry out the idea. Instead, day-dreams had sufficed to dispel some of the bitterness in his soul. Or at least they would have sufficed, if it hadn't been for the passer-by who'd chanced to die in his arms that day.

Mansour had been coming out of the bank, as he usually did around noon, when all of a sudden he was assailed by sniper fire coming from a nearby alley. Shortly thereafter, the man who'd been walking right in front of him keeled over.

The man fell at Mansour's feet. As a result, Mansour tripped and fell himself, and they both ended up on the pavement. A bullet had landed in the man's head. He didn't scream. He didn't seem to be in pain. He didn't even close his eyes. Mansour couldn't recall whether, when he took the man in his arms, he'd been intending to give him first aid or just use his body as a shield against the sniper's bullets. He didn't know whether he'd been trying to unbutton the stranger's jacket to help him breathe – since there still remained the possibility that he wasn't dead, but just unconscious – or whether his actual motive had been to look for the man's identity card.

He wasn't sure. He didn't really want to think about it. All he knew for certain was that for ten years he'd dreamed of carrying some other man's identity card and of being able to muster the courage to do what he'd done today.

It was a dream that had haunted him for ten long years, ever since he'd begun working at the bank. From the very beginning, the process of counting the money at the bank had caused him a kind of subtle, indefinable pain. He was in dire poverty and it was costing him fantastic sums simply to buy painkillers for his mother, who was suffering from a terminal illness. Consequently, all his money had been ending up in the doctor's pocket. At the same time, though, he was quite fond of the doctor and used to thank him from the bottom of his heart when, at the end of every month, he deposited the sum total of his modest earnings in the man's hands.

Mansour had no access to women, since women – lovers and wives alike – wanted to see the money first and then the man. He'd missed out on the chance to complete his education, since it seemed that the professors were more interested in collecting tuition fees than they were in dispensing knowledge. He was even deprived of such simple things as laughter, joy, friendship, a coat to keep him warm in the winter or a soft shirt for the summer. Instead, he was obliged to keep wearing the same clothes all year round, until they hung threadbare and tattered on his weakened frame. Yet he never forgot to thank the doctor. That is, until one day...

He was standing in the teller's booth, counting the money that had come in that day, when suddenly he saw a huge bundle of blue-coloured notes being placed in front of him.

He looked up and who should he see standing before him but... the doctor! As usual, Mansour greeted him warmly, with all the conventional polite words required in such situations.

'Welcome, Bey!' he said effusively. 'At your service! What can we do for you today, sir?'

The doctor wanted to deposit 10,000 Lebanese pounds in his account — 100,000 blue-coloured notes which he'd brought in five gargantuan bundles.

Mansour began counting the money, turning the notes over one by one with the speed and dexterity he'd become well known for. As he did so, his fingers were afflicted with the same mysterious ache that he felt every time he counted a large sum that didn't belong to him and which he knew would quickly pass from his hands to someone else's. It was as if he'd been allowed to handle it for the sole purpose of tormenting himself — kindling dreams and aspirations that he knew he could never attain and thereby reopening the wounds left by one disappointment after another.

And then suddenly, he saw it... His own signature on four bills which represented about two-thirds of his monthly pay. He'd got into the habit of signing all the paper money that he collected as wages, as if this were a way of keeping it in his possession for as long as possible. By 'branding' it the way a rancher brands livestock, he could be certain that even if it passed on to someone else, it would, in a certain sense, always remain his.

Yes, it was his signature all right. And they were his notes, the ones which, if the doctor hadn't devoured them, he could have used to buy himself a winter coat or a bit of meat more than once a week. He could also have bought himself the book he'd seen in the display window of the bookshop next to the bank which he lusted after every time he passed it on his way to work in the mornings. He might even have acquired himself a wife to keep him warm during the bitterly cold nights he'd been spending listening to his elderly mother's pained sighs and groans.

On that day, the pain in his fingers was transmuted into a fierce hatred and resentment. He began counting the doctor's money with ever-increasing speed, his fingers like a machine that had suddenly begun working faster and faster until it was on the verge of exploding.

From that day on, he began suffering excruciating pain in his fingers whenever anyone brought him a gargantuan bundle of cash to deposit in his account. He kept thinking about all the things that such money could do for him and for thousands of other unfortunate souls.

However, the 'maniacal dream' had begun on the day he was promoted. In reward for his trustworthiness and honesty on the job, he was made responsible for overseeing the vault where the safe-deposit boxes were located. In his new position, his duties were restricted to receiving customers who rented safe-deposit boxes, unlocking various doors for them and escorting them through a number of underground passageways to the vault itself. A high-security chamber containing scores of iron safes whose locks could be worked in five minutes or less, the vault was like one giant cashbox.

When escorting clients to the vault, Mansour was expected to walk behind them with all due respect, since people who rented safe-deposit boxes (where one could keep jewels, documents relating to big business deals and the like) were of course among the extremely wealthy. In other words, they were the *de facto* rulers of this wretched, pitiable country of his. He was supposed to open the armoured door leading into the vault, then step aside so as to let the client go in ahead of him. Mansour brought one key and the client another, since the safes were designed in such a way that they would open only if both keys were used. Personally speaking, he found the entire operation something of a farce. However, rituals are rituals, whether they take place in a church, a mosque, a temple – or a bank.

After opening someone's safe, Mansour would pull out a drawer which lay nestled in its bottom. The drawer was in turn covered with a lid which was intended to protect 'client confidentiality'. After placing the drawer on a special shelf, he would pull up a chair for the client so that he or she could sit directly in front of it. Once the client was sitting comfortably, Mansour would stand nearby, with his back turned to the proceedings in a theatrical about-face that suggested respect for the client's precious secrets. Consequently, the client could feel free to put into the safe whatever he or she so desired: jewellery, gold ingots, a box of fancy soap – even a time bomb!

Once the safe had been put away again and relocked with both keys, Mansour and the client would re-emerge from the vault. Mansour would bolt the room shut, accompany the client back out through the underground passageways, lock the entrance securely, then escort the client to the door of the bank. And so on and so on...

He had to admit that sometimes he did steal glances at the

things people deposited in their safes. Some of the jewels he'd seen were so dazzlingly enormous, he thought they must be glass.

Then one day, who should come to see his safe but the doctor. This time, Mansour didn't content himself with furtive glances. On the contrary, he stared unabashedly, indifferent to the doctor's irritation and discomfort. He took a good look at everything, including the sumptuous antique jewellery that sparkled under the fluorescent light of the vault.

'These belonged to my mother, who passed away a week ago,' the doctor told him, disguising the pride he took in them beneath a tone of complaint.

'May she rest in peace,' Mansour replied mechanically. 'God grant you patience in your affliction.'

But to himself he thought: *His* affliction? And what about mine? What about all the times I've had to listen to my mother's loud weeping and lamentation all night long because my salary had run out before the end of the month and I couldn't afford the painkillers she needed to keep her in reasonable comfort?

It was that night that the dream came...

Mansour dreamed that he was one of the people who rented safe-deposit boxes in the bank and it so happened that his safe was immediately next to the doctor's. He went into the bank, where he was received with a bow and a scrape by the employee responsible for the vault. Once inside, he placed a bomb into his safe. Then he was escorted out by the bank employee, who bowed again respectfully, taking him for some wealthy patron who'd just deposited the crown jewels in the vault. No sooner had he emerged from the bank than the bomb exploded. Destroying precious jewels and 'vital' documents, it sent up in flames the obscene wealth which surrounded it on every side – wealth that had been amassed by its owners by prostituting their souls year after year. At the end of the dream, Mansour was sitting on the pavement outside the bank, wearing his holed shoes and the tattered rags which he used for clothes. As he sat there, he began laughing uncontrollably until an intense, blissful rush coursed through his body. Then he woke up, still in a state of euphoric arousal.

After this, the dream had remained no more than a dream – that is, until the day the stranger died in Mansour's arms. For in so doing, he left his identity card in Mansour's possession, thereby making the dream's realization possible.

This would be the first time Mansour had betrayed the institution whose ranks he had joined so long ago. On the other hand, one could say that he wasn't exactly betraying it, but rather just putting to personal use some of the weapons that it had placed at his disposal.

Or, let's say that he misused them. But no… he didn't even do that. Rather, it was simply that the dream was too complex, too abstruse, too opaque for him to be able to explain it to anyone and too profoundly truthful for him to apologize for it.

In order to carry out his plan, he went to another bank. He'd hoped to be able to fulfil the dream down to the last detail, but reality has its limitations. In any case, he showed the bank employee the slain man's identity card, having disguised himself as well as he could to look like the card's original owner. The man had been a member of a well-established family in Beirut, so the employee received him with the utmost respect – just the way he'd always done with the patrons of the bank where he worked. He signed the necessary papers, paid the yearly rental fee, then descended to the catacombs, where he made his way through the bank's underground corridors until he reached the vault. After the safe had been opened, Mansour turned to the employee and –

in a straightforward, pleasant tone of the sort that real rich people never use – asked him to look the other way.

As he placed the bomb in the safe, it seemed to him that his heartbeat and the ticking of the bomb's timing device were in a race against the clock. Then he left the bank, went outside and sat down on the pavement. And although the blast wasn't as loud as it had been in the dream, he still laughed and laughed as if he'd never be able to stop...

Nightmare 137

Khatoun the fortune-teller woke up in a terrible fright. Someone was shaking her bed so violently, she nearly fell on to the floor. She wondered if it might be one of the jinn in whose name she claimed to speak without even believing in their existence. Or might it be an earthquake, or a bomb that had struck the building next door?

She heard several horrendous explosions, one after another. They seemed to be coming from the room where she practised her magic.

She ran in, only to be met by a sight which was beyond belief. Her crystal ball was aglow with lights that grew alternately brighter and dimmer, and inside it she saw a series of explosions go off in splashes of red, blue, green and grey. The sound of the blasts was deafening and the entire ball was quaking on top of the table where it was kept. She tried to flee, but the glass ball was emitting what seemed like electrically charged particles that fixed her glance right where it was, preventing her from looking away. It was as if the ball were a powerful magnet that had emerged from the depths of myth and legend. So rather than running away, she found herself drawing nearer to the glass sphere and staring straight into it.

Inside, she saw the land of snow-capped, cedar-covered mountains and blue-gold beaches going up in flames. However, the fire was extending to other places as well. The chasm caused by the earthquake was growing wider and longer and reaching into new regions and countries, while the earthquake was sweeping over the entire globe. Despite the sparks that had begun spewing out of the ball, she drew still closer, gazing into it so intently that the flames inside it singed her face and the ends of her hair. Yet she kept on looking, trying her utmost to identify which way the earthquake had been moving and to which neighbouring country the chasm had advanced.

Khatoun could see clearly all that was happening. But before she could open her mouth to utter the country's name, the earthquake grew more violent. Meanwhile, the sparks emanating from the ball began coming thicker and faster, until at last the ball itself caught fire. After this, it rolled to the floor, heavy with the weight of the frightful happenings raging inside it. Then finally it exploded in a fleeting, flaming instant.

The following morning, Khatoun the fortune-teller was found dead in the room where she'd been known to engage in her occult practices. Apparently something had exploded in the room, burning her to death and destroying her crystal ball. Younger people said that someone must have planted a bomb in the room for some unknown reason, while those of the older generation maintained that one of the chief jinns had destroyed her with fire for revealing more of their secrets than they'd given her permission to.

One thing at least was certain – namely, that no shell or bomb had entered the room from outside. When Khatoun's body was discovered, all the doors and windows leading into the room had been locked from the inside and remained untampered with...

Nightmare 138

Oh, nightmares, nightmares...
Oh, how the darkness seems to linger when the distance between life and death is no more than a single night's wait.

How slowly the black sands of darkness slip through the hourglass when every single grain has turned into a nightmare.

And oh, my library!

I still couldn't believe that if I climbed the stairs to my flat, I wouldn't find even so much as the door that had once led into my library, or that if I'd reached out to take down one of my many books (whose locations and arrangement I knew like the back of my hand), all I'd get would be a handful of soot and blackish water.

Once more I was overcome by a sense of mortal distress...

The very thing I'd most feared had happened: my books had gone up in flames. I could feel the tears running down my cheeks and I thought: No doubt my tears are black, just like the water that's dripping right now on to the remains of my charred papers.

So I cried a little. Or perhaps I cried a lot – I don't know. In any case, I could feel that mysterious, invisible 'motor' revving up inside me now that everything else had stopped working. I heard a joyful, transparent voice coming from somewhere in my depths, like the siren on a submarine going off at the eleventh hour.

'You dunce!' it said. 'Why are you crying? Don't you know that every three minutes a new book is released somewhere in the world? So what are you lamenting over?'

I realized how true this was and that all owning a library had really meant for me was that I'd donned a veil which limited my peripheral vision and kept me from seeing the horizon at its fullest expanse. Now I was no longer in possession of a single one of my thousand books – which meant that I'd have to read a thousand books more.

Then I heard the same voice repeating: 'Remember, somewhere in the world a new book is published every three minutes!'

I found myself whispering: 'That's true. But it was *my* library that burned up! It's also true that there are more than 3 billion people living in the world and that Yousif was only one of those 3 billion people. But he also happened to be... my beloved!'

Then I began thinking back on Yousif and on all the magic that used to be produced during our times together in forests, on riverbanks and on seashores. It was as if a cocoon were being spun around us, its threads made from the sense of serenity and well-being that became ours whenever we cast off our protective shells and drew each other close, stripped naked of our weapons, our fears and our doubts – both our mundane day-to-day uncertainties and those borne of the times of crisis in which we'd been living.

All that I'd held most dear had now gone up in smoke: Yousif and my books. As for my attempts to comfort myself by thinking about the number of new books published every three minutes or the size of the world population, they made about as much sense as trying to console a mother who's been bereaved of her only son by telling her: 'There's no need to grieve over your little boy. After all, worldwide, more than 80,000 children are born every day!'

There seemed to be only one thing that offered any consolation – namely, the thought that the fire that had consumed my home might be part of a greater conflagration which would purify this suffering homeland, and thereby deliver it from its distress.

Nightmare 139

I felt a sharp pain that picked me up, sent me soaring through the air, then flung me into outer space, far from the planet of sorrow to which I'd grown so accustomed.

Soon I found myself stepping on to a bitterly cold planet made of glass. Its surface was covered with slick spots on which one might easily slip and fall. However, I quickly mastered the ability to walk over its treacherous surface. The force of gravity was also weaker here than on Earth. I was apparently the only living creature on the entire planet. However, rather than being distressed by this discovery, it gave me a feeling of marvellous freedom. I'd lost everything and, as a consequence, I could now reclaim all the liberty that had once been mine.

Whenever a person gains a new possession, he becomes a bit heavier. Yet here I was – possessionless, as it were – as transparent as a teardrop, as free as a bird. My house had burned down and its walls had tumbled to the ground. As a result, the horizon had once again become my sole 'window on the world'. My body was once more both my only permanent residence and the site of my poetic creativity, while the roads I now travelled were the darkened, timeless paths of night. It was if all possibilities had been replanted in my mind and heart, whence they could sprout and grow anew like grass in the springtime.

Everything we lose restores to us some part of ourselves which we had been dissipating in our attempt to hold on to that very thing. Now I no longer possessed anything whatsoever. Nor was there any part of me that was busy trying to hold on to Yousif or to protect my precious books from the flames.

I was now as I wished to be: utterly, completely free, able to make my choices anew, as if for the first time.

Nightmare 140

Oh, how the darkness tarries when nothing stands between life and death but a single night's wait...
How slowly the night's shadowy sands creep downward through the hourglass when every grain has become a nightmare.

As I lay there, the rain continued to pour down. I hoped the following day would be overcast and stormy as well, since that might reduce any sniper's chance of hunting me down. If only the tank would really come. If only Amal had explicitly said, 'tomorrow'. If only I could go to sleep for a while and stop trying to force time's melancholy sands down through the hourglass. If only I could take off for the City of Slumber and Oblivion, rather than spending the night in futile attempts to goad the Earth into rotating a little bit faster...

The rain kept coming down in torrents. I thought back on how I'd stood outside and allowed the rain to bathe and cleanse me. My hand was still covered with black soot, despite having washed it time and time again. The traces it had left on my skin terrified me, as if they were the 'blood' of the things which had been destroyed. I decided to get up and wash my hand once more. However, the water was still cut off. In fact, the taps no longer even gasped when I tried to turn them on, as if they'd given up the ghost once and for all. And now the sight of them ranged along the outside wall of the building made me think of corpses laid out in a mass grave.

I knew that if I didn't have the good fortune to escape from this infernal place by the next day, I'd definitely start to get very thirsty, which meant I'd need to put out containers to catch rainwater in. I wouldn't be able to boil it in the regular way, since the cooking gas had run out as well. Instead, I'd have to bring in wood from the garden and boil the water over a fire. However, the wood in the garden was soaking wet from all the rain, not to mention the fact that going out to the garden would expose me to danger from snipers. Consequently, I'd have to bring in the wood after dark, then leave it to dry. In fact, I'd have to put out the containers right away. After all, it might not rain the next day. And the tank might not come.

In preparation for my nocturnal errand, I lit a candle, which was promptly blown out by a gust of wind. In the end, I didn't go out at all. I didn't collect rainwater and I didn't bring in sticks to be dried for firewood. It was as if I refused to believe that the tank wouldn't actually show up the next morning to rescue me.

I drank a little water and, in the darkness, I could feel the lime that I couldn't see clinging to my tongue. I didn't try to light my candle again. I'd grown accustomed to moving about the house in pitch darkness without bumping into the furniture, just the way sightless people learn to do with the passage of time.

I pressed my back up against my orange travel bag and rested my hand on the revolver, running my fingers over it in the darkness like a new bride discovering her husband's body for the first time. It contained a large number of protrusions and valves that I'd never noticed in the adventure films I'd seen. I'd ceased to see it as nothing but a hideous black blob. In fact, I'd begun to see it in an entirely new light. However, I couldn't stop a shudder of horror sweeping through me as I ran my hand over it. It was as if my relationship with it were a sort of forced marriage to which I'd submitted only to be assured of my daily sustenance. I stood in need of it, yet I still loathed and despised it!

Nightmare 141

I wasn't asleep and I wasn't awake. I was just waiting.

Was this really the dawn that had begun casting its ashen hue over the blackness of the night? Or in my haste to see it arrive, was I imagining things – seeing it the way a thirsty woman imagines an oasis on the desert horizon?

But no, I thought. It really *is* morning.

Yes, it is... No, it isn't... Yes, it is... No, it isn't...

But no. It wasn't. I *had* been imagining things after all.

Whatever the case, I knew that daybreak couldn't be far away. I knew it, because the fatigue I was feeling was the kind that afflicts only those who've spent the entire night awake. I was so sleepy, I was having to exert an extraordinary effort just to keep my eyelids from closing. They felt so heavy that to hold them open was a mighty struggle indeed.

I mustn't doze off! After all, if the tank came while I was asleep, I'd miss my one and only chance to reach safety.

I thought of the city streets strewn with the bodies of the slain. I thought of those who'd lost the ability to distinguish between the combatant and the robber, the warrior and the murderer, the dispossessed and the dispossessor. With thoughts like these running through my head, I found my hand tightening its grip on the revolver. In a jungle of terror, those monstrosities commonly known as weapons may become one's only means of survival.

But even so I wasn't sure I'd be physically capable of killing someone...

Nightmare 142

I apparently fell into slumber's trap – for a while, at least. I may have dozed off just for a second; I may have slept for a year. In any case, I woke up to a suspicious-sounding movement behind the window, as if someone were trying to open it. I flew into a wild panic, as if an overpowering electric current had been sent through my body.

Then, before I was fully aware of what I was doing, I suddenly raised the revolver in the darkness and fired a shot in the direction of the window!

I heard a faint, dying gasp, then the sound of something falling to the ground. Both noises came through with extraordinary clarity. Or maybe it was just that my senses were extraordinarily on edge. And at almost the same moment, Amin let out a loud scream.

As I lit the candle, Amin asked in a trembling voice: 'What happened?'

My voice sounded cold to me as I replied: 'I've just killed someone who was trying to sneak in through the window, that's all.'

'My God!' he wailed. 'Maybe there's more than one!'

He's right, I thought apprehensively. And if so, they won't be content just to rob the house. Instead, they'll resort to murder to avenge their partner's death.

I realized then that a weapon wouldn't solve any problems at all – on the contrary, it could only complicate them. It would obviously be necessary to look for other ways of surviving! However, I didn't have time to think about such things just now.

What was really worrying me was a disturbing fact that had just struck me – namely, I was capable of murder!

Well... not murder exactly, since at the moment I fired I hadn't been committing *murder*. Rather, I'd simply been... well... firing. I hadn't been attacking. I'd been defending. I hadn't been seeking to snatch away someone else's life. I'd only been trying to preserve my own...

Yet even so, the result was the same: I'd pulled the trigger!

By this time, the misty light of daybreak was bathing the world in a melancholy glow. I ran with Amin to the window and, looking out, saw the body of my victim, who turned out to be none other than... a dog!

Amin let out a nervous, slightly hysterical laugh. As for me, I found myself repeating over and over again: 'But I pulled the trigger! That's all that matters, as far as I'm concerned!'

And, of course, he had no idea what I meant.

Nightmare 143

The sound of the shot continued to ring in my ears for quite a while and the smell of gunpowder lingered in my nostrils. It may have been around 6.00 a.m. or perhaps a bit later, and I was keeping my ears skinned for the sound of the tank.

There had hardly been any shelling since around midnight. As for the sound of machine-gun fire, I didn't pay much attention to it any more. Besides, neither of these could hinder the tank's arrival. The only things that might actually sabotage my flight were bombs and, even more so, certain kinds of missiles.

O God! I prayed, please let the fighters doze off for a while, at least long enough for me to sneak out of their war zone! After all, what do I have to protect me but a laughable pistol, which is about as useful in the face of this inferno as Don Quixote's sword was in fighting windmills? Please, God, let them take it easy, and be easy on others!

Hardly had I finished my prayer than a barrage of heavy artillery fire began!

Nightmare 144

With every bomb blast, my hope of emerging from the hellish prison in which I found myself weakened a bit more, fraying like a rope into threads so fine they wouldn't have been strong enough to bear the weight of an ant.

However, I got ready just in case. I picked up my orange bag, went and sat down in front of a window that looked out over the front garden, and waited.

And waited...

I listened hard for the sound of the tank's peculiar roar, which by this time I'd come to know well. I also made an attempt at combing my hair, which for days I'd forgotten even existed, trying to see my face in a small mirror by the dim autumn light coming in through the half-closed window.

When Amin saw me looking at myself in the mirror, he realized – perhaps for the first time – that I really was preparing to meet the outside world. In other words, he finally woke up to the possibility that I might actually leave and that he'd find himself alone in the house.

'Are you leaving?' he asked in an unsteady voice.

'Of course,' I said. 'Why don't you come with me?'

'But the house,' he protested, 'they'll plunder it!'

'They'll do that whether you leave or not,' I reminded him.

'This is my house,' he said in a determined voice, 'and this is where I'll die. I have no intention of living as a homeless refugee.'

'Well,' I said, 'you'll be a homeless refugee even if you stay here. There's no such thing as stability in a homeland which has itself become homeless.'

'You're just talking this way because your flat burned down and you can't get it back!'

'Even if it hadn't burned down,' I said, 'I still wouldn't be willing to die for the sake of walls that I can replace with others like them. Anything that money can buy is, *ipso facto*, not worth dying for. You can buy a new house, but you can't buy a new homeland! And in order to fight for the sake of having a real home and not just a tomb, you've got to stay alive.'

'You're just saying that because your flat burned down and you've got nothing left!' he repeated.

'That's not true,' I objected. 'My library – which you considered to be my "rare treasure collection" – could never make up for the loss of the sea, the forests, the sky, the grass, sunsets, the glitter of the stars, flocks of birds, rain and snow, travel, wonder and awe, love, life, warmth, swimming, a hot cup of coffee in the rain, music, thinking, crying, riding a bicycle, working or finishing a new book... Life is a precious, marvellous gift and in order to give it up for something, that "something" has to truly merit such a tremendous sacrifice. When you place your life in danger for the sake of your treasures, it's because you've mistaken them for your true "home".'

'Like I told you,' he retorted, 'you're just talking this way because you don't have a home any more!'

'Maybe so...'

Nightmare 145

As I was on the verge of giving up altogether, I heard the sound of a tank – just the way it happens in adventure films! I picked up my orange bag and took off running. I didn't say goodbye to Amin (the way people do in adventure films), since I wasn't entirely sure I'd survive the barrage of gunfire that I might be exposed to on my way out. Besides which, more than one tank had already tried unsuccessfully to pick me up before, only to have to leave me behind, like a beggar standing forlornly outside hope's closed doors.

I went out to the garden, then ran towards the gate. On the way, I nearly tripped over the corpse of the dog that I'd killed. When I finally reached the pavement, I didn't find anyone waiting for me. Yet I kept hearing the sound of the tank without being able to see it. I was beginning to think I'd lost my mind, that I was just hearing what I wanted to hear.

I looked up and started surveying the windows in the surrounding buildings. The top floor of the Holiday Inn across from my 'deceased' flat was still ablaze. As for the windows facing me on the other side of the street, most of them were shut tight. However, on the third floor of the building opposite me, one of the windows cracked open slightly and I glimpsed the head of a woman who was staring at something towards the end of the street – that is, in the direction of the Jumblatt Building. Then she began gesturing to me to look that way.

I understood...

She was trying to tell me that the tank was there but the garden walls had been blocking it from view.

At that point, I no longer felt anything but the desire to reach it. All my fear and hesitation now gone, I emerged from behind the stone door jamb and came out into the street for the first time in at least ten days.

And there it was... the tank.

For the first time in my life I appreciated the meaning of the expression: 'She didn't believe her eyes.'

At moments such as these, there's a blurring of the boundaries between the misty, grey land of dream and the sharp, black land of reality. Things that are visible seem to be wandering about lost inside one's head and it is hard to know exactly how to classify them, since they're neither grey nor black. Instead, they're the colour of an autumn morning such as this one was, writhing and turning on an iron spit that is hot as hell one minute and cold as ice the next. At that moment, things took on a sense of heightened reality. Every cell of my body was distended, alert and pulsating with vital power, as if on the verge of orgasm. They were stimulated by this new awareness of danger, of the death that threatened my very existence with every shot that still lay dormant inside a gunbarrel and which, were it to be released, might well make my head its target.

There it was... the tank.

At the sight of it, I threw caution to the wind and I took off after it as if it were the last train out of the City of Death.

Nightmare 146

How peculiar the world looks when you're staring at it through the opening in the roof of a tank. How very different.

The tank had no windows. Instead, it had just a single, huge skylight on top. When you ride in a tank, you see the world – or at least the upper portions of buildings and trees – racing by over your head.

We've grown accustomed, of course, to seeing the world from other vantage points – for example, from the upright windows of houses or cars which allow us to see everything in the street, or at least the parts of things located closer to the ground. Either that or we view the world while standing or walking in the street, in which case our eyes can roam wherever they please.

From inside a tank, you see nothing but the portion of the world imposed on you by the narrow orifice in its roof, which includes little more than the tops of buildings that go dashing along against a tiny strip of sky. When we passed in front of the

Holiday Inn, a tense silence reigned inside the tank. However, we managed to get past without having a single shell fired at us. After this, I tried to identify which street we were headed down, but couldn't do it. Looking out of the tank's skyward-facing window, I couldn't distinguish even the streets and lanes near my house that I supposedly knew so well. I felt that I was going along strange, unfamiliar streets towards an unknown fate. Whenever I peered through the open window in the tank's roof, I felt like a paralysed person lying flat on her back on a stretcher, being wheeled through the corridors of an outlandish, spooky hospital.

After a while, I stopped trying to guess which street we were on. Then I began looking around at the men who were with me in the tank. One of them, by the name of Salim Mansour, introduced himself to me, followed by Lieutenant Isma'il Yasin. As for the officer driving the tank, he introduced himself as Lieutenant Mula'ib.

This was the first time I'd seen other human beings – apart from my immediate fellow sufferers – for nearly two weeks. And now that my long isolation had ended, I felt the need to ask all sorts of questions about what had been going on in the outside world. The queries pushed and shoved and did battle with each other inside my throat, each one wanting to be the first to reach my tongue. As a result, they ended up annihilating each other in an excruciating all-out bloodbath. By the time it was over, nothing remained on my tongue but mute silence.

As I watched the sky glide past above me, indifferent and remote, I was gripped by an eerie sensation of helplessness and awe. Then, before anyone had said another word, the tank came to a halt.

'Here you go,' said one of the soldiers as he opened the door for me.

So, through the narrow rectangular opening which formed

the tank's door, I bounced out into the world in a kind of new birth. I emerged like a newborn child, its hands clinging to nothing, its fingers opened to grasp hold of the unexpected, the wondrous and the unknown.

With a wave of euphoria sweeping over me, I accompanied Salim and Lieutenant Isma'il to a nearby armoured car and off we set. After we'd gone a short distance, one of them asked me: 'Where would you like to go?'

'Uh ... I don't know,' I said, feeling a bit embarrassed.

Only then did I remember that during the days of my virtual 'house arrest', it had never once even occurred to me to plan where I'd go in the event of being rescued! The chances of finding my way to safety had been so remote that I never believed, even for a second, that the moment would come when I'd be faced with such a decision.

I didn't feel any particular longing to see my grandmother, or anyone else in my family for that matter. We'd always been more or less strangers to each other and by now they'd no doubt all taken off for my maternal uncles' house in Ladikia.

So I just sat there without saying a word, astounded at the ease with which my exodus had taken place. In fact, I hadn't heard a single shot since the time I'd left my house.

Salim said, 'The "chief" would like to see you in any case.'

I didn't reply. Not long after this, the car pulled up in front of a house. It wasn't until I'd got out that I became aware of the catastrophe that had occurred: when I'd sprung out of the tank like a newborn baby with nothing in its hands but the unknown, I'd left my orange bag inside!

Nightmare 147

I had to get that bag back at any price!

Lieutenant Isma'il said to me: 'Go on in, and we'll try to phone somebody who can help us track it down.'

When I went into the house, I found myself in a room completely devoid of furniture except for a desk with a telephone on it and a sofa where a long-bearded fighter lay sleeping, though he opened his eyes briefly as I walked in. I lifted the receiver, but there was no dialling tone. Not that it mattered, since I didn't know what number to dial anyway, or who I would have needed to talk to in order to retrieve the bag – the bag that contained my passport, what little cash I had left to my name, some memoirs, the earliest beginnings of *Beirut Nightmares* and... oh, yes... Yousif's papers.

I felt rather mortified when I realized that Yousif's papers no longer meant any more to me than Amm Fu'ad's dead body stuffed inside a rubbish bin. Oh, Yousif, I thought... if I had to lose you, couldn't it have happened without a tragedy on the scale of a civil war? Was the war's continuation the only way I'd be able to forget you? And was the only way for me to stop caring so much about *your* death to find myself on the verge of my own?

I had to get that bag back, no matter what it cost me.

Armed with this thought, I ran out to the car and begged the driver to take me back to the spot where the tank had let me off, in front of the Red Cross headquarters. And as if madness were contagious, he agreed!

With its armed checkpoints and lifeless, deserted streets, the way back seemed much longer than it actually was. But at last the Murr Tower appeared, at which point we turned left on Spears Street (going the wrong way on a one-way street, which of course didn't matter, since there were no other cars to contend with anyway). I didn't find the tank in the place where it had dropped me. However, I spotted it at the end of the street, in front of the Sanayi' Park. The soldier manning the checkpoint nearby refused to let us approach the tank in the car, though he was willing to let me go there alone – and on foot!

So I got out of the car, telling my escort to wait for me. Then I made a mad dash towards the tank through a field of machine-guns ready to go off at any moment. As I ran, there were soldiers gaping at me in astonishment, as if I were Matahari on a not-so-secret mission! As for me, I was feeling no fear, no shame, no cold and no pain. My entire being was focused on a single goal – namely, recovering that bag of mine at any price. Once that was taken care of, I could stop to think about whether I wanted to keep what was inside it or cast it to the wind!

There was something about the steely resolve I felt that wiped out all other sensation, rather the way yoga does – so much so that if someone had impaled me with a sword at that moment, I would have kept right on going in pursuit of my lost bag.

However, when I was half-way to the tank, I was unexpectedly halted by an army jeep. With his machine-gun aimed right at me, the soldier driving the vehicle asked me where I was headed and why I was out wandering around in a military zone. But instead of answering his questions, I just shoved his gun out of my way, got in beside him and requested that he take me to the tank, since there was no time to talk. And – wonder of wonders – he did it!

When we reached the tank, I got out of the jeep, climbed up to the tank's open door and asked: 'Where's the orange bag?'

I peered inside, only to find the faces of seven soldiers I'd never seen before peering back at me in bewildered amazement. Sure enough... I'd come to the wrong tank!

Nightmare 148

Nobody believed my story.

Or at least, while some of them might have believed one half of it – namely, the part about my losing an orange bag. But nobody believed the other half – namely, that the lost bag didn't contain any valuables or cash, but only papers – 'mere' papers. It was inconceivable to them that a woman would place her life in danger just half an hour after being rescued for no other reason than that she'd lost some... papers! As far as they were concerned, the only paper that would have merited such a sacrifice was the coloured type printed by the government and called money.

As I was recounting my story for the fifth time, adding to it a critical 'confession' – namely, that the bag in question contained notes for a future novel which I was planning to call *Beirut Nightmares* – I could tell that the man driving the tank, Sergeant Zayn, knew just what I was talking about.

He explained: 'This must be a different tank from the one that brought you out. We've been sitting here for hours now and we haven't changed our crew since we got here. What was the number of the tank you came out on?'

'I don't know,' I confessed.

'Then could you describe the person who was driving it?' he asked.

'Well,' I said, 'he was an officer, with one or two stars on his shoulder. He had a dark complexion and a moustache.'

My description got a laugh out of the soldiers who'd been listening, after which Sergeant Zayn added in his polite, gentle way: 'That description could apply to half the officers in the Lebanese army! Can you possibly remember his name?'

I tried in vain to bring the name to mind, but it kept eluding me, slipping and sliding out of my grasp like so many drops of mercury. It was as if I knew it but didn't know it. Yet I was certain that if I heard the name, I'd recognize it.

I mentioned this to Sergeant Zayn, whereupon he began listing a series of names. When he came to 'Lieutenant Mula'ib', I shouted: 'That's the one!'

'He was driving tank nineteen,' he said.

He picked up his walkie-talkie and started speaking to some invisible person on the other end, recounting my story about the bag, the tank and so on.

I heard a voice reply nonchalantly: 'We've taken note of it. Over.' And that was that.

But no – that couldn't be the end of it!

I said to myself: I'm getting that bag back if it's the last thing I do!

The lines I'd penned by candlelight in horror-haunted corridors and which alone I'd rescued from the flames – how could I even think of letting them be lost! And then there were my memoirs, which I wouldn't have wanted anyone to see. After all, whoever read them would gain access to my inner sanctuaries and perhaps be titillated by the 'mental strip-tease' which such personal confessions might represent to him. As for Yousif's things, they mattered little to me any more – I'd come to see them as a mere heap of ashes.

Turning to Sergeant Zayn, I said, 'Where's tank nineteen? I'll go and track it down myself!'

Some of the soldiers had gone to get some *mana'iche* for breakfast, which they shared with me along with their cigarettes.

Then Sergeant Zayn asked me: 'Where are you headed? We'll try to arrange some sort of "taxi service" for you.'

'I'm not going anywhere,' I said. 'I'll wait.'

Then he called out again on his walkie-talkie. I heard him saying: 'Twenty-one here, come in please. Twenty-one, come in. What's happened to the lady's bag?'

Then back came the anonymous, apathetic voice: 'What bag?'

Those words nearly sent me through the ceiling. I asked the sergeant who he'd been speaking with.

'With the liaison office,' he replied.

'I'll go there myself,' I said.

Perhaps in an attempt to frighten me (or perhaps simply because it was the truth), he said: 'The office is located on Martyrs' Square, which happens to be one of the hottest battle zones in town right now!'

'Well, I'm going anyway,' I said, and I meant it.

He must have realized that I was serious because he added – as if afraid that I might be hit by a shell or a sniper's bullet: 'Wait just a little longer. We may get an answer.'

So I waited.

Seeing a young boy coming past on a bicycle, I stopped him and tried to convince him to rent me his bike long enough for me to go to the liaison office and come back. I knew that the more time passed, the slimmer became my chances of retrieving the bag.

However, the boy refused, and Sergeant Zayn said to me: 'The tank is at the Hilou Barracks, but the officer who gave you a ride may have gone on his way after his night's work. Try to stay calm. If you'll give me your address, I promise you I'll take care of the matter.'

Then another tank passed by. I ran after it, thumbing the driver in an attempt to hitch a ride. It didn't stop.

However, by dint of great effort, Sergeant Zayn managed to convince one of his superiors to let him keep me in the tank until all the soldiers out on patrol had come back and he could get me to the Hilou Barracks. It was clear that he was doing everything he could to help me and I thought to myself:

Kindness still hasn't died out, even in this ugly, cruel world.

As I sat waiting inside the tank, I noticed for the first time that there was a soldier stretched out on the long iron seat across from me. With some difficulty, he opened his eyes, then stared at me with a startled look on his face.

'Good morning!' I said.

He ran his fingers through his long beard, then asked Sergeant Zayn: 'So what's been going on in this tank, anyway?'

With a laugh, the latter replied: 'We're providing a taxi service for the lady here – or, you might say, a hitchhikers' tank-pick-up service!'

Nightmare 149

As I listened in on the conversation Sergeant Zayn was having over his walkie-talkie, I remembered how I'd once eavesdropped on similar conversations via the receiving device that I'd snitched from Amin. I would listen in as bombs rained down all around me. And for all I knew, there might be another woman listening in now over the same 'forbidden' frequency. If so, she was probably wondering about the secret of 'the bag', and cursing because here she was about to die in the crossfire, while the tanks that were supposed to be out rescuing people were preoccupied instead with looking for ladies' bags! How would I ever convince her that the manuscript of a novel – like a newborn child – is a living being?

Time was creeping forward frightfully slowly. I regretted not having kept the bag in my hand at every moment. But regret was of no use to me now. So I decided to content myself with doing everything in my power to get it back.

As the tank set off at last, I found myself pressed in among a number of soldiers with rifles in their hands. The tank moved along at a brisk rate, tossing us this way and that, knocking our bodies up against the walls as if we were in the belly of a huge metallic whale. Despite the circumstances, I was bursting with energy, and began to imagine them 'having' me one after the other on the filthy iron floor of the tank as it trundled through the streets with violent jolts and shudders.

As I grabbed hold of a leather ring that hung from the wall of the tank, I noticed that the soldiers on the seat facing me had their guns pointed straight at my chest. Some of them, obviously exhausted, would doze off for a moment or two, during which the muscles in their necks would relax, allowing their heads to fall on to their chests as if they'd just been shot. They would half-wake, until their next lapse into unconsciousness.

They looked to me like a motley band of weary, arms-laden footsoldiers. The sight of them reminded me that never in my entire life had I made physical contact with such an awesome number of firearms. It also made me think of the revolver that I'd carried along with me in the bottom of my bag and of the 'murder' I'd committed. It was true, of course, that the creature I'd killed had turned out to be 'just' a dog. However, it was also true that I'd pulled the trigger without knowing whether I was shooting at a human being or some wild beast – and without knowing whether I myself was a human being or a beast. Thus I concluded once more that violence isn't something that's thought through logically or justified with reasoned arguments. Rather, it is simply 'done'. It's done and that's enough!

The sky and the tops of buildings could be seen gliding past through the narrow opening in the roof of the tank. When I caught a glimpse of the smouldering Holiday Inn for the second time that morning, a shudder of horror went through me. The tank was bringing me back to the same spot that I'd left just hours before. I wondered if I'd been destined to die on this very street. Had I been fleeing from my divinely decreed fate, only to be forcibly returned to it by this tank? However, I decided to believe instead that if a shell were to blow up the tank now, it wouldn't be because some divinely preordained ambush was lying in wait for me, but simply because someone had fired on the tank.

Even so, I continued to feel a kind of vague, ill-defined dread. As I sat on the iron seat squeezed between soldiers on either side of me, I chatted with a private by the name of Ibrahim, pumping him with questions about himself, but wishing secretly all the while that I could just talk about my own situation.

At last the tank pulled up in front of the Hilou Barracks and a soldier opened the door for us from the outside. When he saw me with my coal-black hair and my unmistakably Arab features, he asked with unthinking, revealing candour: 'How is it that you rescued an Arab this time and not a foreigner?'

His question put a miserable lump in my throat and I thought to myself: No doubt some of the country's 'fat cats' have been making use of tanks like this to get their foreign mistresses out of danger.

Nightmare 150

Where am I? I wondered. Then, regaining my bearings, I realized that I'd arrived at the Hilou Barracks.

And just the way it happens in tacky films, when the happy ending comes, it comes fast.

Within a matter of minutes, Lieutenant Mula'ib was standing before me. He was in his pyjamas, so it was obvious that they'd woken up him especially on my account. Then suddenly I found myself shouting at him: 'So, do I have to go running after you in a tank!'

A few of the soldiers had gathered around us and, figuring from what I'd said that I was an enraged, neglected wife, they turned their heads away, snickering and winking at each other. As for him, he just laughed and handed me my bag... my long-lost orange bag.

I opened it in front of everyone and inside there appeared a large yellow envelope with the words 'Manuscript for *Beirut Nightmares*' written clearly on the outside.

Lieutenant Mulaʻib said to me: 'One time I read a prison report you'd written for a magazine on an Israeli recruit who'd defected to Lebanon.'

Hearing this, some of the other soldiers took a second look at me, as if I were now some sort of special agent who storms prisons and army barracks and uses tanks as taxis in order to rescue (or steal) important, top-secret documents.

After this, the tank set off with me once more. And without knowing exactly why, I began punching the bag angrily as if it were someone who'd abandoned me!

As the tank went on its way, Sergeant Zayn asked me: 'Where would you like to go?'

'Anywhere,' I said. 'Where are we now?'

'In front of the Carlton Hotel, on the side facing the sea.'

'You can let me off here,' I replied.

So the tank pulled over and, as I prepared to take leave of him, I knew that I was indebted to him, that I'd never forget what had just happened as long as I lived and that kindness was still to be found, even in a world full of ugliness.

'I won't forget your kindness,' I said as I got out of the tank.

'Don't mention it,' he replied laconically.

I thought sadly: He thinks I'll forget, just like all the other people he's provided services for in the past. Sure, everybody is excited at the moment of 'euphoria' – at the moment when a favour has just been done for them. With the passage of time, though, emotions grow tepid, promises fade and the imprints left by events on the sandy shores of their souls are gradually erased. What he doesn't know is that I'm 'a woman of granite' and that once something is engraved deep inside me, it remains fresh and indelible, as if time had stood still.

However, it would have been difficult to explain all this to him over the roar of the tank's engine. So, in a voice which I knew was too soft for him to hear, I said: 'I'll never forget the kindness you've done me. I hope you believe that.'

Then the tank's iron door clanged shut and off it went. I found myself alone on the street.

Nightmare 151

I stood alone on the street with an orange bag over my shoulder.

Alone ... alone, just as I always had been. Planet Earth was like one immense 'zero', and I myself was standing at 'point zero' once again.

On the landing outside the hotel entrance, I saw a group of people waiting for me to come up. They'd seen me get out of the tank and now they seemed anxious to hear my story. Who knows? Maybe they even had a box of Kleenex ready for me so that I could dry my tears as I recounted my tale of woe. I was hungry – hungry for food, for water, for sleep, for peace – and my wounds were still open and raw. But as for stories, I had none to tell! In fact, I had nothing to say to anyone. I didn't feel awestruck. I didn't feel afraid. I didn't even feel homesick.

I kept standing at the bottom of the stairs without making any move to go up to the hotel. I felt like myself. I felt alone. And, as a result, I felt on top of the world...

Everything in my life had gone up in smoke, leaving me in a state of weightlessness. In my orange bag I now stored all that I'd chosen to carry away with me from my former, flame-purged world: Yousif's things (or, more accurately, Yousif's 'corpse'), the revolver and my papers. With these, I stood again at point zero.

Time had taught me that 'zero' was actually the largest number in my life. It didn't represent loss to me. It had always been a point of departure, either for a leap that would reach further than those preceding it or for a fall that would be even more painful than those I'd known before. Yet I'd always risen from my ashes. Joy would weep over me, extricate me from the quicksand into which I'd fallen then raise me up above the clouds. Shouting into the night, it would lift me up, saying: I've raised you up, my child, to protect you not from sorrow but from destruction. I've lifted you up to protect you not from disappointment but from falling. I have lifted you up, my child, to shield you not from defeat but from surrender. I've raised you not above error but above passive acquiescence. I've raised you up, my child, to protect you from that peace which is in fact nothing but surrender.

Thus would joy raise me up, circling about me and beating its drum until the break of day. Then, as the sun appeared over the horizon within my breast, I'd emerge from my coffin and unfurl my verses in the wind like the sails of an enchanted ship.

I continued to stand alone, alone at point zero. I stood at the starting point and, in one way or another, everything around me seemed to be taking part in my new beginning. The clouds weren't sending down any rain, but they were about to do so.

The sun wasn't shining, but there was a possibility that it might. The wind wasn't blowing, but there was a breeze happily announcing its approach. Everything around me was likewise standing at point zero, poised in anticipation of imminent labour and birth, the moment of creation, Earth's nuptial union with the rest of the cosmos.

Meanwhile, I remained standing on the first step of the stone staircase leading up to the hotel.

Reaching out to take my bag for me, a young man asked: 'Are you all right? We saw you get out of the tank.'

I heard myself replying: 'Yes, I'm fine.'

'May I help you up the stairs?'

'I'm fine.'

Just then there passed by an airline bus filled with passengers, as if it were suggesting an answer to me in my state of indecision. Should I also go away? I wondered.

No. I'd tried that before and it had done me no good. It was either here or nowhere. Here lay the beginning and here lay the end as well. Here lay the beginning of the thread and its end.

Go away? No. I didn't intend to repeat that mistake. I knew that if I just kept circling about the perimeter of the 'zero', I'd end up right back where I'd begun, more devastated than ever.

It was either here or nowhere. What was called for now was action, not flight followed by fruitless waiting.

I felt as if I were in a waystation preparing for departure, not standing in front of a hotel.

I decided to flee – from the hotel, that is.

I had no idea whether Beirut's taxis were still working or not. After all, I'd grown accustomed to using tanks for my comings and goings of late. But where would I go? And where would I begin?

So I stayed right where I was, glued to the pavement and

feeling the need to be alone. I could see the people waiting at the top of the stairs. They were apparently hoping to hear a story that would distract and amuse them until such time as they could be flown off to their chosen places of refuge. As for me, though, I needed to be by myself. When one is at point zero, crowds just won't do.

On the other side of the street I could see the 'sea hotel', as it were, extending into infinity. There were no staircases rising from its surface and no crowds gathered about it. I'd been overjoyed to see it, since people generally don't know how to walk on water. Otherwise, they would certainly have sullied it with their wild soirées and their curiosity-inspired gatherings.

The young man repeated: 'Let me help you up the stairs. Are you sure you're all right?'

I gathered from his question that I didn't look 'all right'. On the contrary, it was probably easy to see that I was bleeding, exhausted and wounded in one hand and one ear. On the inside, though, I was standing at point zero, where the horizon was boundless once again, where all possibilities were within reach and one's true desires could be set free.

'Thanks,' I said to him, 'but I'm going to walk along the seashore for a while.'

Insisting on playing the role of 'chivalrous gentleman', he held on to my bag and tried to pull me towards the hotel.

'Listen,' I said, 'I'm not planning to throw myself into the sea. I have an appointment to keep there.'

And I wasn't lying. When I got to the pavement on the other side of the street, I found my 'self' waiting for me there. I jumped over the iron railing that runs between the Corniche and the sea and began walking over the rugged terrain that leads towards the water.

I walked along freely for what seemed like the first time in ages. And like a mother who counts her children as they return from an outing to the forest, I took stock of the parts of my body that had managed to escape unharmed – so far, at least – from the bullets and shells that now posed a constant threat to life and limb. As I did so, it seemed as if they were all delighted to see each other.

I went and sat down on the boulder that Yousif and I had sat on so many times before. It was still littered with the same empty, dusty Coke bottles that I'd seen there on previous occasions. (It's as if things which have been emptied tend to stay just as they are – neither filling up nor breaking to pieces.)

I lay down on top of the boulder, imagining it to be a stone ship that was ploughing through the waves. At the same time, a string of familiar voices and faces went gliding through my consciousness. As I saw and heard them, I remembered, then forgot, remembered, then forgot. There was nothing my memory failed to recognize and embrace – those I'd loved, female and male, joys and disappointments...

I remembered, then forgot...

And as I did so, I found that at the bottom of it all there remained the 'I', vast and expansive enough to embrace both sorrow and joy, both falling and rising again. Remembering and forgetting, I poured my days into the sieve of time and truth, allowing its tiny openings to separate the wheat from the chaff.

I remembered and I forgot...

And I looked closely...

I remembered everything that had been consumed in the fire, the entire lifetime which I'd left behind, all those voices that had gone up in flames: the pictures, the papers, the letters and the books. All of these things, I'd digested, I'd assimilated, I'd taken into my soul, whereas in fact, I should have spat them all out long before, since – as had now become apparent – all of them were actually external to myself.

I opened up the orange bag and poured its contents on to the boulder.

Yousif's mangled 'corpse' now lay beside me, along with the revolver and my papers, which were still inside the yellow envelope bearing the words 'Manuscript for *Beirut Nightmares*.'

Meanwhile, I continued sailing along in my stone boat at 'zero' latitude and 'zero' longitude, while my compass, rather than pointing north, south, east or west, was pointing in the 'fifth direction' – namely, straight down into the depths.

I flung Yousif's remains into the sea, gazing intently at the waves that now closed in over our papers, our pictures and our music. Then I placed the revolver and my own papers side by side and stared at them for a while.

Suddenly I saw Yousif... He was sitting at the other end of our boulder, our seaworthy vessel of stone, and moving his lips as if he were calling to me.

Without a moment's hesitation, I grabbed the revolver, aimed straight at him and pulled the trigger. I could see the bullet penetrate his translucent body. With the speed of lightning, his body was transformed into a pile of ashes that were quickly scattered by the winds and a wisp of smoke which soon vanished into nothingness.

However, I didn't throw the revolver out to sea. Alas, such contraptions become a necessity when one is left with no other solutions to the dilemmas at hand. I nestled it in among my papers, letting them close around it the way a mother's womb envelops the child she carries. Then I sealed the envelope containing the beginnings of *Beirut Nightmares* and put all my papers back in the bag with the revolver wrapped inside them.

The sun was breaking through the clouds, one of which was sending down a shower, with the result that it was raining and the sun was shining at the same time. The piercing rays of sunlight that had emerged from between the clouds were blazing a luminous, brilliant rainbow across the sky – and I saw myself stepping on to it with a long journey before me.

Bowing to the rain and the sunshine, I lowered my face to the soil, the gravel and the thorns and rested a bit before continuing on my way. Meanwhile, the pathway of light in the heavens continued to grow more vivid and intense, and when I closed my eyes I could see it more clearly still.

1 *'Mana'iche'* are made of round, flat pieces of dough baked with either a mixture of olive oil, sesame seeds and wild thyme on top, or ground meat and seasonings. They are a popular food, especially for breakfast.
2 The reference is to one of a collection of famous pre-Islamic odes called the 'Mu'allaqat', or 'Hanging Odes'. According to one explanation of this name, they were hung on the wall of the Ka'ba in Mecca in acknowledgement of their superior merit.
3 This is an allusion to a statement attributed to the first Umayyad caliph, Mu'awiyah Ibn Abi Sufyan: 'Between me and others there is a single hair. If they pull it taut, I give it slack. If they give it slack, I pull it taut.' In his dealings with others, this particular caliph was known for his ability to keep his relations with others intact by means of his diplomatic skills and cunning. In the present context, the reference to the hair points to the fragility of the bond between the people concerned.
4 Ibrahim Marzuq was a Lebanese artist who was killed in the civil war.
5 Considered the most important holiday in the Muslim calendar, 'Id Al-Adha (the Feast of Sacrifice) commemorates God's command to Abraham to offer up his son, Isaac, as a sacrifice. Abraham's willingness to obey was then rewarded by God's provision of a ram to be offered up in the boy's stead. On this holiday, it is customary for families to slaughter a goat or sheep, the meat of which is generally distributed among the needy.
6 Qur'an V (The Table): 35.
7 Husnayn is a Muslim name, whereas Maron is specifically associated with the Maronite Catholics, who represent a large and influential sector of Lebanese society.
8 The name Joseph, derived from the French, is associated with Christians in Lebanon, as opposed to the Arabic equivalent 'Yousif', which is used by Muslims.